THE BACK HANDED

A SHERIFF GUS MYSTERY

John D. Desain

ISBN: 1544102399
ISBN 9781544102399
Library of Congress Control Number: 2017903017
CreateSpace Independent Publishing Platform
North Charleston, South Carolina

Additional books in the Sheriff Gus Mystery Series by John D. DeSain:

ACKNOWLEDGMENT

I would like to thank Chuck and Matt Herman of The Midnight Screening, the best damn country band in Greater Los Angeles.

CHAPTER 1

To be wealthy and honored in an unjust society is a disgrace.
—Confucius

The dusk's winter wind was blowing gently through the high plains tonight. Gus zipped up his jacket and leaned back in his folding chair. It was going to be one of those long nights that came with being a sheriff. The county law enforcement was out in force in order to catch a few stupid people doing a very dumb thing. Gus knew they would be out there, because stupidity wasn't exactly a hard quality to find in quantity when you went searching for it. The origin of humanity's stupidity appeared to lie deep within the very alleles of the species; thus, unlike many insidious infectious diseases that plagued the human race, stupidity had no prospect of ever being cured. There was no person immune to its effects, and certainly no person had ever avoided heading down the path toward unsuspecting duncehood on one occasion or another. A quick bout of stupidity was as common as a cold, and luckily most people completely recovered from it.

While most poor souls caught themselves in time before their stupidity cost them something permanent and dear to them, these days far too many people for Gus's liking seemed to root their stupidity as a permanent fixture at the core of who they were as human beings. Stupidity was their new religion, and so they held it most dearly next to their hearts. They wouldn't

1

give up on their precious chunk of stupidity for any earthly prize found in the here and now or eternal prize that was promised to come to them later on in the hereafter. Gus was rather happy about this whole prospect, because if stupidity could be cured in the average constituent, then he'd have a hard time digging up the cash for the monthly department budget. It was, after all, the bouts of stupidity, whether temporary or permanent, that allowed him to pay his bills on time.

Gus's dad had taught him that you simply couldn't fix stupidity; however, thanks to modern marketing tools, a society could hope to rebrand it. That was exactly the course of action the powers that be of Gus's little county had decided on. Rebranding was the best path forward for a governing body when all else had not been tried because it was assumed all the actual solutions were too costly, and all the fake solutions had run their course as platitudes in the popular press. Gus was smack-dab in the middle of a viral spree of reckless rebranding by the city council. Gus's county was tucked away in the middle of the hot-dry nowhere that lay between that big city to the north and the Mexican border to the south. The good ole boys wanted more tourist money flowing down from that big city on the county's northern border. There weren't many good reasons for a city man to come Gus's way, but reality didn't stop a rebrander from trying to get them to come all the same. The rebranders claimed that you couldn't attract tourists with so many criminal elements moving about, and they should know, as some of the biggest criminal offenders in the county were usually the rebranders. A typical rebrander didn't picture criminals as actual criminals; no, usually a mythical strawman made for a better target to try and fix. All this latest rebranding effort meant to Gus was that he was simply going to have to do his duty and catch his share of the multitude of stupid people who refused to not drink first and drive second. The county was trying hard to clean up its image, and this month the cleaning winds blew toward a crackdown on one of the biggest blights of the county—drunk driving. Gus knew he was bound to catch his prey tonight, because these late-night random checkpoint traps always netted a few driving-while-impaired cases every time he bothered to set one up.

Indeed they often worked a little too well. That was the problem with any rebranding plan. If you set about to go out of your way to find drunk drivers and criminals, then you were bound to find a lot of them. It's not like you can fix stupidity. The result of a crackdown was always the same: you ended up having a huge uptick in the reporting of whatever crime you bothered to crack down on. You looked for drunk drivers, so naturally you found a lot of them. Suddenly you're making a lot more drunk-driving arrests, and, boom, someone in the press adds up the numbers and then claims drunk driving is on the rise. Was it really on the rise, or were there just more arrests because you were cracking down on it? That sort of statistical hairsplitting was too nuanced for the general public. For the city council, it was just mathematics and, thus, like all things difficult, very unlikely to be considered, let alone thought about, by them in a logical manner. Gus knew tonight's crackdown was going to have the same result as the meth crackdown, the pot crackdown, and the crack crackdown that they had tried last year. Instead of the rebranding giving the county a better image, it was going to create a negative image in the form of many unwanted headlines about the county's warts they'd spent years trying to hide away.

Tonight's checkpoint had just started up its nightly operation. Gus was preparing to spend his long hours watching his deputies man the DUI checkpoint. He'd rather have spent tonight sleeping at home in his nice king-sized bed, but then again that was the same thought the drunks would soon be thinking when they sobered up in the drunk tank at the law-enforcement complex come tomorrow morning. Gus didn't exactly call his checkpoint a drunk-driving trap. Technically it was a driver's-license verification checkpoint. Gus was allowed by the law to stop motor vehicles to verify that the person driving it did have a proper license to drive and also that the vehicle was currently registered. Driving a car isn't a basic civil right guaranteed by the constitution in this country; no, it's only a privilege. Checkpoints were handy little devices to verify that this privilege had actually been extended to the driver of any given vehicle, and along the way they generated a massive amount of traffic tickets. Sure, you picked up the occasional drunken idiot, but you also caught your fair share of individuals wanted by the police on outstanding warrants, vehicles missing a smog inspection, vehicle tax avoidance, driving without a license, child-seat violations, and of course seat-belt violations.

You also caught your share of illegals, but picking them up was a job for the immigration boys in ICE. If those boys wanted to catch illegals, then they could set up their own checkpoint. Holding prisoners for too long in a costly deportation case chipped into Gus's department budget. It was far more cost-effective for the county to write illegals caught driving without a license a traffic ticket instead of holding them indefinitely on immigration charges. A traffic ticket to an illegal increased departmental funding; a bust of an illegal on a violation of America's immigration policy could potentially cost the department's bottom line, so it didn't take a degree in accounting to see how the law should be enforced to positively affect the county's financial viability. There was no point in rebranding your way to bankruptcy.

Gus yawned while reclining in his folding chair. The night up to this point had been a relatively quiet one. He checked his watch. He knew not much time had passed, but it was one of those things you did when you were bored. No doubt the social-media sites were steering young people away from Gus's checkpoint. These days the young people all had the latest software on their mobile devices that told them how to avoid Gus's preannounced trap. Luckily for Gus, people are vastly more mindful of things like the advice of social-media users on the way out to drink. Their phones were smarter, so it took more alcohol in them to make them forget to use social media to avoid Gus's trap on the way back home. After getting their mind full of sweet, sweet booze, they were less likely to remember Gus's gang was waiting out here for them at this checkpoint.

Gus took his eyes off his watch because he spotted a pair of illuminated dots in the distance. Those headlights informed Gus that a victim was on their way down the interstate heading toward the trap. It was about time for the first wave of the after-dinner crowd to start driving by. As the car closed in, Gus could tell it was a fancy, large dark-blue sedan. Gus sat in his folding chair under a canvas-tent cover watching his deputies do their stuff. The deputies waved red glowing sticks to signal the car to halt at the checkpoint. While the checkpoint should have been obvious to any driver on the road given its glaring floodlights and gaggle of patrol cars lining it, Gus still had his men use the red glowing sticks as a secondary precaution. There were special cases every checkpoint night where you got a really impaired idiot who needed a touch more than the obvious to remember to stop and not run over the deputies. The dark-blue sedan came to a stop in the designated area illuminated by the high-powered lights that beamed in gleaming radiation all around the car's driver. Gus could see Deputy Costner conversing with the unsuspecting victim. It was a long, drawn-out affair, which meant something bad for that driver. If a stop took more than a minute or two, then usually a ticket would be written, and the county revenue would increase ever so slightly. Gus's hand fumbled in his pant pockets searching for his ticket pad in anticipation.

Eventually Deputy Costner waved Gus to come on over, as he had figured the deputy would. The first revenue of the night awaited him. Deputy Costner was one of the better ones in the department. He had two years of community college under his belt. That was two more years than Gus had, but luckily Gus had an elected position, so his résumé didn't matter as much as those of his deputies so long as the voters kept voting for him. Costner clearly thought this car was ripe for a ticket, so it likely meant they really did have a live one on their hands. Gus wondered how much of the department's cash register this driver was about to fill. Gus slid down the side of the car until he reached the driver's-side window with ticket book in hand. The deputy gave way to Gus, revealing a familiar man sitting behind the wheel of the dark-blue sedan. Of all the people they could have ensnared in the trap, the first person caught was Terrance. Terrance was Gus's longtime childhood acquaintance. He'd have classified Terrance as a friend if people involved in politics could be called friends around mixed company without drawing suspicion down on you. The two of them had gone to high school together, and ever since then Terrance had always gotten Gus involved in any political scheme worth or not worth the county's time. Indeed, Gus's current involvement in the rebranding effort was all due to Terrance's bad influence on the city council.

"Sheriff, I thought I'd leave this particular driver for you to handle," said Deputy Costner, rolling his eyes.

"Thanks a bunch, Costner," replied Gus. Gus leaned on the car's frame and chastised Terrance from the open window. "Terrance, what the hell are you doing here? We tell you people well in advance where and when these stops are going to be for a reason. We want to avoid any legal unpleasantries for the good ole boys." Gus did a quick look around. Good thing it was early and the trap was empty of other victims. He continued, "Look, now I got to go handle this situation for you."

Terrance replied, "Handle what? I just thought I'd come around to check out the traffic checkpoint to see how many drunken Mexicans we've caught. We can't rebrand this town into a vacation paradise so long as we got so many illegals breaking the laws and scaring the God-fearing white folks from up north. Those people up north are filled with much unneeded pocket change, and we need to make sure they're willing to come down here to spend it. We got to give them a cleaner, whiter image; then they'll come, Gus. All the consultants say they will, and when have they been wrong?"

"If I recall, even the Bible's version of a vacation paradise had its share of snakes in it, so you'd think if God was okay with a snake or two in his garden, then your consultants would be okay with us allowing a Mexican or two into our county, particularly considering the fact that they got here first. Remember, this isn't my rebranding idea; it's yours. I just work here. But I'm going to need to ask you this: you didn't per chance drink any alcohol at dinner?" asked Gus.

"I might have had one or two bottles of wine. It isn't anything I can't handle." He cupped his mouth and leaned out the window to Gus and began to whisper. "To tell you the truth, I was rushing back home before the alcohol kicks in. I wouldn't want to drive around loaded, you know."

"He blew a 0.088 percent, Sheriff," said Deputy Costner over Gus's shoulder.

"Aw hell! Deputy, write up a ticket for parking on the highway for the gentleman and then drive him home."

"Can't you give me a break, Gus?" exclaimed Terrance.

"That's what I'm doing. If I gave every criminal a bigger break than you, then I'd eventually end up paying criminals for the privilege of breaking our fine county's laws. What would people think about our rebranding efforts then?"

Terrance rambled on. "Speaking of the rebranding effort, I just got to tell you the news. We've got important things going on in the city-council chambers. I have landed a surefire celebrity to come and move into our fair county as part of the rebranding effort. He'll be here in only two days' time! He's one of the most popular men on cable television, and he's coming here to live. How is that for a rebranding effort!"

Before Gus could answer, another vehicle bounded down the interstate and arrived at the checkpoint trap. It was a cherry-red sports car with a convertible top. Its music system was turned to eleven and rattled the teeth in Gus's head. He'd have gone right over and written the driver a noise-violation ticket if he hadn't had Terrance to deal with first. The top on the sports car was up, so Gus couldn't tell much about who was driving that fancy red number, but whoever it was, the price tag on that cherry-red car said that the person had either a lot of cash or a lot of debt. Deputy Drew was handling that car. Deputy Drew was the least abled man in the department. There was office furniture that offered Gus a better day's work than Drew, but Drew was the son of the mayor, so he had his job for life. The dial controlling the loud, annoying music of the red car was finally turned down, and Gus could turn his attention back to the problem at hand.

"You and the city council are in luck, Terrance. In light of your news that I don't care about in the least, I'm giving you a further break. Never say I didn't get behind the spirit of rebranding. I'll tell you what, though. Since I won't be writing you a ticket at all, then you got to promise me that you won't waste any more time on racist banter about the Mexicans. If you want to rebrand the county for this celebrity person, then you might try making the county feel a little more inclusive. You and the city council should go tilt at another windmill for a change."

"Hmm…that is a thought. This celebrity is a little notorious when the subject of the Hispanic community comes up." Terrance paused in bubbly alcohol-impaired thought. He then continued, "I'm going to do just that, Gus. Good ole Gus, you're always thinking up good ideas to help your good buddy out. You might just have given me another great idea there! Now that I've agreed to this scheme of yours, can I drive home? I got to be in a rush before I get so drunk that I black out and forget this great idea we've just had," replied Terrance.

"No, I can't let you drive home. That would be even less ethical than skipping writing you a ticket, and my ethics are on shaky ground as it is right at the moment. Deputy Costner here will drive you home. You will then pay for a cab that will drive my deputy back here. Consider this all a gift from your pal Sheriff Gus."

"Fine, anything to escape the clutches of *the man*," laughed Terrance.

Gus was about to lecture Terrance that the situation wasn't funny and also was entirely his own fault, when Deputy Drew shouted over to him. They were two vehicles into the checkpoint, and they already had two troubled drivers. "Hopefully this one at least brought a working dime in the form of a ticket," muttered Gus. Gus rounded the red sports car. It was a real classy piece of work. The vehicle was a custom job for sure with matching custom plates that read TWRKING. The classless license plate soured the vehicle's appeal to Gus. Gus could see a man who appeared to be in his midfifties sitting in the driver's seat. The man wore a spiffy-looking business suit. It was certainly a designer suit that had cost the wearer a lot of money to walk around sporting the famous name printed on the label. The driver's eyes had heavily fallen into nystagmus as they danced about in their sockets.

Gus tugged on Deputy Drew's arm and pulled him to the side. Gus whispered, "That guy appears to be totally plastered."

"I know, but this darn machine must be broken. He blew a 0.62 percent," whispered Drew back, showing Gus the digits displayed clearly on the Breathalyzer.

"That can't be right. He'd be dead if that was right." Gus stopped talking and stared at the man in the vehicle. The man was humming a tune as his eyes danced around. He clearly wasn't dead. Gus continued, "You sure you know how to use that stupid thing?"

"It ain't a stupid thing; you know, this here is part of the cutting edge of modern police-force technology."

To Gus the phrase "cutting-edge technology" was another way to say "technology that was too confusing to use properly in the field." It was far too easy to misuse this crap. It occurred to him he had just sent Costner away moments ago. The number on this machine had to be wrong, and Costner had left with their only other device. Luckily, law enforcement had been finding drunk drivers since long before technology was around to quickly misidentify them. Gus started in on drunk-driving identification plan B. Gus turned to the driver. "I'm very sorry, but I'm going to have to ask you to step out of the vehicle, mister…what is your name?"

The driver smiled at Gus, hiccupped, and then replied, "I don't remember. I think I have one. I remember quite clearly that I had a name this morning when I left home. It might be on my driver's license, but that could be anywhere."

"I have it in my hand," said Deputy Drew.

"There you go; the mystery has been solved. Quite a police force you have in this county, Sheriff," declared the driver, throwing his hands in the air.

"Sheriff, his name is Sedric Hedgecock," explained Deputy Drew.

"That's a good name. I should call myself that," declared the driver.

"But you do call yourself that now, according to your license," replied Deputy Drew, looking confused.

"I rarely call myself. I can't find my phone. Left it in my pocket, but now I've seem to have misplaced my pockets."

"Have you tried your pants? I usually keep my pockets there," replied Drew.

Gus ended the banter by rather politely ordering, "Please, Mr. Hedgecock, I'm going to need you to step out of your motor vehicle." Mr. Hedgecock rubbed his eyes and then fumbled at the door's lock. Gus signaled Deputy Drew to assist the driver in getting out of his vehicle. Drew reached his arm through the rolled-down car window and unlocked the door. He then proceeded to open the driver's door for him. Mr. Hedgecock watched the door open in amazement as if he had never seen one function before. Mr. Hedgecock made several attempts to pass his body through his car's restraints, which remained fastened, before comprehending the fact that his seat belt did its job rather well. Mr. Hedgecock found the whole matter amusing and laughed uncontrollably.

Sedric Hedgecock called out to Deputy Drew. "Young lad, can you free me from this infernal contraption, so that I may get out of my seat as ordered?" Drew looked over to Gus, and Gus nodded. Deputy Drew shrugged, reached into the car, and hit the release button on the man's seat belt. Unfortunately for the driver, his seat belt was the only thing holding him onto his seat. The driver's body started the slow process of oozing from where it sat inside the car down onto the cold, hard pavement. Eventually the driver stopped oozing and just lay there down at Gus's feet with his legs tucked uncomfortably under his body. Mr. Hedgecock didn't seem to mind the uncomfortable position he found himself in. Instead he started to hum an off-key tune to the open air.

"Mr. Hedgecock, I'm going to have to ask you to walk a straight line for me. Do you think you are up to walking a straight line?" asked Gus.

"You may ask. Indeed I insist that you do ask. I, however, must warn you that tonight I do not appear to be doing requests of that nature. My legs inform me they'd rather drive than walk. The night air is bad for them—germs."

"Mr. Hedgecock, my Breathalyzer here tells me that you might be under the influence of more than winter germs this evening. If you refuse to follow the instructions of my field-sobriety test, then I will be forced to arrest you on suspicion of driving under the influence of alcohol," explained Gus.

"It tells you? Those things can talk! I never knew that. I blew into that device, and it never told me anything. It doesn't like me, I guess. It may even be conspiring against me. I tell you what, don't arrest me just yet based only on its foul words spoken against me. Please, give me an easier one to accomplish than that last one. It was a toughie. I know your speaking alcohol machine is a liar, and I'll show it that I'm not as drunk as it thinks. Why, I haven't had a drink in…I can't remember when I had my last drink. I must have blacked out for a while," replied Sedric.

"An easier one of what?" asked Drew.

"Test, my boy! I am a very important man. I'm very big in the pants. Wait, that sounds kind of dirty." Sedric laughed at a joke only the intoxicated seemed amused by. He then continued, "I sell pants to fat people. I own three stores, big stores for big people. I know; you may ask me to touch my nose. I believe all the cop shows do that one."

Deputy Drew played along as Gus watched. "Fine, hold your arms out and touch your nose."

"Easy, I've been touching my nose for years." Sedric sat up on the pavement. He held his left arm halfway out from his crumpled body. He stuck out his pointer finger in triumph. He then with minimum effort managed to strike his right eye rather hard with that finger. He backed the arm up and swung another time, landing the finger hard into his forehead. He then proceeded to cry, "My nose, my nose, someone has stolen my nose. You fools, don't just stand around doing nothing at all. There has been a crime. I tell you there is a nose missing! Who knows where my nose might have gotten off to?" Sedric began to sob at the loss of his missing nose.

Gus had reached his breaking point. He informed the man, "Mr. Hedgecock, I'm afraid I'm going to have to hold you on suspicion of driving while under the influence of alcohol. We are placing you under arrest. Your vehicle will be placed in the county impound. You have the right to remain silent. The county will insist on a blood test to more accurately determine your blood alcohol level. You may refuse this test, but understand a refusal comes with penalties later on. I must warn you anything you say from now on can and likely will be used against you."

"Why are you afraid to hold me? I don't bite…well, I might bite. I don't remember really if I do bite. Do you think I might have bitten off my nose?" He started crying again.

Gus ordered, "Deputy, grab one half of this man, and I'll take the other half, and we'll dump him into the drunk wagon for transport. When we've finished with that task, drive his car to the side of the road before some other drunken fool runs into it."

Gus left Mr. Hedgecock in a heap inside the drunk wagon they had brought along to gather tonight's allotment of drunken fools. A good DUI case could mean a few thousand dollars, and that was welcome news. Gus now had one in the bank and walked back to his folding chair. He eased back onto his seat. The deputy drove the sports car to the side of the road. The tow-truck men would be coming soon to cart it away to the impound lot. Checkpoint night was always a good night of profit for the tow-truck industry in the county. Gus was watching the long, distant blackness of the road, waiting for his next victim, when Deputy Drew walked back to the tent cover. He was carrying a case of beer.

Gus asked, "Where did you get that?"

"I found it in the sports car. I figured since it's a slow night, we could test it."

"You want to test the beer while on duty?"

"No, you know I would never drink while on duty unless you couldn't see me doing it. I was figuring we could test the Breathalyzer. I would test your blood alcohol level first before you had a beer, and then after you chugged a beer or two down, I'd test you again. It is no use standing out here all night if the machine is broken."

"That isn't such a bad idea," agreed Gus.

Gus took the machine out of Drew's hands. He blew into the plastic tube. The little numbers came up 0.00 percent. That seemed to be all right. He handed the machine back to Drew for safekeeping. He then reached down into the case of beer. He pulled out a brown bottle with a cap on it. Gus held the label up into the floodlights to read it. It had nice big lettering, so he could read it even without his glasses: *Little Red's Mexican Ale*. It was a beer from a rather fine microbrewery. Gus figured Sedric Hedgecock must be doing just fine financially, because he didn't get plowed on any old cheap variety of booze. He was getting inebriated by some of the best stuff this state had to offer. Indeed, Mr. Hedgecock had bought a case of the stuff, and now it was all going to be seized as evidence. Well, maybe not all of it. Gus popped the top off one of the bottles with the pole of his canvas tent cover. He drank down the bottle. The beer was warm, but it was still pleasant enough. It was the kind of beer you wanted when stuck on the black pavement for several hours of the cold night. He finished the bottle quickly and scanned the roadside. There were no more vehicles coming toward his trap. It had been briefly busy, but so far it was shaping up to be a very slow night.

It didn't make sense to test the machine after only one beer. What kind of test was that? A real test of the limits of modern machinery required a few more modern microbrewed beers. It was easier to reach that conclusion when the beer in question was an expensive microbrewed beer bought by someone else. Gus reached down into the case and opened a second bottle. He sat back down on his chair and slowly put that one down as well. A few vehicles passed by in the meantime. Deputy Drew handled them. Nothing major wrong with any car. One driver didn't wear his seat belt and got a ticket. Another had a taillight out. It was all minor stuff. Gus waved Deputy Drew back over when the last one had left. He was pretty sure his blood had sufficiently filled with alcohol by now to give a good and proper test of the machine.

"Give me the machine test again. I think I'm good and ready to test it thoroughly."

Deputy Drew handed him the little plastic stick to blow into, and Gus proceeded to blow a second time into the machine. It read 0.05 percent. That was pretty good. Gus had expected a number around 0.03 or 0.04 percent, but this was a fancy higher-alcohol-content beer. The kind of beer Gus couldn't afford to buy too many cases of. Certainly he couldn't afford it unless he caught vastly more drivers tonight who had drunk too much of it. He glanced down at the nearly full case of microbrewed delightfulness. It seemed like a waste to let all that beer just sit there in the evidence locker. The good news was that the Breathalyzer machine appeared to be working just fine. The better news was Gus had no intention of letting that beer be wasted in an evidence locker, and he had all night to drink it.

Gus instructed Deputy Drew, "I think this thing is working. You had better keep an eye on that drunk in the drunk wagon. If that machine is right, then I don't want him turning all blue on us sometime during the night. That guy ought to be dead. Finally, you better call up Deputy Costner and tell him to pick up some ice on his way back. It is going to be a long night, and we've got to keep this case of evidence ice-cold and refreshing."

Gus held his head in his hands. The world was refusing to be quiet enough for his liking this morning. He had awoken with a terrible headache that insisted on continuously pounding into his forehead even after two aspirins. He concluded that he was getting too old for all-night checkpoint duty. Staying up all night was a job for the younger men. The bloodshot eyes that looked back at him as he glanced into his rearview mirror seemed to be echoing that fact. It was just a matter of time before he'd be too old for any duty his job required. The late-night work hadn't even been worth it in the end. He had only caught two foolish DUI cases, and only one of those could he bring in to the station for prosecution. The rest of the night was spent catching people with minor infractions that wouldn't even pay for the expensive floodlights, overtime for his deputies, and the tow-truck driver's time. Either people were actually getting smarter or, as he suspected, the damn social media was more and more capable of foiling the county's rebranding efforts. Perhaps the stupid people really were getting collectively smarter these days thanks to all that social-media technology. Well, at least he had the pounding satisfaction of making society slightly better by not drunk driving to go along with his headache.

He parked the sheriff's truck in his own personal parking spot at the law-enforcement complex. Parked next to his truck sat a vehicle owned by the vilest organization of the highly competitive policing circuit—a patrol vehicle from the ICE, Immigration and Customs Enforcement. The agents didn't stay long, which was okay by Gus. They started up their vehicle and drove out of his station's parking lot. Gus half wondered what they had wanted at his office and was more than half glad they had left before he got to find out. As long as they didn't want to talk to him, he wasn't going to worry about them. Another source of headaches he didn't need this morning.

Gus opened the sheriff's truck's door. An empty brown bottle of beer beat Gus out of his truck. He exited the vehicle and picked up the bottle. He had fond memories of that beer. A man could forget a lot of things while drinking, but the memory of a great-tasting beer wasn't one of them. The bottle had been expensive stuff and an on-the-house treat from his only DUI victim of the night, but now it was reduced to garbage. He rubbed his temple. He didn't remember putting any empty bottles in his truck last night. He remembered he had drunk a few while manning the checkpoint, but he had done that drinking task only for the good of the community. The community had a right to know if their Breathalyzers were accurate. Still staring at the empty, he could swear almost 100 percent positively that he hadn't taken any beer home with him to drink. Unfortunately, this empty bottle seemed to indicate to the affirmative that he had. The loss of short-term memory was another sign of old age, or so they say. He tossed the bottle into the back of his truck and entered the law-enforcement complex.

The front desk was empty. Its lack of personnel meant the person manning it was busy doing other activities somewhere in the station. Gus hoped those activities weren't ICE related. The last thing he wanted was to get involved in immigration's messes. He passed down the hall heading toward his office and the sanctuary he would find once inside it. His secretary was manning her desk in her usual surly demeanor. Gus put on a false pretense and greeted her happily in hopes that those false airs would be reciprocated. "What's going on today, my sweet?"

Lupita sat writing electronic paperwork on her computer and didn't even bother to acknowledge him with a courteous fake smile. She muttered, "Nothing's new, and it never will be new so long as the old likes of your sweet lazy ass are in charge here. It's disappointing, isn't it, to wake up and find your fat, dumb, and ugly mug greeting you in the mirror each morning? It could be worse, though; you could be the mirror. After all, you have the chance to gaze at pretty faces like mine once in a while, but that mirror in your home only has your ugly mug to look forward to seeing day after day."

Gus was not in the mood for banter and sighed, "I'm glad to hear you've taken a new optimistic view on things. There is nothing wrong with day after day of nothing particular going on. It means that we as a society are maintaining our high standards. That's the whole point of the rebranding effort."

"Some standards you got. You just keep on going down the path you're on. The path you're heading on leads exactly to nothing, so you won't be disappointed in its final destination. They claim hell is paved by the path of good intentions, but that path is tarred by a chain gang composed of bad-intending trash like you that were never bothered by the fact that you were doing nothing all the time."

"That's a cheerful thought, Lupita. You always brighten my morning with these nuggets of joy. Here I was worried I might be lonely in the afterlife, and you reassure me that I won't be. I like the sound of an eternal chain gang that helps keep up the afterlife's infrastructure. At least I now know that down there deep in hell, society still keeps up its infrastructure, which is frankly more than we do up here. Being on that chain gang seems to be an all-right fate by me, because I find that the kind of guy that's dead certain he will be going to heaven is always the kind of guy you'd rather not spend eternity with."

Satisfied nothing was going on and happy to end his daily give-and-take with his surly secretary, Gus reached for his office door. There was only so much of Lupita's brand of sunshine you felt like listening to on a given day. Lupita wasn't done giving out good advice, though. She shouted as he tried to escape, "The wheels of justice turn slowly, but they have a habit of grinding exceedingly fine. You'll find that out. All sinners find that out in the end. No doubt the wretched little murdering girl will find it out too."

Gus nodded in approval. Satisfied that Lupita was done blathering about stuff, he reached for the door again. The wheel of God wasn't the only thing moving slowly today. A thought was slowly grinding in Gus's head. It was preventing him from going through his office door. It was nagging at him through the headache. Then big words flashed across his mind: "What girl?" It seemed to be a question nagging to be asked, so Gus asked it. "Err, what wretched murdering woman exactly would this be?"

16

A smug expression danced across Lupita's face. She knew something, and only now after chastising Gus sufficiently did she release her knowledge to ruin what was already shaping up to be a very bad day. "I mean the seventeen-year-old pretty girl who the state police just brought into our station this morning. She ran away from her home. ICE picked her up coming across the border. They handed her off to the state police in our lobby, and they handed her off to us. We're the nearest temporary jailing facility. She killed her seven-month-old child down in Mexico. Can you believe that? She'll go to hell for sure. First, though, she is going to Kansas. We are awaiting the signed extradition paper to extradite her sinning butt back there. Her parents were none too pleased at her. They got the local DA up there in Kansas to press for first-degree murder charges against her. The commissioner of the state police, Brian Hartline, is in your office right now. He's waiting to tell you the good news on this very bad girl."

Gus had a hard time separating Kansas from hell this morning. It must have been due to the headache. Gus simply replied, "Remember minutes ago when I asked you if anything was going on this morning? Well, that last stuff you just told me would have been a nicer initial answer than your original answer of nothing."

Gus left her and entered his office. Brian Hartline was the commissioner of the state police. He considered himself the end-all and be-all of policing in the state. The fact that local police and sheriff offices existed didn't bother the commissioner because, in Gus's experience, Brian Hartline simply ignored their jurisdiction. Law enforcement tended to be one big dysfunctional family of agencies that rarely talked to each other unless the law forced them to. That meant if Brian Hartline was sitting in his office behind his desk smoking a cigar, then he was there for a reason that made it unavoidable to be there. It was a reason that would likely make Gus's day worse than the headache pounding away at his forehead.

"Nice to see you again, asshole; why don't you have a seat, and I'll explain the situation to you," spoke Commissioner Hartline as soon as Gus entered his office.

The commissioner had a way with words—mostly four-letter words. He had expanded his vulgarity to seven letters already, which meant there must be an extra-special cow pie waiting for Gus in the conversation. Brian Hartline was sitting in Gus's chair behind Gus's desk appearing rather comfortable. There was a simple fact that you didn't want to make a man like Brian comfortable in your office, since he was always lobbying the big boys in the capital to do away with your office's funding. Gus blurted out, "This is my office, so you stand up and tell me quickly why your prisoner is in my jail. I don't do charity work. Each warm body in those cells back there costs me money, and I'm not planning on paying for your state boys' bills."

"The county owns those cells and not you personally, Gus. She's charged in Kansas with murder, and so she is sitting in a cell until the paperwork gets done to formally dispose of her into the fucking legal system." He attempted to blow a smoke ring, but all he managed to do was foul the office air further.

"I didn't charge anyone with any murder. I didn't put her there, and it is my cell." Gus reached down into his pocket and pulled out a key ring. He tossed it on his desk. He explained, "See those keys on my ring sitting on my desk in my office? Those keys open the cell that houses your prisoner. Those keys make that cell mine."

Brian Hartline got up from Gus's desk chair. He put his cigar out on the desktop. He pointed out, "Arguing semantics doesn't get me the fuck out of your office any faster."

"Arguing with you over what will get you to leave my office faster?"

"Don't go thinking I enjoy talking shit to you, because I don't. You're a shit-for-brains elected puppet, and we both know it. If you want just the facts, then that is what I'll give you. Jennifer Louis Bachman is just your average pretty girl from Kansas. She's a seventeen-year-old high-school junior. She was even on the school pep squad or whatever the fuck kids call them these days. To see her is to tear your heart out. She's just a sweet, ordinary Bible-thumper's little girl from Kansas. If only she had stuck to thumping Bibles then you'd be in better shape. She had a boyfriend who went over to Afghanistan for a spell. He blew his brains out in Kabul about one month ago. Depression or some shit like that, who the fuck knows what goes through kids' minds before the bullet does. The fucking suicidal

18

soldier leaves this poster child for innocence back home in good old Kansas seven months pregnant."

"This all sounds very tragic…"

"Stop interrupting and save your tears for the depressing part of the fucking saga. I'm getting to the interesting parts," grumbled Brian. "About two weeks ago, she bolts from her parents' home. Naturally her God-fearing parents get all worried and shit for their poor, innocent seventeen-year-old daughter that is seven months pregnant with a dead soldier's child. Apparently the parents filled her full of God's good word but didn't put in a word about prophylactics. The parents got worried, so they called the Kansas state police. They told the police that their kid got too emotional about this death shit, so emotional in fact that this pure, saintly daughter of theirs left home in destress. This girl's story was a rather sympathetic story, so naturally all of surrounding law enforcement has been keeping a keen eye out for her. We in law enforcement do our job rather quickly, because we're not dumb fucks like you. We found her last night, but when she was found, she wasn't pregnant no more. She was picked up by ICE crossing the border on a return trip back from our friendly neighbors to the south.

"The ICE squad drilled her nice and rough. They got out of her that she had an abortion down there south of border. *Viva México* and all that jazz—a fucking rat nest hole of shit of a border town if you ask me. Stupid kid should have kept her mouth shut to those ICE boys, but the ICE guys spooked her good, and so she talked to them, and it all came pouring out. It is fucking bad news for you. This post-twenty-week abortion shit is illegal in Kansas without magical doctor's approval that her life is in danger that never comes, her parents' consent that wasn't given, a pointless mandatory state counseling that wasn't given, an equally pointless ultrasound that she didn't have, and a twenty-four-hour waiting period, which she decided was better not waiting for. It turns out the parents lied to law enforcement about why their daughter ran away. They knew all along she went for an abortion. They wouldn't approve of her abortion, and so that's why she ran away. Apparently in the parents' view of things, it's okay to lie to law enforcement if it's all for God's greater plan. The parents have a store-bought Bible-worshipping district attorney in their pockets. Apparently they are all Christian-with-a-capital-C type of people up there in Kansas. This DA had the charges waiting for her once she floated back to the surface. It got officially filed last night when the abortion became verified. To make a long story short, they got a murder-one charge in Kansas waiting for our sweetheart as soon as she gets extradited back there. There ends my fucking story."

Gus walked over to his desk and sat down. Brian didn't leave the office, so logically there was something left unsaid. The story was left incomplete. Gus brushed off the cigar ashes onto the floor. He gave it a good minute to see if Brian would offer the rest of the story, but it didn't come. Everyone liked playing games. It was the way you showed other people you were going out on top. Gus at last complained, "That doesn't explain why she's in my jail cell, and you know it. Don't give me the play-by-play and leave out all the action."

"Yours was the nearest facility."

"Oh, don't give me that bullshit."

Brian hit his fist upon the desk. He then walked around to the garbage can. He crumpled his cigar into a ball and threw it down with the trash. He gave the can an extra kick to settle it in. He was a rude, loud, and vulgar man. Gus figured that it was probably impossible for a nicer man to become commissioner in this state. It wasn't that nice guys always finished last when it came to promotions, but there had to be nice guys in the race to begin with. Brian Hartline is what you got when the race came with a stacked deck. Still, he figured when he was done taking out his childhood frustration on the furniture, he would tell the room what was on his mind. Gus figured he knew already, but he also knew Brian wasn't leaving until he got whatever he needed to get off his chest. And so after a short anger-filled pace around the small office, he let loose with the situation as it really stood.

"Well fuck, Gus, you're going to figure out this shit eventually. There is a shit storm on the horizon, and don't sit in that chair pretending you don't know it. We aren't arguing about a jail cell. We're arguing over who wants to be in the path of the shit storm. The new governor of this great state of ours is a chick, right? A chick gets all emotional very easy. She ain't gonna exactly send this girl along quickly back to Kansas. Oh no, she won't, and you can count on that. Those vegetarian San Francisco lesbians will be down here eating fish and putting a flea in our governor's ear before you know it. They'll be a force of protestors at your doorstep on everything from genetically modified turds to circumcision as soon as they get wind of an abortion case going on here. Then if that don't beat all, we also know every irregular churchgoer with no life, but armed with the possession of a Bible and a bell in their favorite tower, will be beating a path down here as well asking for a right to a life. The only right these people have for a life is when they try to ruin someone else's life by forcing them to live like they pretend to. It will be fucking bullshit fuck chaos. The only thing that saves my lucky ass from dealing with it all is that she crossed the border into your county, so in my opinion that makes this your fucking shit storm and not mine. So that's why I made sure ICE picked her up at the border and drove her straight here. The little apple of her parents' eye is all yours, Gus, and if you believe a word of what I just said, then you'll know she'll likely be the fucking biggest dick-suck headache you've ever had. Enjoy it, asshole, because I'm dumping it on you. You can complain to the governor, but I'll tell you you're already behind the San Francisco lesbians and the Catholic priests on her conference-call list."

Gus knew that while not everything Brian said was coherent, the gist of the statement was accurate. Gus was not in a good spot here. He rubbed his temple and muttered, "How long is she likely going to be here?"

"Too long. Of course I'll try to grease our governor's ear for you when I get back to the capital, but like I said, I can promise you our esteemed governor will be hampered by hearing from idiots, which will prevent her from listening to sensible people like me," replied Hartline. Brian laughed at the relief the burden. He had been able to pass the buck down to someone else. He then tipped his hat to Gus and departed.

Gus sat in his chair for a long time too worried to think. He didn't exactly know what to do. His head hurt. He moved over to the minifridge in the office. He opened the door to find half a case of *Little Red's Mexican Ale*. He slid a bottle of it out. He reminded himself he needed to save some of this case as evidence just in case there was a trial. Nothing relieved a headache like a little brown bottle of liquid painkiller. Alcohol was good at numbing the senses even if it wasn't known to be good at it for the long haul. He popped the top off the bottle by using the edge of his desk and started to drink it down.

He had to get his mind off his new troubles, so Gus dug through his in-box on his desk looking over the dull rote paperwork inside. He'd formalize all the traffic-stop paperwork with his rubber stamp later, as his headache made it too much to handle now. He sipped on his beer and dug out a manila folder buried under all that work. Curiosity got the better of Gus, so he opened it. There was a formal document inside from Dr. Armstrong in the form of an official lab toxicology report taken on samples from a sixteen-year-old named Kim Swoops. A few weeks ago, she was suspected of having taken her mother's ample supply of prescription drugs in order to get high. She hadn't lived. The lab just confirmed what he knew already—overdose of Percocet. A certain Dr. Smith liked to write an abundance of prescriptions to the mother of the girl, Mrs. Swoops, but there was not much Gus could do about all that. It was being handled out of state. He tucked the paperwork back in the folder and tossed it in his out-box, feeling even more depressed when Deputy Drew bounded into his office.

"Sheriff, I hate to disturb you, but there's a strange man in the cell block!"

Gus sipped on his beer. Well, he sipped on the drunk driver's beer, but it was almost his at this point. He figured the driver wasn't likely to want it in the recycled state it was bound to be in before too long. Gus shooed his annoying deputy out of his office. He needed time to think about what he could do to get rid of this girl. It wasn't fair that this girl was his burden to carry. She ought to have committed that crime somewhere, anywhere else. Gus informed Drew, "That's just the drunk we picked up last night. Don't tell me you are too hungover to remember the arrest we made last night. Boy, you need to learn to hold your liquor better. I figure Sedric Hedgecock's lawyer will be around eventually to fetch him away from our hospitality suite. Good ole Sedric was an expensive-looking man, so I figure he can afford his own special lawyer for this DUI case. One of those rich specialist lawyers no doubt. Until the lawyer shows up, we better make sure Sedric's bread and water have got plenty of maggots in them. I'd hate for him to be in the wrong frame of mind when he meets his lawyer."

"Not him, Sheriff. That ain't what I mean. I remember the drunk driver from last night just fine. What I meant was that there's a strange man on the cell block. I don't know where he came from."

"Deputy, could you please start making some sense?"

"I can't start making sense because there's no sense to be made. You see, Rusty the Meth-Hating Dog and I were checking on the prisoners to see that they weren't getting up to no good in the holding cells when we found him. Rusty had heard that there was a pretty girl down on the blocks, so naturally we wanted go and make extra sure no one was committing suicide or nothin'. The sign-in chalkboard says we only got two prisoners: the drunkard Sedric and the cute girl from Kansas left to us by the state boys, but I counted three cells filled with people in them back there. Rusty double-checked the count, so it ain't just me. There are three people back there for sure. Now what do you make of that?"

It was a question with no immediate answer. Gus didn't know what to make of that. People don't appear in prison cells unless someone else puts them in there. It wasn't exactly the kind of place a person longs to visit on a holiday. He wondered if Commissioner Brian Hartline was as honest as to all the problems he had just laid on Gus's door as he claimed, but that didn't make sense. If he was willing to formally talk about the young woman, then why'd he leave this other guy out of the conversation? More to the point, the state police had been kind enough to place her on the official record, so why not him? There wouldn't be a reason that Gus could think of in his headache-filled mind. Gus reached over and picked up the keys to his jail cells off his desk. There was only one way to solve this mystery of the new man on the cell block, and that was to go talk to him. He cursed. "Aw, shit. I kid you not, Deputy, all this crap is not what I needed today."

The law-enforcement complex's holding cells occupied a secure location in the back of the building. The holding cells weren't meant for convicted prisoners to spend their days paying off their court-ordered debt to society. Most of those people got sent off to the county lock-up. The real serious criminal felons got shipped upstate to the for-profit super-maximum-security lockup that was located in the middle of nowhere. No one sane longed to end their life up there in that place. Gus's holding cells were few in number and only meant for people just resting a little while in free parking until a judge got to chew over the relevance of their special crime against humanity or until someone came to bail out the temporary prisoner. The individual cells were located on the cell block, which was just a fancy name for a single hallway composed of cement brick and steel bars. The cell block was held secure by a gate composed of bars. Steel bars weren't exactly fancy to look at, but they worked just fine for keeping people in a place they didn't want to be.

In front of the secure gate was a small desk with a flat-screen monitor showing an image from the camera that was set up to watch the cell-block hallway. This desk with its little digital screen was supposed to be monitored at all hours of the day and night by a deputy, but it was a rather boring task. There were plenty of reasons for sheriff's deputies to leave it and draw their attention away from being at this desk watching the nothing that happened on the screen. The monitoring desk wasn't manned, as Gus knew it wouldn't be. The man whose job it was to be at it today was Deputy Drew, and Gus had left Drew back in Gus's office. Gus figured Drew would wander his way back down here to this desk eventually.

Next to the desk was a large roll-up door that serviced the loading dock. It opened to the back parking lot. Delivery vans dumped palatable foods whenever there was a long-term inmate having a full-blown trial. Gus jiggled the lock on the roll-up door. It was secure. Gus looked over to the large chalkboard next to the roll-up door. The chalkboard was meant to show who was who inside the cell block and where they were located among the cells. The chalkboard told Gus that cells two and three were entertaining guests at the moment. Cell two was called the drunk tank. Gus knew that cell two held Sedric Hedgecock, because he had put him in there

24

late last night. Cell three had the name Jennifer written on it. Gus didn't recognize the handwriting, but that wasn't much of a mystery. The rest of the chalkboard was blank.

Gus slid open a drawer on the desk. He pulled out the keyboard for the log computer. The last people to log in and out of the cell block were state-police boys. They had registered one guest by the name of Jennifer. It all sounded exactly like it was supposed to so far. Gus put his key into the lock and typed a security code into the keypad located on the gate of iron bars. Nothing happened. He opened the top right drawer in the security desk. There was a notepad inside the drawer with several sets of numbers written on it. The numbers on the top of the ledger were crossed out over and over again by a pen. There were fresh numbers written underneath all the crossed-out ones. The numbers were the monthly passcodes to the door. You couldn't get inside without knowing them. Gus pulled out his reading glasses. He held the pad with one hand and read it as he typed on the keypad with the other. The door's lock opened with a clunk. He tossed the pad into the desk drawer and remembered to close it. After all, you needed to maintain security in a place like this, so you couldn't have just anyone seeing the monthly passcode.

The cell block was a long, underlit hallway composed of two-foot-thick concrete-brick walls. On one side was a blank wall, and on the other side was a row of bars that marked each of the prison cells. Each cell was separated by another concrete wall. The place stank of antiseptic and the mildew the antiseptic was supposed to be killing. The first cell was empty. It usually was unless the whole block was full. The second cell was the real working cell of the place. It was the largest of Gus's holding cells. The drunk tank served more than those who had too much to drink. It was the daily holding cell for people who had committed their special crime while the eyes of the courts were sleeping. Public drunkenness was an offense, but one generally not enforced too strictly by Gus's department so long as the people could still physically move their body and weren't committing a public nuisance. When they failed that standard, then they got stuck in this cell overnight. Few nights passed when someone didn't drink themselves into a coma out in public. They'd usually walk away with the appropriate bail bond fund in the morning. Most people walked away with just a slap on the wrist so long as they weren't driving a motor vehicle.

The rest of the cells were smaller than cell number two and held only one guest at a time. Gus spied a pair of hands holding on to the bars of cell number two. Gus pulled out his nightstick and walked the cell line. As he approached cell two, he swung the stick hard into the steel bars just below the waiting hands. The hands quickly darted back inside the cell. This morning Sedric should feel lucky, for he had his own private cell to sleep it off in. It was a good thing that they'd only picked up one person last night. Gus figured you couldn't put a guy like Sedric who blew sky-high alcohol numbers in with all the other common drunks. You had to worry a little for a man like that, as he might expire before sobering up. Sedric was up and moving, so he had lived through the night. Gus looked into the drunk tank. This morning the funny drunk Sedric of last night was long gone, along with the alcohol buzz that had fueled him. Now in the morning only a red-faced, angry man called Sedric remained standing in his confined place. Sedric's face was stone sober. The man didn't even have the common decency to appear embarrassed about the fate that now had befallen him. His voice shrieked out of the cell in anger at Gus, "What the hell are you trying to do to me!"

"Quiet, Hedgecock, I got no time to smell the likes of you this fine morning," ordered Gus. The man had been sick all over the front of his nice designer suit. There was a pile of sick on the flat wooden shelf that served as a bed. The smell was not a pleasant one, and it perfumed the cell. Gus complained, "Do you know what I got to pay a month in cleaning bills? If there was any justice, then I'd get to charge you the cost of my cleaning bill. These tidy cells of mine don't clean up on the cheap, you know. Now quiet down, because you got guests down the hall. They don't want to hear you yelling any more than I do. Didn't your momma ever teach you a lick of manners?"

Sedric came back up to the bars of the cell and grabbed them again. He yelled a little more. "This is an outrage! I can't imagine why I am in here. What happened to my car? That is a limited-edition series six, you know. If you fools scratched even a millimeter of paint on her, then I'm going to sue!"

"I'd advise you not to file that lawsuit. Juries in this county don't like people who use the metric system," replied Gus as he walked on by the cell, heading for cell number three.

"I demand to see my lawyer!" he shouted.

"Don't worry; I'll get a deputy to start work on getting your smelly butt out of here. Trust me when I say that I don't see a need for you to keep stinking up my jail cells any longer than you have to. You're charged with drunk driving. You'll be charged with drunk driving if you see a lawyer or not."

Gus walked away from Sedric and his obvious problems. The next cell had a seventeen-year-old woman. She was dressed in an orange prison jumpsuit. No doubt the clothing was a precaution just in case she tried to kill herself. People do from time to time in a jail cell. The makers of this place had taken out just about anything you could think of that a person could attempt a thing like that with, but suicidal people were very creative, and so they tried hard just the same by whatever means they could manage. You could question that if they were that creative, then why did they end up in jail? Likely the answer was that people could be just as creative at causing trouble as they could be at preventing it.

The young woman from Kansas was strikingly cute even as seventeen-year-olds go. A very innocent blonde who should have been a cheerleader in high school up in Kansas and not a prisoner in his cell, but the fates had chosen a different path for her in life. She was curled up in a ball on the wooden slab for a bed. She held her knees up to her chest, and tears ran down her cheeks. She cried silently either for herself or for others. A lot of things worth crying about had happened to her lately if you went by what Brian Hartline had said. The light from the tiny window in the back wall of the cell backlit her to Gus. Her golden hair radiated in the brief ray of morning sunlight. People like that were too young to be in here, and yet a lot of jails were filled with people just that young. It was all enough to break your heart. Still, she was supposed to be here, just like smelly old Sedric Hedgecock was supposed to be here, for she had committed a crime in the eyes of the law. Her crime was nothing to sneeze at either, for she was charged with murder one, according to those people up in Kansas. Gus had come in here searching for a mysterious man; he had found Sedric, and he had found Jennifer. Now he needed to find this mystery man number three whom Drew had talked about. Gus nodded to Jennifer and started to move on down toward the next cell on the block.

As Gus was nearly clear of Jennifer's cell, the young woman whispered something. He turned to face her again, and she spoke softly a second time, "Mister, can you help me?"

Gus shook his head no. "I'm sorry, little lady, but I'm only the county sheriff. I can't help anyone. If you need help, then I'd go say a silent prayer to God and see if he's in the helpin' mood. I don't find that God is often in his helping mood while people are in my cell block, but there ain't no crime in asking."

"I have," she replied a little more confidently. "Sheriff, do you believe in angels?"

"Not since Donnie Moore gave up that home run to Dave Henderson. I had fifty bucks riding on that game. Screw those East Coast teams. Although I imagine you probably meant the kind of angel that floats in the air with feathered wings while wearing fine silken white robes, didn't you?" The girl nodded and began to wipe away the tears with her left hand. Gus continued, "I don't reckon I believe in any such thing, but you go ahead and pray for one to help you in your time of need if you feel you ought to. No one ever got punished in my jail for talking to angels— except maybe a Hell's Angel biker or two. They aren't by far the worst bikers in the world, but they are in my opinion the worst angels I've met. Don't see how it has ever done a prisoner any good, though. Even Jesus ended up a prisoner, and that seemed to suit God's plans just fine. I figure if God was willing to let his own son rot unnecessarily in prison and then let him up and get executed for something penny ante, then this God isn't the kind to get all worked up about how people down here enforce justice. He certainly isn't likely to be worked up about such a concept in a stinky little nothing of a hole like this one." He finally bit his acidic

28

tongue. There was no sense depressing Jennifer when she was already on the downside of life.

"I don't pray to any old God. My parents believe in that God. Parents…" The sentiment was left hanging, and Gus let it stay there. She appeared to have said all she was going to say on that subject, and he started once again to move away from the cell bars when she spoke again to him. "My poor Robin is an angel now. Robin is the name of my little girl. She had trisomy thirteen, or so the doctors all said. Nothing they could do about it. I had to do right by her. I'm sorry for what I done and all. I wish I had the power to change it, but I don't. I had to do right by her. People, my parents and the folks in their church, didn't understand. They all appear to think they're doctors without no degree or training. The doctors at the clinic all told me one thing about Robin, and these friends of my parents all told me another thing. Most people, I suppose, aren't doctors. You'd think the law would allow a person to do right by their children. I never wanted to do nothing but to do right," said Jennifer, holding back more tears.

Gus nodded in agreement. He didn't know what exactly she was talking about, but he figured it didn't hurt to agree to the direction of the conversation. She was a prisoner and very likely to remain one for some time to come. He replied, "I'm sorry, but there really is nothing I can do. You go pray to your Robin. She'll be up there looking out for you from now on, I suppose."

"Do you really think that?"

That was a real shitty question to ask him. No, he didn't really think that. She knew he didn't really think that. He could read it in her eyes that she understood perfectly well how he felt. She was seventeen and had gotten wise to the fact that adults had been telling little white lies to her, her whole life. It wasn't an easy age to be. Gus didn't know an easy age to be, but he understood seventeen was one of the hardest. He gently tapped the side of his head with his nightstick and smiled at her. "It don't matter what I think. If I was good at thinking, then I wouldn't have ended up a sheriff in this place. Don't live your life by my thinking. Is there anything I can get you: an extra blanket, a pillow, a cheeseburger?"

"I just want to be left alone."

She had requested the one thing Gus knew he had no power to grant her, and worse, the one thing that was never going to happen. He replied, "I'll see what I can do about that."

She turned away from him and faced the stone wall. Gus walked on down the cell block. Gus was past the first three cells and stared down the cell block at what he hoped were four empty ones to come. The prisoners in cell two and three seemed to be perfectly normal for prisoners. The fourth one was empty, and that left only three more to investigate. Cell five was likewise vacant. *Good*, thought Gus, *let's keep all the remaining ones that way too*. Gus strolled quickly by cell six, dragging his nightstick along the bars. It was empty as the day it was made. Then Gus arrived at cell number seven, the last cell on the block. It brought an unwelcome sight. That cell was unfortunately very much occupied despite what the chalkboard had indicated. There was a handsome blond man sitting inside the cell. He was sitting on a large wooden trunk that had designer labels on it. The blond man was typing madly away on a flat-screen handheld electronic device like he didn't have a care in the world.

The man was infinitely recognizable to Gus. He was an internationally known computer hacker who had been named Josh Hansen by his parents, although likely he was going by an assumed name at the moment. He always had an extra name or two stored up to go by just to confuse Gus. The man thought of himself as a revolutionary. He was under the belief that all revolutions happen online these days. The fact that there were actual revolutionaries with real guns and bombs blowing themselves up all over the world didn't seem to shake the hacker of this belief. Josh Hansen was beloved by many young Internet users and hated by many governmental authorities for the illegal hacking he so often did. He could hack into any computer system he thought hacking into would help his cause. When he wasn't personally hacking, he ran computer sites that disseminated information obtained by other hackers. Josh considered himself a techno–Robin Hood, but Gus always suspected there was a hint of Prince John in the man. Yeah, Gus always figured his cause in the end was more poetic in appearance than actuality. He was a man who talked a lot about helping society for the better in the long term, while the only person helped out in the short term by all this hacking appeared to be Josh Hansen.

Josh Hansen wasn't just an ordinary hacker either. No, as an added feature to throw into the mix, Hansen had also possibly killed a young woman while in Gus's county some while back. He was certainly involved in her death. That much Gus knew for sure. That was in the distant past now, as the state police had pinned those crimes on another conveniently dead person. Dead criminals were great for clearing the logbooks of past crimes. Gus had longed to put this computer hacker behind bars, but he hadn't expected the man to put himself behind those bars personally. Gus tapped on the steel bars with his nightstick, but the annoying Josh Hansen was playing the quiet game and didn't bother to acknowledge Gus's appearance.

Gus barked, "Hansen, what are you doing back in my county?"

Josh gazed up with an innocent expression on his face. He replied, "I've come to enjoy your county's serene oceanfront."

"We don't have an oceanfront in this county. All we have are grasslands and deserts. If you want an ocean view, I suggest finding your way out of my jail the same way you apparently found your way into it and head your way out west."

"Sheriff, the part of the ocean I like best is the sandy beach. I think of your county not as a horrible, hot wasteland, but as just one endless beach. When you think of the desert like that, it isn't so bad, now is it? You could say I'm a glass-half-full kind of man. I always try to see the optimistic side of things."

Gus stuck his keys into the lock in the cell door. He unlocked the door. He put his weight into it and budged the door open. He then proceeded to slide the steel bars to the side. He replied, "I'm glad to hear you say that, since it means you won't view this cell door as half closed."

Josh got up from his trunk. He walked over to Gus with a friendly smile. He leaned on the bars next to the open door and explained, "I don't see why you are so eager to see me go away. I tend to recall you talked about arresting me at some point long ago in our past. Well, here I am, ready to do the time for my many crimes, both real and imagined. They say if you can't do the time, then don't do the crime. The people who say that, though, are the wealthy whose crimes the system is designed to overlook, so they never do the time. If a common man gets drunk and beats up a man in public, then he finds himself here in your little hideaway. If a president gets drunk with power and orders the beatings of hundreds of men in a torture program, then he gets to spend the rest of his life painting dog pictures at his ranch while the authorities try to look ahead and not behind. It is funny how all that works out, isn't it?"

"It's a tough world out there for you underprivileged types. I feel for you deeply. I'll give you both a boo and a hoo, if that helps fill your black heart with joy. Now scram from my cells. I got real people in here with real problems today. They aren't lucky like you; they can't get their problems covered up by secret government agencies." Gus shook his nightstick at the hacker as if threatening him with physical harm might change his mind. Any other time Gus probably would have loved to keep Hansen locked up and out of sight, but this wasn't the time to play the spy game with a hacker. Somewhere Hansen had powerful friends who liked computer hackers enough to use them, and disliked them enough to occasionally try to kill them. Gus had played with those types once before, and the game didn't appeal to him very much. Too many of the wrong people had died last time around. Josh Hansen, meanwhile, was still alive and well.

Josh Hansen wasn't exactly moved by Gus's current situation. Instead he explained his own current situation a little more clearly. "I was hacking the e-mails of climate scientists from my safe house in the Ukraine for a… let's just call them a concerned client. You know, to help find a little dirt to smear 'big science.' There's a lot of money in big science, and those climate scientists apparently play for keeps."

"I'm finding your story a little hard to believe. I figured you'd be for those climate-science types. After all, their computers keep predicting the end of the world, and that's something you tended to be for last time we met."

"Well, that is true. I hacked the scientists and smeared their names by selectively releasing their hacked e-mail only for the money. A man like me needs money to avoid people like you from framing me for the crimes that

I have happened to actually commit. Climate change can absorb a little more smearing about as much as the atmosphere can afford to absorb a little more carbon dioxide. It doesn't matter if my lies changed a few empty minds into nonbelievers. Climate change isn't Tinkerbell. It doesn't require people's beliefs to be true. I also figure it doesn't matter since the less we do about climate change, the faster the center falls apart. I want the center to fall apart. It is a win-win situation in my book. I hadn't figured on these climate scientists fighting back with deadly force, however. They're tougher than you'd think."

"Are you telling me the climate scientists are trying to kill you?"

"Never underestimate the long-armed reach of big science. One day I was hacking in my safe house with…well, their name isn't really important. Let's just say they were called 'Bob.' I said, 'Hey, Bobby, how's it hanging,' and he didn't answer. His hands, feet, and head had been removed. I found most of him hanging in a closet. This was probably an unfortunate new look for him. I found the rest of him bobbing up and down in the bathtub. I figured it would be me next if I didn't get out of there in hurry. I needed a quick, friendly place to stash myself for a little while. Yes, I needed a little oasis to lie low. And then I thought of you and your pleasant county. Don't worry, though; I'm not staying here forever. I'm only here until I can dig up a little reverse dirt to cool off the climate scientists' warming anger. I knew good ole Sheriff Gus's county would welcome me back with open arms. You do want to arrest me for all the murders I accidentally caused here last time I visited, right?"

Gus watched the man's eyes. He could never tell for sure if Josh was telling the truth or just the version of the truth he thought was true. A self-diluted man's truth isn't always the most accurate thing in the world. He figured he could just shoot Josh, and that would end things once and for all. The problem with that was the fact that Gus currently had two witnesses in the holding area to tell on him. Plus Josh Hansen, although certainly not a great pal, had helped Gus out of a jam previously. Still, he couldn't exactly release him into the public for fear that some bounty hunter would actually try to kill him, and they would end up killing all the wrong people. The safest thing for now was to keep him locked up until he got bored and moved on. As an added benefit, you never knew when you might need a hacker. Gus grabbed the cell door and closed it shut on Hansen. He replied, "Okay, Josh, you're now Mr. Smith, and you're the prisoner in cell number seven. I'll figure out what I'm charging you with later on. Don't do anything I wouldn't do, and don't do anything I would do. If you do get the urge to do anything at all, then I wish that thing that you do is to keep an eye on the young woman in cell number three. Mind you, just keep an eye on her, and the rest of her you don't get to touch. She looks like she could use an eagle eye on her. Most of all remember, and this is a real important point, don't do anything that gets another person killed."

"The girl in cell three is the one they just dumped in here this morning. I heard her crime was engaging in sex, and her punishment was being inflicted with pregnancy. No doubt the righteous will come down hard on her for escaping what they perceive as God's justice placed upon her. It was a sin to have sex, and God's punishment is pregnancy. Now that's a fucked-up view, but many people have it. It is unjust in their eyes to exercise her rights to medical access. In more civilized cultures, God does not exist, and women have the right over medical procedures to be conducted on their own person. People complain that too many women fake that their life is in danger to get an abortion. Then the foolish idiots make it the law that it is so hard to get an abortion that soon the only way to obtain an abortion is to lie. They make criminals out of saints all in the name of a God that isn't there. They wish to return to the fake traditions of the world they don't understand written in a book they don't read that describes a fantasy world from two thousand years ago that never existed and wasn't all that great to begin with. This poor girl is going to jail because of this male-obsessed world around her that wants to control her body. If the modern world followed Sparta's lead, then all those weak men that feel the need to control a woman so they can feel more like a real man would have spent their days as stains scattered inside the *Apothetae*. They should be careful what they wish for. It is a great little free country you got here. Don't you worry; I'll keep an eye out for her, boss." Josh gave Gus a friendly wink to end the rant that Gus hadn't bothered to listen to. A phone went off in Hansen's prison cell. Hansen walked over to his trunk, opened it, and retrieved his phone that was inside.

Gus explained, "You can't have a phone with you inside my cell block, Mr. Smith."

"Don't worry, Sheriff; it's a cell phone."

Gus shrugged and took whatever that was as an agreement to not make trouble, but only perhaps a little philosophical noise. He made his way back down the cell block with a headache and a lot of added worries stacking together fast.

CHAPTER 2

Justice is my being allowed to do whatever I like. Injustice is whatever prevents my doing so.
—Samuel Johnson

A bad day was like all other workdays in that they finally ended no matter how bad they had gotten. Brian Hartline was a prophet of judicial jurisprudence because, as predicted, the governor had taken no immediate action on Jennifer's extradition papers. Word had come down the grapevine to Gus that no action was expected any time soon. Thus, the young woman from Kansas would remain Gus's prisoner for some time to come. Sedric, the drunken driver, was far better off than her. Sedric's lawyer, while rather slow on the move, had managed to siphon off enough of Sedric's money targeted for beer purchases to make bail by that afternoon. Josh Hansen was free to leave anytime he wished to, and Gus wished the man had never come at all, but he was still back there among the jail cells playing on his computer widget. Gus had decided to charge Josh Hansen, aka Mr. Smith, with lewd conduct in public. This charge wouldn't be processed ever, and tomorrow Gus would have to figure out another fake thing to charge him with that wouldn't get processed either. Hopefully the hacker would get bored and move on to greener pastures before someone on Santa's naughty list found out about Mr. Smith hiding inside Gus's prison and tried to delete Josh permanently from the parish register.

Gus stepped outside the law-enforcement complex heading for home. The early winter darkness had already crept in. There were only two abortion protesters outside the law-enforcement complex holding a candle vigil. One was an elderly woman, and the other was a well-dressed man. Two wasn't all that bad a number. Brian Hartline had promised Gus a zoo of activity, but two was more a like a monkey house rather than a whole zoo.

"Evening, Sheriff," said the elderly woman as she tried to shove a prayer book into Gus's hand.

"Evening," replied Gus. Gus looked down at the prayer book, titled *Prayers for Life*. He refused her kindly. "I got the full version at home, so I don't need another copy."

"It's good to hear it. Far too few people these days read the good book," said a man's voice in return.

Gus glanced over to the well-dressed man. "And you are?"

"I'm Pastor Uriel Voce of the Christian Brothership Church. We came here to start a daily midnight prayer because we're worried."

"About what?" asked Gus.

"We're worried that the sinner won't get what she deserves and because of it America will end up a godless communist mess just like Canada," said the woman.

"Do not judge, or you too will be judged," replied Gus.

"Don't worry, for we're not afraid to be judged, for we've done nothing but lead a righteous life. We're all very righteous people over at the Christian Brothership Church, and we're all very concerned about keeping up our community's high moral standards," replied the pastor right back.

"I'm glad to hear it. I have to admit that I'm not like you in that regard. I'm afraid to do a bit of judgment. I am, after all, just the local sheriff. You understand that I don't get to judge people; I just get to enforce the law. I don't want people to get to thinking I'm judge, jury, and executioner in these parts. If you want to know if she'll get what she deserves, then you'll have to take it up with the lawyers and the courts."

"The courts," replied the pastor with disdain. "I plan to stay here to make sure Christian feelings are known to this girl. Her slick lawyers will try to convince her to make some excuse to the courts, as that kind always does. In the end she'll claim that her life was in danger or lie about a rape. I can see it in your eyes that she's got an excuse already warming on the block. What was her excuse to God for her special sin?"

"She said it was her fundamental human right."

Pastor Voce replied, "Huh, she must be suffering from post abortion syndrome."

"Well, you're a man, so I guess you'd know all about a feeling like that. Listen, you two, I'd like to chat more, but I'm off duty and would like to go home for a quiet evening. You two stay peaceful now."

"We're always peaceful," replied Pastor Voce.

"I'm glad to hear it." Gus walked over to his truck and got inside.

It wasn't that long a trip from the complex to Gus's home. He pulled the sheriff's truck into his driveway, eager to forget everything that was considered work related. The home was a place that was supposed to bring peace of mind. That was exactly what Gus was figuring to give someone right about now—a firm piece of his mind. The person he was planning on giving it to was his next-door neighbor. The reason was simple. He spied by the electric light of his porch two little girls of about the age of eight standing out in the middle of his lawn. One girl was clearly the daughter of Gus's neighbor, and the other was just a girl of unknown origin. The two young girls were running around like maniacs with a big stick in the unknown girl's hand. The neighbor's daughter appeared to be yelling at this other girl and egging her on to whack into Gus's finely manicured lawn with that stick. Clumps of grass were flying about all over the place. Gus hadn't seen so many divots since Terrance had invited him to that political fund raiser at the swanky private golf course. Two girls that young shouldn't have been out after dark. They shouldn't have been out in the winter after dark without coats on. Most important of all, they shouldn't have been out after dark in the winter without coats on messing up Gus's lawn. All that peace of mind was stirring inside Gus's brain and needed to be delivered to someone.

Gus leaped down from his rusty and quickly dilapidating official sheriff's vehicle and marched across his lawn. As he walked his voice increased in volume. He went from muttering obscenities to himself to a full-out holler directed at the two young fiends. They couldn't have been more than eight, but they were of proper age for yelling at. When he reached within a foot of the two little girls, he let go of a full-throated bark. People that age needed instruction, but all Gus had to offer was a bark. Gus barked, "What are you two little devils doing to my lawn?"

The two girls stopped moving and stood stone still, looking up into Gus's fierce eyes with gazes of innocence. The girl of unknown origin replied with a matter-of-fact tone, "We are just playing."

"That's right; we were just playing Death to Hungry Kids," added the neighbor's daughter as if Gus would know exactly what that title alluded to.

Gus replied, "That sounds like a damn stupid game to by playing on my lawn. There ain't nothing fun about a bunch of kids starving. I have it in my mind to go tell your mama about what you are up to over here. She's going get a piece of my mind about all this playing."

"It is not a stupid game! Everyone at school is playing it. Death to Hungry Kids is just about the bestest book series ever written. They're making them into the bestest movies ever made," explained the neighbor's girl.

"The bestest," echoed the girl of unknown origin.

Gus stopped barking and just looked down at the two with confusion on his face.

"Don't you know what Death to Hungry Kids is?" asked the neighbor's daughter in disbelief.

Gus slowly shook his head. He didn't really care what it was. He cared about what it was doing to his lawn. He paid Miguel and his crew one hundred and fifty bucks a month to keep it in proper shape, and it didn't need two little fiends digging at it with sticks. Indeed, filling these new holes could double the maintenance fee this month.

The neighbor's daughter continued, "It is only one of the bestest movie series in the whole wide world; haven't you been listening to us?"

"The bestest!" the girl of unknown origin agreed.

"I'm a Darvelak of the City Primal. She's just a poor Minimite. She's got no job, no food, and no home. She doesn't matter in this world at all, so she has to entertain us Darvelaks by fighting for her supper. She fights to eat or ends up being eaten. They say it's a game of survival of the fat-test."

"Nope, I don't matter at all. I got to fight to eat!" agreed the girl of unknown origin.

"She's got to bone up and train, or else I won't be entertained, and then it is thumbs down, and another Minimite comes and takes her place on the food lines. The Minimites are a dime a dozen. They also get to wear really neat costumes when they fight to eat. I got all the Death to Hungry Kids collectable action figures!"

"Collect them, trade them, save them 'cause they're the bestest!" added the girl of unknown origin.

None of that made a lick of sense to Gus. He hoped none of that ever made sense to anyone, and yet he got the feeling this movie must be rather popular at the moment. Gus replied to the two young girls, "Well, that all sounds just horrible. More importantly, it sounds like you two should be training on your mother's lawn, since your friend here is supposed to be entertaining you and not me. Miguel has told me he doesn't want you two girls digging any more holes for him to fill in. I believe that I told your mother this already. I didn't want to catch you two over here again digging holes. I also don't want to hear excuses on why you're digging these holes; I just want no holes."

The neighbor's daughter complained, "That isn't what Miguel says to us. He said to us just the other day that it was okay to play here because you are a cheap bastard for not giving him a Christmas bonus. He saw us on my mom's lawn playing just the other day and said come on over and play here 'cause the sheriff's a cheapie."

The other girl corrected her, "That's not true; he didn't say that at all. He said you were a cheap, cheap bastard. He definitely said the word *cheap* twice."

Gus scowled at them both. Off they scurried to go play on the other neighbor's lawn. The problem with kids was that they lied when they should tell the truth and told the truth when it was kinder to lie. Perhaps Miguel really did say that about him, and perhaps he didn't. It didn't matter, because Gus couldn't find a cheaper lawn-care guy than Miguel, so he wasn't about to fire him. Gus quickly surveyed the damage and tried to stomp a few divots back into the ground. Sizing up the pointlessness of his actions and, more to the point, the backbreaking labor involved, he decided to pay Miguel extra to do it for him. Something, however, needed to be done about this horrible situation. He couldn't afford a Christmas bonus, let alone month after month of overtime payments to maintain a Minimite-battered front lawn. Gus took a step onto his neighbor's adjoining lawn, heading for their front door. He stopped himself. He didn't want to miss his opportunity to lead by example for those two children. Gus walked down his driveway and then back up his neighbor's driveway. He climbed the front steps and rang the neighbor's doorbell.

The door jerked open after a few moments. Gus's neighbor hung on the other side of the door momentarily lost for words. There was no hello, hi, or what do you want coming from his neighbor's worried-looking lips. Gus's neighbor was called Rosa Hernandez. She was a plump forty-year-old wearing a dowdy shirt and pants. Since she wasn't in the greeting mood tonight, Gus started things off. "Hi there, neighbor, I guess we both know why I've come over to chat."

"But the note said two weeks. I still have two more weeks," replied Rosa.

Perhaps *we* didn't both know why Gus had walked over, as Gus didn't understand that response at all. Gus clarified things. "I don't know anything about a note or two weeks. I'm here because your daughter is digging holes in my lawn again. We spoke about that matter three weeks ago and not two weeks ago. I'm sure you'll remember the conversation. I can bring over a divot of grass or two to remind you if needed."

"You...you're the sheriff in these parts, right?"

"Hole or no holes, I'm still sheriff in these parts. I'm hoping on the no holes part."

She wasn't listening to him. She appeared to be off in her own little world of thoughts. They were thoughts Gus didn't exactly care about at this moment. He had come to talk about holes in his lawn and not some note. Unfortunately, she momentarily left the doorway. The doorway hung open. Gus took a few steps back to the edge of the porch to spy out what those kids were up to now. They were still over on the other neighbor's lawn digging more holes on account of the undue influence of some kid's movie and the accompanying book series. Gus had always been suspicious of reading, and these holes seemed to justify that suspicion. Rosa returned to the open door with a sheet of legal paper in her hand. She handed it on over to Gus. "See, here's the paperwork. It says I still got two weeks. I'm not leaving, and you got no right to force me out for two more weeks."

Gus took the paperwork from her. He slid his reading glasses out of his pocket. All he wanted was to stop her daughter from digging up his grass. Everything was more complicated than it needed to be these days. Gus scanned down the front page. It was a letter from the Arroyo National Bank. Apparently they were foreclosing on this property due to an unpaid mortgage bill. The letter warned that the sheriff's office would be evicting Mrs. Hernandez from her house in two weeks' time. Gus read the total amount past due on the mortgage—two dollars. Gus took his glasses off and cleaned them on his shirt and read that last line again. He looked up from the pages and asked her, "You can't pay two dollars?"

"No, they won't let me pay it. They say I have to pay it all or nothing. The remaining mortgage owed is a whole lot more than just two dollars. You see, I've been trying to catch up on all the bills ever since I got tired of feeling the back hand of my no-good loving husband and threw him out six months ago. He hadn't worked in a while. He was secretly blowing all our money on drink. When I confronted him on it, he'd hit me. That was his solution to all our problems. I couldn't take it anymore, so out he went. I've been working two shifts down at the maid service trying to catch up on the bills. I've been awful behind lately on paying everything, but last month I finally got everything just about paid off, but those two dollars. I didn't have the full amount to pay the mortgage off, but I was only short two dollars. I figured they wouldn't care if two dollars were late. They did care, and they cared plenty, because they foreclosed. I've tried giving them the stupid late two dollars now that I got it, but they don't want my money. They want my house."

Gus took the front page off the paperwork and folded it up. He then slid it into his pocket. He explained to her, "My office isn't evicting anyone on account of two lousy dollars, so you stop worrying about this, you hear. I'll personally stop by the bank and pay the two dollars for you. There has to be some mix-up. You know banks are always having mix-ups. I ain't losing a neighbor on account of two dollars, holes in the lawn or no hole in my lawn."

"Thank you, Sheriff," Rosa replied.

"Thank me by keeping those kids off my lawn."

As annoying as the neighbor's daughter was, you couldn't risk losing a neighbor. There was always someone vastly worse who could move in next door. This neighbor at least kept her house's appearance up well enough. Nope, the fact was Gus could do a lot worse as far as neighbors went. For instance, Rosa could have left, and the husband could have stayed.

Gus walked across the neighbor's lawn to his property. It was the shortest path between two points, and his leading by example was wearing thin on him the later the day got. He was late for his dinner, and he was hungry. Gus walked up to his porch and passed through his front door. After a nightmare day at the office, it was always good to be inside his home and be safe and sound. No unexpected problems worse than anything at his office would be in there waiting to bother him.

That last part was always a bit of an exaggeration. Once in a great while, something at home was worse than it was at the office. For instance, a pair of thugs working for Big Gustavo's Mexican drug gang could be waiting just inside the entrance hall of Gus's house wielding aluminum bats. They could hammer down onto each of Gus's supple knees just as he passed through his doorway. Now the odds on any given day of this event happening were very, very slim. Today just happened to be that one-in-a-million unlucky day. The bats made a dull ping and not the crisp sound you get off an official MLB wooden baseball bat. There was something disappointing about the sound of the strike of an aluminum bat for a baseball purest. However, for the cheap thugs the aluminum bats were just fine for the smashing up of kneecaps. Gus fell face forward onto the hallway floor with an unceremonious thud. His wife had always insisted on hardwood flooring, and Gus really appreciated the hard part of the floor as he struck it. He reached out his hands to brace himself but only managed to jam his wrists upon impact with the cold, hard flooring. The extreme pain didn't come all at once. No, it lingered back for just a moment until the body realized the true horror of the situation. Then in unison his nerve endings fired pure pain into his brain.

There wasn't much Gus could do to ease the pain. He figured trying to get up would only result in another round of batting practice. Gus slowly flopped over onto his back. The two thugs stood towering over him with a look of menace on their faces. Gus didn't know them. They were only a pair of cheap rent-a-goons. They'd be dead before long one way or another. The odds of working your way up the drug-gang ladder weren't as good as the odds of falling off it completely. Eventually the stupid idiots would do something worth getting rid of them, and they'd be gotten rid of. There were dozens of goons on the open market to replace them. In a drug gang, it was the people at the top who got all the money, and they were all that mattered. Gus was trying to feel bad about their fate, but the pain in his knees was blocking his otherwise empathetic feelings at the moment. Gus watched them for a minute, waiting for them to talk or swing again, but neither event happened.

Gus risked it and shouted out, "All right, I've had enough, so can I limp to my feet, or are these two esteemed employees going to whack me again?"

Gus could smell the fumes of a vaporizer lighting up. A three-hundred-pound Mexican in a white three-piece Italian designer suit waddled into the entrance hall from Gus's kitchen. He was no doubt disappointed in what he had found lurking in Gus's understocked kitchen, but then Antonio Victor Minnelli could afford to miss a few meals. Antonio gave off an unconvincing air of Italian romance that was as real as most of his working girls' double Ds, but if he wanted to pretend to be more than he was, it didn't usually matter to Gus. It only mattered now because Antonio had seen to it that Gus's knees got bashed. Antonio was Big Gustavo's right-hand man. Big Gustavo was the Mexican crime lord who controlled a big chunk of territory just south of the border. The area was mostly wasteland, but he controlled it like it was the Garden of Eden. He foolishly thought this side of the border was also his. Gus lying on his back viewed Antonio looming over him and understood that some days it was hard to argue that this territory wasn't Big Gustavo's. Gus desperately searched his brain, trying to think about why Antonio might be making an unwanted call to his home. The pain in his knees wasn't helping jog his memory, although that pain had overcome the headache that had been bothering Gus all day.

Antonio took a long drag on his electronic cigarette and blew the vapors over Gus's head. It smelled vaguely of peaches and nicotine. A rather terrible combination, but one you'd probably tolerate if they had you hooked on the drug. Antonio took his time sizing up the situation. He wasn't a man to be rushed into anything, including making a judgment, if you went by his large frame. Gus just lay there not making any sudden movements. He didn't want to encourage Antonio and go do something stupid to suggest that he was a threat and that his knees needed more bashing. After a long, silent moment of smoking, Antonio waved his two men away from Gus's fallen body. He then leaned against Gus's empty coat rack and spoke.

"I have a lovely son. His mother has raised him to be big and smart, a very good son. I have five daughters, but only one son. You understand what it means to a man to have a son," said Antonio.

Gus didn't understand, because he didn't have a son. He only had a daughter. She had gone off to college on the West Coast and never come back. He considered telling that to Antonio, but it didn't exactly seem a wise decision. Gus replied, "It is always nice to have a son."

"My son is *muy* smart. He gets it from his *padre*, no doubt. He got into the prestigious George Taylor University up in your big city to the north. His dear mama is worried those big-city girls of yours will be too much for him. She wanted him to get a good education closer to home and then become a noble man like a doctor. Whose mother doesn't want them to be a doctor? She is afraid that he will instead become a vile *pajero* with so many pretty women around in that school. She has convinced my son not to live up in the city by the university he goes to, but to live down here, closer to his real home across the border. He has a lovely apartment not so far from where we stand now. He drives up every day to his classes in that school, and every weekend he travels over the border to see his dear mama. That is the kind of good son I have. No loose women in my son's life will you find."

"It all sounds really nice, Antonio. Can I tell you the story of the two good knees I used to have? They were very good knees. They weren't perhaps as good at being knees as your son is at being a good son, but I was kind of partial to them just the same. A funny thing happened to my good knees. You see, some idiots with baseball bats hit my two good knees. They better not have done that act just so I could lie about on my own hardwood flooring in pain while hearing stories about your one son and how good he is to his mother. Is there a point to this little walk down family lane or not?" asked Gus.

Antonio took another long drag on his vaporizer. He blew out the mist and replied, "Sheldon Nickelback is the point."

Gus shouted back, "Who the fuck is this Sheldon Nickelback? Don't just blurt out stuff like I'm supposed to understand!"

"Do not get so grumpy, my friend. If you want to play dumb, then I will remind you of that subject which you pretend to forget. Your rebranding efforts in this county have not gone unnoticed by Big Gustavo. He doesn't care so much about these petty crackdowns you've been having. They've not harmed our business significantly. However, he is not very happy about the fact you've cleaned up your county's image enough that a certain Terry Tang has decided to move into the area. You comprehend my drift?"

Gus understood. Terry Tang was a West Coast mover of illegal prescription drugs. He was tied to some gang out there. If you had developed more than a hankering for sedatives like Xanax, Klonopin, and Valium or opiates such as Percocet and OxyContin or even stimulants like good old childhood-helper Ritalin, then Terry Tang was likely on your best-friends list. Terry didn't bother with your doctor's worries about addiction and was happy to refill your prescription drug even without your family doctor's okay. They said a doctor was a fool to have themselves as a patient, but the Terry Tangs of the world were there to sweep up the fools who felt they were smarter than their doctor in knowing what their body needed. Gus had been watching Terry Tang's gang slowly move into town for a good six months now. He had a dead young woman resting on a slab in the morgue that created a strong desire to shut him down. The case was held up due to formalities. There were plenty of homegrown dealers of illegal drugs to deal with, and a sheriff couldn't arrest everyone with a bottle of painkillers taken to erase the edge off their dull, unenlightened lives. There was also the fact that rich people used legal prescription drugs to get high semilegally, and they were the kind of people who had political pull. Terry Tang had a few customers among the movers and shakers, and he had this semilegal Dr. Smith handing out prescriptions to them like it was candy. That helped matters stay as they were, with Terry free to sell his product while the city council wanted crackdowns on other types of illegal dealers. It might make Big Gustavo plenty mad, but it didn't have anything to do with anyone named Sheldon Nickelback as far as Gus knew.

"That doesn't jog any memory for me. What does a penny-ante serial prescription writer like Terry Tang have to do with anyone called Sheldon Nickelback?" asked Gus.

"Nothing, but it demonstrates that things are slipping up here in this county. First this Terry Tang moves in and makes us *muy* angry. Then this little *marica* named Sheldon Nickelback is invited to live in this county. It is an affront to anyone like my son. People like my son are not safe in this county so long as that man Sheldon lives here. I leave it in your hands to make sure he doesn't get a friendly welcome in this county. Do you understand me? I leave my child *en las manos de* you, Sheriff. It is a great risk you are all taking, asking Sheldon Nickelback here to live. If anything should ever happen that breaks my son's poor mother's heart, then I shall break your heart. How can I enjoy my time I spend with my mistress when I know back home there is a good mother whose heart is breaking? I just came here to explain this all to you."

"That didn't exactly tell me who the hell this Sheldon Nickelback is," complained Gus.

Antonio took one large step and placed his well-polished imported Italian shoes onto Gus's chest. He pressed down with three hundred pounds of force. He took a long drag on his vaporizer and blew the mist straight down into Gus's face. He gave Gus a wicked criminal smile. He spoke softly, "No more games, *amigo*, please. I have told you what is to be done. This Sheldon Nickelback is not welcome here. Not now, not ever. You make sure he is not welcome, or my boys will be back, and they won't be as loving in their touch next time."

Antonio took his foot off Gus's chest, and Gus sucked in a few missing breaths' worth of air. The front door opened, and Antonio left. The two oversized baseball fans disguised as goons soon followed Antonio out the door. Gus started to try to sit up when one last goon came down the hall. He gave Gus a comical sneer that was meant to strike fear into Gus's heart. It didn't. Two thugs were placed up front, and one was hanging out in the back of the house. It was the type of information that was handy to remember, because you'd probably need to recall it later.

It was only an hour after the unexpected visit by the local unfriendly drug dealers, and all Gus had managed to do post visitation was crawl to his living-room sofa. It wasn't much of an accomplishment. Still, given the two severely black-and-blue kneecaps, Gus felt he'd chalk it down as one of life's little accomplishments. Not one of your accomplishments that you'd brag about by texting messages to all your immediate friends, but all the same an accomplishment in a day with almost no other success. Gus wasn't exactly enamored with the concept of the social media. He was a little too afraid that posting "beaten up by the Mexican mob until I can barely move" might get too many likes and followers on any social-media website. Still, he had to call someone for help, because he needed actual help at this moment. Until that help arrived, all he could do was lie there on the sofa in intense pain.

Today problems had become like seeing a bunny in your backyard garden. You knew if there was one out there today, then soon there would be ten more. He was in desperate need of a plan to get out of these many sticky situations before they kept multiplying out of control. The first task before him was that he was supposed to be thinking about ways to remove a Sheldon Nickelback from his county. The motivation for doing this was to escape a second beating. The problem with forming any plan of attack on conquering this dilemma was that he honestly hadn't much of a clue as to the identity of this Sheldon Nickelback. Intense pain is a great way to focus your mind on the source of the intense pain, but a lousy way to focus your mind on other tasks. Thugs like Antonio failed to understand that simple concept, but that failure didn't surprise Gus too much. Gus figured Antonio didn't care so much if the people receiving a beating in his organization got the message or not, because they generally didn't last long one way or another in those types of places. The point to dealing out messages in a drug gang was for the survivors to be the ones who got the message and not the person whom the message had been delivered to. It was managing by Darwinism at its finest. The thugs who understood the messages he sent best survived, and those who didn't went extinct. The main message received by Gus tonight was that he would need to figure out a way to teach Antonio some type of lesson in return, or else he'd risk continuing being Big Gustavo's personal punching bag. But his mind was drawing a blank on how to teach that type of person any kind of a valuable lesson.

He took his mind off the pain in his knees by focusing on another burdensome issue he wished to be freed from. He reached over to the end table next to the sofa. There was a black-and-white photograph in a sparse metallic picture frame. His dead wife had bought the frame a long time ago at a garage sale. Inside the picture frame was a faded photograph of a young girl in a pep-squad uniform. The young girl was his daughter, Samantha. The photograph didn't feel like it was taken that long ago, and yet now it was nearly ten years ago or so. The time had slipped away fast. He couldn't remember now if his wife had been still alive when he had taken this photograph. He guessed not, but he was only guessing. Time robs you of your crisp, focused memory. Try as he might, he couldn't remember the timeline of events. His daughter was inconveniently nearing thirty and living far away, so he couldn't exactly ask her for the details. It really didn't matter anyway. He was staring at the picture to get his mind off his problems with Antonio.

The picture worked because it focused his mind on his other problem. His daughter in that picture was nearly the same age as the young woman from Kansas sitting in his jail cell. The poor, innocent young woman was waiting to be returned to the authorities of Kansas so she could be put up on trial for first-degree murder of her own child. All he knew about any of that was the fact a child shouldn't be having a child. Then again, a child shouldn't be forced into war either, and yet that's where the child's father had gone. He had died there too. The worst kind of death there was in war. He had died at his own hands. It was too many cruel fates for one young unhappy family to deal with. Yet her parents seemed intent on making more misery for her and not less. His daughter in the photograph was talking to Gus, and he didn't like what she was saying. "If it was your own daughter, then what would you do?"

"What are you doing?" asked Dr. Armstrong as she strolled into the room casually with a bottle of painkillers in her hand.

"I'm thinking," replied Gus, tucking the picture frame down between the sofa and his side.

"I hope you're not thinking about doing something stupid."

"The key to doing something stupid is to not to think about it at all before doing it. Thinking just ruins the whole process of doing stupid things. I can assure you, though, that I'm not going to do anything stupid in my current situation," he said, pointing at his swelling knees. "There are only so many stupid things a man can do at one time and still remain brilliant in the visions contained in his own mind. I would say that I have enough stupid things going on in my life right now and thus have no desire to intentionally introduce yet another new form of stupidity to plague me."

Dr. Armstrong started to examine his knees. "As a doctor I've never witnessed there being a limit on the number of stupid things a person could do at one time. You, for instance, are my only patient that calls me up to make a house call on account of them being accosted in their own home by thugs wielding baseball bats."

"I believe that is only because all your other patients are dead," replied Gus.

She stood back up. "My prognosis is that you'll live. You should cheer up, because I don't get to say that very often to my patients. I brought my best painkillers for you, and now I'm going into your kitchen to retrieve two bags of ice and a set of towels. I want to get the swelling down. You keep waiting right where you are."

It was a doctor's order that Gus wasn't likely to disobey. Dr. Chloe Armstrong was the county coroner. It felt like just yesterday she was the newbie on the law-enforcement block. Now she had been around for a couple of years. She was one of the few people Gus felt comfortable calling when a problem arose. She was everything Gus was not: college educated, young, attractive, intuitive, and intelligent. He envied her enthusiasm for the job. All the young deputies on the force pined for her, but she was dating a computer programmer, which seemed to let the air out of any potential relationship. Not that Gus was pining for anyone at his age. At his age the pine box came soon enough. She might be everything he wasn't, but they had a lot in common. There was the little fact that Gus had his own computer programmer to deal with at the moment. He wasn't exactly dating the computer hacker hiding in his jail cell, but he was having a hard time getting rid of him all the same. Josh Hansen was less a bad penny that kept turning up than a bad relationship you were afraid to end because there was nothing else better waiting for you after that.

Gus reached over to the end table where she had left the painkillers. He snatched up the bottle and tried to remove the childproof cap. He tried reading the little arrows on the cap to open it. He failed to make much progress. He slipped his reading glasses out of his pocket. They were currently in less-than-stellar condition after being fallen upon during batting practice. Gus found one good corner of the right lens and attempted to open his bottle a second time. In small triumph, he succeeded in opening it. He wanted to down half the bottle, but he vaguely remembered hearing on the news that painkillers often had bad side effects. One kind of pills was bad for your liver, and the other kind was bad for your stomach. He could never remember which one was which. He took out two pills and downed them without water. It wasn't an easy task, but he gulped them down eventually.

As the pills went down his throat, Chloe came back carrying two towels filled with ice. She gave Gus a friendly smile. She then ordered him, "Okay, now off with your pants." Gus gave her less than a friendly expression in return to that order. She added, "Come on now; I'm a doctor."

"My pants are rolled up high enough. I can get the ice on my swollen knees without having to reveal too much. You should let a victim of violence have a smidgeon of dignity. Plus, I wouldn't want to get a certain computer programmer all hot and bothered over all this extra attention you are giving me. I've got too many problems with my own computer programmers to start having problems with yours as well. When your computer programmer is a hacker like Josh Hansen, you don't exactly need another one in your life."

"So you guys are on the search for him too. I heard twenty-seven different governments were after him for revealing classified information. I wonder where he is now?" asked Chloe.

"I wished I wondered that too," mumbled Gus as Chloe pressed the ice towels to his bare knees.

"I take it you know something about Josh Hansen's whereabouts?" she asked, pressing the ice to his knees.

"Me…well, not really," lied Gus.

"Then why'd you bring him up?"

"I'm trying to get my mind off the pain in my knees."

She changed the subject. "Your pants will get wet, and then you'll have to sleep in soaking-wet pants all night."

"Let them get wet."

"Fine, but I'm definitely ordering you stay home from work tomorrow. I know you'll ignore that order too, but as a doctor I have to at least offer good advice to my patients. Don't worry about offending me by refusing; the cadavers never take any of my excellent medical advice either."

"Don't think I don't appreciate all you've done for me, because I do. I would stay home if I could, but I have to go into work tomorrow. Terrance is supposed to unveil his big celebrity news as part of the town rebranding effort. There is going to be big festivities going on in downtown tomorrow. The county bigwigs have been planning it for months, and they all expect me to show up for it. If you want a little scoop on who the secret celebrity they're unveiling is, I have a sinking feeling they are introducing *the* Sheldon Nickelback to our fine community." Gus ended the statement with a shrug. This was a guess on his part. He was fishing in hopes that the name Sheldon Nickelback rang a bell with her. He didn't know the name and wondered if she wouldn't either. She apparently did. Sometimes playing a hunch pays off in this business, not often, but it does happen.

Chloe was just a bit more than annoyed at the news. The name seemed to remove the gentle touch of the good doctor, and she started tightening the ice bags to his knees a little too tight. Chloe didn't love the entire scope of ideas laid out by the good ole boys who Terrance worked for. She was of a younger generation and didn't appreciate the good ole boys one bit. It probably had to do with her actually being good and not ole or a boy. It was one of those things Gus liked about her. After all, besides their money there wasn't much to like about them good ole boys that Gus had ever noticed.

"I've never heard of this Sheldon Nickelback. What is he, one of those new teenage-scream Internet celebrity singers?" asked Gus in hopes she'd focus more of her displeasure on thoughts of Sheldon and not on thoughts of tightening those ice packs to his knees.

"Oh, Gus, really sometimes I think you live in your own little world. Just look at this room. You still have an entire shelf of DVDs when the rest of the world is downloading and streaming movies."

"When they start streaming *Barnaby Jones* for free, you let me know. I'm not about to pay for something I already own. Anyways, my being old doesn't tell me who Sheldon Nickelback is. The men that hit my knees didn't like this Sheldon guy. The expression on your face when I brought up the name tells me you aren't in love with him either. I figured there must be a reason why."

The doctor was done with his knees and stood back up. She then lectured him, "Sheldon Nickelback was home alone late one night when he claimed to have seen a suspicious Latino youth hanging outside under a streetlamp in front of his house. He went out to confront the young man. What happened next was up to conjecture by the jury, but ultimately we know that Sheldon shot that fourteen-year-old boy in what he claimed was self-defense. He stated that the youth jumped him without provocation and accosted him. Most of the papers I read were calling for Sheldon's head on a platter. He was heavily speculated to be a huge racist, and popular opinion was that the murder was racially motivated. I can't believe you don't know all this. The trial was the most covered story in the news last year. The man's lawyer, Wilton McDermott, is practically a household name because of it."

"Oh yeah, that Sheldon Nickelback…remind me to remove the streetlights from the block that he happens to move onto here. Normally communities put them up for safety, but with Sheldon coming to town, I'll have to do the reverse. As I recall it, Sheldon's jury bought his story, which makes him a celebrity to some in these parts and a coldhearted racist murderer of Latino youths to others. Either way the story goes, it was the main story on the news for a good half of last year; thus I tried very hard to avoid it. Remind me to thank Terrance for bringing such a well-known celebrity to our town. Only Terrance could land that quality of famous celebrity for the rebranding effort. I'm sure tomorrow is going to be a real blast."

"From your comments, I take it the introduction of this *celebrity* is what they plan for city hall tomorrow?" asked Chloe. Gus nodded. "Well, then I think I'll head home and get an early start in calling in sick so I can miss witnessing the disaster in person."

She started for the door, but Gus didn't want her to leave. He asked her, "Chloe, do you believe in angels?"

She stopped dead in her tracks. "You aren't going funny on me, are you? A lot of people get religious when they get too old and fear death. I didn't think that would happen to you, though. You only got hit on the knees. It isn't fatal."

"I ain't afraid of nothing not holding a baseball bat, and I ain't funny in the head. It's a perfectly legitimate question."

"Do you mean the white-robe-wearing kind of angels that live among the clouds?"

"Don't be funny. I mean…well…I don't suppose you've ever heard of trisomy thirteen?" asked Gus.

"That's a funny sort of question to ask and a funnier way to ask it. Trisomy thirteen is caused by an individual having three copies of chromosome thirteen instead of the normal two. We doctors call it Patau's syndrome. It is generally a fatal genetic flaw, and most people with it die within the first year of life if not the first few days of life. It's basically a death sentence."

"I got a young woman in a holding cell awaiting murder charges because she had a late-term abortion illegally done in Mexico without her parents' consent. They got a whole set of rules to follow to have a late-term abortion back where she's from. Parental consent, forced ultrasound, waiting period…they think they have a case. They want to bring her to justice. She told me she wanted the child. The husband is dead, you see, so it was the only thing she had left of him, but the child had this trisomy thirteen. Would you, as a doctor, tell her to have an abortion if this fetus had it?"

Chloe sat down on the sofa next to Gus. She reached down and scooped up the photograph of his daughter. After seeing what it was a picture of, she looked up from the picture and over to him. She explained, "I'm a coroner, Gus; all of my patients have been aborted by this world by the time they've reached me." He didn't laugh. She smiled at him anyway. She added, "Abortion is a common experience: At current rates, about one in three American women will have had an abortion by the time she reaches age forty-five—a shocking statistic to many, but a real statistical number nonetheless. As a doctor I would tell her the prognosis, allow her to explore her medical options, and let my patient decide the best medical outcome for her and her child."

Gus lamented, "The law up there sees it differently. As soon as our esteemed governor signs the extradition papers, she'll be at the mercy of the Kansas courts. I think her parents are likely to do her in. Even if she escapes the accusations of the prosecution, her life is going to be fucked, because worse still, a whole mess of people on this and that side of this issue will be down here making trouble for her. Compared to Sheldon Nickelback's little appearance tomorrow, I think this is going to be a real pain in the ass."

"I don't see why you're so worried about this issue. There is nothing you can do about it. The best thing to do about the Sheldon Nickelbacks of the world is to ignore them. That is what I plan to do. As for this young woman, I'm as concerned about a miscarriage of justice as the next, but you can't let it get to you psychologically. They say that true peace of mind is not merely the absence of tension, but it is the presence of justice. Perhaps the justice system that failed for Sheldon Nickelback will actually work for that young woman. There is no reason to go into this with such a pessimistic view. There is no reason to feel so tense about an issue that is yet to be resolved, justly or unjustly."

"There is another side of this thing people call justice. They say that justice is really a form of love. The process of love is supposed to correct those awful occurrences that revolt against the idea love. I read that in a supermarket tabloid while waiting to check out. There and on cat posters are where all the best platitudes can be found. I can't help feeling this young woman did something out of love that ought not to be judged. She's going to be judged all the same, because that's what the law says to do. They probably got a legal term for it when you kill someone out of mercy to prevent them from a long, pointless, slow death."

"You mean euthanasia?"

"I'm sure there are young people in Asia, but I'm not sure what it has to do with what I'm talking about."

Dr. Armstrong laughed. She walked over to the end table and placed the picture frame back on it. "I'm going to ask you this question again, this time as your doctor. Gus, you're not thinking about doing something stupid?"

He didn't answer right away. Gus felt the cold ice pack on his knee. Finally he admitted, "I just for the life of me can't think of what I might do. But, yes, I think whatever I end up doing, it might be something stupid, so yes, I admit it that in this case I just might end up doing that."

Driving the sheriff's truck with two defective knees was a challenge, but it wasn't as big a challenge as driving through Main Street in downtown on this particular morning. Main Street was effectively shut down by the day's activities at city hall for anything other than foot traffic. People were driving in from all over the county for the grand unveiling of the county's newest and only actually famous celebrity. There were even folks driving down from the big city to the north to get a gander at what the television ads promised would be a big surprise. The identity of the super celebrity lured by the city council to come live in this county was a carefully guarded secret that only a few people were supposed to know. Gus thought he knew it and wasn't exactly excited by the prospect of that man moving into his county. Gus gave up driving through the growing mob on the street and pulled his truck into the courthouse parking lot. This parking lot wasn't open to the public today, for it had been set aside as the meeting place for the VIPs of today's event.

Deputy Wilson was standing in front of a barrier blocking the court-house driveway entrance. Gus waved a friendly hello, and the deputy mechanically moved the barrier to the side and let Gus inside the parking lot. The lot was reserved for the elite of the town for today's ceremony. If you listened to Terrance's rebranding-effort advertisements, then this county was in desperate need of new elites, but you wouldn't know it from the volume of vehicles in the parking lot. Almost every parking space was already full. There were still plenty of handicap parking spaces available. He pulled the truck into one marked with a blue handicap sign and parked. Gus opened his glove compartment and took out his trusty ticket pad and quickly wrote up a parking ticket for his own truck. He got out of the vehicle gingerly and proceeded to place the ticket under his windshield wiper. A ticket under the wiper should prevent another one from appearing on it later. He promised himself that he'd remember to tear that ticket up after the conclusion of today's events. After all, he believed in giving a guy who accidentally parked in a forbidden spot a break once in a while, particularly if that guy was himself. If you judge people, then you have no time to love them, or so a fortune cookie once told him. It was easier to judge people favorably when that person was you.

Gus hobbled up the courthouse steps and then through the front door. He knew that a small gathering of the muckiest of the high-mucky-mucks would be situated inside the entrance hall. The unveiling of the celebrity was to be done on the grand marble steps of city hall, but the parking was more secluded at the courthouse. Gus counted the mayor, the deputy mayor, and several members of the city council standing among the rabble. The rest of the rabble consisted mostly of the movers and shakers of the county, or to put it another way, old white people with money. They were all decked out in their Sunday best. The old men had their best sports coats and ties, while the old gray-haired ladies wore spritely spring dresses and brightly colored hats. A person could easily have mistaken today for Easter morning. Among the gathering crowd there was both a sense of relief that the big day had finally arrived and a sense of excitement as to who would be revealed as the new county super celebrity. It wasn't every day that the county could offer up a real live famous person to dazzle a crowd. Some people get famous for the arts, some people get famous by inheriting wealth and beauty, and some people get famous by shooting a fourteen-year-old minority under a streetlamp. Yeah, it was just like Easter Sunday, thought Gus, except he was pretty sure that fourteen-year-old boy wasn't about to rise from his grave today.

Gus used the highly polished metal of the entrance hall's copper pillars to straighten his white cowboy hat on his head. Gus hated wearing the hat, but it made him appear statelier for the gathered crowd and more importantly covered the bald spot on his head. A familiar head appeared behind him. He gingerly turned to greet his old high-school pal Terrance, who happened to be more sober today than the last time they had met. Terrance was standing next to an attractive young Hispanic woman. She didn't appear to be a day over twenty-five. She had long black hair and a well-toned figure. She stood out to Gus for two reasons, the first one being that she wasn't Terrance's wife, and the second one being that she wore a new and pressed deputy uniform.

Gus extended his hand to greet Terrance. "I have to admit this whole celebrity thing is going well for the city. I have my reservations as to if everyone will appreciate the guest of honor after he's unveiled, but so far so good. We've got a great turnout."

Terrance was happier than usual. He took Gus's hand and shook it with force. He agreed, "The decision I made wasn't an easy one. It was a choice between our great unknown celebrity and Cecil Lauper the big-game hunter. He's the guy that generated all that media attention a few years back for hunting rhinos."

"I remember him. He's the guy that poached that famous rhino on the protected game reserve. I have to admit I'd take a poacher over a murderer any day if those two were my only choices," replied Gus.

"Murder, hunter, or poacher, what is the difference when it comes to fame, if you ask me. I was looking for people who get search-engine hits. Gus, in this day and age, search-engine hits sell products. The guy was famous, and famous is what this county needs to turn its image around. Things were getting plenty hot for ole Cecil in his hometown. Deranged people were threatening him constantly. He was ready to find greener pastures, and although due to the lack of rain our pastures are typically brown, he was considering my offer. It is just too bad Cecil died last month when a rogue elephant stampeded him while he was poaching on an African nature reserve. It was a tough break for us on the planning committee. Luckily we had a fallback option, and he accepted."

"Don't feel bad, Terrance. When the last rhino is gone, there will be no more rhinos, but with Cecil Lauper now gone, there are still plenty of ass-holes out there to replace him. I just wish you found a replacement asshole a bit less controversial than a poacher. Fame is one thing; creating a pain in the ass for me is quite another."

"You seem to know all about my secret. I hope my secret hasn't leaked."

"Don't worry; I'm just a good guesser," lied Gus.

"There is no doubt about it that our secret celebrity is a bit controversial. In the media it is controversy that brings in the ratings and ratings that bring in the bucks. Politically incorrect sells these days. Half the audience watches politically incorrect nastiness to hate it, and half watch it to love it, but they all watch, and getting eyes focused on our county is what rebranding is all about. That's why I took what you told me to heart the other night. I got to thinking this rebranding thing needs to offer something for everyone, and since you were so concerned for the inner feelings of our minorities, I went out and hired this chick deputy here for you. You have to admit that your department is lacking in both chicks and spics. I killed both demographics with one hiring, as she's both a chick and a…" Terrance glanced over at the woman and then continued, "Latino. Her name's Chiquita Lopez. You know, Chiquita like the banana."

"When were you going to consult me on this new idea?" asked Gus.

"I consulted you on it already! Has your brain gone soft or something? Let's both remember that at the traffic stop, it was you that recommended this idea to me and not the other way around!"

"Does this idea come with any additional funding to pay for this new deputy?" asked Gus.

"Gus, the devil is in the details. Don't think about funding; think about how by hiring her I've helped soften the blow to the Mexican community I'm about to land by having lured 'mustn't say who' to live here in this community. I'm sure we'll work out later how we…you pay for her! Now go ahead and greet your newest member of the law-enforcement department with enthusiasm. I've already set up a photo shoot for both of you to appear in to help put in the newspapers to sell the idea of our new concept of brotherly love. It should counteract the backlash of today! Pros and cons, Gus, it helps sell the controversy and gets keen eyes focused down here," replied Terrance, starting to shove Chiquita toward Gus.

Chiquita flashed an impish smile at Gus. He figured she had to be one hell of a good sport to tolerate Terrance's company. To Terrance she was two demographics filled in one blow, but to Gus she was a deficit on his balance sheet that he had no idea how to fill. His department's vehicles were ancient, his jail was so outdated Josh Hansen could come and go as he pleased, so he didn't need more people producing red tape in his budget books. Still, there was a bright side to the matter; Chiquita was just about the prettiest deputy the county had ever hired. If you went by Gus, then you'd think ugly went with the job title. Gus nodded back at her. He put out his hand to greet her. "Where'd he find you?"

"I just graduated from community college with a degree in criminology. You could say that I was on the hunt for a job in these parts, but was languishing on the waiting list to get into the state police academy when this rather lucrative offer suddenly came my way. After meeting Terrance the other day, I found it hard not to pass up his offer and not throw up at the same time," she replied.

Gus pointed over to Terrance with his thumb. "The politics of the matter can be a little gruff, but on my force everyone is equal. It also helps to remember to be hard of hearing at times when politics comes our way."

Chiquita replied, "Oh, don't have any fears about the whole chick-spic thing; I would have to respect a person who said a thing like that to me in order to take offense at their low opinion of me."

Gus smiled and patted her on the shoulder. "You're a good kid, Chiquita. You're going to work out just fine on my crack team of criminologists."

"What's my first assignment?" she asked.

"The city is filled with people today, and there aren't nearly enough legal parking spaces for all of them. Go out and write me some traffic tickets so I can pay you. I just want you to keep in mind to ignore a certain sheriff's truck parked illegally in a certain parking spot. All the other cars are fair game if you want to be paid a salary to go along with your new job."

"I got into this job because I was sick of the injustice in this world and hoped I could start to dispense a little of it."

"And you will. You can start by dispensing a few traffic tickets. Think of them as distilled justice in paper form." He handed her his ticket pad. Chiquita frowned at it and then turned and headed for the door. There was going to be trouble when the boys at the office found out about her.

Terrance shouted out to her, "Don't forget the date for the horse-riding photo shoot! We need your lovely figure to help advertise the rebranding effort!"

Chiquita never turned around to respond. She just gave Terrance the solid thumbs-up salute with her left thumb. It probably wasn't the digit she wanted to stick up in the air at Terrance. Not that Terrance would mind one way or another. Terrance was a man focused on image and not reality.

Gus whispered over to Terrance, "I don't know how to ride a horse."

Terrance whispered back, "You're a sheriff; of course you know how to ride a horse."

"I repeat, I don't know how to ride a horse."

"What is there to know? You get on a horse's back with the lovely, photogenic Chiquita Lopez, and we shoot a few photographs. We then place that image on billboards, magazine covers, and our county social-media pages. It is all for our rebranding effort aimed at restoring the county's image. There is no actual horse riding involved."

"Terrance, when did this county ever have this positive image that you think it can be restored to?" Gus's further arguments against the idea were squelched as the mayor's aide took that moment to shout at the gathered crowd. It was time for the festivities to begin. Gus scanned the crowd, searching for Sheldon Nickelback, but there wasn't anyone he recognized from his television set standing among the crowd.

Gus dutifully took his place among the rank and file as the crowd was escorted down into the basement of the courthouse. Gus knew for a fact that a long, dirty tunnel ran between the two buildings. It was originally built as a mutual air-conditioning conduit but had also served as an emergency escape route for a city-council member in more than one dicey situation. Today it was serving a different purpose. The event organizers had gone all out and decorated the conduit with lines of paper cutout decorations and a red carpet. There seemed no end to the rebranding effort. Gus walked along the conduit wondering where the budget for all this shock and awe was coming from. The answer was no doubt that it was coming from all the future income the rebranding was supposed to bring in.

The tunnel ended inside the basement of city hall, and the crowd pushed onward up the stairs toward the city hall's grand marble staircase at the front entrance to the building. Gus exited the front door to see that the grand marble was not to be enjoyed today, because it was covered up by a large plywood platform covered in official bunting. To the right side of the platform stood a wooden bleacher grandstand painted white, and to the left was a large wooden ramp that led down to the street level. There was something big covered by a tarp at the bottom of that ramp. The VIPs along with Gus were escorted to the recently constructed grandstand. It was the same grandstand that was erected every summer to house the judges for the annual July Fourth parade. Gus knew it well. Even a new coat of paint couldn't disguise it from him. Before sitting down, he checked the paint to make sure it was dry. It was. He took a rickety seat between a city councilman's wife and an octogenarian who no doubt was one of Terrance's many fund raisers or at least the funds part of the raising effort. Gus didn't know the man, but that was likely due to the man having retired and moved to spend his golden years in Florida. A lot of Terrance's best funds came from people who had long ago left town but still felt the need to interfere with the day-to-day life of county folk back home. Terrance must have advertised far and wide to get a man like this back for today's event.

Gus scanned the crowd below the marble steps to see just who had come to watch today's unveiling of the secret celebrity. The area closest to the podium was filled with vocal members of the PTA, local gun enthusiasts, and concerned church groups. Gus assumed Terrance had strategically arranged to leak out enough vague information to these organizations that they'd be wise to come today to just the right people in order to assure he got a favorable crowd up front where the cameras from the television crews were sure to pick them up. Judging by whose cameras were here and whose were absent, it appeared that the story had been selectively leaked to just the right news stations as well. Terrance had selected the ones that would report the news today only in a positive light, if you went by how they had covered the original trial. Toward the back of the crowd, Gus could make out a few signs of protest, but they were far away and only a few. Terrance had done a good job keeping the actual identity of the celebrity a secret from the general public; thus, the rest of the crowd was likely totally unaware of who the celebrity coming to town really was.

Gus's attention was torn from the crowd as one of the lesser councilmen opened the day's events by turning on the microphone on the podium to a roar of annoying feedback. The councilman then proceeded to make a few lesser remarks that fit his position in life. They were forgotten by the crowd even before they were said. He then left the podium to a round of light clapping from people who wanted to see someone famous and knew clapping would hasten the activities onward to that point. Gus sat there ignoring the activities by trying to come up with a plan. He needed one to avoid another beatdown by the Mexican mob.

His mind was still drawing a blank on how to do that when the mayor distracted him with his noisy arrival to the podium. The mayor was only recently elected but extremely familiar to his post, as he had previously been the mayor for years and years. He had won back his old post after the sudden demise of the previous mayor. He had won his office back not so much by the popular demand of his constituency as by the low attendance of it at the polls during the off-year emergency vacancy election. He was at least sober today, which was a bonus in some regards, but not when it came to making the speech livelier. The mayor's remarks were long, uninspiring, and lacking direction, which pretty much described all his previous terms in the office. Gus joined with the crowd in giving the mayor a deeply felt halfhearted clap upon his vacating the podium.

The mayor's speech was supposed to be an introduction for the man who was going to introduce the man of the hour. Only most people, including Gus, had forgotten to follow the speech, so he didn't understand exactly why Skip Lipschitz was now being called to man the podium. Gus knew Skip well. Skip was the head of the local gun-enthusiasts club in the county. Two attractive cheerleaders from the local high school pulled off the tarp from the object at the bottom of the ramp. The crowd appreciated the unveiling. There was a sparkling, brand-new customized white Corvette under that tarp. It was the kind of car Gus dreamed to buy when his rich relatives died and left him their inheritance. That idea was a dream mostly because most of his relatives were already dead, and none of them had bothered to get rich first before passing away. Skip was in the driver's seat hanging out the window. He gave everyone a thumbs-up salute, and the front section cheered madly. Skip then drove the car the short distance from the bottom of the ramp to the top of the stage.

Skip waved to the cheering crowd from the car's window a second time. Given the ample frame of Skip, the feat of fitting inside a Corvette was worthy of praise, although Gus figured most of the cheering was actually due to the fact of Skip's leadership role in the local gun-enthusiast club. From his leadership position in the club, Skip was known to be one of the more vocal members of the community. Skip was a man who wore his gun strapped to his thigh at all times as if it were a normal wardrobe accessory like a tie or a belt. To distract a person from his sidearm, Skip always managed to wear a suit and coat one size too small for his ample frame. A small ring of white belly fat peeked out at his waistline from his off-the-rack suit. The crowd didn't seem to care as Skip emerged from the Corvette. The crowd in front had come to life at his appearance and now shrieked in annoying fashion. Many of the crowd members near the stage proudly waved Gadsden flags. Skip enthusiastically grabbed the microphone in one hand, releasing another chorus of feedback as the crowd in front continued to roar with approval. Skip waited for the right moment in the crowd's noise level to proceed to introduce the guest of honor.

The wife of the councilman next to Gus whispered to him, "I'm lost. Do you understand what is going on?"

"History," whispered Gus back.

Skip laid it into the crowd. "It is not often these days this county has the great privilege to seduce a celebrity to live down here in this beautiful county with all of us red-blooded common folk. I feel this county has to offer some of the best and God-fearingest Americans that this country has ever produced." The crowd went crazy.

Skip played up the positive crowd noise and then lowered his hands to hush the audience. He continued, "When I heard the plight of our newest resident, my heart was moved to tears. He might be a celebrity, but we need to remember that he's also a victim. I was watching the news on my seventy-two-inch plasma television one night, and on it I saw a man as American as you or me. He had been driven out of his previous home by insidious hate. He had been forced into poverty by the vile courts fueled by radicals driven to lock him up over their hatred of his rights. He said right there on my television set that he was looking for a new home where people lived without hate and prejudice. I called the mayor and said to him, 'If ever there was a way to rebrand this county in the image of brotherly love and peace, then it was by giving this poor wrongly tortured soul a new home here among our community!'" The crowd erupted again. There were chants of the county name among the members of the crowd. They started to wave mini American flags to join the Gadsden flags.

Skip let the crowd noise die down again and continued, "This man that I introduce to you all today was subject to defamation beyond the limits that any among us could understand. He was branded a murderer and a thug for doing what every American should have a right to do: defend his own home. Here today we offer this man a new home and a new chance at peace of mind. If a man is wrongfully accused of a crime and the jury finds him totally guilt-free of those charges that were laid out against him, then in this nation he ought to be given a fair shake and a clean slate. In my country, the greatest on God's green Earth, a man is innocent until proven guilty in the court of law. When that court finds him innocent, then he ought to remain innocent no matter what the facts say. But there are those among us who don't believe that. They have hounded this man. They have hounded him from his house, from his home, from his money, from his loved ones, but I tell you his hounding days are over! Let me introduce you to the man of the hour. The most famous man living in this county today! The man that the media dedicated more airtime to last year than even the president of these United States! Ladies and gentlemen, I give you the newest resident of this fair county, Sheldon Nickelback!"

The passenger's-side door of the Corvette opened, and Sheldon Nickelback exited the car and walked onto the stage. He was dressed to the nines and, much like Skip, wore a gun strapped to his leg. The crowd's reaction was mixed. The front of the audience roared in approval, but they were the canned audience placed there for the cameras to do just that.

The middle pack of the crowd was the crowd who were just down here to see the show and hopefully to see someone famous. Their reaction was more mixed. More than a few didn't appear happy to see the man even if he had appeared often on their television set. Drowned out in the far back were a few protestors. The wife of the councilman next to Gus clapped her hands in approval and said to Gus, "Oh look, it's that man from the television news. I remember him. That courtroom stuff was just like the TV shows I like to watch. It's so nice to see someone so famous up close! He doesn't look as fat as he did on TV." She was apparently unaware that the felony trial involving this man had taken place for reasons other than just to entertain her. Gus scanned the rest of the VIPs, but he didn't see any unhappy faces. They had shelled out big bucks to Terrance to lure a celebrity into the county, and they all seemed happy that he had done just that. You could look at the crowd and see jeers and cheers, but you didn't see that many who didn't know who Sheldon Nickelback was. Terrance had certainly gotten his man. Gus sat back in his bleacher seat and tried to enjoy the show. He would enjoy it more if it ended sooner.

Skip passed the podium over to Sheldon, giving the man two healthy thumbs-up in approval. Sheldon thanked the audience and pulled a written speech from his pocket to place on the podium. The paper routine was just a show. Terrance would have no doubt only hired the guy if he was smart enough to memorize a speech. The cheering finally subsided, and Sheldon spoke into the microphone, "My dear new friends, I feel warmly welcomed by you with that bursting reception and this beautiful gift of a brand-new Corvette! It was such a generous gift from your local gun club for your humble servant, me. As many of you know, it was a hard year for me last year, but I've pulled through it. By the grace of God above, I pulled through. God shone down through the murky clouds of hate to enlighten my troubled heart that had fallen low by false demons of accusation. I couldn't have done it without people like you out there to spiritually support me. The struggle and trial have left me without a job and heavily in debt to my lawyer, but worse, it left me with so many unintended enemies. The lying liberal media has smeared my good name in many a leftist place in this great country, even though I was found totally innocent of malice by a fine, noble jury of geniuses. Justice has been done to everyone but to me. Do I find anger in this? I tell you I do not. Why? It is because my heart still has nothing inside it but a pure joy for my fellow man. Let the haters hate, because they can't break a God-blessed heart like mine. I tell you fellow citizens that we ought to always deal justly, not only with those who are just to us, but likewise to those who endeavor to injure us with false allegations. I say to you if you let your heart render an evil for an evil, then only evil will dwell there. I will not let this totally unintended incident turn my bountiful heart into a heart of stone. I love my enemies and wish only that they find the peace I now find in your grand community. I ask only of you that you take me *tabula rasa*, and I promise to do the same to each and every one of you in return!"

The crowd erupted once again into cheers. Even Gus had to admit it was a well-rehearsed and written speech. Another man might doubt if this man meant those words, but he couldn't deny they were skillfully delivered. Skip went back up to the podium now with something in his hands. Skip spoke to the crowd, "I have here in my hand the key to the city. I want you all to put your hands together and welcome our county's very own Sheriff Gus to the podium. The sheriff is here today to personally hand over this grand city's simulated gold key to Sheldon as a sign of our newfound trust and friendship between those falsely accused and law enforcement!"

The crowd cheered as the gallery of VIPs all craned their necks in Gus's direction. The wife of the councilman next to him patted him on the back. "It's so nice of you to admit your accusations were in error, Sheriff." Gus wanted to remind her that Sheldon had been arrested, tried, and found not guilty in another county that was actually located in a completely different state. He wanted to do that, but he doubted it would be of much use. Apparently Terrance had left out discussing with Gus the part of today's ceremony where Gus was going to line himself up to anger Antonio even more.

Gus slowly rose from his gallery position and hobbled through the bleachers, heading reluctantly to the stage. He did his best to mask the pain he felt at this moment; some of that pain was even in his knees. He faked a smile to Skip and took the foil-wrapped wooden key from his hands. Sheldon came immediately over to Gus and placed a hand on the key. If you couldn't trust a man like Sheldon with a simulated gold-foil key, what could you trust him with, figured Gus, as he let go of the key. Skip spoke once more into the microphone. "Lord, please let this passing of the city's key represent to Christian America that this county firmly stands behind the traditional concept that every free American has a solemn and sacred right to live his life in peace under our God. Every free man has a right to a life in our county. What we do today is just the start. Today this county opens its heart to the downtrodden, and tomorrow our neighbor does, and then the next county beyond that. Soon it will be all of America that believes the innocent have a right to a life."

The television cameras swooped in. Flashes started going off from those cameras, cell phones, electronic video recorders, electronic pads, and any other thing media reporters could push their way through the crowd with, pointed at Gus and Sheldon. The front of the crowd started to roar again in good cheer. The flags waved as they roared. A chant started from the front and moved in a wave over the crowd, "Right to life, right to life…" The media stopped flashing onto the stage and turned their cameras on the crowd. The event couldn't have gone off better had it been scripted. Indeed, the general public in the audience wouldn't have understood the simple fact that the whole event was likely carefully scripted by someone. They were just a few feet from someone famous, and they all loved it. The fame that Sheldon Nickelback represented appeared to be all that mattered to them as more and more got swept up in the moment. Up here on stage was the man the media couldn't stop talking about. His trial was the trial of century, or at least the past few years. It was as if a favorite television show had come to life and, more importantly, come into their own little town.

Skip tugged on Sheldon's shoulders, and Sheldon departed with the golden-colored oversized novelty key draped over his shoulder. Skip and Sheldon both boarded the new white Corvette. The car started up with a roar that was barely audible over the din of the cheering crowd. It rolled backward slowly down the ramp, leaving Gus standing alone to face the crowd. It didn't matter, as no one in the crowd watched Gus. They all had their eyes on the car. The crowd parted as the car slowly paraded down Main Street with a sheriff's deputy walking on either side of the vehicle. The media scurried behind the Corvette flashing cameras in ecstasy the whole way.

The man of the moment was now gone, and the gallery started to break up at once. Gus hobbled down the ramp before anyone dared to talk to him. He slowly limped through the crowd down the street. Occasionally he got a pat on the back from a fellow well-wisher. Gus would make the appropriate grunt of acknowledgment for every back pat. The deed was done, and Terrance had gotten his spectacle. Now Gus needed to figure out what it all meant for him. He hadn't stopped Sheldon Nickelback from coming to town. More than that, his face holding a key welcoming him to the city would be on every twenty-four-hour news station from coast to coast and possibly beyond. Wherever news was meant to distract rather than to inform, this story would be playing. The news would be reporting and commenting on the latest story about good old news-generating Sheldon Nickelback. To many a newsperson, Sheldon Nickelback was the golden calf that just kept giving. A man whom the audiences couldn't get enough of for reasons no one understood.

As Gus neared the rear of the crowd, he noticed once again the small gathering of opponents. Most of them were of Mexican descent and carrying signs that read simply "Assassin." There were no cameras focused on them. They were invisible to the massive crowd of well-wishers. Gus pulled his cowboy hat tight to his head and ducked it low in hopes of passing by the small protest without being noticed. You never knew if one of them worked for Antonio or not. Mostly, though, he guessed not. They were just citizens whose children looked a lot like the forgotten other star of last year's highest-rated news program—the shooting victim. The well-wishers like Skip were the optimists who saw the glass half full. This small pocket of protesters were the pessimists and saw the glass as half empty—the void in the glass having been created by Sheldon's gun. Gus knew in his heart he was not one of the pessimists. There were the glass-half-full people and the glass-half-empty people, and then there were people like Gus—the people stuck in an occupation in life who could only see the unsightly spots that lay all over that glass no matter how much stuff was inside it.

Gus made surprisingly good time limping down the block toward the law-enforcement complex. He'd send some deputy back to fetch his truck later. He wanted to disappear into his office faster than the crowd covering the street would have let him by driving down here. There was the added unpleasant fact that if he had stayed onstage with the crowd, then Terrance, the mayor, or someone in the gallery might have talked to him. The last thing he needed was another problem to deal with at this moment. Unfortunately, problems can't only be walked away from; they can also be walked into. There in front of the law-enforcement complex was another gathered crowd on this busy street. This crowd meant a new problem. The crowd of two abortion protesters from last night had grown. It was now a force of twenty or so. They had their own signs, they had their own slogans, and they chanted to any of the dispersing crowd from today's celebrity-unveiling event who happened to walk down the street from city hall. A few in the crowd were stopping to listen to Pastor Voce. Worse than that, a few were stopping and joining in. The main protest crowd all wore the same unison white shirt that the pastor wore, and they all handed out free shirts to anyone who would proudly wear it with them. The shirts all read "Pro-life." The pro-lifers seemed to have no problem welcoming to their ranks the people who had cheered the arrival of Sheldon Nickelback a few moments ago. Indeed, the more people here protesting, the merrier it was for them.

Gus acknowledged the new crowd with a halfhearted wave in the direction of the pastor. The pastor didn't wave back. He had three fresh meats on a hook and appeared focused on reeling them into the cause. Brian Hartline had warned Gus they would be coming, and now they were here in force. This was only the start of them. The media cameras had been distracted by the Sheldon Nickelback issue, but they'd be here too in greater and greater numbers until Gus rid himself of this meddlesome problem. In the meantime there seemed no sense in making even more enemies of the people in the crowd. He slinked on by them, trying not to say a word. He was heading for the office door when a young girl at the end of the protest line shouted out to Gus, "Truly children are a gift from the Lord; the fruit of the womb is a reward. Give that child murderer the justice she deserves!" The crowd cheered their agreement with those sentiments and answered the young girl with, "Execute the murderer in the name of the Lord!"

Gus froze in his place. The Lord that bestowed woman with the blessed vessel of a newborn soul was also the one that placed in every one of those souls original sin, at least according to Saint Augustine. A Lord that did that was certainly something of a bastard at heart if it was true. Then again, you could doubt its veracity due to the fact that Saint Augustine got that quaint idea of original sin from a bad Latin translation of the Greek text. It was a fact that probably didn't bother this crowd. Gus didn't know if that sin was originally in the text or not. People's fingerprints were easy for Gus to find, but their sin was often a lot harder to detect. Sin was like the holy in the holy water. They told you the water was holy, and you just had to believe them. Someone told you something was a sin, and you just had to believe them. No person had invented a Breathalyzer to detect the holy or the sin that was unseen inside. Gus doubted Saint Augustine's original sin was in there from the start for these people, but it didn't make him right.

Against his better judgment, Gus turned to face the protest crowd. There stood a fourteen-year-old girl. She knew nothing of the world, and those standing around her weren't likely to explain it to her. Certainly Pastor Voce had nothing to gain by telling her about the world as it really was outside of his fantasy tales of martyrdom. Her shirt called her a pro, but she was just one of the rank-and-file amateurs. The professionals of the issue were few and far between. They understood all the arguments and had catchy sound-bite comebacks to defend against them. They profited by convincing these people to advertise the hate. There was a good deal of money to be made from hate. The professional would never teach this young girl practical things that might help her in life; they never taught her about sex education, birth control, family planning, incest, or rape, and they never talked about all the women who didn't want abortions but found themselves faced with the terrible reality that they were now faced with—the reality of possibly needing to choose to have one. To this girl all that stuff was just lies. Lies were a thing Gus had to deal with as sheriff on a regular basis as facts. This girl couldn't understand that the young woman in his cell had told him she had wanted the child. How could you explain that to an amateur when the professionals had done such a good job of preparing her to never accept the absolute realities of life? Gus replied coldly, "That's the second time one of you asked me for justice. What would justice be in this case?"

The young girl replied proudly, "The Bible says an eye for an eye, so I would expect no less from you than the word as commanded by the Lord."

Gus shrugged. "So you demand temperance in the justice dealt out for the woman in my cell, do you? Just an eye for an eye, but no more vengeance than is merited by the crime. I wonder if that is really what you meant."

The young girl said nothing. She didn't understand. A lot of people didn't understand that Bible verse. Gus ducked into the station door. He was admonished by his internal voice. He should have kept his mouth shut. He started for his little place of solitude against the crazy world around him. He headed for his office. A man in a slick two-piece suit and a black cowboy hat sat on an uncomfortable bench in the front lobby. He appeared to be a tall drink of water, a well-built fellow of no more than thirty-five. Gus figured he wasn't likely to be any man's lawyer. His suit was too nice for that lowly a position. Even a bad lawyer would also have enough pride to not waste his time waiting in a stuffy lobby like an over-worked watchdog. Gus had the strongest desire to not get to know this man better, but he knew instinctively that wasn't a very probable outcome. The man sprang up from his seat as soon as Gus entered and was quickly cutting the distance between the two of them. Gus avoided eye contact so as not to advertise his availability. The man didn't seem to care; he was coming no matter what. The man pulled his sports coat apart to expose his shirt below. There was a badge pinned there on his chest along with a shoulder holster carrying a firearm. These two new pieces of information didn't exactly increase Gus's desire to meet the man.

The man made sure his path stood between Gus and Gus's path to his office. The two stopped abruptly before colliding in the law-enforcement-complex lobby. Only then did Gus look the man square in the eyes. This man didn't even extend a hand to offer a handshake. Instead he bluntly spoke to Gus and said, "I see you're the sheriff of these godforsaken parts, so I guess it is you I got to speak with. I'm here to see you and only you. The governor of the great state of Kansas has sent me here to this station for one task only. I'm Trooper Major Scott Dundee, and I'm here to pick up a prisoner of yours by the name of Jennifer Louis Bachman. I'm not here to become buddies or swap stories in front of cameras. I got a criminal that committed a crime, and I got to take her into custody to stand trial so the victims can have justice. The sooner you give her to me, the sooner we leave. I can't be any more direct than that."

"I need a paper with some governor signatures on it before all that can happen. You know all that as well as I. You got them papers in one of your pockets, Major Scott Dundee, or not?" asked Gus.

"Nope, but I got a man of mine delivering them personally to your governor as we speak. They'll fetch a signature out of your governor mighty quick and then bring them on down here for you and me to gawk at. Then all the fun begins."

"Well, when you get those signatures you need, then come around talking to me. Until that time you're just another man loitering in my station that I can't the find the time to see."

"I understand the feeling, but I just wanted you to know I was out here waiting. I wanted you to know I'll be watching this station. The San Francisco bleeding hearts can get all the lawyers they want to try and stop the great state of Kansas from bringing law and order to this matter, but as soon as I get those papers, I'm handing them to you, and you're handing Jennifer to me. Those lawyers can bitch and moan to the media cameras all they want, but it doesn't make any difference to me. I got a job to do, and I will do it. I won't let a lawyer obstruct justice. A person commits a crime in Kansas, and I put them in jail in Kansas. That's how the law works in my state. The bleeding hearts can talk all they want about their platitudes about social justice and morality, but platitudes don't mean as much to the law as a signed bunch of extradition papers. I'm a letter-of-the-law type of man, and I wanted you to know that. My governor sent me here special to make sure those papers and the law get followed in these parts."

"I'll repeat, when you get those papers that we all are supposed to follow to the letter, then you come hollering to me," replied Gus as he brushed the Kansas lawman aside. Major Dundee didn't follow him. The Kansas lawman just went back to sit on his bench and returned to watching like the good dog he was. Gus sensed inconvenience from the man, but not exactly trouble. There was nothing that man could do without his papers, and they both knew it. Without those papers he was just another lawman outside his jurisdiction.

Gus made his way to his office. The demonstrations didn't exactly leave him in a good mood. The rebranding effort was quickly turning the whole county into a zoo. The national press was covering the Sheldon Nickelback story today, and because of it, no doubt, this new abortion story could blow up big at any moment. The people from the state police knew it, the people from Kansas knew it, and Gus knew it. He wondered if the governor understood just how big this might get. If not, perhaps she'd sign those papers sooner rather than later and end this mess before it got too sticky. Gus arrived at his desk to see his secretary missing. Deputy Drew was sitting in her place. There weren't many reasons to ever want to see Deputy Drew, let alone want him assisting you as your office assistant.

Gus demanded from Drew, "Where is Lupita?"

"She called in sick today. She said that she was going to have some tests. I figured since no one was here and so many people were stirring about outside that I'd help you out by manning her station. You know, fill in here until the temp agency sends us a temporary replacement from their secretary pool. That's good thinking on my part, huh, boss?"

"What test was she getting done?" asked Gus.

"Don't know."

"Didn't you ask?"

"Nope."

"Deputy, you are about the least curious person in my department."

"I'd hate to ruin my retirement strategy. You know what they always say about it being curiosity that killed the cat."

"Yeah, that may be as it may, but it's also true that curiosity got that fat cat off the couch once in a while. A cat can't spend all day smoking doobies while watching reruns of *What's Happening*. How are our prisoners doing back there?"

"The young girl from Kansas seems rather depressed. She hardly eats a thing at all, and I've been serving her decent food and not the stuff we reserve for lowlifes. Nothing I do seems to be cheering her up either. The mystery man, Mr. Smith, that I ain't supposed to tell anyone about, keeps escaping after you go home, but don't you worry; he keeps coming back by the morning. Since he ain't under that much arrest, I reckon it's all right him going and coming like that," explained Drew.

"I wasn't worried a lick at the moment about our Mr. Smith. You just don't tell anyone about him until I figure out what there is to do about him. If we don't pay him any attention, then we might get lucky, and he might go away on his own accord. That man's trouble with a capital T, so stay away from him—well, possibly only a lowercase t at the moment. There are so many troubles floating about I just can't get worked up over that one man. I just hope no one in the press identifies him while he's coming or going."

Gus reached for the door to his office. Inside he would be safe from Josh Hansen, the Kansas Troopers, and the rest of the idiots who seemed doomed to plague him today. Deputy Drew added one more comment before he could escape. "There's a lawyer in there waiting for you to show up."

"I thought you said you wanted to help me out today. If you're helping me out, then how come there's a lawyer in my office?" grumbled Gus.

"I figured it was better than leaving him out here with me. Only a fool wants to spend time with a lawyer when they can do something to avoid it, like letting him wait in your office."

Gus rubbed his temple. He had to admit it was good thinking on Drew's part. He reached for his door one more time, and Drew spoke,

"Sheriff, one more thing before you go inside that's been bothering me. Can I ask you a serious question?"

"I reckon you can."

"Do you really think there's a pool out there filled with hot secretaries for me to swim around in?"

"No," replied Gus as he passed through the door and into his office at last.

Gus had two old, worn wooden chairs in his office. They were barren pieces of furniture that had been purchased with the sole purpose in mind of making sure only the most desperate of people would consider using them. Inside the office on a cold, worn chair sat a man dressed in an expensive suit. He was the kind of man that would sit in a shark's mouth for the right price. The price paid for his services was not as much money as the fame he could generate from your name. The man didn't bother to acknowledge Gus's entrance by turning to see who had entered the door. He simply barked out at the air, "I'm here to see my client."

"You could have gotten any number of untalented deputies to do that. There was no point in waiting around in here for me to arrive to tell me the obvious."

"I wanted you to know that I was handling this case," replied the man as he stood up. He straightened his suit not because it needed it, but because his suit was expensive enough that it mattered if it was straight or not, and he wanted Gus to know it.

Curiosity got the better of Gus, and he circled around to the chair behind his desk to get a better view of this lawyer's face. The lawyer had a good head of hair on him and appeared fit enough. He was good enough for the cameras and smart enough to convince juries. It was Wilton McDermott standing right here in Gus's office. There would only be one client interesting enough in this jail to draw a made-for-television defense lawyer. Well, two if you counted international hacker Josh Hansen, but Gus wasn't counting him. Gus replied, "You look taller on my television set. I might have to adjust the aspect ratio next time your show is on the air. I take it you expect to be back on the air soon with your new client. She was made for television pretty, and we both know it. I guess you're the man the rich San Francisco bleeding hearts hired to defend Jennifer. I figured you had made enough money from your last case, so you wouldn't need to do these high-profile gigs anymore. Oh, and for your information, your former client was just up the block a few minutes ago. You should have stopped by and said howdy for the TV stations. They'd have loved it."

"I don't do this work just for money. I also do it because I believe every man deserves to be defended to the full extent that the law allows. If they deserve it in front of television cameras, then so be it; I don't mind the extra press. As for getting rich on my last case, I'll have you know that Mr. Nickelback hasn't fully paid me for my services yet, but I'm sure he will in the due course of time so long as the press stays interested. I got a feeling his fifteen minutes of fame will last far longer than time should allow. Lucky for you, I'm not here about him. I don't care about him anymore. I won that case in front of the cameras, and that suited me just fine. I'm here to win again. I also want to add for the history books that I wasn't hired by anyone from San Francisco. I was hired by a concerned group of citizens up in Kansas."

"Sorry for my coarseness just now, but my sources misinformed me. I hear there's a lot of that misinformation about stuff up there in Kansas these days. Your client preferences came to me from a tall drink of water from another set of concerned citizens up in Kansas. A state trooper by the name of Major Scott Dundee. He might not be the most accurate fellow with his facts, but I do believe he's correct in one important fact: as soon as my governor signs the extradition papers from his governor, your client is no longer my problem. There's nothing in my law-enforcement complex for you to win. I don't see what a fancy-dressed man that bills by the hour can do about that fact. You don't need to see me."

The lawyer bent over elegantly and picked up his briefcase. He stood up straight and tall and walked to the door. He motioned with a wave of the hand for Gus to follow him as if Gus was a lapdog in his service. In this case Gus unfortunately was. The young woman in the cell had a right to see her lawyer, and he knew it. The lawyer said confidently, "I am going to speak to my client now, and then I'm going to speak to your governor.

I'm going to do my best to prevent her extradition to Kansas from ever happening. Now if you would kindly show me to her."

"You do understand by talking with my governor and getting her to delay those extradition papers, your job here is not to free your client, but to keep her down here in purgatory indefinitely. Meanwhile I'm going to have every form of crazy lining up outside this sheriff station picketing for and against her demise. Doesn't that seem to you kind of a cruel fate to leave her in, let alone me? Don't you think it's better to hasten your client's departure from my doorstep?"

The lawyer turned and gave a devilish smile to Gus. He explained, "My job is to defend my client by using all the power of the courts at my disposal. We both know she stands a much better chance down here in this state than she does up there in Kansas. The longer I drag this affair out, the better her chances become of either a trial down here or my firm stance being able to reduce the severity of the charges up there so that her extradition doesn't have unfortunate political ramifications for the governor. Delaying might seem cruel, but punishing Jennifer for a crime she didn't commit is far crueler. I know what I'm doing. Justice will prevail; I can assure you."

Gus sat down at his desk. He replied, "I see where we all stand now. You can stand there at the door waiting until hell freezes over for me to take you to see your client. I got a deputy sitting at a desk outside that door that will show you to her anytime you want and twice on Sunday. I don't need to see her with you. I already know what she looks like. She looks like money to a guy like you, and we both know it. The only justice that will be done is to your bank account by the time this is over."

"Like I said before, my last client hasn't even paid me yet."

"That's not the only way you make money from these cases, and we both know it." The lawyer didn't reply. Instead he effortlessly slipped out Gus's door to begin the process. Yesterday had been a bad day, but today was thoroughly rotten. Gus folded his arms on his desk and put his head down. The cowboy hat slumped off his head. He didn't care. His knees hurt, and he needed to think. He had to rid himself of these problems, but he couldn't think of any path forward as to how to get out ahead of these matters. To his annoyance the phone at his desk rang. He didn't lift his head. He simply focused his eyes over to the annoying ringing thing on his desk. It likely had more problems on its line waiting for him to hear. He reluctantly reached his hand over to the desk and picked up the receiver.

"This is Sheriff Gus in complete and utter despair right now. If you think you have something going on in your life worse than what's going on in Sheriff Gus's life, then I advise you to dial a nine followed by two ones."

Terrance's exuberant voice boomed from the other end of the line. "Gus, why didn't you tell me that we had another about-to-be-famous person in town, and more to the point, in your jail cells! Gus, do you know how exciting an opportunity it could be for this county to have a real live celebrity trial right here in this county? This is the kind of thing that could put this county right back on the map!"

"It must have slipped my mind. Besides, I thought as part of the rebranding effort we were trying hard not to advertise how many prisoners this county generates, since it has gotten us into trouble before."

"This is different. She's going to be national news! The national news is already here covering our newest celebrity, Sheldon Nickelback. I'm hoping they stay a long while covering him as he readjusts to normal life after the tragic shooting he committed. I got them all up here at city hall, and I'm going to send the press gaggle all down to your law-enforcement complex so you can keep them abreast of this abortion situation and see all the lovely protestors I just saw outside. As I said, this moment in time is our one great chance to put this county back on the map, and more importantly, to put plenty of coins into our political pockets."

"How are we going to do that?"

"I just told you, by going out there and talking to the national media. Just think, Gus; tomorrow your face could be splashed in heavily edited sound-bite segments that distort every word you say in a perpetual closed loop of information noise that runs morning, noon, and night on at least three major news stations. If we are really lucky on this one, it could even go global! You'll have talking-head experts whose only expertise is getting in front of a camera with a hot mic talking about you and this county in languages you never dreamed existed! You can't buy that kind of free advertising. Hell, you might end up a television star out of all this."

The pain in Gus's knees throbbed. He held back his excitement over the chance at instant celebrity status for putting a seventeen-year-old woman in jail for life. "You're making it all sound awfully tempting. Honestly, Terrance, I don't want to talk to the national press. This whole thing is going to be one huge headache for me. It's going to be me that will have to wade through the protestors every damn day just to get to work."

"Don't worry; it is going to be easy. I'm sending them down to your station right now! All you got to do is talk to them. You know; just go out and tell them what they want to hear."

"I give up; what do they want to hear?"

"Anything!" And with that Terrance hung up.

Gus put his head back down on his desk. There was no escaping the trap he was now in. There was a knock on the door, and someone new entered. Gus tilted his head up slightly to examine the new unwelcome office visitor. Deputy Wilson stood at the door. He was Gus's biggest, meanest-looking deputy, although looks were often deceiving.

"The guy in the jail cell charged with nothing told me to tell you he wants foie gras for dinner."

"Well, if you find any frogs in the grass, feel free to feed them to him. Now leave me alone; I'm thinking."

"Sorry about disturbing your thoughts. It looked an awful lot like you were sitting there with your head down sleeping to me. What are you thinking about, boss?" asked Wilson.

The *what* struck Gus in an instant. Perhaps it was the bulk of Deputy Wilson that put the idea in his head, and perhaps it was just the only thing now he could do to escape. A plan suddenly crystalized in Gus's head. It wasn't much of a plan, but it had become a clear and welcome start. He had been on the receiving end of a lot of stuff the past few days, and it was time to start being on the giving end. It was time to flex his department's muscles. Gus sat up. He ordered the deputy, "I was thinking about you, me, and Deputy Lopez going over to a certain man's house later on today and arresting him. It is about time this department inflicted a little pain on someone besides me. Just go back to your office and wait for Deputy Lopez to return from her present parking-ticket assignment. Later on we're going out to bust a head or two and enforce a little of the law."

"Who is Deputy Lopez?" asked Wilson.

"Don't worry; you'll know her when you see her," replied Gus.

"Her!"

CHAPTER 3

Fear follows crime and is its punishment.
—Voltaire

Gus didn't bother to meet with the national press despite Terrance's wishes. Instead, Gus had utilized that service entrance next to his cell block to sneak out of the law-enforcement complex the back way. He had done it with no intention of heading home. He'd had a completely different destination in mind.

It was now going on five in the afternoon when a new man appeared on the driveway he was watching. Gus followed him with his field glasses as this new man stepped out of a freshly detailed Audi. This vehicle had pulled into the driveway only moments ago. This rather smartly dressed man had gotten out of his perfectly wonderful car to do a very mundane thing. He was just leaning against the Audi's expensive wax job while waiting. A dirtbag who went by the name of Terry Tang came out of the house to greet the Audi-driving enthusiast. Terry was decked out in a wife-beater T-shirt and a pair of cheap sunglasses. He also had a gun obviously tucked into the waistband of his blue jeans. Terry went over to the driveway and talked to the smartly dressed man for a solid two minutes. Gus figured they weren't talking about car detailing. Terry nodded a lot and then went back into his house. The other man went to the trunk of the Audi and retrieved from it a plain brown paper bag. The Audi driver carried the brown bag to the driver's-side door and leaned against it again. The man appeared happy enough as he checked out his receding hairline in the side mirror.

The scumbag Terry reappeared from the house carrying a similar brown paper bag of his own. The man with the Audi perked up at the sight. These two men were apparently interested in having a brown-bag dinner together. Well, not quite dinner, as it appeared to be much like your typical grade-school brown-bag lunch affair with these two men. That meant, as all grade-school lunches meant, that the other guy's mom had made a more attractive lunch than the one the first guy's mom had made. They opened them up and took a peek at what the other guy's mom had to offer. Yep, as Gus suspected, each man coveted the other guy's handmade delights. You could see it in their eyes even through the sunglasses they wore. The two brown bags exchanged hands right out in the open on Terry Tang's driveway. If they were feeling guilty about something they had just done, then they kept it a well-hidden secret.

The bad guys also weren't attempting to be quick and discrete about this affair. Instead, Terry was killing time out on his front lawn shooting the shit with this other man. Luckily, the shit could be shot without the use of that gun in his waistband. That other man had found some interesting subject to talk over with high-school dropout Terry Tang. Gus watched the two men through his binoculars from a full block away, wondering what they possibly could find in common. He figured he knew, but he couldn't know for sure. He didn't want to know for sure, so he sat patiently waiting in the sheriff's truck. Gus wasn't working particularly hard to shield who he was from them, and they weren't trying very hard to shield what was happening between them from Gus. Gus figured either Terry Tang was confident that his high-profile addicts were big enough wigs to shield him from the law, or Terry was rather stupid. In reality those things weren't mutually exclusive, and thus it was probably a combination of both. The only definite thing was that they were annoying Gus by shooting the breeze instead of letting the more important man leave the crime scene. There was nothing to do while he was around. Once again, Gus didn't 100 percent want to know for sure what that man was doing. It was Terry he wanted to see, and he needed to see him alone.

This situation was the hardest thing involved in this kind of work. There were simply clients whom you wanted to nail badly, and there were other people you were supposed to be less than vigilant about when observing them breaking the law. The richer and whiter they were, the worse your eyesight was supposed to get. The guy with the Audi was the type of man you didn't want to arrest, because he came with a heap of trouble. Gus knew him vaguely. He worked up in the big city to the north reading the news on local television. He was just a minor celebrity, but still a man not worth ensnaring in a dragnet. It might have been wrong to purchase the substance in that brown paper bag, but he didn't need a man with a clean image and a bad drug habit causing negative news from his television gig. His image was clean, so it wouldn't matter what the facts were. There were enough negative stories to churn about in the news without creating artificial waves over nothing. The foolish man was purchasing something he shouldn't be, but that was its own punishment as far as Gus was concerned. Wealthy addicts would end up with a slap on the wrist and rehab, so what would be the point of Gus arresting him? If you wanted a man like that to be punished, then you were better off letting him continue to feed the addiction or die trying. Not that Gus was going to let that happen. That was why he was here.

The only thing that mattered to Gus right now was Terry Tang and his house of ill-gotten goods. Terry had been treated with kid gloves up until now because many a rich person was buying his prescription drugs thinking they weren't addicts. They considered themselves just sick men and women in need of a little medicine. No doubt Terry Tang did nothing to persuade them of that notion. Gus had gotten what he wanted. He had observed a buy right there in the failing twilight. Now he wanted Terry alone so he could explain to him one-on-one that Terry's West Coast drugs were no longer going to be tolerated in this county. It was the merciful thing for Gus to do. Gus knew that if he didn't explain things to Terry, then Antonio most likely would eventually explain this fact to Terry by a more lethal lesson. There were important people behind a man like Terry Tang, but when push came to shove, no one with something worth losing was going to stick their neck out for an ordinary thug who sold drugs.

Gus gazed up into his rearview mirror. The trooper from Kansas was sitting a full block down the road in his patrol car. He was likely watching Gus watch Terry Tang. That was the way it was going to be between the two of them, and Gus took note of that fact. Gus heard a car start up its engine, and he looked back into his field glasses. The smartly dressed man in the Audi had finally packed himself back into the expensive vehicle, and it was roaring down the road. Soon the rich man would be happily sedated. Terry gave a glance down the road toward Gus's truck. It was just sitting there on the side of the road doing nothing. If Terry Tang thought something about Gus being here, it hadn't prevented the business transaction from going down. Terry lingered for a few minutes before casually reentering his house. He appeared to be a man without a care in the world. That was about to end.

Gus opened the truck's door and stepped out onto the street. He now casually strolled down the sidewalk. The neighborhood was shabby enough to believe a drug dealer might set up shop to sell here, but not so shabby that men in expensive Audis wouldn't come here at twilight to buy drugs. In other words, it was a nice place to set up a prescription-drug ring.

Gus knew that the drugs here came in from Los Angeles. How they got here Gus didn't know for sure. Somewhere back in Los Angeles, there was this Dr. Smith associated with a pharmacy that was very loose in the handing out of prescriptions and the drugs those prescriptions prescribed. The district attorney had explained to Gus two weeks ago that while the whole thing looked unethical, it was technically legal in appearance. The DA assured Gus that top people on the West Coast were looking into this organization. Terry's agency was only a delivery service between this pharmacy and the needy patients. It all sounded good on paper even if, as Gus suspected, many of these drugs were stolen out of warehouses by the pallet straight from the manufacturer. Still, some doctor called Smith was writing prescriptions for people who didn't have them. Many prescriptions likely got written after the fact, but they were written. This doctor lived out west and so never met his local patients, but that didn't hamper his intuition on what they needed. He was getting in return a very nice cash reward. That was the setup. It sure felt illegal to Gus. That was obvious to anyone with eyes who cared to look.

Gus didn't bother watching Terry Tang's house as he strolled down the sidewalk. Instead his eyes were fixed on a blue sedan parked farther down the street. The car was conspicuous in its shared interest in the drug house. A pair of binoculars stared out of the back seat of that particularly menacing vehicle. They hadn't bothered glancing once at the sheriff's truck the whole time Gus had sat there by the curb. No one seemed particularly scared of law enforcement in this county. Gus wanted that to change. It was healthy to instill a little fear and loathing among the rabble. Operation one in that regard was about to begin. It should make the man in that blue sedan very happy, or at least his bosses very happy. The thug in that blue sedan was likely just a goon doing what he was told with no idea what the ultimate stakes were going to be. Antonio had told the thug to watch the house and not to watch the sheriff, and that was just what he was doing.

Gus stopped his casual stroll down the street when he had come alongside a rusted-out white sedan parked directly in front of Terry Tang's house. It was the department's only unmarked patrol car. The man in that blue car probably had lived in this county his whole life, and so he knew it by sight. Terry Tang as a newcomer to town apparently didn't. Gus pulled out his nightstick and pounded it on top of the roof of the white sedan. Rust flaked off the body of the vehicle, and the two front doors opened up. Deputy Wilson and Deputy Lopez came out. They had been ducked out of sight of the car's windows for over an hour in the failing heat of the day. They were stiff and unhappy, which meant they were in the right mood to handle Terry Tang. Gus had wanted a word with Terry alone, and it was better to be alone with a drug dealer with a couple of friends along with you. Gus gave quick instructions to the two. "Lopez, you take the back door just in case our suspect wants to jackrabbit out of sight. Deputy Wilson, you walk over behind me to help greet our new West Coast friend."

"The suspect had a gun. Should I return deadly force with deadly force?" asked Deputy Lopez.

"Don't go shooting anyone on your first day. A guy running away from us is trying to get away. If there's deadly force needed, then it will be needed at the front door, and it will be used by me," replied Gus.

"Then maybe I should take the back and leave the front door to you two trigger-happy people," suggested Deputy Wilson.

"You just stick with me, Wilson. I want our suspect to get a good look at your size. I'm hoping he thinks he's smart and will come along peacefully, but I don't plan on too much smarts from this man."

Deputy Lopez ran off to the back of the house as quick as can be. She appeared enthusiastic for the job. Gus strolled across the street to the suspect's driveway. He didn't rush it, and Deputy Wilson walked even slower. He walked just a few paces behind Gus, swinging his nightstick. The window curtains were rustling, so someone was at home watching them. Gus had only counted one man, Terry Tang, inside that house the whole time they watched it. It didn't mean that he was alone, but Gus figured he was. They strolled on at their casual pace right up the stairs and to the front door. Gus rang the doorbell. Nothing happened. He rang it again, but still nothing happened. He might have bolted out the back door.

Gus turned to Deputy Wilson and nodded. Deputy Wilson shook his head in disgust and walked along the porch until he came to the front window. The deputy took one long, swooping swing with his nightstick, and the front window imploded into the house. Gus rang the doorbell again. Now there was the sound of frantic activity inside as Gus could hear the steps of a resident echoing behind that closed front door. The door knob fumbled a few times, but finally the door jerked open until stopping hard on a chain. The suspect had limited security on the house's front door. Through the door crack, Gus could see Terry Tang standing there slightly cut by the broken glass of the window.

"What the fuck gives you the right to break my window?" yelled a rather angry Terry.

"I don't have a right. I never thought I did. It was wrong of me to do that, and I'm sorry for it having been done. I just wanted you to answer your front door so I could talk to you, and you did, didn't you, because I broke that glass," replied Gus as he watched Terry's hands. Gus was playing it cool but careful, just in case Terry went for his gun.

"Try ringing the doorbell then!"

"I did, twice."

"I saw you over there watching me. You and your trained gorilla here are a pretty suspicious pair. What do people like you want with people like me?"

"What kind of people are you?" asked Gus.

"If you don't know…" replied Terry as he motioned to close his front door.

Deputy Wilson pushed his large foot in the doorframe to prevent the door from closing. Gus smiled to Terry, friendly-like, and then replied, "I'm the local sheriff in these parts, and you've been operating in my territory for quite a spell. I thought it was time we talked and made some arrangements. Don't the people back on the West Coast make arrangements? Nothing in life is free, and you don't even do nothing, do you, Terry? Something in life costs you much more than doing nothing, and you're the kind of man that does something that should cost him plenty."

Terry relaxed. He replied, "Why the fuck didn't you say so from the start? I'm not a greedy man by nature. I never expected to get something from you locals for nothing. How much something did you need to do nothing about me? I saw you limping on your way to my door. Our Percocet is fifty percent off this week, but perhaps I can do better than that even if we're going to be friends."

"Shit, boy, don't just leave me standing on the porch; offer me a seat inside and a cold drink. Didn't you boys from out west ever learn you some proper manners?"

"Awe, fuck, man, I'm sorry," replied Terry. He flexed the door to remove the chain when he hesitated and stopped. He said, "You can come in, but your monkey stays outside, okay?"

"It's all right by me, if it is all right by you. Deputy Wilson only speaks with his fists, so he won't be needed. You and I are the only ones that need to sit down and talk."

Deputy Wilson pulled his foot from the doorway and stood back. Terry Tang's body now completely relaxed. He flexed the door and slid the chain back. As soon as the chain moved off the door, Gus took one small step to the side, and Deputy Wilson had a free path to the doorway. The deputy never hesitated for a second. He burst forward with a full head of steam into the front door. The door jerked immediately backward with violence. It impacted with Terry Tang in the most unpleasant way. Terry's nose exploded with blood as he fell backward. Deputy Wilson pounced upon his prone body, and before Terry knew what had just happened to him, he was lying facedown on his living-room floor with Wilson sitting on top of his back. Deputy Wilson not so delicately yanked Terry's arms one by one behind his body and secured him in handcuffs.

Now Gus strolled through the wide-open front door. He closed it behind him. There was no need to advertise to the spying neighbors what might be happening to poor Terry Tang inside. Gus patted Deputy Wilson on the shoulder and with great effort bent down to relieve Terry Tang of his gun still tucked in his pants. Gus tucked it into his own waistband. There was no point in letting a nice gun go to waste on a man like Terry Tang. Gus ordered Deputy Wilson, "Wilson, be a nice fellow and help Terry here onto the couch while I go retrieve Deputy Lopez from the backyard. After we've had a nice search around the premises, I might be back to have a second chat here with poor bloody Terry."

"I know my rights! You can't come in here and search my place without a warrant," yelled Terry.

"Why, Terry, don't you remember that you just invited me inside?" replied Gus.

"But I did that when I thought you were only coming inside to ask me for a bribe!"

"Your problem, Terry, is you thought you could think at all. If you're smart, then you'll never make that same mistake again, but you're not a smart man, are you, Terry?"

Gus left Terry to struggle under the crippling vice grip of Deputy Wilson. Handcuffed and bloody, he wasn't likely to put up much resistance.

Gus wandered quickly through the shabbily furnished house to the back door. He opened it and took one step outside. He then blew a whistle, and Chiquita's head appeared over the neighbor's hedges. She placed her gun back in its hostler and proceeded to come inside to join the party. Gus let her search the basement and attic while he stuck to the main floor. He spent the better part of a half hour in vain, because the stuff wasn't around in an obvious hiding spot. Eventually Deputy Lopez appeared with her hands nearly empty as well. She was holding a shoebox filled with slips of paper in one hand and a brown paper bag in the other.

"What's in the brown paper bag?" asked Gus.

"Money, Mr. Tang has a whole lot of it in bills. I found a cardboard box upstairs filled with these brown paper bags. Each bag is filled with a nice stack of twenties and bank deposit receipts."

"Which bank?"

She read out loud to Gus, "Arroyo National Bank. Should I go get the whole thing and bring it to the station as evidence?"

"Nah, don't do anything rash. It ain't illegal to have money, even a whole lot of it." Gus ignored the bag of money and focused on the shoebox. "Okay, now go ahead and tell me about the contents of that box."

Deputy Lopez pulled out a slip of paper. "I think they're prescriptions." She read it out loud, "OxyContin, fifty milligrams, take twice daily. There's a name on it, Nancy Mayer. There's also a doctor's signature, Dr. Joseph Smith."

"That's the game all right."

"What's it all mean?" replied Deputy Lopez.

"People have a doctor give them a drug. They like the drug. They want to keep taking it, but their doctor knows the drug is habit-forming, so their prescription ends on purpose. The patient doesn't like that much, so they go searching for another doctor until they find a doctor like Dr. Smith. They call him up. He writes them a prescription if they got a conscience and feel like they need to follow the law more or less. He doesn't if they don't, but he always sends them here. The thing is they don't go to a pharmacy to fill that prescription. They come here to where Dr. Smith sends them. Terry Tang doesn't report doctor shopping to authorities and wants Dr. Smith to hook his patients. The business is good for both parties involved. And like I said, the prescription signed by a doctor makes the patient feel like they're not doing something wrong."

"What's the next step?"

"Give me one of those bank receipts." She handed one over. Gus tucked it into his pocket. Then Gus relieved her of the shoebox. "Wait here; we haven't found the good stuff yet, but I'll be back."

Gus took the shoebox back into the living room. Wilson had spent the half hour placing Terry on the couch. Blood had dried all over the front of Terry's shirt. Deputy Wilson stood towering over the man to make sure he sat patiently awaiting Gus's return. Terry didn't appear to be a happy man. He was about to get unhappier. Gus took the remains of a decaying pizza box off a chair in the room and sat down to face Terry. He plunked the shoebox of prescriptions on the floor. Terry's eyes followed that box of prescriptions with interest. Then he looked right back up into Gus's eyes. He didn't say a word.

Gus asked, "Terry, my good buddy, why do you have so many prescriptions written out for other people?"

"You know why," replied Terry.

Gus let the insolence pass by. He asked another question instead in rapid fire. "Then where is the why?" Terry didn't answer. Gus dipped his hands into the prescription slips. He pulled out a slip and held it out for Terry to see. "Oh, Terry, Terry, Terry, I knew a mother that had more than a few prescriptions for drugs from a Dr. Smith just like this one here. Her daughter OD'd on them drugs rather recently. It broke my heart to watch that dear momma cry as the coroner carried her daughter's body away."

"Fuck you!" shouted Terry.

Gus nodded, and Deputy Wilson hit Terry hard in the gut with a closed fist. Wilson flexed his hand after the punch. Gus felt bad for the deputy. A man shouldn't have to earn a living punching people like Terry Tang. Gus knew Wilson hated doing this kind of stuff for a lot of reasons. For one, it wasn't worth the pain to your hand. For two, Wilson was a decent sort of fellow, but Terry didn't know all that. Out had come a little more blood from Terry's mouth to decorate his shirt. Gus let the man cough up a little volume before explaining things to Terry. When Terry was good and silent again, Gus continued, "I think you are going to find that I'm your friend. I'm your very best friend in this county."

"You could have fooled me, asshole!" yelled Terry.

"Anyone could fool you, Terry, because you're a moron. You also happen to be a moron with a hell of a lot of prescriptions for drugs. I know you're not Dr. Smith, so you must be the prescription filler. I think this pharmacy on the West Coast you deliver for is a scam. These drugs you got stashed away here are illegal, so I'm obligated to do something about all this."

"Fuck you, I got the prescriptions right there that say these drugs of mine aren't illegal!" yelled Terry.

"But these prescriptions aren't made out to you. You got some quack out west to print these out for whatever some client tells you that they need. It's almost legal. This house is a profit-making machine that runs on every Joe Blow that needs a little more than his normal doctor will allow. I grant you it is a good business. You know who else thinks it is a good business? Big Gustavo. You know that name, don't you? Are you afraid of Big Gustavo, Terry?"

"We can handle a spic like him," replied Terry.

"You better be good at handling them, because Big Gustavo has a thug sitting out there in a blue sedan watching you work. I don't think Big Gustavo likes you too much, Terry."

"Fuck you and Big Gustavo!" replied Terry.

"Terry, you shouldn't speak that way to a good friend." Gus nodded again. Deputy Wilson rolled his eyes and then punched Terry hard in the face with a closed fist. Terry lost consciousness for a second or two. Deputy Wilson grabbed the man's hair to hold his head steady.

"I think he's had enough," said Wilson.

Gus didn't reply. He waited for the cobwebs to ebb before continuing to talk to Terry Tang. "Terry, old boy, don't go falling down and bumping your head like that, because you might get permanently hurt. I'm very concerned for your health just now. I mean, I'm deeply concerned. As I said, about a block or so down there is a blue car filled with a man from Big

Gustavo's esteemed thug force. After I dance you out of here and take you to my pristine jail cell, what do you think that man in that blue car is going to do? I'll tell you what he will do; he'll tear your house apart until he finds the stuff. There won't be a board left standing if it is really hard for him to find the stuff. That sounds like it could be a big loss of investment on your part. If only there was some way to prevent that loss." Terry's mouth hung open, but it didn't make a sound. Gus finished, "Now I got a plan that might prevent this all from happening. You want to hear it, Terry my boy?"

Terry didn't answer. He was conscious but confused. He gingerly nodded his head in affirmation. He wanted to know what he could do. He knew an opportunity to bribe when it came. Now Gus finished his thought. "The thug down the block might see my deputies walk out of here carrying your drugs. Those drugs would then spend a pleasant air-conditioned night in my office, and I guarantee you the man in that blue car sure as hell won't break into there to get them. You see, you're going to jail for the night no matter what. Your drugs can risk their luck with either the likes of Big Gustavo's men or my men. Once again, I think we know who might be easier to bribe into retrieving them when the courts get done with you, don't we?"

Terry didn't say anything in response. Gus rubbed his temple. He got up from his seat. He started to exit the house. He said over his shoulder, "It appears to be a no that I'm hearing from you. That's too bad. Well, okay, Wilson, you can tie Terry here up in the bathroom and then torch this place to the ground with him in it. We'll chalk it up in the official report as a victim of gang warfare. Perhaps the next guy this West Coast outfit installs in this county will be easier to negotiate with."

Terry became faster on the response. "Torch! Wait, wait; I think we can come to some agreement. I mean, the first plan is a good plan! I'll take your first offer. The drugs are in the refrigerator."

Gus stopped and turned around. He said to Deputy Wilson, "Take the idiot to the patrol car and book him for drug peddling."

Deputy Wilson tugged the sad sack off the couch. Gus didn't stick around to watch him depart. He made his way back to Deputy Lopez. He motioned her to follow him into the kitchen. He opened the refrigerator door. It wasn't full of drugs. It wasn't exactly filled with food either. It was empty except for the shelves. He started yanking out the shelves. When they were all removed, he slammed his foot hard into the floor of the open refrigerator. It echoed. Gus turned to Deputy Lopez. "Don't just stand there; please help an old man out by lifting the refrigerator flooring up."

Deputy Lopez bent over and slid the fake bottom off the refrigerator. It revealed a dark hole with a ladder. She looked up at Gus, who pointed for her to go down into the hole. She turned on her flashlight and did just that without complaint. She returned a minute later with a medium-sized box in her hand. She explained, "There are about a dozen boxes like this down there. All filled with prescription drugs." She was smiling with a sense of victory.

"Good, take them to my truck and put them in the back."

"Do you think this evidence is enough to get rid of this slime once and for all?"

"Get rid of him? I doubt that. People like Terry Tang are very hard to get rid of. You remove one, and another pops up in his place. They're like the hydra in that Greek story from long ago. Cut off a head in this drug-peddling business, and two more grow back. The only way to kill them is to strike at their body, the vast body of users out there who won't admit they have a problem and who society pretends don't have a problem. As long as we fail to admit our society has a drug-taking problem, the losers like Terry will always be around to profit from that fact. We could hurt their business profits by focusing on rehab of the inflicted instead of building more jails, but the whole business won't go away forever, because some people will always want to get high for stupid reasons. There must be something awful bad about being alive that makes so many people want to live comfortably numbed by addiction. Got me what it is; stupidity I guess."

"Then what good did this little raid of ours do?"

"Good? Why, Deputy Lopez, you just earned your first paycheck; isn't that good enough for you?"

She apparently agreed, because she went back down the hole to retrieve the other boxes. This little war waged by Gus on drugs might not be doing society much good, but it was going to do Gus a lot of good. He kept that little piece of knowledge to himself. For the first time in the past few days, Gus felt like he was getting ahead of the game.

Terry Tang was tucked away in a jail cell for the night, and Gus was ready to call it a day. He'd call it a bad day at that. He had been happy to be heading home when the call had come in over the dispatch. It was truly the week for problems, and there seemed no end to them. He wasn't about to make it home just yet because of this rather bad news the dispatcher had told him. Gus knew that in this job, there were problems your deputies could more than handle without you, and then there were problems like this one that you had to handle personally. Luckily, by the time Gus's truck navigated the maze of suburban pathways in the development section of the county, the fire had been put out by the local fire department. The development was the newest urbanized section of the county. It was a suburban jungle built for city people who longed for the city life but couldn't afford the city prices. They lived here in Gus's county and commuted north to work, play, and shop. All the houses there were built up to the latest fire codes, so it was unlikely for one of them to catch fire by accident. It was nearing ten at night, and his knees reminded him he should be anywhere else but here watching the large hook-and-ladder truck and two small emergency vehicles wind down their professional activities.

It would have been annoying for Gus to have driven all the way out here for nothing, so he was happy to see that there really had been a fire after all. The firefighters milled about on the front lawn with flashlights in their hands. The firefighters' boots and their hose water had turned the lawn's turf into the consistency of pea soup. The mood was casual and light among the fire crew. There was the extra security in knowing that no one appeared to have been hurt by this trivial blaze. The only injury was likely to the psyche of the neighborhood who had just found out that there was a price to pay for having a celebrity living in their secluded little corner of the world. Sheldon Nickelback stood on his porch in defiance, watching the display of the fire-handling experts on his newly acquired front lawn.

All his neighbors besides the ever-faithful Skip Lipschitz kept their distance from the crime scene. They weren't so far away as to be minding their own business inside their own homes like a normal person did at ten o'clock at night. No, instead the whole neighborhood was outside watching the activities with excitement, but they were doing it from the safety of their own front porches. They probably weren't acting unneighborly to Sheldon on purpose. These neighbors were being about as neighborly as they thought they could afford to be. No doubt every single one of them knew Sheldon Nickelback by sight and figured the person who lit this fire would be taking notes on who came to his aid and who stayed home. It was thus a neighborly thing to do to make sure that other people didn't end up unnecessarily with burning crosses on their lawns as well, or at least that was how most of the neighbors saw it from their own point of view, figured Gus. Gus didn't blame them for having their own point of view on these events either. The result, though, was the same; Mr. Nickelback was basically alone, defiantly standing on his porch in his nightclothes. It was just him and Skip Lipschitz against the world, and tonight the world appeared to have fought back just a little bit.

From the safety of Gus's truck, the situation seemed rather obvious. Some person or persons unknown had taken the bother to erect a cross of wood on Sheldon's front lawn. A lawn that one assumed the previous owners had paid good money to be excellently manicured so that a person like Sheldon Nickelback would purchase this house. The perpetrators, not satisfied with a little crucifixion display, had bothered to set the cross ablaze to warm Sheldon's heart. The exact reasoning as to why someone burns a perfectly good cross Gus didn't know. It all felt a little too old-school 1950s-style hate for his tastes. More than that, though, was the fact that the victim, Sheldon Nickelback, felt like the type of man who should be on the hating side of an event like this rather than on the hated side. Strange times must make for strange scenarios, and this was as strange a time as Gus had ever been wrapped up in. There was too much happening all at once. He thought he had just started to get ahead of the game when tokens had gotten tossed onto the playing table to propel events deeper into chaos. The implication of a blazing cross seemed clear enough at this distance. A couple of angry minorities had set a cross on fire to symbolize an odd sense of irony about the reversal of fortunes. They didn't want Sheldon Nickelback in this community and weren't afraid to advertise the fact. The only bright side of the current situation was that some other minority would likely be paid handsomely to return Sheldon's lawn to its former state.

Gus popped out of his vehicle and made his way over to Deputy Lopez. His first task was a hard one. He needed to shoo the admiring firemen and the idiot Skip Lipschitz away from his newest and hardest-working deputy. The sight of the raven-haired beauty apparently wasn't missed by the hardworking men of the county fire departments. They all seemed to be finding her with no difficulties even in the cool night by the glow of their flashlights. It was the kind of thing once illuminated you'd hate to give back to the darkness of the night. Not that Gus had ever known a fireman to have a hard time finding an attractive date. In his experience, women liked an athletically built man in a uniform with a good-paying job and a pension. As to which was the most attractive element of that mix, Gus didn't exactly know. It was starting to become rather clear that of all the county's rebranding efforts, the hiring of Chiquita was the only one bringing in rave reviews from all sides. He hadn't met someone who didn't enjoy seeing her yet. Well, except possibly Terry Tang, but you could excuse the drug dealer for his poor taste.

Gus walked through the sloppy grime of the lawn until he came upon Skip Lipschitz on his hands and knees poking about. He kicked him softly on his big, round bottom. Gus ordered, "Skip, the sheriff has arrived, so there's no need to mess up my crime scene further."

"I was searching for clues. The foul fiends that did this must pay dearly for ruining our pristine county's image! A man ought to be able to feel safe in his own home."

"Cheer up; I've heard of people being treated worse in their own home lately."

"It makes you wonder what's happening to this world," lamented Skip.

"Yeah, well, the professional clue searchers are here to bring a little justice to this event. I want you to help me out by going up on the porch and comforting poor Mr. Nickelback."

"Okay, Sheriff, if you insist, but Sheldon is one tough cookie. I doubt he needs any comforting. He's got his gun, so no bad man is going to ever get him. The only thing that keeps this world sane and safe is a well-armed citizenry."

"Is that a fact? You better hustle and talk to him to make sure that gun of his is loaded then. I want to know he's safe so that the next burning cross on his lawn he can just shoot at until it goes out instead of calling in the fire department. All these hooks and ladders cost the county money."

Skip didn't reply. He got out of the slop and made his way toward Sheldon Nickelback. Civilians like Skip were always trying to help Gus's policing, but mostly they just got in the way. Skip was right about one thing. Gus watched Sheldon on the porch, and he gave off the impression of a man not exactly afraid of the implications of the burned cross. He was a man who appeared to be used to being hated. Sheldon was just standing on his porch surveying the scene like he was cock of the walk. Sheldon gave Gus a casual nod when he noticed Gus looking at him. Gus nodded back at the man of the hour.

He was turning his attention away from watching Sheldon when several of the firemen lingering around the cross came up to Gus to try and brag to him about their firefighting prowess. It apparently hadn't been a big blaze, and it took a very short time to put out. Still, any amount of fire was enough to get these boys worked up. When there was a pretty deputy around to impress with their fire stories, the flames tended to get bigger and more dangerous than they appeared to have been. He concluded from a brief survey of the crime scene and his important chat with the fire boys that indeed the cross had been set on fire by someone, and then the fire crew had put it out. Not every investigation had to be filled with mysteries. His investigation now needed to move it up a notch. He wanted actual helpful information on who had done this. He succeeded in prying Chiquita a few feet from the admiring eyes of the firemen and asked her,

"Since you seem to be my Johnnie-on-the-spot today, can you tell me what the hell happened here?"

Deputy Lopez replied, "When I arrived, the cross was on fire. It wasn't that scary a thing. These guys put it out quick enough. Big, brave men if you ask them. The only question left to know is who did this. I was examining the wood to see if there were any identifying marks. They used cut two-by-fours, which means the wood had to be purchased somewhere, so knowing where that was would go a long way to identifying the suspect. Then we will get to make the suspects pay for their crime. The rest I imagine the fire people covered already."

"Possibly. Did you see anyone suspicious hanging around the burning-cross scene when you first arrived?"

"No, I just saw the man up there on the porch and a huge bonfire in the form of a burning cross."

"How soon do you think you got here?"

"Probably five minutes after the call came in. I was fortunately driving around the development on a scouting mission. I'm trying to get the lay of the land because I'm new here. Like I said, the only one stirring about the scene when I got here was the man up on the porch. Then the fat, ugly one called Skip arrived. I notice Skip is the same idiot as from the show this morning, so it can't be him. You don't donate to a man an expensive car and house and then burn a cross on his lawn in the same day. What would be the point? The neighbors all came out on their porches watching once the firemen and their sirens arrived. It could have been one of them, but I doubt it. I figure whoever did this is long gone."

"It all sounds a little odd. You don't start a fire to scare a man and then leave before you get to see how scared you made him. It's going to be an odd one; I can feel it."

Deputy Lopez said, "I'll catch the ones that did this; don't worry."

"I like your attitude. You're my hardest-working deputy already. When searching with the flashlight around the slop of the lawn, did you happen to come across a fuel tank or a match, torch, or other incendiary device?"

"Sorry, between me and the fire boys, we did a pretty good job scouting the area, but we didn't find anything useful like that."

"Yeah, I saw them all scouting out the area just now. Some of those firemen even had an eye out on the ground briefly while scouting the area. Do me a favor and get them to focus on the ground and not on you for the time being. We might get lucky and find out what they used to light our cross up. One little clue is all we need, I think, to figure this whole thing out. It might be an odd little crime, but my gut is telling me it is also a very simple crime," replied Gus.

"I'll do my best. Those firemen shouldn't be too hard to convince." Chiquita winked, and off she went back toward the firemen.

Not only was it odd to do something like this and not hang around to see your handiwork, it was also odd to set a thing like this on fire and scram fast enough to not be seen in a dense neighborhood. They had to have moved fast and yet been slow and careful enough to remember to carry away the spent fuel tanks used, the matches used, the shovels used, the hammers used, and the torches used; they had quickly scrammed and yet methodically scrammed. It just felt odder and odder the more Gus thought about it. It didn't mean that it hadn't happened just that way, as the facts seemed to speak for themselves.

Gus shuffled up the mud pit that was once a lawn to go talk to the victim to gather more facts. The victim saw Gus walking up the lawn and gave Gus a big, friendly wave. He appeared rather happy to be getting a going-over by the sheriff. Well, that wasn't unusual; he was just like any other celebrity Gus had run across. They were all whores for attention whether it was good or bad. Sheldon just stood up on the porch smugly watching and waving for Gus to come to him. Before Gus stepped up onto the porch, he looked back and glanced over the area from this perspective. The cross was plenty obvious from the front porch. When it was lit up, it must have been quite an impressive sight. He looked over from the cross and saw that Deputy Lopez had gathered the firemen into an effective search team. They were setting out through the surrounding area to search for anything fire related. If it was out there in the night to be found among the mud, then they'd find it. Every fireman wanted to be the man who delivered what the pretty deputy asked for. She used her feminine charms rather well. A normal person might be offended to see people manipulate others with their attractive features. Gus didn't mind at all. Good looks were an effective tool, and if you had them, then you had them. You could teach a person some degree of book smarts, but you couldn't teach a person to have and use their charisma effectively. Charisma was a thing people either had or they didn't. If Gus had had it, then he had lost it a long time ago, so these days he got by ordering those with it to do his work for him. The result was the same: a team of firemen setting about with flashlights to search the neighborhood for a clue to the origin of the fire, and that was just what Gus wanted. Gus stepped onto the porch to see Sheldon up close. Sheldon had it too, charisma that is.

Gus reached out his hand to Sheldon Nickelback, and the victim took it. Gus said to Sheldon, "Hello." He then turned to Skip standing next to Sheldon on the porch. Gus had sent Skip up here. That was a mistake. Gus barked out an order to Skip. "They are setting up a search team. Why don't you help me out by searching with them?"

"I thought you didn't want me to mess up the evidence?" replied Skip.

"I haven't got any evidence to mess up. Why don't you do Sheldon and me a big favor and get out there and find some. I'm sure he'd appreciate it. He's had a hard night, and we owe it to him."

Like a happy, helpful dog Skip bounded his round frame off the porch in hopes of glory. Gus and Sheldon watched him depart. The Skips of the world were easy to exploit if you knew how to talk to them. Gus apologized for the situation to Sheldon. "It's a bit of a tough luck break for you here, mister. I wouldn't worry too much about it, as it was probably only a collection of kids out tonight doing stupid stuff. Kids do stupid stuff all the time. You've had trouble with kids before, haven't you?"

"You could say I've had a spot or two of trouble with young people before, but nothing I couldn't handle." He patted his gun on his side. He stood under his porch light dressed in his nightclothes with slippers on his feet. A pistol of some type was strapped on his waist. It was an odd combination.

"Good, then cheer up. Now that they got all our attention, they likely won't be back. They know my boys will be watching the house from now on."

"The thing is that I rather doubt that this was the work of kids, Sheriff," replied Sheldon.

"Then you saw the perpetrators? That is good news, as it will go a long way to helping us find the perpetrators of this crime. Please give me as accurate a description of them as you can," replied Gus, taking out a pen and a small notepad.

"I didn't say that. I didn't see anyone. I didn't hear anything suspicious. I was getting ready for bed when all this stuff started out here. It was rather late at night, remember. What I meant was, given the facts about who I am, I rather doubt it was just a bunch of foolish kids. Old prejudices are hard to kill no matter how innocent a man is on the inside. People who didn't even know me are calling me a racist in the press all the time based on how I chose to defend myself against an attack. You got to remember I didn't pick the race of the young man that attacked me."

"So you think this cross burning was organized?"

"You know those types of people. They're pretty easily influenced by the media. One group of activists or another did this. They love to cry racism then ask for special favors. Those reverse bigots did it to me back home, and they're doing it to me here. They love to persecute me because of my innocence."

Gus asked, "This is the first cross burning on your lawn, though, right?"

"This is something new. I have to admit that."

Gus could see the certainty in Sheldon's eyes. It was possible these were really meticulous, organized firebugs with a grudge against Sheldon Nickelback, although Gus's gut said to him that the meticulous people involved in this case wouldn't set a cross on fire to begin with. There were half a dozen Latino organizations now formally protesting his arrival to Gus's humble little county. Gus knew most of the leaders of those groups from city-council meetings. The members of those organizations were likely at home tonight writing their opinions up for the paper and television news shows. They weren't here tonight, because they made their pastime complaining with written non-legally-actionable letters and blog posts directed at the media and city-council members. That's what meticulous people do when a Sheldon Nickelback moves into their town. What they don't do is generally set fire to crosses, or at least until this cross tonight, he hadn't figured on them ever having a cross-burning agenda. The press was going to love this burning cross, and Gus knew it. Sheldon Nickelback was news. His trial was over, but his story just wouldn't end.

Gus finished that thought and was ready to say something more to Sheldon when the press arrived. The whole lawn scene exploded with a strobe of bright light. Then it exploded again in rapid fashion. Gus glanced out across the spoiled front lawn to observe the first of the news hounds who had smelled out a late evening story. There in the distance stood Marty Liard armed with his digital camera with a big nighttime flash lamp. Marty was most of the press in this small county on a typical day. Where Marty smelled a story, no doubt the professional national and state journalists would soon follow. There had been plenty of those at today's event, and no doubt some had stayed in town for the night, because by now those national press people had heard of Jennifer and her problems as well. They were probably staying the night at the convention-center hotel. It would take them time to hear about this new story, and time to drive over, but they'd get here eventually to join Marty. There was no way a cross burning on Sheldon Nickelback's front lawn was going to stay a local story for just Marty Liard's small-time county paper to exploit.

Worse than the thought of the national press making trouble here was that Gus could see now that crafty old Marty had lined up a nice shot of Deputy Lopez on her hands and knees searching for evidence among a gaggle of beefy firemen. Her rather shapely posterior was pointed right at Marty's lens during one of those flashes. It was disgusting what some people called news. It wasn't like Gus hadn't ever had a female deputy on his staff. Well, actually it was, until recently, exactly like that, but it still shouldn't be a story now that he'd hired one. There were ideas about equality and all that stuff these days, so actual equality in action shouldn't be the news.

Gus turned back around to face Sheldon to finish his thought. It remained unfinished as Gus noticed the man's eyes. They weren't exactly the eyes of a man upset to see his humble house tragedy turned into a front-page story. Sheldon Nickelback had eager eyes and they were focused in on Marty. Sheldon waved a friendly hand at Marty, beckoning him to come up to the porch. Gus forgot all about his prior ideas on the potential perpetrators of this crime. Instead he said to Sheldon, "I'm sorry, Mr. Nickelback, for this untimely intrusion of the local press into your private life. I'll go get rid of them for you."

Sheldon protested, "Oh, you don't have to do that."

Gus didn't have to, but he left the porch anyway on a mission to do it. He walked between Marty and his prize shot of the search party and then continued closing the distance between him and Marty. Marty for his part did his best attempt to shoo Gus away from his shot. Marty complained, "Out of the way, Gus, I think I see a front cover in the making. It is about time the county readers got to know your newest deputy better from all angles. I'm thinking of turning this little cross burning into an exposé on her."

"I reckon you're exposé-ing enough of her as it is. I hope you do your readers a favor and don't put her best photograph in the centerfold. I find the staples always cover the parts of the exposé you wished had been exposed more."

Before Marty could reply, Gus had grabbed him by the shoulder and strong-armed him down the lawn to the edge of the street where they could be relatively alone. Here on the edge of the street was just about the only place they could be alone. The neighbors were now all huddled on the edges of their lawns, the firemen and Skip were gratefully helping Chiquita search the victim's lawn and the neighboring lawns for clues, and the victim Sheldon eagerly eyed Marty and his poison pen from his perch on the porch. Marty looked up to the overhanging streetlamp they found themselves under. He said, "You don't mind strong-arming me a little farther away than this. I heard our man up there on the porch isn't the type you want catching you hanging out around his streetlamp. I figure that cross over there says someone else objects to his anti-streetlamp-standing stance as well."

"The man's innocent, if you would care to remember, Marty," replied Gus.

"Innocent? No, not guilty, if you buy what you read in the papers, and I'll read between the lines of what got published in a slightly safer location," chuckled Marty as he moved on to Gus's parked truck.

Gus took a few steps and followed him. "Marty, now that you mention the trial's verdict, I want to know what the real story was that all you in the media were not writing about in that Sheldon Nickelback case. You know, the facts in the case not factual enough to be put in the trial but factual enough to be the true stuff the general public never gets to hear."

Marty shrugged. "It's no secret the man had his issues with Hispanic kids. He had gotten in a few tussles with some Hispanic boys before if you go by the local hearsay. It was claimed there were gang members persecuting him. That's what his lawyer said, even if he couldn't find a single gang member to sit on the stand and swear to it. The local police didn't know anything about anything gang related either. Sometimes the authorities don't know about these things, so who is to say what's true? According to his lawyer, the trouble was brewing in quiet for a long time, and I guess Sheldon got sick of it. That don't mean he killed that kid in cold blood as retaliation, though. They never proved it in the trial. It was self-defense, according to the verdict. Whether the kid was in a gang or Sheldon just thought he was didn't matter. The kid started a fight with Sheldon, and Sheldon shot him dead because of it. I never heard anything more than that. Now if you don't mind, I need to go talk to the victim. He looks eager to be interviewed again. The man's always great with a quote."

Gus grabbed Marty by the shoulder once more. "Don't depart from me just yet."

"Gus, why are you trying to get between a journalist and his story? I got a mob of unruly Mexicans burning a cross on a vigilante's front lawn. Not only do I have that, but I beat the rest of the national press to the scene. This Sheldon Nickelback is a real piece of work. He's an honest-to-God celebrity. You have to love the modern world where a man like that is famous! Isn't America one hell of a great place to live? There, that's the information you wanted to know; now I need my story on the Mexican pyromaniacs."

"How do you know who did this?" asked Gus.

"Isn't it obvious?"

"That's what Sheldon said to me. Not everything obvious is real."

Marty patted Gus on his round tummy and patronized him. "I tell you what, Gus. When you get evidence that says differently, then you come tell me what you learned, and I'll print that too. The press loves to build a man up, and then they love to tear a man down. I'll print either story so long as my readers care about the man. The man up on that porch is famous, so they'll care about news about him. Oh, and how they'll all care about this crap. Unknown Hispanic kids shot dead before the general public ever got to know them the people at home don't care about so much. You have to understand that there's no continuing story to unveil with a dead person."

"Marty, doesn't it ever bother you that a million poor people can protest for poverty or against war and the press hardly gives them five minutes of their time, but one famous rich man holds a press conference to complain about his taxes and it becomes a four-day news event?"

"I only get bothered when that famous rich man fails to call me first to tell his wonderful story in an exclusive for my readers. Now if that is all, I got a story to cover."

Gus let Marty run up the muddy lawn to cover Sheldon Nickelback. Gus limped on over to the sheriff's truck. He popped the trunk and dug into one of the evidence boxes in the back searching for a bottle of Oxy-Contin. You weren't supposed to use it without a doctor's prescription, but your knees weren't supposed to be beaten by baseball bats either. Gus took his bottle with him to the front seat of the truck. He popped open the door and climbed his tired body inside. The whole day had been one long nightmare, but it would end. The sun was bound to come up again before too long. Nightmares typically ended when you woke up from sleep, but today's nightmares would end when Gus finally got to sleep. Gus knew the most warped parts of his mind couldn't dream up a nightmare worse than his current reality.

He fumbled trying to open the bottle. The damn thing had a child-proof cap on it. Apparently Terry Tang was a conscientious drug dealer and didn't want any children to get into his treasure trove of addictive numbness. He hit the button to turn on the overhead light on the ceiling of the truck roof. It didn't come on. The bulb must have burned out ages ago. He slid his broken reading glasses on and tried to find the sweet spot in the cracked glass so he could read the bottle top's arrows. This exercise was useless in the dark. He tossed the unopened bottle onto the passenger seat. He should just drive home and write up a report in the morning. He didn't leave. He had to see something first. He leaned his head back into the headrest of the seat cushion. He was tired. He was too old to keep doing this forever. The question of whether Sheldon Nickelback was a murderer was a fact already decided by a court of law. It wasn't Gus's job to figure that historical mystery out. Somewhere past midnight in the front seat of his truck, he closed his eyes and aimlessly drifted into sleep.

The horn in his truck sounded, and he woke up. The night was still black around him. He put on a good face and casually glanced out of the side window of the truck. It felt like he had slept for seconds, but he could tell a good deal of time had passed. The neighbors had long since gone to bed. The news crews were swarming all over the place now. He stared down at the arm that held the hand pressing down on his horn. It was the arm of the talented Deputy Lopez. She was standing there with his driver's-side door open. He asked her, "Did you find me something?"

"Not a single thing. Worse, we won't find anything now with this circus in town. I imagine this is going to be big news," she said.

"I reckon so," replied Gus.

"Maybe the coverage will tip someone off, and they will come forward so justice can be served."

"Maybe," replied Gus.

"You don't think so?"

"Deputy, are you so sure this guy didn't put a quarter in his ass and play himself?"

She paused a long moment. She then replied, "You think he did this? It hadn't occurred to me that he did. A lot of people around this town don't like this man very much. I don't think we'll have a problem finding someone willing to have done this. On the other hand, why would he want to do this?"

Gus looked at the reporters all standing in a gaggle listening to Sheldon lecturing them from his porch pulpit. He replied, "Every time the camera is on him he gets rather eager eyes. Now all I have is a hunch about those eyes, but when I see him up there holding court, I think my hunch is correct. You don't go making big statements like this and then get camera shy, so where are the people who did this? That bothers me too. Maybe tomorrow morning they will put out some manifesto on the Internet, and it will prove me all wrong. I thought at first it was kids out for a prank, but nah, that ain't it at all. Right now I think this whole setup stinks. You could say it came to me in a dream. A lot of people have done less for fame and money. I imagine the ever-helpful Skip Lipschitz will have every person in his organization writing checks for the poor, downtrodden Sheldon Nickelback. Sheldon will be called into news shows by morning to be interviewed. Look at the media fawning over the man. Two years ago he was no one; now he's still the center of attention when his trial is all over and he's free. He'll probably get speaking engagements because of this all over again. I understand the why in why someone would want to do this, and I'm not even sure I care if he did. I tell you what, Deputy, I'm tired, and so I'm going home. You keep up the good fight for the department so that justice can be served. If you find out anything interesting, you let me know. I can't help but feel somewhere there is something interesting here to be found. I told you what I think. Prove me wrong if you can." Gus closed the door and started up the sheriff's truck. He had stayed here to see what he wanted to see now—Sheldon and his ever-adoring press. He drove off home.

It was nearing three o'clock when Gus finally crawled his truck into his own driveway. He had officially arrived home. He turned off the engine and looked into his rearview mirror, watching the street. A few minutes later, a Kansas patrol car streamed by his house. There was no doubt about it. Major Dundee wasn't the trusting sort of man. He also wasn't a very sleepy man. Well, let him watch. Gus wasn't doing anything Major Dundee would object to at the moment. The worst part of getting home this late was the creeping knowledge that he had to get up in just a few hours to go back to work and do everything he wanted to avoid doing all over again, and that included talking to the Kansas state trooper.

He looked over at his neighbor's house. There was someone in the community he wanted to keep. No one burned a damn cross anywhere to protest the losing of her and her daughter's house to a bank. No one seemed to care. That apparently included him, because he had told her he was going to look into it, and he hadn't done a damn thing all day to help her. Well, truth be told he'd done practically nothing to help her, he had done one small thing for her that he'd keep to himself because it might not be needed. She couldn't be less important than the fate of Sheldon Nickelback, so he'd have to start getting on top of that issue.

He shuffled his feet down the pavement toward the safety of his own front door. There was someone waiting to speak to him standing under his porch light. Gus did his best to ignore that fact. The porch light only illuminated a small patch of his front lawn, but that small arc of illuminated area was all that was needed to see the new damage to the lawn. His beautiful manicured lawn was now filled with more unsightly holes. Each hole dug into the lawn represented yet another losing battle of a stalwart Darvelak to the friend of the neighbor's child. Then again, she might be the Minimite; he honestly couldn't remember the difference. It was just childhood games to them, but to him it was getting to be more and more expensive holes in the lawn that he would pay through the nose to repair. He couldn't remember the fictitious names of fantasy movie races that came from books he'd never bother to read, but he could remember vividly telling the two of them not to play this game on his lawn anymore. His reasoning had been sound. He had told them it would make a lot of unwanted holes, they hadn't listened to him, and now there were more holes. He'd remind himself sometime in the future to yell at the neighborhood children more. Now was not an appropriate time, as they were tucked into their beds to savor their hostile Poaceae dreams.

The person standing on his porch coughed to get his attention. Gus put his hand on his gun and walked up to the porch light. It wasn't a friend or a foe waiting for him. It was just Pastor Voce standing there under his light. Gus relaxed. He was embarrassed to have his hand on his gun in front of the pastor. He said, "Sorry about that, I thought you were a different angry citizen here to protest to me about how I'm doing my job." He moved his hand from his gun.

"It's about those other angry people who I came here to speak with you. I know it's late, but I also know where you've been. We at the unborn-child prayer circle heard about the terrible unchristian act done to poor Mr. Nickelback tonight. Something has radicalized these liberal Mexicans; I don't know what it was, but it has got to stop. We can't have radicalized Mexicans wreaking havoc in God's country, Sheriff."

"I suppose not," replied Gus. He walked past the pastor and placed his ear to his front door. He rang his own doorbell. He couldn't hear any noise on the other side of the door. Antonio's boys must have either given up for the night or were waiting to waylay Gus someplace else.

The pastor coughed again. "Are you okay, Sheriff?"

He turned around to face the man. He took his ear off his door. It was a little awkward to explain your fear about getting jumped by the Mexican mob to a member of the clergy at three in the morning on your front porch, so Gus didn't bother to try and do it. After all, it might inflame the man's imaginary fear of hostile Mexican cross burners further. Gus said, "Everything's just hunky-dory; why do you ask?"

"You looked worried."

"You look worried too. It's three in the morning, so let's cut to the basics. You're on my porch to…" Gus paused, hoping that void would get filled. He wasn't disappointed.

"Violence, Sheriff, can't be avoided when dealing with those types of people. They aren't like us good Christians. You'd never see a pro-life Christian man shooting up a place, burning a cross, or causing violence. The Bible says thou shalt not kill, and we in the pro-life movement don't kill. Occasionally a false Christian abortion advocate kills people at an abortion clinic in order to smear our Christian name, but it is all part of the clever con of those types of people. Once again, a true Christian pro-lifer never kills. Do you understand my meaning?"

"I'm not sure I want to."

"To be frank, Sheriff, we need some protection. If they'll burn a cross to try and force out a God-fearing Christian man like Sheldon Nickelback, then they won't hesitate to use violence against us peaceful, life-loving protesters at your station. I want a guarantee you'll have armed deputies guarding my people. I don't want anyone too afraid to come on down and join in the peace, love, and protest. The church can't raise the money to do God's work if people are too afraid to join in God's activities. As soon as I got wind of this terrible tragedy tonight, I came over here to get your word that you'd protect us."

Gus mumbled, "I'll have my top people at the law-enforcement complex securing the place. You got my word on that."

"Then I can tell my people they're perfectly safe?"

"Yeah, you go ahead and tell them anything they need to hear. I figure you're used to doing that already. You got my word that I won't let violence intentionally come to my station." He took out his keys and opened the front lock. He waved good-bye to the man of God and went inside. He was at last home again. He walked in, and to his relief there was not another soul waiting inside. He was finally and truly alone. It was a welcome feeling.

He kicked off his shoes one at a time and left them by the door. He shuffled around in his stocking feet to the kitchen. He dug his hand in his pocket. He had the bottle of painkillers in his hand and a terrible pain in his knees. He plunked the bottle on the kitchen table and went to search through his cupboards for something to drink. He found a bottle of gin unopened. It was a beautiful feeling to break off the wrapping of a virgin bottle. He poured out half a coffee mug of gin. He then found the steak-knife drawer and pulled out a knife. The knife was advertised that it could cut through a brick and then cut through a tomato. Gus had never had the need to cut a tomato and a brick during the same meal preparation, so he wasn't sure this knife actually worked as advertised. He was going to test the limits of his knife set tonight. He pinned the pill bottle down with his left hand. He started sawing away at the childproof cap with the knife in his right hand. Sure enough, the knife cut right through it like it was made of butter or possibly a brick. Gus spilled OxyContin pills from the bare, lidless container across his kitchen table. Part one with the Terry Tang plan was done with, and he'd need these pills tomorrow for part two of his master plan. He left the pills scattered on the kitchen table and grabbed his coffee mug of gin. Drinking it down was the best idea he had had in days.

He stared at the pill bottle. The crap was habit-forming. He warned himself that only a fool would take them without a doctor's prescription. He would need to get rid of that box of pills in his truck to prevent him from getting carried away by temptation. That would be the right thing to do, since getting rid of that box was part of the bigger plan. He didn't want to move too fast on his plan, but he might have to. Things had a habit of moving faster than you planned just when you didn't want them to, so he decided then and there to move quickly on part two of the plan tomorrow. He didn't know for sure if the high-priced lawyers could delay the extradition case too long. Eventually the lawman from Kansas was going to take Jennifer away from his jail, much to the delight of the protestors outside it. He knew eventually all the money in the world paid to lawyers by people far removed from the pain and suffering of the situation wasn't going to prevent it all from happening. The only question was how well the sides could play the governor, and Gus didn't know the governor well enough to answer that, but on this matter he was very much a pessimist.

His body started to numb from all the pain. Sweet, sweet gin was always the answer unless you were out driving late at night. It wasn't that he didn't hurt anymore; it was just that due to the gin, he no longer cared. It was long past time for bed. He had an option of climbing the stairs up to the bedrooms on the second floor or shuffling along the hall into the television room to spend the night alone on the sofa. He didn't want to sleep another night on the hard sofa even if it was technically early morning. He didn't want to climb the stairs. Life gives people few good options when they're hurting. He was glad to at least be alone to make his choice between the two bad options. When life only gives you bad options to choose from, funny enough, people will still find it in their heart to blame you for choosing a bad option anyway.

He painstakingly climbed the stairs. It was a hard task, but it was accomplished the old-fashioned way. He took it one stair at a time until he reached the landing. He shuffled slowly down his hallway to his bedroom where his lovely bed awaited him. He'd forget to set the alarm clock. He'd wake up late. He was his own boss in a way, so there'd be no one to complain to him that he had arrived at work late. He passed by the door that belonged to the room of his long-absent daughter. All her stuff was still there even if she was not. Then he passed by the bathroom. It was the most dignified place in the house. Finally he passed by the spare bedroom that he used as a den. The word *den* was a convenient word people used for the place in the house where you abandoned all the crap you don't want guests to see, and thus you kept them behind one convenient door that remained forever closed.

Gus shuffled past the den without giving a moment's notion of entering it, since it was a place not to be entered. The funny thing about tonight was that Gus could swear he was hearing clicking noises coming from inside the den. Gus stared down the last bit of hallway between here and his waiting bedroom door. Inside that bedroom was a comfortable king-sized bed waiting for him. It was so near, and yet suddenly it felt so very far away. There shouldn't be anything clicking inside the den. There wasn't anything to make a clicking noise inside there. It was just a room filled with garbage, or as his wife had called them—spare odds and ends. They were the lovely things Gus never found the desire to part with and seldom found time to use. He had collections of sporting equipment from sports he never played. He had sewing material his wife had bought that was still waiting for her to return from the dead to use it. There was also an antique desk his father had owned that he was storing until he found the exact right place for it. He had even stuck an old desktop computer on it that also never got used. He did enough computing at work and thus never wanted to compute more at home. The clicking sound came again from behind the den door. It was the sound of someone clicking on the keyboard of that computer that no one was thought to ever use. It was an unmistakable sound. Someone was using it right now, someone who shouldn't be in his home. Gus reached into his waistband and took out Terry Tang's gun. He reached for the door handle and opened the door.

There was a blond man sitting at that antique desk. He was typing away on that computer no one used. Finding him there would have been a surprise on any other day, but this week it seemed like just part of the new normal. On a box of Christmas decorations long ago abandoned to the den sat Josh Hansen, much to the perplexed annoyance of Gus. Gus in frustration tossed the gun down on a box of clothes marked to be eventually donated to charity. Gus figured if he waited long enough to donate them, the styles might come back in fashion. Gus's legs were too tired to make the distance between him and the hacker. He simply yelled from the doorway, "Hansen, what the hell are you doing in my house?"

Josh continued clicking on the ancient keyboard in rapid fashion. He merely responded, "Shhh...I'm Mr. Smith now, remember. I came here because I knew your house would be a quiet place to write and think. I need to finish updating my blog so my fellow passionate cyber-revolutionaries will know the latest wisdom from my ever-flowing fount. I could no longer concentrate at that jail of yours. The constant noise that crowd makes is so irritating. I can't imagine what those people think they can accomplish. A bigger collection of fools I've never seen in one place. People with that weak an understanding of modern biology and philosophy don't even have the common decency to protest in silence at their silent vigils. I wonder why is it that Christians are always a collective bunch of loud-mouthed nobodies? They should try reading Matthew 6:6 for a change. Don't they know they should leave us criminals alone in peace and quiet? They can go evangelize someone that wants to hear that barf. I thought that was the point of all those churches. Let those types of people congregate together without bothering the rest of us with their magic thinking from a mythical God. We placed them in their tax-free churches to keep their loud, thoughtless ideas away from decent society so we normal people could have a moment's peace of mind, but they refuse to stay there. Instead they are up at all hours of the night lighting candles and singing praises to the Lord so that he may punish the wicked. Obviously they don't understand that the only ones being punished are themselves—punished at the hands of those who use them for their own gain. In this world of ours the institutions of punishment, jails, laws, legislatures, church confessionals, and so forth, are systems of illusion. The common people who believe in them are foolish dreamers or radical followers. We all know the three people who will never accomplish anything worthwhile in their lifetimes are the foolish dreamer, the radical follower, and the person who spends all day correcting other people's grammar on Internet discussion sites. Justice remains just a tool of a few powerful interests, and the law's interpretation will continue to be made to suit the convenience of their abuse of power. Distractions like poor Jennifer sitting in your jail cell are to be judged by those idiots to keep us from thinking about true social justice. True justice is in the hands of the people if they choose, like me, to use it. Most people choose not to use it. A just man is not a person who strives to avoid doing harm to others, but one who has the power to harm but not the desire. The just man uses his power to enhance, liberate, and create pathways toward the happiness of others and not to create spurious causes that enable a rancid dialogue that brings fame and wealth to only himself."

Gus yawned. He wasn't in the mood for an ontological discussion with a fugitive from justice. He was never in the mood for that kind of discussion with anyone. He replied, "You know, Hansen, sometimes your libertarian mumbo-jumbo just sounds like the boring greetings from a badly selling atheist Christmas card. You just keep on talking like that, and I'll see you when we end up in hell with all the other sinners."

"The closest I've ever come to hell was opening your refrigerator. You know, those expiration dates on food are like dates in history books. It is handy if you both notice and remember them and act on that knowledge. You can't just move the date to another time period because the truth is inconvenient."

Gus wandered over to the old mattress he had forgotten to have the junk collectors pick up and slumped down into it. The mattress didn't have that much life left in it, but it beat the alternative of standing about in the doorway talking to Josh. He noticed Josh had propped up a spritely life-sized plastic sex doll in a seat not too far from him. It wasn't the cheap blow-up kind, but the rather an expensive silicone affair that had cost thousands. It was almost lifelike. Gus had received it as a rather obscene birthday present from Josh Hansen at one time. Gus had tucked it into this den and forgotten all about it, or her. That was what the room was for. Now Hansen had bothered to take her out, dress her up, and prop her up in a broken chair next to him. You hoped that was all he had done with her.

Gus pointed to the doll. "What did you drag that thing out for?"

"I found her in here! A fine way to treat my birthday present to you. Do you know how much that would have cost me had I used money instead of hacking the sex-doll company's computer and generating your order? Plenty I can tell you."

"I didn't know what else to do with her."

"Poor Sheriff Gus, you really must be getting too tired and old. When a girl looks as attractive as that doll, you should know exactly what to do with her, plastic or not plastic."

"Sorry, Hansen, but I like my women in the flesh. If I wanted a plastic woman, then I'd have moved to California."

"A beggar can't be a chooser," replied Hansen, working hard on the computer still.

"I thought it was *the man* that made beggars of us all in your philosophy."

"Now you are sounding more like me. I like it."

Gus sighed and sank further into the mattress. "If I sound like you, then you must be right. I must be too old and tired." Gus could see the computer screen and what Hansen was typing on it from his mattress vantage point. Numbers were scrolling fast and furiously about the screen. His eyes couldn't focus on it. The gin had diminished the pain in his knees, but he was still a beaten man awake long past his bedtime. He wanted Hansen gone so he could sleep. "I thought someone was trying to kill you. Wasn't the whole point of hiding in my jail to keep a low profile so that they don't find you and kill you? I'm saying this not out of concern for someone killing you, but out of a strong desire not to keep finding you in my house. Is it wise to go parading in front of a bunch of midnight-vigil attenders just to get here to do whatever it is you're doing? What if someone recognized you during your departure from my jail?"

"That's a lot of rhetorical questions in a row. Gus, I wore a disguise when leaving, so don't you worry. Also, I know how to protect myself. I studied in Madagascar with Tibetan monks well versed in the ancient art of Gymkata. There is no one more deadly in hand-to-hand combat than me. It is just that I don't like violence. Granted, people do have a habit of dying around me. Anyways, I came straight here, where I knew I'd be safe. Granted, there were some people from the Mexican mob around the house looking for you when I arrived. I told them you weren't home. I think they might come back, though. I guess we both have people who want to kill us now. In retrospect, I should have chosen another house to work at tonight, but I figure I'm safe enough for the time being so long as I'm around you."

"I don't know; I might just shoot you myself for trespassing."

"Bah, you put the gun down when you came in the room."

Gus yawned. He didn't want to argue, particularly when he didn't know what they'd be arguing about. He leaned back on the dirty mattress and closed his eyes. He spoke, "That might just have been a mistake. I don't like it when people lie to me, and you're lying to me right now, aren't you? I don't think climate scientists are out to kill you."

"Me, lie? I am the conduit from which free information flows. I am the ultimate hacker that steals the secrets of governments and disseminates them to the world. How can you accuse a person like me of lying?"

"When it comes to free information, you get what you pay for. I noticed there are a lot of numbers on that computer screen and not that many words. It is a funny way to write a blog. I figure you came here because you're up to no good, and you don't mind if they trace that no good back to my computer. That's mighty nice of you. So tell me, honest man of the people, what all those numbers mean in case the FBI come by and ask me all about them."

Josh stopped typing. He turned around on his box to face the nearly sleeping sheriff. He shook his head at the sight and chastised him, "You need to get with the times or have them pass you by, my friend. Each one of those numbers represents a virtual coin. They call them Vitcoins; personally I call them shit coins, but to each their own. Fiat money, like the

118

little greenbacks in your wallet, derives its value from a government. These virtual coins do not. That is their inherent value."

Gus opened his eyes to see the hacker watching him. He reluctantly sat back up. He replied, "So you idiots created your own money supply. Well, what the hell is the purpose of all these shit coins of yours?"

Josh smiled, "Purpose? I'll tell you a little story about the purpose of things in this life. There once was a man that had reached a prosperous middle age. Yet he was a tired and lonely man that lived alone in a rich house down by the seaside. He had worked hard his whole life and made heaps of money. He should have been happy, and yet he discovered, much to his dissatisfaction, that more and more he wasn't. He tallied the material wealth, which he had by the truckload. Then he counted the inner spiritual wealth and discovered it completely lacking. He fell into despair, for his life he had determined clearly lacked a purpose. Night and day the nagging idea racked his brain that he would not find a true purpose in life before he reached his final judgment day. Troubled by this perpetual haunt of knowledge, he decided that if his life was destined to end without a true purpose, then he would rather end it now than continue unabated to a natural hollow ending.

"He went down to the beach at the foot of the sea near his home. It was wintertime, and the beaches were desolate. He climbed the rocky wave break out to the end. There he planned to jump in and sink to the bottom. He readied his body to spring into the sea, but a sight in the waves unsettled him. There at the end of the rocky wave break was a porpoise splashing happily in the waves. The porpoise noticed the unhappy man and beckoned him to join him in playing. The man leaped upon the porpoise's back. Off dashed the porpoise jumping and dancing through the white foam of the collapsing waves, heading toward the beach. When he was hungry, the porpoise caught a bountiful supply of free fish, and they both ate their share as they frolicked in the sea. When he was tired, the porpoise napped among the lapping tides. They danced, ate, played, and napped for hours on end until the man had completely forgotten his former sorrows. As the day grew long, the porpoise swam back to the wave break and let the man off his back. The man begged the porpoise not to send him back to his former life. He stood at the end of the rocks and gave a heartfelt explanation to the porpoise that today had been the first real day of his life. Today he had truly lived. It was a day where he had experienced unbridled joy, he had eaten freely when he wanted, he had slept where he pleased, and he had never had a moment's worry or heartbreak. This was life as it should be. He pleaded with the porpoise to allow him to swim forever among the porpoises where life had a purpose. The porpoise simply waved good-bye to him and exclaimed as it dashed off in the waves, 'Oh, silly human, I'm but a dolphin and not a porpoise.'"

Gus lay back down on the mattress and shut his eyes. He replied, "That was a really great story."

Hansen chuckled then explained, "To answer your question, the advantage of nonfiat money is that it doesn't derive its value from any government. It thus isn't exactly subject to regulation by any state's law. It is created by the traffic of the peer-to-peer world, and it is moved from person to person via virtual transaction within that reality. Since it is not subject to the whims and laws of a government, there are also no agencies like the treasury department out there to see that the Vitcoin marketplace is an honest one. That can be handy for drug dealers and hackers like me. It is particularly of interest to people like me because, you see, there is no one out there policing the Vitcoins to protect them from hackers like me stealing them. More to the point, a Vitcoin is considered property by your government, and thus like any property I am free to counterfeit my own. It is illegal to counterfeit a country's currency, but I ask you, is it illegal to create out of thin air a new car just because Ford or GM makes cars or any other form of property? It isn't, so you can legally make new property any time you want. Thus by default it isn't illegal for me to make my own Vitcoins out of thin air. It is a handy device for a man accused of spying and on the run from several dishonest governments to keep enriching himself by using the untapped shit-coin market and the pure, foolish greed of those who utilize that market."

Gus started to snore. Hansen kicked the mattress from his sitting position to wake the poor sheriff up. Gus made an appropriate grunting noise. He wasn't about to open his eyes to encourage more conversation. He didn't care. All he wanted was rest. He managed a grumble. "Look, can't you please leave me alone? Go run off and bother some other sheriff in some other county. I don't have time for you. Just today I had to deal with a rebranding celebration, a lobbyist, self-defense protestors, abortion protestors, a lawyer, a Kansas lawman, a drug dealer, a pyromaniac, and a talkative hacker, all the while being on the lookout over my shoulder for the cold grasp of the Mexican mob."

"What was the purpose of dealing with all that?"

"I don't know. I did this all for the sake of the community. Enforce the law, you know, justice," grumbled Gus back.

Hansen let out his chuckle. He replied, "Sheriff, that sounds like a dolphin and not a porpoise. I tell you what I'm going to do. To reward you for all your hard work and as an incentive to keep me alive, I'm going to make a little account here on the Vitcoin Vault website and create a few million dollars' worth of coins in it for you." He turned and tapped on the keyboard. "There you go. Right there on the virtual coin exchange under the name of Morton Salt is your millions. The password to the account is *porpoise*. Keep me alive, and the money is virtually all yours, Sheriff."

"I always knew I'd get rich from working in law enforcement."

Josh got up from his box and walked to the door. "I can see all this justice enforcing has plum worn you out, so I'll let you sleep and think about our deal. I like being alive, and other people would like me dead. I'm safe here for the time being, but how long is that time being I don't know for sure. Help me stay alive while I'm here, and the money is yours." He reached the doorframe, turned back to the nearly sleeping Gus, and added one last thing. "By the way, there was a message on your home phone's answering machine when I came in. A certain district attorney said something vaguely about you being due bright and early for court at ten o'clock tomorrow morning, or more technically, this morning, judging by the current time. You're in luck, though, as it is only three thirty, so you've got plenty of time to make it to that court date. I'll catch you back at the office. Oh, and between you and me…that new 'drug dealer' guy you put in the jail is kind of a jerk. He's very unpleasant to be around. Worse than that is the fact that I think he is a bad role model to have around our impressionable teenage girl, Jennifer. A man like that should be locked up somewhere far away from innocent young people like her and me. I mean, in a just world, there just ought to be a place you put people like that so they don't bother decent society. If I were you, I'd think about a good plan on how to rid our fine cell block of this filthy criminal."

Hansen left. Gus was alone at last. He didn't bother to get up from the stale mattress. He simply closed his eyes and longed for sleep. He knew it was a matter of time before he fell back to sleep. The trick was how to get back up. He needed to wake up on time for court. There were things that needed to be done. He had his plan on how to deal with things, and he needed to make sure that his plan stayed on track. Yet there were so many side tracks before him. It was easy to get distracted. He was the sheriff, and it was his job to make sure justice was served in this county. He wasn't going to let a bunch of lawyers and protesters get in the way of that. Nothing would get it the way of that if his plan worked out. Somewhere tonight a little part of the plan had just gotten easier instead of harder. Only he couldn't think about how that was true. His brain needed a rest. Not a long rest but just a brief moment's rest, and then it would be time to start the whole hot, sticky mess all over again.

CHAPTER 4

It is more dangerous that even a guilty person should be punished without the forms of law than that he should escape.
—Thomas Jefferson

Gus arrived at the courthouse still extremely sleepy but at least showered and shaved. Gus also arrived dressed in his Sunday-best uniform and had even bothered to polish his badge and shoes for the occasion because you never know what might catch a judge's eye. He didn't feel like he'd be of much use, given his current condition, but luckily his job today was a simple task. The county lawyer would do all the real work. He just had to appear in court. He was up to appearing. Thus, he had arrived at the courthouse not to do a little courting of Lady Justice, but just to watch the prosecutor try to persuade the judge to see things from Gus's point of view. It shouldn't be that hard a courtship between those two men, as this case was a simple driving-while-under-the-influence case. *Influence* was not a strong enough word for what Sedric had been caught doing. He was driving while his condition bordered on the near-comatose state. This was an open-and-shut case if ever a case before this court was open-and-shut. Still, like an eager suitor courting a mate with even the loosest of moral standards, the prosecutor wasn't taking for granted the pleasant idea of putting this one straight to bed, so he made sure Gus was here just in case Gus was needed to put in a kind word with the judge.

Gus had to admit he felt a little better even after so little sleep. Mostly he felt this in his knees, as they bothered to bend slightly more this morning than the day before. That medicinal gin was like a magic elixir. He had the open bottle of pills in the front seat of the truck next to him. He picked it up and tossed it in the back. It landed in the box that contained the rest of the evidence he had acquired from the ever-helpful Terry Tang. He had it on good authority from Deputy Costner that Big Gustavo's man had stormed Terry Tang's place after they had left with Terry. All those paper bags full of cold green money were stolen by the Mexican mob. Gus doubted Terry would bother to file a formal complaint with his department. Terry should be happy Gus had saved for him at least the drugs. Not that Gus planned on using them as intended. He was on normal over-the-counter painkillers today, and that was all he needed. He bounded from his truck and headed up the steps of the courthouse. Finally a little something was going to go his way. The courthouse was generally a good friend to ole Sheriff Gus, and that was due to the fact that all the right kind of old-time judges were sitting on their collective benches still. Today there would be no unexpected problems for the sheriff to deal with.

Gus paused on the staircase. Ahead of him hustling up the steps was Bernie the Attorney. He wasn't as television-friendly and charismatic as the likes of Wilton McDermott, but on the other hand, he was the best lawyer who practiced his art in this county on a regular basis. It was then Gus remembered how nice and fancy the car was that this particular drunk had been driving. He also remembered fondly the expensive free beer he had pilfered from that expensive vehicle. The drunk had lots of money, and he had bought one of the best lawyers in the county to defend him. Well, that was okay by Gus. If a man wanted to lose both the case and ten thousand dollars for Bernie's expert advice, then that was what the system allowed. Bernie was smart enough to know a loser when he saw one and also smart enough to know how to keep that loser's courtroom loss off his permanent record. Nah, figured Gus, there'd be no trial today. Bernie would likely work his backroom magic and come to some arrangement in that back room before he "lost" the case.

Gus smiled as he climbed the steps at the thought of a plea-bargain deal. So it would be a plea bargain instead of a full-blown DUI charge. That was still all right by Gus. As long as the drunken idiot learned some type of lesson about driving around stupid drunk, it was worth the deal to get some speedy justice. Sure, you could claim copping a deal would be the rich man's avenue to avoiding any real responsibility for his actions, but at least he'd plead guilty to something. There were a lot of people who might tell you the legal system didn't work. They'd be wrong if they ever watched people like Bernie work the legal system. The legal system worked just fine so long as you had the capital in your bank account to make it work. The best part of it all would of course be that Gus would be able to sleep in the courtroom gallery, because a plea deal meant he was guaranteed not have to testify in court. That was a real win in his book.

Gus walked the courthouse halls, heading for the courtroom. The courthouse floor was made of a hard marble. It gave the building a noble feeling, as if this place had a true sense of dignity and power. Above each courtroom door was a small pedestal that was set aside for a small statue also made of marble. There stood Lady Justice. In the statue's right hand was a set a scales, and in her left hand was a double-edged sword. The scales were there to weigh the evidence fairly, and the sword was there to wield the power of the court system. The sword was double-edged because the court's reason and justice were blind and could be unleashed upon either party as the strength of the facts in the case dictated. It was a finely crafted piece of historical artwork. The whole building was finely crafted and dated from another age when people had cared about more than just the bottom line when building public buildings. A place like the courthouse demanded respect and had been built accordingly.

Bernie the Attorney was a few paces ahead of Gus and walked effort-lessly into courtroom number six. It was the honorable Judge Frank Under-hill's courtroom. Outside the courtroom door stood Dr. Chloe Armstrong. Gus pause a second to talk to her.

She waved a friendly hello and asked, "How's the knees?"

125

"They're doing much better."

"I noticed that you're following my advice and keeping off them."

"I can't afford to sit around. Has someone died in there, or did you come to watch the slow wheels of justice turn?"

"The DA asked me into court today. He said there were some questions about the evidence against one Sedric Hedgecock that I might need to clear up."

"Did he say what those questions were?"

She shrugged. "Nope, I was hoping you knew."

Gus shrugged back at her. He replied, "It's been a long time since I knew something. I guess we can both go inside and find out."

The local DA was seated behind a cheap wooden bench. He was dressed modestly in a suit his mother had likely picked out for him. To his left sat Bernie the Attorney alongside his client Sedric Hedgecock. Bernie and Sedric were like Gus in that they wore their Sunday bests, but their Sundays were a little nicer than Gus could afford. Hedgecock scowled at Gus when he entered the courtroom. It was an ugly look for a man dressed in such a beautifully tailored suit. There were some people who were just more pleasant to be around when they were drunk. There weren't that many, but Sedric was clearly one of them. Bernie appeared cool, calm, and collected. If the DA had asked Dr. Armstrong here, then there was something up in the air about this case, but Gus was at a guess as to what that was. Gus reminded himself to stop jumping to conclusions, and then he proceeded to conclude there'd be no plea deal today. No doubt in a minute or two the cat would be out of the bag as the Honorable Judge Underhill entered the court. The judge was slightly under eighty and had one bad leg. He was entirely bald except the hair that grew from his ears. He methodically made progress toward his bench as he clicked his cane on the marble floor the whole way. Gus found a seat behind the DA and sat down next to Dr. Armstrong.

The DA whispered over to Gus, "What did you do a fool thing like arrest Terry Tang for? As I told you two weeks ago, his pharmacy he delivers for was under investigation by the authorities in California, and some pretty powerful people wanted us to lie low until they were done."

"Don't worry; I wasn't going to charge him with anything. I was just going to put him in my jail cell for a spell. It will help him reflect on his business practices," replied Gus.

"You can't just arrest people because you feel like it," replied the DA.

"It don't seem fair, as I've got people I didn't feel like arresting in my jail at this moment, so it seemed only natural to have someone in it I did feel like arresting," replied Gus.

The DA didn't get to comment further as the bailiff commanded the proceedings to order, and everyone in the courtroom rose, the respective parties promised not to fib too much, and then finally everyone was allowed to find their seats again. The judge then fumbled for his bifocals and placed them on the tip of his nose. He peered over the top of the glasses and began the proceedings. The judge was old but still had a booming voice that filled the chamber. "This hearing is to clarify if enough evidence has been gathered to allow the DUI case against one Sedric Hedgecock to proceed. According to the briefings filed by the defense, some of the evidence gathered against his client is being called into question. The defense feels there is no case without this evidence, and thus the case should be dismissed. Has the DA seen this briefing, and are they ready to comment today on the validity of the evidence gathered?"

"I have, Your Honor!" the DA stated boldly.

Now Bernie the Attorney strolled up to the judge's bench and dropped off a sheet of paper. He then strolled back to his seat as the DA watched him cautiously. Bernie explained, "Your Honor, that sheet of paper contains the blood alcohol level that supposedly was coursing through my defendant's veins on the night in question. I wish you would examine that number closely. The sheriff's office stated my client blew a 0.62 percent. I repeat, he blew 0.62 percent! It claims that my client's blood was drawn and measured by a testing lab and that it confirmed a 0.62 percent. Your Honor, the limit that causes death from alcohol is between 0.4 and 0.5 percent in any DUI textbook that I have ever read in my life. My client, according to the very evidence of the district attorney, shouldn't be in your courtroom today. Instead my client should be pushing up daisies. I think this evidence alone is enough to suggest to the court that clearly some mistakes were made in ascertaining the blood alcohol level of my client on the night in question."

Bernie finished his argument and returned to his seat without expressing a hint of emotion. Sedric Hedgecock appeared cocky enough for both of them. He puffed out his chest and tried to give off the air of being above it all.

The DA stood up. He said, "I object, Your Honor. The defense is mischaracterizing the nature of the evidence before the court. I have a witness that can correctly state the evidence, if it would please Your Honor."

"If that witness is our lovely lady coroner sitting behind you, then it would please me to no end," said Judge Underhill.

The DA replied, "It is." He then turned to Dr. Armstrong and whispered, "I need you to explain away Bernie's interpretation of the blood results, but don't get too technical."

Gus could see that Chloe was more than confident she could do just that. She also brushed off the judge's sexist comment and stood up. She patiently explained, "Your Honor, I believe there is some confusion in the defense's argument over the meaning of the term *LD50*. The lethal dose fifty is the amount of a substance, usually measured as a percentage of body weight, that is required to kill fifty percent of a test population. A patient reaching this concentration level in their blood doesn't mean they will be guaranteed to die every single time. It only means there is roughly a fifty-fifty chance of death at this point. There is nothing magical that happens at this number. Instead, it is merely the peak in the distribution around the LD50, and many patients will not be as lucky as Mr. Hedgecock and will have expired before ever reaching the LD50."

Chloe sat back down with a look of triumph on her face. She gave a victory smile to Gus as if what she had said had sealed the deal. Gus gazed over to Bernie the Attorney. The man did not appear shaken by her facts presented to the court. Instead, he took no time after Chloe sat down to spring back up from his chair. Bernie the Attorney announced his rebuttal to the judge. "I'm very glad the county coroner came here to explain exactly what the LD50 means. I suggest to you, Your Honor, that her presence in your courtroom today is very much like the blood alcohol level placed into evidence. Both facts stress the very idea that the state believes my client is dead. Your Honor, either the LD50 limit was passed, or it was not passed, just like either a man is dead, or he is not. I place before the court that the man sitting in the defendant chair is my client, and he is unequivocally not dead!"

The judge nodded and replied, "I do have to admit that these facts when placed together are pretty strong arguments in your favor."

The DA now sprang back to his feet. "Your Honor, the blood alcohol reading is not the only evidence before the court!"

Bernie the Attorney was not one to back down and pounced on this opening, "This is true, Your Honor. My client informed me that when he retrieved his vehicle from the impound lot, a rather expensive and unopened case of beer was missing. I should think the facts in evidence speak for themselves that this case of beer was stolen, and the DA and local law enforcement have done nothing about it. Instead he stands in this courtroom persecuting my client for a crime he'd have to be dead to have committed."

The judge banged his gavel, and the two attorneys quickly returned to their seats. Once they were properly seated, the judge acted on the new evidence. "This is a very disturbing matter brought up by the defense. I would ask the pertinent question on this subject before proceeding: was this theft reported to the sheriff's department?"

"Well, of course not. Given the security of the county impound lot, it was assumed this case of beer was registered into evidence and thus fully known to the local authorities," replied Bernie.

"I see," replied the judge, who turned his attention now over to Gus. He addressed Gus, "Seeing that the sheriff is right here in my courtroom, I would ask him what he knows about this alleged crime. Gus, know anything about this beer?"

The courtroom turned their collective eyes toward Gus. Gus knew the details of this alleged crime down to the exact detail. He didn't feel like sharing those details with the court. He stood up to address Judge Underhill. He took off his cowboy hat and held it in his hands. He replied, "Begging the court's pardon, but this is the first I've heard of this case of beer being missing. The sheriff naturally feels this is a very serious matter, and I plan on putting my very best people on this task. I can assure the judge I have every intention of getting to the very bottom of that case of missing beer."

"I'm sure you will," replied the judge.

"But, Your Honor…" protested Bernie.

"I will hear no more about this case of missing beer. The sheriff, now dutifully informed, will look into this other crime. There is no evidence available to ascertain its relevancy toward the charges before your client. Unless you have further comments to make as to the evidence before the court, I would suggest you sit down," replied the judge to Bernie, who reluctantly sat down. His body posture suggested more needed to be said, but his demeanor was jovial enough.

Gus, seeing no need to be standing anymore, sat down as well. Chloe leaned over to him and whispered, "What is he delaying for, a plea bargain?"

Gus whispered back, "Look at the concern on our young DA's face. I'd say Bernie is going for a complete dismissal. He appears confident that when it comes to scientific facts in a court of law, justice can be blind, deaf, and especially dumb at certain times."

Chloe sat fully back in her chair in complete displeasure. The day was not lost yet, and the DA was back up on his feet fighting. The DA pulled out the arrest report. He now addressed the court. "If it pleases the court, I would like to finish my statement I was trying to make before being interrupted."

The judge replied, "Fine, you make your statement first, and then I'll tell you if it pleased me."

"Very well, I would like it to be known that the blood alcohol reading is not the only evidence before the court today. We also have the official arrest account from the arresting officer that states that the defendant failed a field-sobriety test. He could not walk, not even one step. Nor could the man touch his nose."

Up bounced Bernie the Attorney with a quick rebuttal. "Your Honor, my client's inability to walk is exactly why he was driving on the night in question. If they felt that the fact he couldn't walk was all that was needed to prosecute him, then why test his blood alcohol level at all? I fail to see why a handicap or ailment is held in prejudice against my client. Would the prosecution ask the court to lock up every man without feet who drove through this county? I think we both know the answer to that question. Furthermore, as to the alleged fact of his lack of ability to touch his nose, I ask the court, since when did nose touching become integral to the functioning of our automobiles? I would further like to add one last bit of sound reasoning for the court to consider. My client freely admits he was driving under the influence on the night in question. He was driving under the influence not of alcohol but of grief due to the account of his beloved mother's death. I doubt very much this influence is illegal even in this state! My client may have been driving erratically due to this grief, but he is not charged with that today."

Judge Underhill didn't respond quickly but nodded and wrote something down. Eventually he asked one question. "So his mother died recently compared to the date in question?"

"Yes, she did, Your Honor!" confidently answered Bernie.

"At what time?" asked the judge.

"She died ten years ago to the day in question."

"So the night in question when he is alleged to have been drunk driving, he was in fact crippled with grief on account of the tenth anniversary of his mother's death. Does he normally lose all motor control of his legs on such anniversaries?" asked the judge in disbelief.

"Well, no, but there was a very cute barmaid at the bar he was drinking at whose posterior reminded my client of his mother, and that just set his emotions on fire."

"Duly noted, the court has heard that a woman's posterior may affect a man in such a way from time to time. Although, perhaps not due to the fact of their resemblance to a dead mother."

Bernie sat down with confidence. The DA sat down in frustration. The DA turned now to his last hope. He gave a sad puppy-dog stare toward Gus to do something to save the open-and-shut case. Gus took a deep breath and stood back up. He addressed the bench, "Your Honor, I would just like the court to know that I did in fact field-test the Breathalyzer in question on the very night of the arrest of Sedric Hedgecock and found it to be in perfect working order. The man was above the legal limit according to this very accurate gauge. It is a technological marvel of modern law enforcement."

Bernie bounced right back up. "Your Honor, this man is not a qualified technician, and thus his statement is irrelevant to the case."

Judge Underhill asked Gus, "How exactly did you test the device?"

"Well, to be honest, me and the boys drank a few beers on the night in question and blew into the device. We were worried about that high reading, so we wanted to make sure the machine did work. First I blew into it before drinking anything, and then I had a few beers. When I was done drinking, I blew into it again. The thing read perfectly fine. I simply state we tested the device, and it worked. It correctly told me more or less just how much I had been drinking on the night in question when I arrested this man." Gus sat down and put his hat back on.

Bernie now protested, "Your Honor, the arresting officer has just testified that he was drinking on the night of the alleged DUI. Isn't it possible that his judgment was impaired and not my client? I think we can throw out all the field-sobriety evidence based on this new fact. The man giving the test might have been impaired even though my client absolutely was not!"

Judge Underhill was busy writing a note down. He took his patient time. When he was done writing, he replied, "I've known the sheriff plenty of years now, and I've never known his poker playing to get worse the more he drinks. He plays his best hands after a few cold ones. I don't see how his judgment could be impaired by drinking."

"Your Honor..." pleaded Bernie. The judge motioned him down, and the attorney sat down. For the first time, he appeared a little shaken. That last statement didn't go over well. There appeared a glimmer of hope in the courtroom that the case might go to a full trial after all. The judge wrote a few more notes, and everyone sat in anticipation.

Judge Underhill addressed Sedric Hedgecock directly. "Before this court decides on the weight of the evidence before it, does the defendant have anything to say in his own defense?"

Bernie the Attorney nodded and winked to his client, and then Sedric Hedgecock stood up to address the court. He put his hand over his heart. He pledged, "Your Honor, an unjust law is no law at all, and I was clearly brought to this court under false pretenses. And yet, I can honestly say that today has taught me a valuable lesson, and if I am found to be the innocent man that I am, then I will tread more lightly from now on. For while I am rich in wealth, this fair and honest procedure today has taught me that I am also rich in your court's humble wisdom. You won't have to tell me a second time about the dangers of drinking and driving after today; I guarantee it."

Judge Underhill replied, "I'll take you at your word." Sedric sat down. The judge wrote more notes. Everyone sat there in silence. Finally, after a five-minute feast of silence, the judge banged his gavel and motioned for everyone to rise. Judge Underhill addressed the court.

"For the record, in this country we don't prosecute the guilty because of the victims. We prosecute people in the name of society, because the crimes are thought to be against society and their locking up a form of mutual protection for us all. Prosecution is not a form of revenge, and it is not a form of punishment for Mr. Hedgecock; it is merely meant as a form of protection for society at large. The question before the court is if there is enough evidence to find Mr. Hedgecock a menace to society and, more to the point, if there is any probability at all of a guilty verdict based on the evidence that might be thrown out. It is always hard to ascertain exactly the weight of the evidence in any case. In this case, there appears to be some conflict in the evidence. I must also factor in the reputations of those involved. In light of the evidence brought forward before the court, I must find that there is insufficient evidence to bring this case to a full trial. I am thus, with some reluctance, dismissing this case. Without a full trial, no reputations should be in jeopardy, and both parties can leave today knowing their reputations in the eyes of the court are intact. I warn the defendant, Mr. Hedgecock, to go lightly on his drinking before getting behind the wheel of a car in this county, because he might not be so lucky a second time. I further warn that accusing the state of theft is a serious charge, and serious evidence should come to bear before entertaining such charges in my courtroom." The judge finished his statement by increasing the volume in his voice. "This case is dismissed!" He proceeded to bang down his gavel. He then picked up his cane and started the slow, painful walk out of court and to his chambers.

Bernie the Attorney snapped his briefcase closed and quickly made his own exit. There was neither happiness nor celebration on his part. It was just another day and another paycheck in his bank account. His client was not so humble. He took his time leaving the court. He made sure to give a big middle finger to Sheriff Gus and the rest of the prosecution team as he made his way out of court.

Dr. Armstrong was angry and not afraid to show it. She blurted out to Gus and the DA, "There was a gross miscarriage of justice today if I ever saw one! That man nearly killed himself with his drink alone, and because of it he got off without punishment. If he had merely been stupid with drink instead of well past the LD50, then there would be no question of his alcohol level, and he would lose his license at the very least. Despite this enormous luck in living through being that drunk and getting off without facing the charges against him, that fiend still has the nerve to act like that to us afterward. We are trying to save him from a horrible conclusion. I drive on those roads too. We all do! Look at that fool; he doesn't care that he was drunk driving, and he certainly isn't going to go carefully from now on."

Gus nodded. "You know what they say: the problem with self-reflection is that it is only used by the people in the least need of it."

The DA consoled the two. "It isn't the first case we've lost, and it won't be the last. It is better to lose it at this stage then in a full trial, and that's what the judge was doing today. He spared all our reputations. You two can't let something like this bother you. Some days the court just doesn't go your way. Think of it this way; it isn't clear a man like Sedric can be punished. Only the man who has it in him to feel the injury of the penalty can be punished by the law; the others can only be hurt. A man like that, who you try to punish by taking his license, doesn't give a shit about drinking or driving. He would still drive with or without his license and likely drink and drive without it."

Gus put his hat on his head. He grabbed Dr. Armstrong and led her toward the door. He whispered over to her, "The DA can afford to be high-minded, as the judge just saved him a loss on his official record. Come on, Dr. Armstrong; let's go buy a few rounds of beer to dull our anger. We can't punish Sedric, but we can punish a few of our brain cells."

"Are you sure that's a good idea?"

"No, but I was going to do it win or lose. Plus, having a few drinks with you prevents me from doing something truly stupid, doesn't it?"

"Gus, you aren't still planning on doing something stupid, are you?"

"You never can tell, but I promise I'll go about my stupidity more carefully than Mr. Hedgecock does."

Lunch with the good doctor had been nice, but now it was time to get back to business. One of the best places to conduct business was at a bank, so long as you weren't expecting to deal with a business as nice as your lunch. Arroyo National Bank was located only a stone's throw from the sheriff's office on a pleasant rural street corner in what was once considered one of the best parts of town. It was a national bank in the sense that it had one branch in the entire world that was located not only in this nation, but more importantly in Gus's town. It also flew the flag of the nation right out front just in case you forgot where you were. A lot of people from time to time accused each other of doing just that, so you couldn't get more national than to remind them.

Gus parked the sheriff's truck in a conveniently vacant space right in front of the bank. It was also right in front of a fire hydrant, but Gus didn't let that bother him. He turned the emergency lights on top of his truck on and headed toward the bank's front door. A security guard stood on the other side of the glass door in a sparkling blue uniform. He had a gun in a holster by his side. Gus nodded a friendly hello to Clarence the guard as he passed him by. There hadn't been a bank robbery in this county in quite a long spell. Not a single old-fashioned one with a gun, a mask, and a note saying "This is a stickup" had occurred while Gus had been on watch. Gus figured that Clarence's job was to act more as a deterrent than as an actual crime-fighting force. He was always situated by the front door of the bank just to be seen. A smart guard would use that door and be the first one to run toward safety if any real trouble started. Gus hoped Clarence at his salary level was a really smart man. You had to pay a man pretty well to do something stupid like actually trying to stop an armed robbery in progress with no real training on how to do that. Still, Gus figured the friendly Clarence did an all-right job doing his main task at the bank: preventing people from stealing the pens off the center counter. There was nothing more annoying than trying to write out a deposit slip and finding all the pens were gone, so the guard's service to the bank was invaluable as far as Gus was concerned.

Gus didn't need to use the little counter today, as he wasn't dealing with his own account. There was only one teller window open, and there wasn't another soul in line. Young people today direct deposited their checks in banks. The money went straight from their employer into their bank account and then out to their credit cards without them ever needing to see a bank teller. It was a great way to decrease a bank's need to hire people, which also meant fewer people employed, and thus there were fewer people making a paycheck to be direct deposited somewhere. It was also a great way to obtain a customer for life. Once people signed up for direct deposit, they were much less likely to switch banks and go through the hassle of changing all the paperwork involved in setting up that direct deposit. In a day and age when banks failed regularly, it was odd to Gus that so many people placed such loyalty in any one banking institution. None of that mattered to Gus today other than it meant there was no line for him to wait to see Frank Patterson. He spied Frank Patterson at his teller window waiting to service any customer who walked through his bank's front door. Frank ran the bank. He likely owned the bank too, but Gus wasn't 100 percent sure on that last part.

Gus walked up the teller window. Frank's demeanor was jovial enough. "Sheriff Gus, what can the bank do for you today?"

Gus fished the note Frank's bank had written to his neighbor Rosa Hernandez from his pants pocket. He unfolded it and placed it down on the counter. Frank turned the paper to face him and quickly scanned the wording. Frank didn't seem overly concerned by the information he was reading. A banker was a lot like a doctor in being able to check his emotions at the door. Gus figured they guarded their emotions out of fear they might lose a cent due to any empathetic transaction of emotion. Gus fished out two one-dollar bills from his wallet. He placed them on top of the note that was sitting on the counter. The appearance of money didn't perk Frank up any, and the man merely shrugged at the two bucks lying before him. Frank explained, "Sorry, Sheriff, I can't take that money."

"Why, is your arm broken or something? Sure you can take it. That note says your bank is owed two dollars by Rosa, and I'm paying you two dollars. I don't want to see my neighbor get foreclosed. If I pay what she owes to you, then you got to take it, don't you?"

Frank shook his head. He explained, "The law says I don't have to take it. It is written in black and white inside the legal books. I'm sorry, but the law is the law. I can't take that money."

"But you're foreclosing on the house based on these two dollars owed, aren't you? If I pay it, then it isn't owed, and the whole matter can be settled to everyone's benefit."

Frank nodded in affirmation. "Well, don't get to hasty on that last part, Gus. Yes, it's true what the bank is doing is that we are foreclosing on this house. The owners should have paid their mortgage on time. It was not the bank's fault they became delinquent. Once the foreclosure proceedings have begun, we will only take the full amount of the debt owed and not just the amount late. It is all written into their agreement with the bank that they signed."

"But they're trying very hard to pay you what they owe, which as of this moment is only two dollars. I mean, it feels to me like you're intentionally kicking them out of their house just so the bank can take it. It's almost like stealing."

Frank balked at the accuracy of the accusation. "I...I think if you'll read the note right there, then you'll find that we're not kicking anyone out of any place. Since it will soon not be legally theirs anymore, we will exercise our legal rights and call upon the sheriff's office to enforce those rights, so technically you're the one evicting them and not the bank. The bank is not stealing anything. This institution will of course put the house up on auction. This bank doesn't want to own this property. We're not in the property-ownership business. The bank only wants mortgage payments from people who want to borrow money to buy property. We also want to be paid the mortgage on time and in full. The current occupant was short in that regard, so a new occupant will get the chance to satisfy the bank's needs when we resell the property at this auction. The current occupants will of course have the same chance to bid on it just like everyone else."

"So instead of taking their two dollars to catch up on their payments, you'll be making how much more money on all this when you auction their house off instead?" asked Gus.

"I'm not at liberty to say."

Gus tapped his finger on the two dollars sitting on the note on the counter. He asked one last time, "Are you taking those two bills as fulfillment of the amount due or not?"

"Law's on my side, and the law unequivocally states that I don't have to take it, and I won't take it. It is not, after all, just these measly two dollars that are in question here, but the honesty and integrity of that sanctified, signed mortgage that is at stake. The borrower signed a contract with the bank in good faith to pay their mortgage on time and in full at a set payment rate. They failed in their obligation. It might be a small matter, but a contract is a contract. If I let one debtor slide by still owing the bank two dollars at the end of the month, would that be fair to all the other debtors that I don't let slide by? Is one thousand too much to owe, three thousand, a million? It's a slippery slope that this bank refuses to slide on. I treat everyone equally no matter the amount past due. I gave them three months to catch up, as I'm legally obligated to do by the contract. They missed by two dollars. Please, as the sheriff, make sure they leave the bank's house promptly on the eviction date. Sometimes those vagrants try to linger around and even damage our property. I don't like the homeless hanging out on bank property. It brings down the auction price."

Gus snatched his two dollars off the counter along with the note. "Thanks for your help, Frank; I won't forget it." He left the teller counter behind, stopped, fished something out of his back pocket, and showed it to Frank. "I got one more thing to ask on a totally unrelated matter if you can spare the time."

Frank circled his head around the empty bank. He shrugged and replied, "I got the time."

"Can you verify that this deposit slip made out to one Terry Tang originated from your bank?"

"I can, because that's what this deposit slip says," replied Frank.

"Thanks again for your help. Have a wonderful day." Gus shoved the deposit slip in his pocket and headed back to the sheriff's truck. He gave the guard an unfriendly scowl as he passed out the door. He felt bad about it as soon as he reached the truck. It wasn't Clarence's fault the bank wrote their own rules against their own customers. The day was shaping up to be another bad one. The whole week hadn't been that hot. Today was two tasks down and two complete mission failures in a row. That didn't bode well for the tasks left to come. If it hadn't been for those beers at lunchtime, he'd be considering throwing in the towel on the day. Luckily, he had other things to investigate this day that he felt he would be more successful at. You couldn't control the banks or the courts, but as a sheriff there were things you could more easily control. He drove away from the bank and headed toward his next destination.

The question at the moment that lingered on the precipice of Gus's mind didn't have to do with an important matter. It had to do instead with a very basic form of matter. The matter was wood, or more precisely, it had to do with lumber. Lumber was a weighty matter, but rarely an important one. Lumber might grow on trees these days, but you didn't exactly cut down your own backyard to obtain it. No, in a civilized society most people purchased their lumber at a store. This was particularly true in a county where trees were often hard to come by. A sheriff who wanted to trace the purchase of a few boards of lumber was at a slight disadvantage. Society didn't feel sufficiently threatened by the odd cord of lumber, so it wasn't a controlled substance. No man needed a doctor's prescription to purchase it. Worst still, there were lots of places like stalled construction projects where a man could go and cart off a trace scrap of lumber without attracting a moment's notice. For the less criminally minded, there were large box stores completely dedicated to homes and their improvement. Inside them, there were plenty of lumber and other tools for the handyman that people bought thinking they were the handy kind of people. The basic fact that most people weren't handy didn't seem to prevent these box stores from being filled to the brim with more and more optimistic customers.

These large box stores had other problems for lumber buyers with criminal intent on their mind. These larger chain stores were much more likely to have a computerized system that tracked purchases than your local small-time ma-and-pop lumber store. A criminal could get around being tracked by his credit-card usage by using the good old-fashioned cash of yore. Of course, using plastic and virtual debits had become so common that someone who used cash to buy something might be remembered simply by virtue of using it instead of a credit card. Added to these worries was the unfortunate fact that these modern stores were so untrusting of their own customers that they often had security cameras. They might not be worried over an occasional lumber theft, but they were large box stores, so they had actual valuable things to purchase in them. More to the point, they were chain stores with billions in profits at stake, and so they tended to be greedy entities that felt the need to count their lumber down to the last stick lest they lose out on ever more profits. They weren't shy to announce the fact that you might be on a security camera either. No, they proudly proclaimed it on a yellow sign with black lettering right there at their front entrance. Most customers being honest folks didn't ever bother to notice those signs, but the criminal-minded ones sure did.

Gus pulled into Connery Lumber's parking lot. He was playing on a hunch. His hunch was a rather simple one to put to verse. He figured his criminal was the kind of man who thought he was smarter than everyone else. Everyone else in his inner circle felt the same way, which only reinforced the illusion of intellectual superiority. A normal criminal-minded man would buy his lumber at the big box store. He'd do it with a credit card. The criminal wouldn't give a rat's ass about the security cameras recording him or the credit card being used to trace the lumber back to him. No, a normal, basic criminal just isn't that suspicious in nature. A normal criminal would have a simple, normal plan and because of it be virtually shielded from discovery. No one at the box store would ever have remembered him. Those security tapes got erased probably every night or so, and even if they weren't, no one was going to watch countless hours in an attempt to spot him buying lumber. What sane person had that much free time? The credit-card receipts could be traced back to the criminal, but who would give a sheriff a warrant to request such things based on a flimsy hunch about wood? An abnormal man who overthought things and was far too clever for his own good, though, he would be too paranoid to purchase his ill-gotten goods from a public place like those box stores.

Connery Lumber was a family-owned place in the middle of nowhere. The sheriff's truck kicked up dust in the mostly empty parking lot. The store didn't exactly have a parking lot so much as a large dirt area that a man could park his vehicle in at random. There were rarely enough patrons at the store at any one time to worry too much about getting your truck exactly in a proper parking spot. Most people these days went to the large home box stores up on the highway closer to the big city to the north. Only the old-timers of the county and loyal handymen who worked on the cheap even remembered Connery Lumber was still in business. Art Connery had run the store ever since his dad's untimely death at age ninety-four. Art was not exactly of the computer generation. It had been said he only kept the lumber store open as an excuse to get out of the house once in a while. But given the lack of customers, Gus was pretty sure a new guy showing up out of the blue to buy such a very small quantity of lumber would be an act well remembered by Art. Art's memory was always clear as a bell.

The main structure of the lumberyard was a converted wooden barn. A chain-link fence surrounded the structure, enclosing the yard part of the lumberyard. In the yard were piles of bricks, tiles, and timbers that came in a variety of shapes and sizes. Gus got out of the truck and walked through the open double doors of the barn. The front of the store was filled with rows of assorted household hardware. Gus walked past all the aisles as he made his way toward the back of the store, where the old-style register was located. In front of the register sat two older men around a folding card table. They sat on makeshift chairs made of crates. The two men weren't playing cards at the card table. They were playing chess. One of the men Gus knew immediately as Art Connery. The other man was Calvin Fox. Calvin did odd jobs around the county for as much of a living as he could make. Gus knew why Calvin was hanging around the store. Occasionally a customer would come by the store and give Calvin a few days' work painting a fence, mending a drainpipe, or digging out a stump. Most days he simply made no living at all and played chess all day with Art. On a good day, there might be a half-dozen people like Calvin sitting idle waiting for a chance to offer up their services, but today it was just the two of them sitting there playing chess.

Gus moseyed on up to the card table. Neither man bothered to notice a new man in the store. There was chess to play, and they seemed intent on playing it. Gus casually started the conversation flowing. "It seems like an absorbing game."

Art replied while studying the board, "Passes the time, Sheriff; it passes the time."

"Which time?" asked Gus.

"The present," answered Calvin, making a move. The move seemed to delight Art, which was probably not a good sign for Calvin.

"Who's winning?" added Gus.

"I don't like to make predictions about the future. In a game like this, you never know for sure the outcome until it is over and done with," replied Art, moving a pawn into a precarious position. He lifted his fingers from the chess piece and finished his move. Art finally gave Gus a quick glance and a wink that might have meant something, but it didn't mean much to Gus. He didn't understand chess other than you could win it, lose it, or withdraw.

Calvin moved his knight quickly and took one of Art's pawns. He then said, "Now, I'm the complete opposite. I only make predictions about the future. You can always be proved factually wrong when speculating on the past, but no one can prove you wrong speculating on the future. For instance, I could say a silly thing like aliens will visit Earth tomorrow. It is clearly a totally bad guess on my part that you might be sure that I'm bound to be wrong about, but now here comes the beauty of it all. When are you going to know if that bad guess was right or wrong? You'll have to wait all day tomorrow to see if I'm wrong. Then when the end of the day comes and another tomorrow begins, you'll know for sure that there weren't any aliens that had come a-visiting. You might then say to me, 'Calvin, you idiot, you were wrong about the future,' but you can't say that, you see. While you clearly have evidence that my prediction about the future was completely wrong, you only know it after the time in question that we used to call the future, which is what I made my predictions about, has become the past. Thus I was only wrong about the past, and not about the future. You keep those speculations always progressing ever onward toward the future, where you can't never go wrong in life, and things will always work out fine for you in my book."

He finished his meandering lecture just as Art moved his queen to threaten Calvin's unsuspecting plastic king. Calvin frowned and scratched at his head a little. Art appeared to be satisfied about the present situation and asked Gus, "What brings you here to my fine lumber store on this lovely afternoon?"

"I reckon I came here to ask you all a question or two," replied Gus.

"About the past, the present, or the future?" asked Calvin as he moved his king to safety.

"I'm here to talk about the past. Not the long past, but the past all the same. I wouldn't want to ask you anything you weren't sure about the facts on."

"Ain't you been listening? He has already said he might be wrong about the past," replied Art as he quickly took Calvin's exposed knight.

"I'll risk it," replied Gus.

"The qualities that distinguish the good from the great chess players are an enormous ego coupled with an acute intuition that aids in the ability to take educated risks at a critical moment," replied Calvin as he stared at his hopeless situation on the board. He played with his pieces before deciding on racking up another pawn with his remaining knight. Calvin added the word, "Check."

Art quickly swooped in with a bishop, taking Calvin's remaining knight, and replied, "The present situation isn't in your favor, because that's checkmate. It was a nice attempt at a gamble, but we're all getting too old to take risks, particularly with our knights."

The two old men now spun around on their makeshift chairs to face Gus. He wasn't exactly sure what to say to them. The bluntest question probably was the best, he figured, so he led with it. "You boys didn't sell any wood to a stranger these past few days, did you?"

Art cleared his throat. He answered, "I sell mostly tile these days, or more to the point, terra-cotta. I got some nice Spanish terra-cotta that comes from over the border. People used to like the word *Spanish* tile, but now it's all terra-cotta this and that these days. People love it in their kitchens, their gardens, and their bathrooms. It's all hand glazed and fired. You don't get many strange people just looking for the odd stick or two of wood in my store. I get Mexican handymen coming and going all the time from here, and they do get the odd bit of lumber to mend a fence or patch a drywall, but I figured you didn't mean people who I know by sight if not also by name, so they're not strangers to me."

"This would be a man you knew but didn't know. A man you probably recognized plain as day, but he wouldn't have ever shopped here before. I figure he recently came in, bought a few lengths of lumber, and no one would think twice about the fact. It was after all only some lumber."

"I think the answer to that question is yes then," added Calvin.

Art gave Calvin a nasty little stare. There was something he knew, but he didn't exactly desire to risk offering the knowledge to Gus. Calvin shrank back deep into his seat from the admonishment. It was his second defeat in the last few moments. Art delayed for a time, hemming a bit and scratching his head as if he were trying to remember something that he remembered clear as a bell.

"Now, Gus, I liked your daddy swell and all; you're good folks, but I'm not so sure I can exactly tell you about my customers' private business. There is such a noble thing as the sacred bond between a lumber merchant and his client. After all, our Bible isn't exactly filled with a list of Jesus's carpentry customers for a reason. This sacred bond of the lumber is not to be divulged and broken for any ole willy-nilly reason."

Gus replied, "All right, Art, then how about answering another question for me? This wood that the man we can't identify or else betray the sacred brotherhood of the wood bought, how exactly flammable was it on a scale of one to ten?"

"Aw, hell, if you knew already, then I guess it can't hurt anything to tell you," said Art. Art got up from his seat and walked over to his counter. He pulled up a copy of the county's daily newspaper. He walked it over to Gus holding the photograph on the front page up so Gus could see it clearly. It was a photograph of the downtown rally that had introduced the county to Sheldon Nickelback. In a full-color spread stood Sheldon Nickelback, clear as day, receiving his brand-new limited-edition white Corvette. It was a magnificent machine, and it photographed well even in newspaper ink.

"Sheriff, do you think he did with that lumber he bought here what Calvin and I figured he did with that lumber?" asked Art.

"I figure he might have. He doesn't seem the hardware-store type of a man to me to be doing handyman things around the house. He just got the house new, so what handyman things would need to be done?" replied Gus.

Art tossed the paper onto the chessboard. He went over and sat back down. He seemed upset and didn't feel ambivalent about showing it. He blurted out, "Well, hell, I can't figure out why he'd do a thing like that, a good Christian man like that. Pastor Voce spoke kindly about him in church just the other day. It doesn't make any sense. I had liked the guy too. Not that I knew him except from the TV set. A man ought to be able to defend himself in his own yard by any means available. The media portrayed his case so eloquently that I honestly never doubted his innocence. I was hoping he'd get off, and then he did. I should have trusted my old papa. He always said that from such crooked wood as that which man is made of, nothing straight can be fashioned."

Calvin interjected, "I always thought he was no good and a murderer to boot. I still do, but the past proved me wrong again. The jury let him off. A lot of my Mexican handyman friends are none too happy about that bastard moving into our friendly county. One of them could have set that fire too, I imagine." He gave Gus a hard stare. Gus didn't react, and Calvin's brief rant continued. "But I suppose they didn't do it. If he was guilty about shooting that kid, then it doesn't seem exactly fair how things work out. Some men's kings can't so easily be checked, I guess."

"Setting that fire shows a guilty mind, don't it, Sheriff?" asked Art.

Gus replied, "Maybe, but sometimes a fire is just a fire."

Art wasn't game to the idea. He seemed pained to see his television hero brought down into reality's realm. He asked, "Do you think maybe he murdered that Mexican boy just because he's a racist after all?"

There really wasn't much to say to allow Gus to confirm a solid yes or a no to that matter. Gus simply tried to bid his farewell to the two men. "It doesn't matter one way or the other. He can't stand trial for the same murder twice. He's innocent until proven guilty, and they didn't prove it, or so the jury said. In this world that makes him as innocent as you or me, Art. Don't feel so bad about selling him a little wood. You can sell that type of stuff even to a convicted felon. If a man wants to harass himself with a cross of fire, then that's his own business. It might make him seem a little weird, but why he did it is his own business, and you remember well the business part of the idea. Stranger men have done stranger stuff."

"You aren't going to arrest a man for setting fire to his own front lawn?" asked Art.

"Nope, can't see what law was broken except wasting an officer's time. That time's been wasted already. It's in the past. I'm thinking about the future at the moment. I'd like to know where I stand for the future, and now I think I do. I don't think I'm wrong about that. They say that wood burns because it has the proper stuff in it, and a man becomes famous because he has the proper stuff in him. Sometimes that stuff is the same combustible mixture, and the wood and the famous man aren't that far apart. The only advice I can tell you is that if I was you, then I wouldn't go donating to that man's welcome-to-town fund when the collection plate comes passing by you," said Gus. He started to leave.

"I never was planning on it," replied Calvin. Art said nothing in response. He just set out cleaning up the chessboard. His local celebrity had let him down. He had known the truth but hadn't wanted to accept it. Now Gus had forced him to, and the truth was that it wasn't all that bad. An old man like Art didn't really have that much invested in a minor fraud like Sheldon Nickelback. Gus wasn't too sure that a lot of other older men weren't just about to be taken for a ride, though. They lacked Art's special knowledge of this man's true nature. Gus never doubted the man's true nature, but you can fool some of the people all the time and all the people some of the time; that rare "some of the time" only has to be one jury decision to allow a man to walk away innocent for the rest of his life.

Gus made it back to the sheriff's truck. He admitted to himself that internally he was now conflicted. He picked up the sheriff's radio and made a call to the station. He waited patiently as the dispatcher located the deputy he needed to speak with. There weren't any patrons milling about in the parking lot, so Gus just calmly waited without anything to distract his attention. A nice, quiet place this county could be if you went to the right parts of it. Gus was aiming to make more of the county feel like this little lumber store. They didn't need to rebrand the county; they just needed to appreciate the county they got.

The radio line came to life. "Sheriff, this is Chiquita here. The dispatcher said you needed to speak to me. I'm down in the industrial district getting the lay of the land."

"You've been downtown, in the development, and now into the heart of our industry. It sounds like you've really gotten to know the county pretty well this past week. I called you up because I wanted to know how well you got to know Sheldon Nickelback the other night after I left."

"I got to know him better than even he might think. He was easy to sweet-talk. After you left, he brought me inside for a drink. I claimed I needed to go to the restroom, and I got to scope the place out pretty good. He had an empty gas can in the garage with a box of matches sitting on top of it. The whole place smelled of the fumes. Your hunches are pretty good. I think he's our man. I wrote it all down in my report and put the report on your desk, but I guess you haven't read it yet. You just give me the word, and I'll go arrest him for you."

This new news from his deputy worried Gus more than just a bit. Sheldon Nickelback seemed to be going out of the way to be an easy catch. Gus replied, "Well, we can't do that."

"I don't understand."

"Now, your little bit of information ties in with my little bit of information I just gathered, so I think we can safely put this yard-fire case to bed. Luckily for Sheldon Nickelback, I'm not about to help him be a martyr to the cause, not that I'm one hundred percent certain that I understand the cause. Fear and business, I guess. There are a lot of people afraid these days, and they're easy to convince you're on their side the more afraid of the other guy you make them. When the right talking head sides with you and takes up your cause, then people will support you no matter who or what you really are. It is nonsense, but it is also reality. Sheldon Nickelback hasn't exactly got a lot of money at present. Sheldon Nickelback does have a lot of lawyer debts. Those are on the negative side of the ledger for our friend Sheldon. Sheldon has a lot of fame. That's on the positive side of the ledger. Sheldon Nickelback got a loan to buy a new house and was given an expensive car because of this fame. Shelden Nickelback needs more people to keep on giving him money, and he found out this county is a place where he can get people to give him money. If we go arrest Sheldon Nickelback for setting fire to his own front yard and lying about it to the sheriff's office, then he'll just say that we're all part of the conspiracy of the legal system out to get him. We'll just be verifying his version of the events in these people's minds. Then he collects even bigger profits, while I probably can't even get the DA to press a single charge against the man.

I'm not about to do that. I'm not about to help him take these fools to the cleaners just to enforce a few penny-ante laws. I'm not stupid."

"Compassion for these fools is no substitute for justice. The man is guilty, and he should pay for his crimes. I would make him pay if I was in your place."

"So that's the way you see it, Deputy?"

"An injustice anywhere is a threat to justice everywhere, so I say let justice be done to this man even if the tiny world of these self-deluded fans has to perish. We should have the honesty to risk losing in court for the right reasons rather than let this man make us his fools. I know if a man slighted me in the least and thus did an injustice to me, I would never let this man get away with it. I would track him down and find him. I would punish him severely if I did ever find him."

"Deputy Lopez, I admire your spirit, but you won't last long in this world if you don't know how to pick your battles. Sheldon Nickelbacks of the world may not go to jail or get disgraced in public for the worst thing they've ever done, but they often get theirs in the end. They can't help themselves."

"There would be no helping them if I was in charge!" said Chiquita.

"There is no need to shout. So you got a little justice streak in you, do you. Good, I'll tell you what. I want you to drive over to Arroyo National Bank and figure out the vehicle of every employee of that bank. Then I want you to start writing those people tickets. I want parking tickets, moving violations, and all the rest. Hell, don't stop short of public decency. I don't care what you write them down for, because all I want is a high volume of tickets; do you understand me? Most important of all, I want you to follow the owner of that bank around town. Ticket him if he has a moving violation, but more importantly, call me if he ever has a large sum of money on him. If he ever has a large amount of money on his person, then do not, I repeat, do not go near him until I arrive. I don't want to spook him in case of that event."

"And this is bringing about justice how?" asked Chiquita.

"You let me worry about that."

"I do not understand you, but if you want me to unleash the devil upon this bank, then I will do it." She hung up.

Gus honestly admired her passion for the job. He also liked that his hunch had paid off so handsomely. He had come up on the negative end twice today, so he was happy to land one in the win column, not that he got anything for being right. He now understood Sheldon Nickelback as well as he would ever need to know him. He wasn't going to waste any more time searching for arson suspects who didn't exist. The problem with finding out the truth wasn't the same for Gus as with Art or Chiquita. Art had lost a moment of hero worship for a man not worthy of it. Chiquita had lost her sense of purity in the system. Gus had only lost a little puzzle to keep his mind occupied away from heavier issues. This case of the burning cross was all too easily solved. It was disappointing to have solved it so quickly. He had read Sheldon good and proper, so it was bound to be easy. Now came the harder part.

He knew exactly what he wanted to know, but he knew not what to do with the information. Fill out the paperwork and set his hound Chiquita after him was one real possibility. The facts told Gus to act, but the facts were not very convincing. He had told Chiquita he wouldn't act, and now he had to decide for himself if that was really the course of action he would take. He might always do something stupid. He hadn't told his deputy about that possibility. It was better Chiquita didn't know that stupid was still an option.

Karma was the idea that what comes around goes around. It was a form of cosmic justice. Good intent and good deeds contribute to good karma and future happiness, while bad intent and bad deeds contribute to bad karma and future suffering. It was the grand idea that bad things happened to bad people, and thus they got what they deserved. Only thing about that grand idea was that most adults figured out people rarely got what they deserved. Bad people got rich, slept with beautiful women, and lived to be miserably happy and wealthy old men. Many a good person was born into a state of poverty, lived their whole lives in poverty, and then died in it without ever receiving a reward for their suffering. In the Western world, people convinced themselves such punishments and rewards came after death in heaven and hell. It was as wishful an idea as the idea of karma. These noble ideas, however, allowed people to sit idly by while watching bad people repeatedly do bad things to good people while doing nothing about it, because most people assured themselves bad things were waiting for the bad people on this earth eventually or in heaven after the fact. But there was little proof that things actually worked out that way.

Still, it wasn't Gus's over trusting nature as to the balancing effects of karma that would keep him from acting. It was something else entirely, but he knew now he would not act on this information. No, Sheldon wanted him to act, and by acting he would help the criminal more than ever, and so he would not act. His inaction might keep a buck or two in a deserving man's pocket rather than give that man a false reason to donate it to Sheldon Nickelback. Sheldon had fought the law and won before, and the law was wiser now from the experience. He wouldn't act now or ever on the information he had received today. Sometimes doing nothing at all was the most just solution to an act of crime. He might do something stupid in the future—you never knew about the future—but today was rapidly becoming the past, and he wasn't planning on doing something stupid today.

Yucca Flats was an apartment complex in an unincorporated part of the county. It was located up near the county's northern reaches. The complex was situated just off the great highway that flowed north by northwest. The highway was just about the only way in and out of this tiny residential oasis. In older times before the highway, the area was used mostly to house the many ranch workers the county had once needed, but in more modern times it housed mainly day trippers to the city. It was the easy access to the highway leading north to the big city with its noble airs of civilization that lured the residents here. Yeah, getting out of here fast was the main and only attraction of this small strip of civilization carved out of the dry basin. To Gus the urban city was a government system that was invented from a choice of mixed components and was easier to idealize in the minds of today's youth than to realize in practice. Even if this grander idea of the city was ever briefly realized, there didn't appear much future for it. Everyone dreamed of going to the big city, but more and more they spent their days in it and their nights at home in Gus's small county where a man could afford a bed. However, that civilization up north included a large private university and a state college, which no doubt explained why Yucca Flats catered mostly to college students in need of reasonable rents and access to the grand ideals of city life up to the north.

Gus walked the edges of the two-story eyesore that was the apartment complex. It was a long stucco building that doubled back on itself to form a grand, looping structure surrounding a central commons. The complex was decorated with fuchsia and tangerine accents. The paint covering the wood doors and accents was sun faded and chipped. The brass door handles were corroded from the many years of disinterested handling. The cement pathways of the complex were cracked and uneven. Gus passed by a small, termite-ridden fence that blocked the view of each patio of the lower apartment units. Drying laundry hung out in the sun peeked over the fence on many of the units. Overall the place appeared to be lightly defended from a break-in. This was likely due to the residents having little to steal rather than the area having a low crime rate. Gus figured he could jimmy open any one of these apartments' front doors without taking too much of his time or attracting too much residential worry. There was no need to try to do that, however.

Gus found what he was searching for inside the complex's commons. In the center of the complex sat a small hut structure, which was also composed of aged stucco. The sad little structure resided next to the communal swimming pool. The pool had passed its glory years on by, but it maintained functionality for any guest brave enough to try a dip in it. The cement facade may have been crumbling, and the poolside furniture's appearance suggested it was in a state of haphazard repair, but the water sparkled with an inviting blue hue due to the faint smell of chlorination. There were no residents milling about the cement poolside to enjoy the blue waters today. No doubt the active students were all still up north in winter classes learning or whatever one did at college these days. No doubt this pool would be bustling come the weekend. The sign on the roof of the hut read "Manager." The hut's windows were all fully open, and the front door was propped open by a fan that managed to blow ever outward into the barren heat of a mild midwinter day. The air outside smelled of tobacco smoke. The doorframe was stained from years and years of bad habit. Gus maneuvered around the blowing fan and entered the stale, smoky air of the hut.

Gus was greeted by a cobweb-covered air conditioner in disrepair on the floor in the center of the room. There was a small front desk with a tiny steel bell. A small, dust-covered plastic sign next to the bell read "Press bell for management assistance." Out from a recess behind the front desk, there came the sound of a television whose volume was too loud. Gus depressed the button on the bell and let it ring out in an attempt to attract the attention of anyone lurking in the recess beyond the desk. He stood patiently waiting for half a minute. No one bothered to come to the front desk. Gus took it upon himself to lift the wooden flap in the front desk and entered the office proper. Behind the desk was a vacuum cleaner, a safe, a small amount of maintenance tools, and a few assorted pens and pencils. Gus walked over to the recess and knocked hard on the frame of the entranceway. From the entrance he could see that the recess gave way to a tiny inner room that held a dirty bed, a disheveled dresser, and a small reclining chair that faced a huge wall-size flat-screen television. On the chair sat an old man in his soiled undershirt and shorts. He was smoking a cigarette with his right hand and dumping its ashes into a glass ashtray that was precariously perched on the recliner's right armrest. The tiny room smelled of burned tobacco grime. The old man did not acknowledge the knock any more than he had acknowledged the bell or the grime that surrounded him.

Gus headed back over to the front desk and picked up the bell. He returned to the recess and stood in the entrance ringing the bell repeatedly to obtain the old man's attention. The sound echoed in the small room but didn't gain much of a rise from the room's inhabitant. Gus yelled out, "County sheriff here, I'm looking for a Kyle Minnelli."

The old man continued to watch his television. He did manage a reply. "You'll have to come back later. I'm on break and watching my shows."

"Can you tell me if a Kyle Minnelli lives here?"

"I can, but I'm watching my shows."

"What channel are you watching so intently?"

"Game Show Network."

"What's on?"

"Game shows."

"I can see how it would be hard to tear a man away from all that important stuff. Unfortunately, I need to see Kyle Minnelli's apartment immediately. You can stay there watching your shows, because all I need from you is for you to tell me where I can find the keys to Kyle Minnelli's apartment. I'll fetch them and let myself inside."

"Nope, I can't do that. I'm the manager of this here place. The owner doesn't pay me to just hand out keys to our apartments for free. You gotta pay rent here to get a key here. We got rules in this place. You don't pay rent, so you get no key. That's the rules, and the rules are the rules. I never apologize for being right by the rules."

Gus sighed and pulled out his badge. He walked from the entrance heading for the sweet spot between the old man and his prized television. He clarified the situation to the old man. "I'm the sheriff, and this here is my badge. I'll ask again nicely; can I have the keys to Kyle Minnelli's apartment? If your answer to my request is another round of noes, then you'll have me to deal with. I'm sure the owner doesn't want criminals living in or managing his apartments, so don't force me into making you a criminal."

"I've never noticed him caring one way or the other on that matter. The rules are based on quantity of the rent payment and not quality of the rent payer. Speaking about rules…Sheriff, eh…don't you need a search warrant or something to go messing about in another man's apartment? I don't think I can let you have no keys without a warrant. That's what the television always says to me. The television never lies."

"Life is a little different than television. You spin a wheel on television and win ten thousand dollars; you spin a bottle in the real world and end up seven months into an unwanted pregnancy. That's real life for you. More to the point, our constitution says I don't need a warrant to search apartment rooms, so you'll have to hand those keys on over to me. The law is the law in America, just like the rules are rules in your apartment complex."

The man put his cigarette out in the glass astray. He paused, either lost in thought or else more likely completely thoughtless. The absolute constitutional truths of American life were an important unknown to him, so he gave in and replied, "Oh, I didn't know that. I guess television script writers don't read the constitution much. Since you say that it's in the constitution and all, you're legally proper. The master keys are right there under the front desk hanging on a peg nailed into the wall. Kyle what's his name's apartment number can be looked up in the book under the front desk. Help yourself to looking it up, but just make sure you put my keys back where you found them when you're done with them. I don't like it when people go stealing my keys."

"Sir, I want to thank you kindly for helping out the local sheriff's office."

"Yup." The old man lit up another cigarette and continued watching his game shows.

Gus walked out of the recess. He leaned down and snatched the keys off a peg. According to the college, Kyle Minnelli's current address was listed as unit number ninety-nine Yucca Flats. Gus took out the ledger under the front desk. He ran his finger down to flat number ninety-nine. The name matched the college records. It was nice when people were truthful in life. It made Gus's job easier. Too many criminals were dishonest about things like their address.

A quick survey of the complex's numbering scheme suggested that apartment ninety-nine was, much to Gus's misfortune, on the second floor. To get to the apartment, Gus would have to climb up a narrow set of winding metal stairs. There was no easy going in the field of law enforcement. Gus climbed the stairs using the cold steel rail to assist his aching knees. It was a tough climb, partially due to Kyle's father. Gus counted the doors off by using their cheap brass numbers that were nailed to each door's center. Each door had a small peephole like you would find in a hotel door. The glass in the peepholes generally was in filthy condition, and Gus figured not many residents could possibly be using them for peeping. The sights outside their doors weren't much to peep at anyway. Arriving at number ninety-nine, he did a quick survey of the apartment. The second-story apartment's patio was in the back, so it offered no help from the front for a man wanting to peer into the apartment. In the front there was only an opaque door with a dirty peephole that faced the wrong way to be of any use to Gus. There were no windows to peek through. Kyle wasn't much of a homemaker. He had no welcome mat or potted plant to greet a visitor. Gus rang the doorbell located to the left of the doorframe. If it rang, Gus didn't hear it. Gus resorted to pounding on the door a few times with a closed fist.

The next-door neighbor opened her door. The head of a blonde of college age stuck out of the open door to see what was going on. She clearly identified the sheriff and immediately headed right back into her apartment without saying a word. Her reactions just went to show that some smart people did go to college these days. The door in front of Gus didn't answer to his ringing and knocking, so Gus took it as the lucky break that he had been hoping for. He stuck a key of the master key ring into the lock. It took five keys to find the right one to open the door.

Gus went inside. The apartment was no better maintained than the grounds around it. The main room served as a dining room, living room, and kitchen rolled into one. Off to the side was a small room that housed a messy bedroom and a bathroom in much need of cleaning. The living room was cleaner and housed simple, cheap furniture. There was a reclaimed wooden kitchen set, a couch with sheets draped over it, and a couple of unstained particleboard wooden stools that matched a particleboard coffee table. The coffee table came complete with water-stained rings from coffee cups that had forgotten to land on the nonexistent coaster. A few college-mathematics textbooks with stickers on them that labeled them as used sat in a haphazard pile on the coffee table. The only expensive thing in the room was a huge wall-mounted television entertainment center. Gus bounced his hands on the battered back of the couch. A cloud of dust kicked harmlessly into the air. The air smelled stale but free of normal college vices like tobacco or pot.

Dissatisfied with his initial impressions, Gus moved to examine the garbage can in the attached kitchenette. It contained mostly the remains of cans of soda pop and boxes of frozen dinners and not the remains of the feasts of a champion. The garbage smelled badly of the need to be taken out to the Dumpster, but it wasn't filled with beer cans or liquor bottles. A quick search of the drawers in the kitchen and bedroom yielded no butterfly knives or guns. Kyle seemed to be more and more exactly like the good kid of legend judging by the refuse in his apartment. His father, Antonio, made more money a year than Gus would amass in a lifetime, and yet Kyle was living like any other teenager of college age. It bothered Gus a little that Kyle was exactly what Antonio had made him out to be. It would be easier had he been a monster in the making. It would be easier, but it wasn't going to change what needed to be done. The conscience might be the chamber where justice lay, but having too much of it could lead to its own problems, and at this particular moment Gus ignored his own conscience. Things had been set in motion by forces beyond Gus's control, but he could still control his small sphere of the world. The current plans that went with it were all that mattered. It didn't matter what Kyle was really like any more than it mattered what Jennifer had really been like. The law was the law, and justice would have to prevail, and it was Gus's job to see that it did, so at the moment Gus's finer points of conscience weren't going to be able to do anything to prevent it.

Gus left the apartment. The female neighbor was back out on the balcony eyeing apartment ninety-nine with curiosity. She quickly scooted off the balcony and back into her apartment as soon as Gus reopened the front door. Gus ignored her and headed swiftly back to his truck. It was just a normal college apartment complex filled with people who wanted to know what was going on, but they were unsure if they desired to actually get involved in what was going on. In other words, it was full of young people. The neighbors were noisy but shy. The stairs were easier to navigate in the down direction than going up. The thought of a second visit up those stairs was looming, but it had to be done.

Gus headed over to his truck and opened the back. He momentarily stopped what he was doing and glanced around the back of the truck's frame. He eyed the Kansas trooper vehicle parked about thirty yards away on the side of the road. The winter sun glared off the driver's field glasses. Gus gave a friendly campaign-patented wave to the driver of the patrol car. Satisfied, Gus went back to what he was doing. Inside the back of Gus's truck sat a box filled with prescription drugs kindly donated to law enforcement by Terry Tang just the other day. Terry was a real helpful, ignorant loudmouth son of a bitch whose gift of illegal trafficking of painkillers for the medicating of the wealthy was the kind of gift that kept on giving. Gus opened his little black bag and took out a pair of black gloves. He put them on. He took Terry Tang's gun from the black bag and stuck it in his waist. He picked up the box from the back of the truck and carried it back toward the Yucca Flats apartment number ninety-nine. Navigating the box up the flight of stairs was a big challenge. The pain in his knees would have prevented a normal man from completing his task, but Gus was a man who was now on a mission, and he was willing to forgo the lack of pain in the knees to reach the required ending.

The young woman was back out on her balcony and was now joined by a second young woman. They were chatting in hushed tones, no doubt about the recent developments of the day. Upon Gus's return to the balcony, they quickly hushed up. Gus was tucked behind a large box and walked slowly, retracing his footsteps right to Kyle's front door. He dropped the box down in front of apartment ninety-nine and unlocked the apartment for a second time. He thrust the door open and then gave a wave to the two gawking young ladies. They froze like deer illuminated by headlights and made no action to inquire as to what was going on other than to gawk. He then reentered the apartment with his prized box of goodies. The ladies had respected their own business and were not to be busybodies, but still they were curious as a result of human nature. He kicked the door closed behind him to alleviate them from any further need to inquire as to his business.

He stuck the box down on the center of the reclaimed kitchen table. He took his preopened drug bottle out of the box. With a hard flick of the wrist, he scattered the pills out of the open mouth of the bottle and onto the stained rug covering the floor. He walked over the pills to grind them into the carpet fibers. He then started emptying the contents of Terry Tang's box onto the kitchen table. The writing was too small to make out the pill labels without his reading glasses, so he sorted the bottles roughly by size. He left half the contents inside the box. He took the remains of the box and placed it under the kitchen table. Last, but not least, he took Terry Tang's gun out of his waistband. He placed it square on the dead center of the table as exhibit A. The stage was now set for the play to begin. He grabbed one of the wooden kitchen chairs and moved it around so he could watch the front door. There was nothing more he needed to do but wait. Patience was a virtue, and his soon-to-be criminal would return to his home to play the part of the victim for Gus.

Gus sat on the seat flipping through the only reading material he could find. The math textbook he took from the coffee table was flavorless and boring. It was just numbers begetting more numbers. It was a book of proofs that were true within the world of numbers. They were valid whether the reader knew about them beforehand or not, or so the text claimed. It was satisfying within that collegiate world, because it pleased the mind to know something could be proved by logic to be true even if it was only by the simple logic of mathematics. A person adds a one to another one and thus makes a two. You could create a whole philosophy based on it by just assuming that somewhere out there were mathematical proofs of things like temperance, wisdom, and courage that worked just like two ones making a two. Those ancient philosophers of logic thought that justice became a cause and effect by following those three cardinal virtues. It would be nice if you could prove all that with a mathematical proof. Math was hard, but it was much easier than dealing with the real world where things like justice reduced to working at that to which a man was naturally best suited. In Kyle's case that meant learning mathematics in college, and in Gus's case it meant arresting Kyle for selling another man's illegal drugs. That was what justice was boiling down to at the moment, and you couldn't prove it with ones and twos. That was what Gus sat there waiting to do while bored to tears reading about mathematical proofs.

Gus could hear voices at long last from the other side of the door. Those two young women were talking to someone out there. Young people were shy around old people but talked freely among themselves. It was probably a boy they chatted with, judging by the change in the tone of their voices. The door handle jiggled and unlocked. Gus tossed the math book under the kitchen table next to the half-filled box of drugs. He put his hand on the butt of his gun as he stood up from the chair. A young, handsome Mexican teenager walked nonchalantly into his own apartment. He wore a basic red T-shirt and a pair of blue jeans. He called out into the apartment as he entered, "Is there anyone at home? No use hiding, as the girls already said someone came in here."

Gus mustered up his cold, harsh officer voice and ordered, "Put your hands up in the air and plant your face to the wall. You're under arrest."

The young man relaxed when his eyes focused better to the dimly lit apartment after entering it from the sunlit world of the outside. Kyle could finally see Gus and his uniform clearly. The young man didn't seem alarmed to see the law in his apartment. Instead, he smiled an innocent smile as if this was all a terrible prank that was about to be played on him. It was no joke, and Gus was not in a joking mood. There were lives at stake, and that made it all a very serious game. Gus pulled the gun out with one hand and flipped his badge out with the other. He ordered, "Hands up and turn around to face the wall. I don't want to ask you a third time."

Kyle was no dummy and knew a man with a gun pointed at him meant business—serious business. He placed his hands high on the wall and pressed his face against it. Gus forced Kyle's legs far apart with a knee. He poked the barrel of his gun into Kyle's back to remind him not to do anything sudden. Gus proceeded to go through the motions of frisking Kyle. He didn't expect a weapon on the boy, and those expectations were fulfilled. Gus reached up, grabbed the left hand, and forced Kyle's arm behind his back. He clicked an end of the handcuffs on the left wrist. Then he followed that action by securing the Kyle's right arm behind his back. Gus marched the handcuffed boy over to the dirty couch and pushed him forcefully into it.

Kyle hadn't muttered a word the whole time. His face read as a person in complete disbelief. Now sitting sunken into the depths of his own couch due to the furniture's failing support springs, he uttered a response at last, "I don't understand this. Are you arresting me just because I'm Mexican?"

The boy, being secured in the handcuffs, was easy for Gus to ignore, so Gus ignored him. He was busy calling for backup with his phone. He got Deputy Wilson on the other end. Gus made it short and simple. "Sheriff Gus here. I was answering a call about some loud music over here in the Yucca Flats. It's a dirty little apartment complex just off the highway with a bunch of college kids as paying guests. I didn't find any music, but I found a treasure trove of drugs. It appears we have more than one prescription-drug peddler in our midst. You boys better come on up here to apartment number ninety-nine and pick up the drugs and the suspect. I'll hold him until you arrive."

The deed having been done, Gus put the cell phone away. Kyle said to him, "That is all a bunch of bullshit. I'm being framed as a bad joke by someone. I don't have any drugs. I don't sell any drugs. I don't even know anything about drugs. I was raised right. Drugs destroy your mind. This is some fantastic story. I wasn't even home to play loud music, and even if I was, what neighbor would call up and complain about me playing it? All my neighbors are college kids like me and like their music loud. I find your whole story very derivative of a weak movie plot."

"Really, I thought it was all very integral to the current plot," replied Gus.

"What is all this? I hear about this shit all the time—you really are just harassing me because I'm Mexican, aren't you? That's it, isn't it? I dared to come to your country and go to your college, so you're going to harass me. You're another piece of trash that can't stand a foreigner taking advantage of the educational system you were too privileged to bother using. When my father hears about this, you are going to be sorry. He'll have the best lawyers in the county so far up your stupid racist ass you'll wish you had gone to college yourself just so you'd be intelligent enough to think of a better lie than the current one you are using."

The boy struggled on the couch in a bit of a hissy fit, but he was smart enough not to do anything that required Gus to use force. Gus asked the boy, "Do you know what your father does for a living?"

Kyle replied with pride in his voice, "My father is the best. He buys and sells avocados. He's one of the biggest and best merchants in all of northern Mexico. Everyone about town respects and admires my father and his business sense."

The boy stated it like he believed it. It was one of the noble lies one tells oneself to make the world a saner place. Gus could tell the boy the truth, but likely he wouldn't believe it if he heard it. The boy sat there naïve and helpless. Gus knew he could go for an eye for an eye like the maddening crowd-promised parts of the good book said. He could rough Antonio's son up with his nightstick the way Antonio's thugs had roughed him up. There would be some satisfaction in doing just that. It wasn't part of the greater plan as Gus had worked it out. He had framed Kyle for grander reasons than a simple excuse to beat the crap out of him. Had he only wanted to do that, he wouldn't have needed to work so hard. As sheriff he could beat the crap out of just about anyone and get away with it, as history had proved to him. Gus was playing a role in the farce that wasn't of his own creation. He hadn't started the play, but now that he was an actor in it, he was going to make sure the damn thing ended the way he wanted it to before the curtain went down. In this play he was in the role of the grand philosopher, whose job it was to be the least susceptible man to the corruption around him and therefore the most just. Only to be a just man at this moment required more than its share of injustice, beginning with the arrest of Kyle. Gus couldn't prevent Sheldon Nickelback from roaming about town, but he could prevent Kyle from doing the same. After all, Antonio had wanted Gus to make sure his son was safe, and there was no safer place in the county than Gus's secure little cell block. How could Antonio complain about Gus just doing what Antonio had told him to do—keep his son safe? Funny enough, though, Gus knew Antonio would object and object loudly to today's turn of events.

CHAPTER 5

…questions of justice only arise when there is equal power to compel: in terms of practicality the dominant exact what they can and the weak concede what they must.
—Thucydides

It was an unjust world when a man couldn't find peace and solace in his own home. Granted, the bank usually held the mortgage on that home, but so long as the monthly payments went out, home ownership would eventually come to those who waited. That was unless the bank tried to steal it out from under you by using the finer print in the contract. That scenario was unlikely in Gus's case. He owned his home outright. No, what he was likely to find in his home tonight wasn't a banker, but a very angry confrontation with Antonio's goons. Kyle had already made his one phone call, and he had made it back home, so the meeting was set in the stars. The next meeting was coming eventually anyway, which was why Gus had made sure to stack a loaded card inside his deck. Antonio needed Gus to remove the charges from Kyle's record, and that gave Gus a little leverage in the current situation. This fact would come in handy, provided Antonio didn't run off and do something stupidly rash like kill Gus first and think of why he shouldn't have second. Gus was pretty sure the latter scenario was distinctly possible.

Gus slowed the sheriff's truck and turned a block earlier than usual. The car following him did likewise. It wasn't a very prudent idea to just drive straight into the nest of the gunmen who were waiting to kill you in cold blood on the asphalt of your own driveway. It was also just an added annoyance that someone was following you home to watch it all go down in flames at the same time. The Kansas patrol car had been following him since he had dropped Kyle off at the law-enforcement complex. The silent lights sitting exposed on top of the patrol car had given the identity of the tailing vehicle away.

There were far too many hotheaded idiots about potentially risking Gus's life tonight. He swung the truck down a street that ran parallel to his own. He parked the truck along the side of the road. The patrol car following him drove on past as if that action would convince Gus he wasn't still being followed. Gus had been followed enough to know if he was or wasn't being followed. Major Dundee was apparently willing to follow him to hell and back again as a constant little reminder to Gus that he was still around. What a nice man. The papers Dundee needed weren't signed yet by the governor. No doubt the governor had faced a rough day of lobbying by all sides interested in the case. According to the radio news, Wilton McDermott had a team of ACLU lawyers working the governor over. She had also gotten her own midnight prayer circle of pro-life advocates surrounding the governor's mansion. All that lobbying by both sides had produced the much-predicted gridlock. The lack of papers gave Gus time to work on his problems, but it also gave Dundee time to jeopardize Gus's life needlessly by potentially giving his scheme away. The major was everything Gus couldn't afford around at the moment. Gus suspected the major's presence at his home would be a poor excuse for a trigger-happy goon to panic and start blasting away.

Gus waited for the Kansas patrol car to turn out of sight farther down the street. He then focused on a plan for the rough task of going inside his home. Gus searched the street carefully. There didn't appear to be anyone around tonight, suspicious or otherwise. Good, that meant there was no one on this street to get spooked by the people from Kansas. The hired goons must all be concentrated on Gus's block. They weren't watching the surrounding area, which gave Gus a chance. Gus turned his gaze from the roadside back toward the house that neighbored his backyard. Gus's backdoor neighbor was an inconvenient friendly type of fellow. He didn't adhere to the neighborly rule that good fences made for good neighbors. Instead, the man insisted on having no proper barrier between the two properties. His backyard would not give Gus much of a chance to sneak up and spy on the goings-on in his own home. Instead, Gus's simple plan was to move one house over from his backyard neighbor. He would travel through the adjacent house's yard and then be able to slip unnoticed into the backyard of Rosa Hernandez. Inside Rosa Hernandez's backyard, there was a good, proper fence that stood between Gus's house and Rosa's house. A noisy young child was a good incentive to build fences, and so fences surrounded Rosa Hernandez's house on all sides, not that they had a prayer of keeping those kids at bay. Once safely there in Rosa's yard, he would then be able to safely peer through the fence to see what was going on in his own backyard.

He figured on something happening in his own house tonight. It would be foolish not to expect it. More than foolish, it would be damn disappointing, as his plan was counting on it. It was pitch-black in the backyard of Gus's backyard neighbor. It was a good neighborhood in a small town, so no one thought anything about leaving lights off at night. The extra darkness was good cover for his movements. While his neighbor Rosa had a nice, high wooden fence that faced his backyard, she had only a low chain-link fence guarding her backyard from her backyard neighbor's yard. Gus reached the chain fence unnoticed with relative ease. As an extra fortune in tonight's luck, he arrived at the chain-link fence and discovered that Rosa Hernandez had kindly left her back porch light off tonight as well. Gus made his way down the fence line until he came to the back gate. He grabbed the back handle of the gate and twirled it. Nothing happened. There was some annoying plastic device on the gate. His neighbor had placed a childproof lock on it. There wasn't time to figure out how the child-defeating device worked, so Gus decided to climb the fence.

First he stuck one foot through the metal rungs, and next he scissored one of his legs over the top of the fence. He then eased his body over the crest. Slowly he let one side slip down the other side until his foot hit dirt. This was working well, and if he'd been twenty and flexible, he'd have been in good shape just about now. Instead he was fat and old and thus found he had ended up doing a rather unnatural split upon the fence. The easiest way to remove his suspended leg was simply to fall backward into the dirt, which he did out of necessity. He landed with a loud thud. This move had hurt a lot, but he decided it was wise to not advertise that fact to the outside world. He screamed in pain in the recesses of his mind but kept his fat mouth shut.

He stood back up on his feet and dusted the dirt off. He reached around his waist for a flashlight. Gus made for the wood fence that lay between his house and Rosa Hernandez's house with his flashlight now firmly in his hand just in case of need and his gun secure in its holster, because you never knew if you'd have a need for it. He knew that there was a good-sized knothole in the middle of that fence. Gus had often noticed the kids spying on him through that very knothole. Why kids wanted to spy on a fat old man lying on a hammock during the summer was an unanswerable question. This hole was a handy little thing to know about tonight. It was very high up on the wooden structure, which meant he wasn't even required to bend over to look through it. Gus walked the fence line searching with his hands, trying to find the hole in the darkness. His fingers pressed down at last into nothingness. He had located the hole, and he pressed his body to the fence and peered through it.

There was one poorly dressed thug wearing a black hoodie smoking a cigarette sitting on his back porch. Clearly he wasn't a man exactly into doing a good job of menacing. He was sitting down right under the back porch light, so the whole world could see him staking out the porch. The thug was hunched over on the back steps reading a magazine of some type by the dim yellow glow of the porch light. The thug had an automatic rifle resting across his knees, so he was still a very dangerous, if not a very good, lookout. The thug signaled that inside Gus's home was Antonio. No doubt Antonio wanted to make sure Gus heard a new message about Big Gustavo's displeasure. Gus planned on turning that idea around and being the one sending messages tonight.

The chain-link fence gate screeched in the night. It opened and closed in the darkness. Gus took his attention from the thug on his porch. The noise made him worried that a smarter thug had actually thought about staking out his neighbor's backyard as well. Perhaps the adjacent street had a man watching it after all. Gus could hear padded footfalls in the backyard grass but couldn't make out anyone walking through the darkness. He could still hear faint footfalls in the grass moving toward him, though. Gus turned around fast and hit his flashlight toward the faint noises. The image of two small girls appeared in the illuminated area. Gus clicked the flashlight off quickly. He didn't want to draw the attention of the thug next door. He glanced back through the hole, but his thug hadn't bothered noticing the creaking gate or the flicker of the lights next door. The magazine that he was reading must have been a good one.

Gus took a few steps away from the fence. There were no-good thugs next door, so he needed to get those darn kids indoors to safety. You never took chances with stupid thugs, even if they appeared at least to be literate stupid thugs. Gus squinted and tried to make out the exact whereabouts of those children as his eyes readjusted to the darkness. Try as he might, though, he couldn't make them out. Where had those two kids snuck off to? Then he felt a tug on his pants. He flicked the flashlight on, and there standing right beside him were the two little girls. The two noisemakers had somehow silently snuck right up upon him. It reminded him that kids, though they might be noisy a lot of the time, can be extremely silent when they want to be.

"Mister, what's going on?" asked the neighbor's girl in a soft whisper.

"Shhh," replied Gus with a finger to his lips. He turned the flashlight off again. He continued with his own whisper, "There's a man over there on my porch, and me and him are playing kind of a quiet game."

"Is he a Darvelak or a Minimite?" asked the neighbor.

"He's a bad guy, and I'm a good guy. He wants to hurt me, and I'd rather he didn't hurt anyone," replied Gus.

"Good guys and bad guys sounds like a very boring type of game to play. There are no bad guys and good guys in Death to Hungry Kids. There are just the lucky Darvelaks that get to live in the beautiful golden City of Primal and then the unlucky poor Minimites that have to fight each other to entertain them so they get thrown some scraps of food to eat.

That sounds like a much more sensible game to play to me," whispered back the girl of unknown origin.

"Well, be that as it may, Sheriff Gus needs you two to run along inside and play indoors. Good guys and bad guys is more of a grown-up game and not for you two kids to go about getting mixed up in. I'm sure you got some dolls inside, so go play with them," whispered Gus.

The girl of unknown origin whispered back, "Don't you know nothing? I can't play with them, silly, because I'm the Minimite. I have to give my dolls to a Darvelak and then watch her play with them. It wouldn't be right for a Minimite to play with dolls, since they are supposed to have nothing. That kind of stuff isn't in the movies, and those movies are the bestest."

"Bestest," echoed the neighbor's girl in a low voice.

"Well, you two girls run along and maybe just switch roles. She can be a Darvelak for a while, and then you can be one for a while, and that way you both get to play with the dolls," explained Gus in a hushed but rising voice.

"That's stupid. What Darvelak would give up being a Darvelak just so a Minimite can play with some dolls? It definitely isn't like in the movies," replied the neighbor's girl.

"Those movies are the bestest. The last sequel comes out tomorrow. We can't wait to see how it all ends!" replied the girl of unknown origin.

"Fine, play any way you want to play, but do it indoors. It is nighttime out here, and little girls ought not to play around in the dark because, ah… it's hard to see how bestest the game is being played when it's being played in the dark."

The two girls nodded in agreement to that statement; then the girl of unknown origin said, "Come on, let's go inside; I can't wait to watch you play with my dolls!"

"If you watch me play real good with them, maybe I'll let you eat something tonight," replied the neighbor's daughter.

"Bestest!" answered back the girl of unknown origin.

The two girls ran quickly into Rosa's house through the back door in rather amazing silence. He waited until the sound of the back door of the house could be barely heard opening and closing. He made one last attempt to spy on his own house next door through the hole in the fence. The generous thug was still reading his magazine. The man must be blind, deaf, and dumb, but an avid reader.

Gus slipped away from the fence. He clicked the flashlight back on. He made his way back to the gate in the chain-link fence. There was no reason to be in darkness if the thugs were going to volunteer such lack of attentiveness. Gus placed the light on the childproof device. It was a simple little plastic thing. There was tiny writing on it that could have been in Egyptian hieroglyphs for all Gus knew without having reading glasses to read them. Gus tried depressing the central button on the device while gripping it hard. The plastic shell engaged the metal handle of the gate. He turned it and opened the chain-link fence. It was a small victory for an adult against the childproof world of parents. Gus now turned the flashlight off and slipped down the fence line. He reached the corner where the chain-link met the wooden fence. He peeked around the corner at the inattentive thug with the expensive assault rifle lying on his lap.

There were three hundred precious feet between Gus and the thug. The light on the porch made the backyard too bright to hope to move to the porch unnoticed. There was one thug on the porch, but who knew how many lay inside waiting. Gus kicked his shoes off. He'd be more silent moving in his stocking feet. There was only one thing he could do. Gus rapidly moved through his own backyard straight at the thug. He had the flashlight raised in his right hand to use as a club. It was an ineffective weapon against a man wielding an assault rifle but an effective one against a thug who didn't seem eager to use his weapon or his own eyes. The thug paid no attention as the rapidly moving death closed in on him. Gus moved right in, and his flashlight hovered over the back of the man's head. Gus briefly saw what the man was reading that drew so much attention. The man was watching the pictures of a nudie movie playing on a flat-screen widget. He was not the first man to be done in by paying too much attention to a pretty woman and not enough attention to his job. It happened to every man at one time or another. Gus drew down the flashlight onto the thug's head. The flashlight exploded as its head shattered on the man's thick skull. The batteries, shattered plastic, the flat-screen widget, the assault rifle, and the thug all crashed down to the porch pavement with a thud. Gus kicked the thug in the gut to make sure he was either dead or unconscious. The thug didn't move, but he was still breathing. Gus relieved him of his assault rifle.

Gus opened his own back door and stepped inside. He was in a small, enclosed porch. It was designed as a mudroom by an architect who apparently had never visited this dry county. Gus quickly moved through it. He pressed himself to the wall and gazed into the kitchen. There at Gus's kitchen table sat the rotund Antonio casually eating a churro while waiting for the thugs to signal him that Gus was about to stroll through his own front door. Gus crept up to the chewing Antonio and pressed the tip of the nozzle of the assault rifle into the exposed small of Antonio's neck. Antonio didn't make any sudden motions.

He casually swallowed the bit of churro he was gnawing on and said, "*Amigo*, I will get to the point quickly; I believe you have my son."

Gus replied harshly, "Your beliefs have nothing to do with it. Whether you believe it or not, I have him."

"I've come in peace and friendship. I don't mean any harm, so can we dispense with the weapon?"

"There was an armed thug on my back porch, so you can see how I got the wrong impression about your meanings."

"The thugs were to protect me and not harm you. I could not harm you, Sheriff Gus, without Big Gustavo's *bien*. So please put the gun away and tell me what you want in exchange for my only son."

Gus pulled the gun from the back of Antonio's neck but kept it pointed at him as he maneuvered around the table to converse with him face-to-face. Gus replied, "Let me limp over and get a good look at the man that doesn't mean me any harm. The last time you came by in peace, my knees ended up black-and-blue. They still hurt, you know. What was the point of all that hitting and warning? I can't stop an idiot like Sheldon Nickelback any more than I can stop you idiots from moving about. We both know how ineffective the law is against a man like Sheldon Nickelback."

Antonio took a bite of his churro. He replied with a full mouth, "I'm just a messenger of Big Gustavo. I meant you no real harm. This business is nothing personal between us. Now that you got that off your chest, tell me what you want. I told you what I want. I want my son back and free of these false charges you have laid upon him."

Gus dug his hands into his front pocket and pulled out a yellow sheet of notepaper. He placed it down in front of Antonio. He explained, "That is my plan. It is all pretty simple to follow. You wanted to know what I want, and it is all written down there. I dotted the i's and crossed the t's, so you shouldn't be confused as to what I'm asking from you and what I need you to do." Antonio shoved the rest of the churro into his mouth to free his hands of it. He wiped his hands on Gus's tablecloth and then picked up the yellow note.

He was a fast reader. He turned to Gus and said, "*Amigo*, this is a lot of *dinero* to be asking for."

"It's not your money, and I'm possibly willing to share it with you if you can retrieve it. But to do that, you first have to retrieve it and then launder it for me. I need it clean without any strings attached to this county. It is possible that I'm sick of this life here and willing to let go of it all for the right price. A man only has so many knees to bash in."

A voice came out from the front of the house. "*Escuché voces, te encuentras bien?*"

Antonio replied, "*Todo está bien!*" Gus had no idea what was said. Antonio hadn't agreed yet to the deal. He was fumbling with the yellow paper in his hand. He was a careful man, because great care was needed to stay on Big Gustavo's good side. Antonio said, "And Sheldon Nickelback, you will be forcing him out of town then?"

"I can't do anything about him," replied Gus.

"No, no, no, no," Antonio let go of the yellow sheet of paper and let it drop onto the kitchen table. He slammed both his hands down and repeated, "No! There is no deal then."

"I can't do what you want me to do. I won't let you help that man out. You'll just have to trust me on the fact that the less I do about him, the better off we all are with him."

"I do not understand, my friend."

"I'm saying to leave that man alone."

"We leave him alone? It was not Big Gustavo that did that thing to his house. We don't work that way. The way Big Gustavo works is he kills those he thinks needs to be killed. We just want him to pack up his bags and leave. He killed a boy for nothing, nothing. My organization is at least a good businessman about whom we kill, and that's why I won't personally kill this Sheldon Nickelback. It's bad for business. We just want to make him go away and leave our sons and daughters alone in safety. He's not welcome here."

Gus replied, "He set fire to a cross on his own lawn to blame people like you to get people like me to do something about it all. I won't stir up more shit than is needed. He's bad news, this man, but he's good press. I won't help him get press of any kind if I can help it. Leave that man alone. Don't play his game."

Antonio placed his hand on the yellow piece of paper. "Games, it is you that wants to play games," replied Antonio. It was then that the home phone took the inopportune time to start ringing. He said, "You might as well answer it. It isn't for me, my friend."

Annoyed, Gus tossed the assault rifle down on the kitchen table and went over to answer the phone. The goons Gus feared, but Antonio wasn't about to shoot the only man who knew his son was innocent. Certainly he wasn't going to shoot him now that he had a simple deal to free him with no strings attached. Gus watched Antonio pull the yellow sheet out from under the rifle. Antonio was as interested in watching Gus as Gus was interested in watching Antonio. No one in the house knew exactly what was going on. There was a deal out in the air to consider, but one phone call could change everything. Gus jerked the slim line-white phone from the kitchen wall. "Hello, this is Sheriff Gus in the sheriff's house. I am busy being assaulted by a gang of Mexican thugs, so if this is a law-enforcement emergency and you need assistance, please hang up and dial a nine followed by two ones."

The voice broke up into laughter. It was Terrance on the other end of the line. Terrance replied, "I am glad to find you in good spirits, because I have just terrible news."

172

"Is this news more or less terrible than a Mexican gang member pointing an assault rifle at me in an attempt to murder me?"

"I'm sure I don't know the answer to that question, but it is terrible news nonetheless. It's about our gold prize. I'm afraid we are losing it just when they were starting to bring name recognition on the national airways for our fair county."

"Well, that's a shame Sheldon Nickelback is leaving town. We all have a cross to bear, although they usually don't burst into flames. Tell me when he's done packing up, and I'll be sure to show up and kick him in the behind to wish him good luck grifting a few dimes away from some other county's good-natured suckers."

"What! Oh, not that gold prize. Don't be silly, Gus; Sheldon is very happy here. I heard from him just this afternoon about how much money they've raised for him already. That cross burning was terrible news and has thus shaken a lot of sympathetic dollars free. We'll raise even more after the photo shoot with you and Deputy Lopez together on that horse tomorrow. Right now we're only collecting from a select few. The image of our county, represented by you, being friendlier with minority relations will help loosen a broader spectrum of pockets."

"Do you really think one officer getting hired is enough to erase years of racial profiling from people's minds?"

"Hmm…Gus, don't sidetrack my thinking. I'm thinking about the lost prize tonight. All those fancy high-price civil-rights lawyers have lost their appeals to our governor. The governor has gone and lost her good senses and is planning to sign the extradition papers tomorrow! Can you believe that she would want to rob this state of a chance at weeks of daily national attention? The networks can't show enough of the antics those abortion protestors are doing in front of the capitol! There must be thousands of them by now. Think of all the publicity! It's the best thing to happen to this state since we rejected fluorinated water based on our fear of communism."

"You're telling me that the camera-lens-friendly gawking zoo that is growing and growing day by day in front of my station as well as her governor's mansion is the stuff the governor doesn't strongly desire to continue to be shown on national television? I guess you're right, Terrance; that is a surprise. I thought it would be another week before she figured that out."

"Exactly! I wish there was something that could be done to prolong this blessed event."

"If I think of something, then you'll be the last person I call, Terrance." Gus hung up. Gus had just been proved wrong at the worst possible time. He had planned on this thing dragging on for ages. Never in his wildest imagination did he think the governor would act so quickly. Politicians in general weren't known these days for taking swift action or any action. The national professional second-guessers and critics with no better ideas would be howling now that she had decided. It made sense, though, now that he thought about it. Mistakes become clearer only once they've become the past. The national circus would now travel to Kansas to start the zoo all over. The governor would take a few days grief for making a decision, and then it would all be forgotten as the traveling dung-feast dug into the Kansas governor. The governor had done the smart thing and passed the buck. Gus had never planned on a politician arriving on the smartest path so quickly. He was in trouble. He rubbed his temple, trying to stimulate a new plan.

Antonio spoke, "Did that phone call ruin this little yellow paper filled with your plans?"

Gus stared at the eyes of the fat Mexican at his kitchen table. This stupid problem had really originated in Mexico. It should be their problem, not his. Then somewhere in the back of his brain a voice called out, *Then make it their problem!* Gus pulled the drawer open and took out a pen. He went over to the kitchen table and wrote another sentence on the yellow sheet of paper. When he was done writing, Antonio picked it up and read it quickly. Antonio balled up the piece of paper and tossed it to the table.

He declared, "This is an impossible task to do in such a short time. I am not sure even I can convince Big Gustavo to do such a thing. It may bring national attention to him. He doesn't like to have any attention drawn on him."

Gus unballed the paper and placed it in front of Antonio again. He explained, "It doesn't have to be real. You know people. Dress them up and have them play the part. It only needs to complicate matters long enough to give me perhaps just one more good solid day. That should be enough time for you to get the money together to pay me for your only son. Then everything else on the paper happens as planned. There is a lot of money potentially to be made from all this. Big Gustavo likes money. We all do. I know you like money. You cleaned out Terry Tang's house of the stuff just the other day."

"Did we?"

"I sure hope you did. I arrested him and took his drugs and guns away, but I left the money for your goons to find. They found it all right, didn't they? You see how I'm trying to help you, Antonio. All this is for you and Big Gustavo. I'm a team player. I just need a little bit of help from your side of the team."

Antonio got out of his chair. He picked up the sheet and folded it into his suit pocket. He nodded in agreement. "Pretend for a moment that I do not like such dishonesty as a rule, but understand that I am willing to do this evil act for my only son's sake. I am sure Big Gustavo will do it just for the money. It is a hard game you will be playing, but it's your pretty little neck on the line if things go wrong. Big Gustavo won't kill a man like Sheldon Nickelback, but if you harm my son, I will make sure he kills you." He got up from the table with the note in his hand and started to waddle his fat behind toward the front door.

Gus called out to him, "Don't forget to pick up the trash in my back-yard."

Gus yawned and looked at his watch. He was hoping a little more of this morning's future had come to be written down in the history books as the past while he slept, but a late start to the day wasn't to be. He hopped down from the sheriff's truck and made his way to Deputy Lopez's patrol car. She was sitting on the hood drinking coffee from a foam cup and eating a churro from a white wax bag by the light of the dawn's sun cracking over the roadside minimarket. Gus sat down on the hood next to her. The car's shocks gave way a little more, and they both sank closer to the earth. Gus said, "Chiquita, you seem like a woman on a mission. Not that I didn't welcome your call this morning, but don't you ever sleep?"

"Churro?" she asked, offering the bag to him.

Gus took a deep breath. The bag filled with churros smelled heavenly. His figure, however, had already had one churro too many ages ago. He sighed. "How do women end up looking like you by eating crap like that? It doesn't seem fair somehow, if you ask me."

"They invented this thing called exercise; perhaps you should try it now and then."

"Is that right? Big science, you never know what they'll invent next. Speaking of which, science that is, you haven't seen any climate scientists hanging around the station lately, have you? I have it on authority there might be a few hanging around town causing trouble."

"You're a funny man. I never know what you're going to ask next. I can assure you that there are a lot of people hanging out by the station, but I think lessons in modern science are gladly missed by most of them."

"Hmm…I didn't think there would be, but I had to ask. Well, I've come to an important decision. I won't exercise, but I will eat one of your churros anyways, because I got a feeling it would make you feel better if I did."

Gus slid a churro out of the bag. Deputy Lopez dug her ticket booklet from her pocket. She plopped it down on Gus's lap. It was rather light on account of it missing a bunch of pages. Gus scratched his chin and ignored the pastry for a second. He took out his reading glasses, found the sweet spot left in the lenses, and then flipped through the stubs. There were a lot of familiar names on those stubs. Names you knew like old friends if you were a frequent customer, like Gus was, of the Arroyo National Bank. It was fast work. Deputy Lopez had nailed just about every bank employee on multiple moving violations. One name was missing. It was the key name. "You didn't get anything on Frank?"

"I could have, but I didn't. I followed my commanding officer's orders to the letter. This Frank Patterson left the bank a little after closing, rolled a stop sign, but I resisted the temptation to nail him for it. I was smart to do so, for he goes around after hours picking up drop bags from the local business. You're a trusting little small town here in your county. He didn't drive these bags to the bank for safekeeping for the night. I got curious as to why. I watched the money in the trunk all night. The reason was most likely laziness and a false sense of trust. It turns out he had a few more stops to do this morning. There is nothing criminal in this that I can see, although it certainly seems unwise. He should hire an armored-car company to do this work."

"I figure the local businesses don't make enough money to worry old Frank. Where is he now?"

"He's in the Laundromat next to the minimarket picking up another bag."

"How long do you think he'll be?"

"Don't know. Bank opens in a few hours, so I figure he'll be done collecting by then."

"Which car is his?"

"He owns the black BMW in the minimarket parking lot."

Gus whistled. "That's one nice car if you can afford it. A fancy car like that only takes premium gas. I've never owned a vehicle like that, Deputy Lopez. I don't see the point. Buying a car that runs only on premium gas is like paying extra for the prettiest hooker on the street when all you want is blow job."

"You're a very classy man."

"The funny thing is I don't even try to be. It just comes natural to me. I'm a very classy man that's gonna go peak at the contents of that BMW's trunk. I got a hunch there's drug money inside that trunk."

"I already told you what's in it, and I got a whole list of legitimate businesses where the money came from. I don't think any of them small businesses are a front for drugs. He's just picking up money to drop in their accounts in the bank."

"I know that, but I also know there's a drug dealer or two in my jail. One of them has deposit slips from that bank. That means there's drug money about in Frank's bank. I got suspicion, and the law says I don't need proof, only suspicion in this instance. Facts on the innocence of that money in this case will be for Frank Patterson to prove in open court. Technically it will be his money's job to prove its innocence. Frank is innocent until proven guilty, but in this great nation of laws, his money isn't so lucky. I can seize it, lock it up, and throw away the key no matter how innocent Frank is based only on my suspicion that Frank's money isn't so innocent. It's easier for me to suspect his guilt the more money that's in his trunk."

"It sounds like stealing to me."

"When the police steal from you, they call it asset forfeiture. Isn't the law great, Deputy Lopez? I heard Frank, our boy over there, is a real by-the-books type of man when it comes to the fine print in contractual law. He's going to enjoy learning this little part of the law. It's my right to take his money, and I'm going to take it and wrap it up in so much red tape he'll be lucky if he sees it again in this lifetime."

"Why do it? He's no money launderer."

"Oh, don't worry about it, because I got a feeling Frank will get his money back faster than you think. I'm not a thief, and I don't want his money. This is just like all the tickets you've been writing for those bank people, a small indication to our friend Frank to consider more than the letters of the law."

"I don't understand."

"It doesn't matter that you do at the moment. The less you know the better it is for you. Good work, Deputy. I'll see you at the photo shoot this morning."

"What shoot? Terrance called me last night and said it was off."

"He didn't..." Gus stopped short. Frank left the Laundromat with a red bag full of cash. He opened his trunk and placed it in. He then went over to the minimarket with an empty bag in hand and went inside. "Sorry,

I'd like to talk more, but I got to move while I have my chance." He took out a screwdriver and headed toward Frank's BMW.

He had cleaned out twelve red bags in total from the trunk of Frank's very fine BMW. Each bag was partially filled with spent greenbacks. Gus had to jimmy Frank's lock with a screwdriver. The cost of that repair on the back trunk might be more than the total amount of money Gus had stolen from Frank, or forfeited for the greater good of society, depending how you viewed the law. It wasn't like local business was booming, so Gus knew the cash total wouldn't be very high. Gus figured he didn't net more than five thousand in all. It wasn't a large sum of money he wanted from Frank. The knowledge that the sheriff's office was seizing money from the bank due to its alleged laundering of cash for drug dealers would be enough to hurt the bank's reputation far more than the five thousand dollars taken from it. The bank's money would eventually win in court, and Frank would get the money back. But who of sound mind would put their hard-earned money away inside a banking institution where you never knew if someone was going to seize it and make your assets disappear into worthless credit to be paid later at any moment? Perhaps a few people, but the stock market scooped up most of that business already. The looting of Frank's BMW was another small step toward a larger goal, but Gus felt frustrated all the same. There were more important things to do today, and all this silliness with the bank wasn't one of them.

Frustration is the desire to do something, but not the ability to do it. For Gus the limiting factor in his newfound impotence was time. Time was ticking away this morning, and yet there was no place to go to spend it unwisely. He knew for a fact what time the governor was going to sign the extradition papers today. There was a press conference called for in the state capital at twelve noon sharp to broadcast it live on television. It would be on the news coast to coast and perhaps even around the world. When she was done putting her John Hancock on those papers, a lawman from Kansas was planning on personally driving the signed papers down to Gus's law-enforcement complex to hand them to another lawman from Kansas. That lawman would hand them to Gus, and his half-week nightmare would start to be over. The lawman from Kansas with the doomsday papers was due to arrive at the law-enforcement complex at approximately two o'clock, depending on traffic. That meant if things went well today, then this county's nightmare would be over, but the tragic tale of the Jennifer Louis Bachman show would go on and on. The only thing that would change for her show was the venue of the set. For poor Jennifer, the show would likely never stop. Win or lose in court, the press would hound her until the day she died. For many she was the symbol of the heartless killer who never should be allowed to walk this earth free. There was nothing Gus could do to speed up the process to draw the curtains to a close on her tale as it pertained to him.

The news on Gus's truck radio of the governor's acquiescence had spread like wildfire since last night. It was the only story being addressed on the talking-head chatter that substituted for radio news channels this morning. Gus was sitting in his truck finishing off another bag of churros—you couldn't just eat one—and listening to news about his own workplace where everyone was broadcasting live from. Those media types were making sure to give this story wall-to-wall coverage. Each channel had its own talking-head expert who claimed to know everything on any subject. They talked about Gus's county like they were all longtime residents. Mostly what they claimed to know was wrong, but there was no one with any real knowledge on set to correct them. Listening to the media was making it difficult to finish his churros. The only news Gus got out of listening to it was that they were sure making it seem like today was a good day to be anywhere else but inside that law-enforcement complex. You wouldn't envy the poor sucker who was going to have to march that poor young woman out of there into that media feeding frenzy and crowd of victorious pro-lifers. That sucker was going to be him.

Luckily, no bad idea from Terrance ever went completely away, and thus Gus was fated to fill some of the waiting time in purgatory in the blessed place he most wanted to find himself in—anywhere but the law-enforcement complex. Terrance's value system on good and bad could be questioned, but when you wanted to avoid the hellhole at work, doing Terrance's little photo-shoot stunt could be considered good. So that was why Gus set down his bag of churros on the dashboard and started up the truck again. He was going to waste Jennifer's last sane hours of ticking time driving through the ranchland of the county to find Terrance's little photo-shoot set rather than sitting in purgatory waiting to condemn the alleged criminal to a very public damnation.

The trial balloon of Terrance's photo-shoot idea hadn't gone away, but Deputy Lopez had left the plot, which meant Terrance was up to something. He hadn't filled Gus in on the new details in his plan. This assignment was only expressed as a simple little procedure. Gus was supposed to show up at Lester Cravitz's ranch. Then he was expected to ride a few horses around waving a cowboy hat in the air so the national cameras from the networks could see a real live lawman from the county in action. The people in favor of sending Jennifer Louis Bachman to the gallows would naturally assume that old-time cowboy sheriff was on their side, the people in favor of a woman's choice would naturally assume the old-time cowboy sheriff was not on their side, and lastly the vast majority of people who didn't care would naturally assume a place with a great old-time cowboy sheriff was a great place to spend tourist dollars. This logic train was what Terrance was banking on, and you never got poor banking with the public's dollars.

The only problem with this fine plan was that first and foremost, Gus didn't know how to ride a horse. A not-so-trivial second problem lay in the fact that Gus simply hated horses with a blinding passion. Perhaps hated was too strong a word. Scared to death of the beasts might come closer to the truth. The only use Gus had for the animals was placing bets on them in the casinos, and even then the horse rarely did him a lick of good. The horses seemed to have a sixth sense about which one he had bet on, and even the deadest cert was determined to fail when Gus's money was placed on it. Still, getting trampled by a horse for the good of the national media's cameras felt like a better activity for wallowing away the morning hours than heading down to work so as to make a larger target for the few thousand screaming protestors. When you're spoiled for choice, the choice that kills time wins, and the photo shoot would certainly do that.

Gus pulled the sheriff's truck into the dusty driveway of Lester Cravitz. It wasn't that long ago Lester had sold the drilling rights to his land, but so far no one had bothered to exercise those rights. Lester had thought those rights might make him rich, but he hadn't figured drilling rights were rights better written down as theories and would be seldom used in practice. What all that meant, as Gus figured it, was that Lester was highly motivated to attract a few extra dollars from another revenue source. Terrance had sized up the situation correctly, no doubt, and thus gotten Lester's approval to use his horses for this morning's media spectacle.

Gus made his way through the gathering of media that had bothered to show up for the event. The media turned out to be exactly like Gus. Since they were all dressed up but with no place to go until the two o'clock deadline, they were more than eager to fill their twenty-four hours of air-time with any old crap someone was ready to feed them. Going out and getting news was hard work; just showing crap people gave you was easy, and no one ever accused the national media of working hard. Terrance was giving them a crap-feast of an event to shoot, and they seemed more than eager to cover the crap event with all the skill they had at their disposal. The media's crap was everywhere. They brought cameras, lights, makeup, and personalities. The real talent stayed in the studio. The future talent had to travel to counties like Gus's to cover absolute crap, but they were personalities all the same.

Terrance and Lester were standing next to the paddock surrounded by cameras. It was a slow news day, but it still seemed like too many people were here for just a feel-good story about a county sheriff hiring an attractive minority woman who wasn't even at the event. Certainly they hadn't all come here just to see fat old Gus. He examined his watch. It was only ten. There was still too much time to kill. Gus didn't want to think about it anymore and went into the fray.

A horse poked his head out of the stable door as Gus approached the paddock. The horse had a little of the Luis Suarez about it as it bared its teeth. Gus went up to Terrance and Lester and patted them both on the shoulders. He then turned to give a good solid wave of the white cowboy hat to the cameras. The cameras weren't shy and shot him greeting them all with a howdy. Having satisfied the media beast, Gus sized up the situation; he figured if he placed Terrance between him and the horse sticking his head out of the stable door, he'd be safe for now. The grand goal was somehow to correct Terrance about his notion that Gus could ride a horse.

"Gus, we have to make this whole thing work quickly. The media won't stay here too long before they'll get antsy and head back into town. Lester here was going to just pop you on Diomedes here, and we'll ride the two of you out into the paddock for a nice photo spread. Look at the cameras over there. They'll eat this whole thing up. People love this old-time Americana bullshit. A real live cowboy in real live cowboy country; they'll love it," greeted Terrance.

"I'd love to meet this real cowboy; when does he show up?" replied Gus.

"Good one, Gus. I'm glad to see you're in a cheerful mood. I want a big smile for those cameras out there. Remember, you're selling this county to the people on the other end of those cameras."

"I'm surprised to see so many cameras out here, to tell you the truth. I know the show don't begin up in the capital until noon and downtown until early this afternoon, but I figured these boys would all be jockeying for the plum spots."

"Naturally I did sweeten the pie a little for them this morning."

"How sweet did you make that pie?"

Just then Sheldon Nickelback rode out of the stable on a black mare. He dug his spur heels into her and seemed to be enjoying the riding experience. The cameras just about exploded at the sight of him. The crowd rushed by Gus and pressed against the wooden paddock fence. Each newsperson wanted to be the first to get that killer shot of last year's most famous television celebrity murderer-to-be.

Gus gave Terrance a sour look, and Terrence simply replied, "I'm losing one star today, but I sure as hell am not going to let those boys with the cameras forget we still got Sheldon Nickelback in this county with all his glory. When you attract a star to live in your city, then you use that star, Gus!"

"No doubt someone is getting used in all this."

"No time for that; I need you on this horse. I got to have someone representing this county out there with Sheldon to advertise this county to America. I want every American watching their television at home to know what this county stands for."

"What do we stand for?" asked Gus.

"An awful bunch of bullshit, but so long as it pays the bills," said Lester out of the blue. He then grabbed the saddle for the horse and headed into the barn. "C'mon, Sheriff, I'll take care of you." Gus shrugged and followed Lester. Lester guided Gus through the barn to the business end of Diomedes. Lester saddled the horse while Gus nervously watched. A horse wasn't that bad up close. The back end could kick the shit out of you, and the front end might bite you, but Gus reminded himself it was all part of the job. Lester then went over and got a ladder and placed it next to the horse. He motioned to Gus. "I use this ladder for the kiddie parties, but since you're a novice, I thought you'd need it. There ain't no nothing to be afraid 'bout. This here horse is as friendly as they come. You climb up there and sit on his back calm-like. Then I'll hold this here reins and guide good ole Diomedes out. You don't do nothing but wave your hat. Bunch of bullshit for the cameras, and them city folk will eat it up, I guarantee yah. They's out there are a stupid, ravenous bunch."

Gus nodded in agreement on that part. He climbed the rickety ladder to the top. The ladder was meant for eight-year-old girls' birthday parties and not a plus-sized man past middle age. Still, the ladder held. Lester motioned with his leg, indicating for Gus to swing it around and sit on the horse. The horse craned his neck around and appeared to give Gus the evil eye. A horse has the good sense to know a phony from the real thing. The scent of fear must have been percolating off Gus. The horse played with him by flaring his nostrils once with a hard blow of stale air. Lester responded by laughing and feeding the horse something out of his hand. Gus closed his eyes and swung his leg out. Somehow his buttocks landed in the saddle of the great beast. He was no sooner down in the safety of the saddle when Lester started to guide Gus out of the stable door into the paddock. Gus was white with fear, but as long as he kept his eyes closed, he managed things all right. His mind flashed the idea that riding a horse was just like riding a bicycle, only without the two deaths a day that bicycle riding produced nationally.

Gus shouted to Lester, "This horse doesn't bite, does it?"

"Diomedes doesn't bite anyone; he swallows them whole," laughed Lester.

The response didn't build Gus's confidence up. The horse was striding, and Gus's bottom was bouncing. It was a sore point that Terrance hadn't advertised when pitching the idea. Finally the horse stopped moving. Gus slowly opened his eyes. He was out in the paddock at some distance from the media horde gawking from the wooden rails of the fence. Terrance was sitting on the top wooden rail saying some speech about today's event. Gus couldn't hear it properly, so as speeches go, he assumed it was a good speech. If the media was paying a lick of attention to Terrance, then it was likely due to incredible boredom. Lester was holding the reins firm, and the horse was at least a steady mount when standing still. Gus palmed the white cowboy hat on his head and raised it high into the air. The media crowd went wild, not with cheers of praise, but with simple relief to finally be able to film something for the studios back in New York. Now the attraction they really wanted came together. Sheldon rode his horse side by side with Gus. The media loved it. Terrance droned on and on as media people with their cameras pointed at Gus and Sheldon while talking over Terrance's speech as they babbled to studio people back home. Whatever their interpretation of today's events was, it was certainly a subject of mystery to Gus at this distance.

"Look at them over there, Gus. They're lovin' this shit. I reckon I oughta have charged Terrance double for these horses," said Lester.

"Just keep me alive, Lester, and I'll see that Terrance pays you."

Sheldon trotted his horse in a circle for the cameras and then back up alongside Gus. He was all smiles for the camera. He asked Gus, "Did you find any suspects yet for that fire?"

"I reckon I've narrowed down the list plenty," replied Gus.

"Hispanics?"

"I'm not willing to commit totally in any one direction just yet."

"Good man, you know I don't have much against them personally…"

"No, you just shoot them," interjected Gus.

"It could have been any race of hostile kid under that lamppost that night. I shot who was there. I did it in self-defense. People love a good self-defense story. Well…some people. Other people hate it. Either the love or the hate brings me fame. That's the game, Sheriff; that's the game. Don't be in too big a hurry to solve my little fire. Fan the flames for me, because the press loves a slow reveal, and so do my lawyers. I wrote Wilton my first check yesterday. I think he's blowing the cash on that murderer in your jail, but it's his money to blow. I just need one more score to finish paying him off; then the rest becomes profit. Lester, pull that horse nice and close to me so they can get a nice photo of the happy sheriff with America's former number-one suspect here in this field together. The only thing those cameras out there like doing more than tearing a man down are building him back up."

"You seem to have been managing them all pretty well since the beginning."

"Shit, the lawyers did all the real work. I had a vague plan of self-defense, but Wilton is a genius and knew how to make it hum. The funny thing about my life is that I was truly no one until I shot that boy. Then those cameras out there made me a star because of it. Wilton pumped the media stories about me hating Hispanics, and those media types knew just how to run with it. It got the sympathy of a certain persuasion of people all right. The media out there helped convince the all-white jury too. I've watched my share of the news over the years. It taught me how to properly feed the media and let them make you a star. I always wanted to be a star. The thing I figured out in all this mess was that all this coverage might help keep me out of jail, but it didn't really do me any good otherwise. I'm the star, but they make all the money from their little news shows. It isn't cheap to keep your ass out of jail. As I've said, I got plenty of debts. It didn't seem fair that the stories are always about me and my exploits, and yet I wasn't receiving a dime from that coverage. I was the highest-rated story on the twenty-four-hour news networks for a good solid year. I was a star, but a dirt-poor one. You stick with me, Sheriff, and I'll get them to make a star out of you too. I love them over there as much as I love this horse. I love driving a mustang with or without the cameras."

Gus replied, "I thought the generous people of this county bought you a Corvette."

"They did; they did. The wonderful and giving people in this county; I came here to be saved, and they're saving me with their savings. As I told you, when my trial ended, I was at wits' end financially. I had all this coverage and fame but no money. It was tough, I can tell you that, but the people of this county are helping me get over that and made me appreciate what those cameras out there can do more and more. I needed to find a place with a high concentration of my kind of people. You know, people with generous pockets that were motivated into giving based on what they saw happen to a man on the television. Skip Lipschitz told me there are ample amounts of sympathetic people living in this town, and I can tell you this county hasn't disappointed me yet. First become a star, use your fame correctly, and then the money will flow. I always believed in myself."

Gus grumbled, "If you wander by my law-enforcement complex, I think you'll discover I'm no stranger to the media circus and how it makes ordinary life a little hard for you. I might even sympathize with you a little on account of it."

"Look at that mob at that fence. Tomorrow when Skip's phone-bank volunteers hit the marketplace, we will raise twice the money for me that the sympathy from that cross fire raised the other day. Those cameras aren't going to be around me forever, I figure, so I need to strike while the fire is hot. God bless this little county of yours. I used to be no one, and now I'm a star. In a few weeks' time I'll be a filthy-rich star. Those are the best kind of stars. Stick with me, Sheriff, and maybe I'll make you some money too. The people here are not at all like those where I used to live. I do not suffer fools gladly, so I'm glad to be rid of those whiny fools from my old hometown."

"If you don't suffer fools, then it must be a hard time being you."

187

Before Sheldon could respond, the media gaggle broke up and started hustling to their cars and trucks. Terrance tried to corner a friendly local station or two, but they all had pressing business. Sheldon Nickelback was, after all, only yesterday's news. The fire had kept his limelight lit a while longer, but all these journalists understood that Jennifer Louis Bachman's trial was going to be the future. She was the going to dominate the news in the year to come. Sheldon was a star but a fading one, and Jennifer's fame was on the rise. They had time to kill, and they had killed it, and now it was time to catch a rising star.

Sheldon lamented, "Where are they going?"

"They're sending a young woman up the river due a misunderstanding about biology. I figure they're all lining up to get in the best position to assassinate her character live for the folks back home. If you hurry to downtown, then you might get one last chance to shoot her in order to get back into the news cycle."

"No, thanks. If they got to send someone up the river, then it is better her than an honest man like me," replied Sheldon, and he kicked his horse and rode off.

Gus watched him head back to the barn. The media news wagons were starting to depart back to the city. Even Terrance was departing after flashing a quick thumbs-up to Gus. Gus couldn't figure out who'd desire to visit the county based on a brief media segment that made them all look like clowns in a three-ring circus, but Terrance was happy, so what did it matter. Gus nodded to Lester. "Let's bring the horse inside. I think this dog-and-pony show is over for the day."

By the time Gus got down from the horse, the field was nearly empty. The last vehicle in it was a white Corvette driven by Skip Lipschitz. Gus wandered out of the barn to see Sheldon Nickelback wave him good-bye as he ducked into passenger side of the car, and then he and Skip drove off together. They were likely heading to another fund raiser. It was hard work paying off your lawyers, even for a celebrity. It was harder when you wanted to net a large profit for yourself as well. Gus's plan to not help Sheldon get any more publicity was sure working as well as all his plans worked. Gus took his hat off his head. He had survived the media onslaught up to now, but the real games were about to begin. He headed to his sheriff's truck standing out lonely in the field. An old Mexican man in overalls was standing next to Gus's truck. Gus didn't know the man, and he eyed him with suspicion. The man was standing rather close to the driver's-side door. When Gus got close enough, he barked out in an unfriendly fashion to him, "Did Antonio send you?"

"I don't know any Antonio. No, I am…"

Gus walked by the man and opened the back of the truck. He tossed the cowboy hat inside. It landed on a pile of red bags partially filled with the bank's forfeited money. The propaganda campaign was over. Now he circled back around the truck, coming up on the man from behind. "Ah, you're from the burning-cross people. Excuse me, but there's so much nonsense going on these days even I get lost as to who is who."

"Excuse me, sir, but that is a lie. I don't want you taking that accusation personal, but when I hear a lie, I say so."

"Well, you are a more honest a man than I first thought. I don't see much of that these days."

"It is just that I…we…people I know, they think that this man, Sheldon Nickelback, ought not to be living here."

"He's a free man, so he can come and go as he likes."

"But, Sheriff, he ought not to have come here. He's stirring up trouble. Look at what happened the other day with that cross. I don't condone things like that, but it just goes to show that he's stirring up a lot of anger on both sides of the issue. That man should go before another poor boy is shot. I can't understand when a boy dies how there can be another side of the issue, but I've seen enough television to know they can create a side where no side should exist. The thing is that this reflects badly on the whole community. Surely, you can see that. I saw you out there talking to him. Tell him to go away."

Gus laughed. It wasn't a mean laugh. He wasn't laughing at the man. The man simply didn't understand. Gus replied, "People keep telling me to do something about that man. Understand this; I don't think he'd leave if I asked him. Indeed, the more I insisted he go, the more he'd want to stay. There are too many economic incentives for him not to stay. There are even better incentives if the law starts giving the appearance of oppressing him again. When the economics runs out here, most likely he'll pick up his stakes and run out with them. After all, he was found innocent by a court of law. He's as free to live here as you or I, and I think you should get used to that idea for the time being."

"But…"

Gus cut him off. "What kind of car do you drive?"

"I have a nice American pickup truck."

"I'm glad to hear that. You know what, though, last year an American car company had a defect with their car. They didn't recall it right away, and they told no one about the defect until getting immunity from prosecution in a bankruptcy court. Only after they got that immunity did they divulge the defect in the car. In the meantime thirteen unlucky people died due to that defect. That corporation is as guilty of murder as the man you want removed from this community. Hell, they might be guiltier. There's no court of law to convict them, and even if they could, you can't put a corporation behind bars. Knowing now what you know, are you going to sell that pickup truck of yours?"

"I can't sell my pickup I need it to do my job."

"It is a free country for pickups and people. It might not be a fair country, but the law is the law. Would you want to live in a country where the sheriff can evict people from the county without finding them guilty in a court of law first?"

"I guess not."

"Well, then there is our problem. Thanks for your concern. Perhaps I feel it myself, but I've done all I can do on this matter. There's a gaggle of people outside the law-enforcement complex complaining today, so come on down and join in the group if you want. All I got is time for complaints to me that I can't do anything about."

The old man held his hand out, feeling the air. He said, "Got to bring the horses in. It's going to rain buckets by tonight for sure. I can't leave the horses out in that weather. The monsoon season is upon us." He shook his head and continued, "That man ought not to be here."

Gus looked at the crystal-clear blue sky. The last thing that seemed likely to happen here was rain. He'd have to check the weather report. Gus opened the truck door and got inside. He watched the old man wander back into Lester's ranch through the front windshield. The old man must have been a ranch hand. He was just another concerned citizen whose concerns were ignored. You don't get rich working on a ranch. Nope, the old man was just another innocent American whom the cameras never showed. No money in televising to folks at home an old man doing an honest day's work.

Gus was trailing the pack as they all rushed back from Lester's ranch to the law-enforcement complex for the afternoon massacre. It was still barely past one o'clock, and Gus heard on the radio that the highway traffic wasn't doing the Kansas lawman any favors. The two o'clock exit time was in serious jeopardy of being delayed. Gus's carefully laid plan still existed, but what no longer existed was any hope of parking near the law-enforcement complex. Gus found a spot at the courthouse and did his familiar routine of walking through the air-conditioning tunnel to city hall. He exited the main door of city hall and hit Main Street's bustling sidewalk. He made his way cautiously through the extremely packed street to his work. The curb parking was filled with media vans beaming their signals up to satellites overhead. Several of them were parked with wheels up on the curb. There were certainly a lot of ticketable offenses here, but Gus didn't care for ticket writing at the moment.

The protestors lined the sidewalks and the road. They had become a very diverse group. The constant television coverage had drawn them into downtown like moths to a flame. Gus strolled by a collective bunch protesting against genetically modified foods, which Gus assumed meant that they were some type of creationist society. After them came a bunch of people holding a hunger strike in protest of world hunger. Gus wasn't sure if they were pro or con. The next bunch was Skip Lipschitz's gun group. They were collecting donations to help restore America to its traditional heritage values. Gus assumed none of them owned a musket. This week's donations were going to help get Sheldon Nickelback back on his feet again after his patriotic exercising of his traditional Second Amendment rights. There was a sizable crowd of reporters covering them. Gus figured some people could never get enough of Nickelback. Then again, there was still likely to be hours of news to fill before Gus walked out Jennifer and handed her over to the lawman from Kansas just to appease the masses. The media had to fill that time with something, and Barabbas was apparently busy.

After that gun group came a small bunch of men and women in uniform asking for support to expand veteran's benefits. The television crews ignored them. Apparently these soldiers in their peacetime roles weren't flashy enough for the fast-paced modern news. There were smaller groups protesting the basics: the end of income tax, the end of big government, the end of business regulation, the end of the Federal Reserve, the end of social security, the end of Medicare, the end of persecution of religious freedom, the end of the war on Christmas, the end of the Voting Rights Act, and the end of the world. They were a dime a dozen, and the camera crews could film them anywhere at any time. The majority of the glorious media were setting up to get the obvious ending to the governor's fateful decision. They wanted the huge pro-life crowd's reaction when those papers were delivered. They were here to see and hear; as one passionate conservative protestor put it nicely in cardboard sign language, "I want to see the skank bitch get what she fucking deserves by the immortal power of our beloved Jesus." Hopefully the Internet was going to save all this on digital film for future generations to admire how the modern age had brought society to a new level of civil discourse.

Had anyone bothered to ask Gus this afternoon, he'd have explained to the cameras that outcomes aren't always what you expect. No one was asking for his opinion, though. His job had moved location, but it hadn't changed. They'd shoot him on a horse, but they didn't care what he thought about anything. They'd shoot him giving Jennifer over to the Kansas trooper, but they didn't care what he thought about the whole thing. He was there just to look good and folksy for the cameras as he offered up Jennifer Louis Bachman to the admiring, hateful crowd.

The crowd directly in front of the law-enforcement complex had multiplied tenfold from the other day. Still, the same familiar faces of previous days were there up front to soak the best camera time. People were coming to express their anger, but no one was leaving. Not now when there was a fifty-fifty chance of getting your anger aired on live television. Actors trained for years just to get a lucky break and appear for a minute or two on a bit acting part for a television program. Why did they go through the bother when they could come down to Gus's office, fake some outrage for the twenty-four-hour news networks, and get wall-to-wall coverage in return for their acting efforts? Gus walked by his assigned parking spot in the law-enforcement-complex parking lot. The spot was now reserved as a permanent candlelight vigil for the outrage.

The majority of the newspeople had camped out near the outer edge of the crowd to get a wide-angle shot of the proceedings. This area was also where the crowd was chanting slogans at anyone foolish enough to pass them. They started chanting to Gus as he moved closer to work. Many of the protestors held manufactured signs. Someone was making a buck or two selling premade antiabortion signs. Capitalism held no bounds, so when there was a buck to be made, it made it. Gus figured all this was at least good for the local economy. "Adoption not abortion" was the popular slogan choice among the signs, presumably more because of the alliteration than because it expressed these people's deep inner desire to adopt other people's children over and over again for the rest of their lives. "Abortion is anti-women," stated a well-meaning banner displayed in front of a group of catholic priests who did not allow women into their ranks, "We're safer without abortion," wrote a man who would never be faced with that choice. "Women need support not abort," wrote an antitax advocate who certainly would not be offering said support out of his bank account. "Life begins at conception and ends at Planned Parenthood," wrote someone who had no clue that planning parenthood was likely a good way to prevent unwanted pregnancy and thus avoid an abortion. Gus stopped reading so he could reserve some of today's quota of cynicism for the lawyers who were likely to be waiting for him inside his office.

There must have been supporters for Jennifer somewhere in this world, since they had bought her a rather nicely dressed lawyer, but Gus didn't observe even one in the front of his office expressing much of it. He figured that was probably a good thing. The last thing he needed was a yet another noisy crowd heckling him as he went to work, or worse, violence breaking out among all these people. He arrived at the complex front door to see that a pale-blue plastic kid's pool had been erected in front of it. The front window of the law-enforcement complex to the side of the pool was shattered. No one seemed to care that the window was broken. Instead the crowd up front was occupying their time playing with the kid's swimming pool. One by one a group of protestors were dunking plastic babies into the pool's shallow waters as Pastor Voce said a few religious words and blessed them.

Gus greeted the pastor. "I hope my protection has been adequate for your needs."

Pastor looked up from his latest plastic baby-doll christening and greeted Gus. "Ah, Sheriff, it has been indeed. Your sweet secretary Lupita, God's little spot of sunshine, saw to everything. She even ordered pizza for my flock. If there ever was a person in God's favor, then it is her. I was worried there might be violence down here today due to the godless pro-abortion crowd, but your boys have kept the peace."

Gus looked at his broken window and wondered what unkept peace might look like. Against Gus's better judgment and because curiosity simply got the better of him, he asked the pastor, "What is going on here with all this plastic-baby-dunking business?"

Pastor Voce replied in lofty tones, "The sanctity of a baptized life shall not be denied our baby Amanda. We are baptizing her in spirit because her wicked mother denied her child a more righteous earthly baptism! May her devil-born mother rot in hell's eternal fires for the deed she has done in unholy Mexico to that magnificent child of God."

"Amen," replied the crowd in unison.

"Who's baby Amanda?" asked Gus.

"Our beloved, saintly child of innocence that was wrongly put to death by the vile and wicked Jennifer Louis Bachman!" boomed the gathering right back at Gus.

Gus rubbed his temple. He replied, "The name was going to be Robin. You might want to know things like that before you go and place eternal judgment upon a seventeen-year-old girl and a postmortem baptismal name upon her dead child."

He popped open the complex door before Pastor Voce and his flock returned what would no doubt be a witty reply to him. He was now temporarily safe in his office as muffled cries of "you bastard" came his way. The founding fathers had whiffed on this one. The Bill of Rights promised a citizen freedom of religion instead of granting a citizen freedom from the demands of the overly religious. It was bad enough that they hounded you your whole life that they knew what was going to happen to you after you were dead. Now they were hounding you in your death with a baptism you never asked for. If any protestor for any cause walked through that door at this moment, then Gus was personally going to arrest the person. He was in that frame of mind, but they wouldn't come in. The office's inner lobby was pretty much as Gus expected it to be. It was protestor-free.

There was an overworked deputy on the front desk fielding all manner of helpful tips on subjects ranging from the whereabouts of the Hispanic arsonists who couldn't possibly exist to the meaning of the transfiguration of Christ. There was also that Kansas lawman, Major Scott Dundee, cooling his heels on Gus's bench. The lawman held up a digit to Gus when Gus looked over in his direction. This wasn't an insult but only a signal that the man from the capital was expected to be arriving in an hour or so with the proper papers. Gus didn't have the heart to tell Major Dundee that his deputy would be late due to traffic. Last and certainly least, there was Deputy Drew. The fool was standing next to a brick that lay on the lobby floor surrounded by the glass that had up until last night made for a rather nice front window to the complex. Gus shook his head and walked over to Drew.

"Go ahead and pick that brick up and get rid of it. It can't hurt you now," ordered Gus.

Deputy Drew hesitated. "I'm not sure I should. Some helpful person tossed that brick through our window last night as a message. I was plenty mad when it happened, and then I read the note on it. After I read that brick's message, I had to admit I was mighty confused. I left it just as I found it until you got here to deal with it properly."

"What does the note on this brick say?"

"It is plenty bad, Sheriff. The note clearly labels our brick a *baby killer*. I couldn't believe it myself. A small red brick like this. You see them all the time. There's whole buildings in this county made of the stuff, and to think this one out of all of them would go bad. To kill a baby is unimaginable, and yet here it is; this brick is labeled for all to see as a baby killer. I figured if that brick did kill a baby, then it might be evidence or something, so I didn't touch it."

Gus gave a proper scolding stare to the ordinary red brick on the ground. He then ordered Deputy Drew, "You can't tell the good bricks from the bad bricks these days. Deputy, you might as well put that brick in a jail cell, and I'll ask the DA if he thinks we can build an airtight murder case against it."

"I won't let you down."

"I can't see how you could on this one."

That was one small problem out of so many that was solved. He had gotten Deputy Drew as far away from him as possible, and Drew was working on a task he was the most capable in the office of handling. Windows were expensive to replace, and there was a new deputy to pay for as well. Terrance was in love with all this wall-to-wall news coverage, but it wasn't doing anything for the town except increasing the budget deficit. Sheldon Nickelback was right about one thing; this county was taking all the risks to gain a certain national notoriety, but it wasn't making any real profits from these odd affairs. Gus continued to his office. If Gus's plan worked out, then perhaps there would be a profit in this for someone. He was more than ready for this all to end. Retirement had never sounded so good. He wanted to retire as many problems as he could by today's end. Gus found that Lupita was gone from her post again. Today he needed her, because she was efficient. It was going to take a lot of efficiency to

196

pull today off properly. Instead of Lupita sitting at her desk, there was Josh Hansen sitting happily in her chair typing away on her computer.

Gus barked out, "Aren't you supposed to be under arrest in my jail cell? You came here to play the role of a prisoner, so please for just a little while stay inside my prison. But before you depart me, I want to know what you were doing behind my secretary's desk."

"Nothing nefarious, I can assure you. You're the one helping parade children around for the gawking masses as a sort of sport, not me. I assure you that your secretary left about an hour ago because she was feeling sick, so I'm just filling in for her. I'm having a devil of a time sorting out all your files for you. You really should find someone to update your computer system. The security here is so out-of-date anyone could hack into it. You don't want some no-good computer hacker looking up all your files, do you? Trust me; I found lots of things you'd rather no one saw. Identity theft is running rampant these days, so be careful. I know what I'm talking about; I got twenty-five separate identities to protect me from the clutches of the various governments. I stole almost half of them."

"Did you buy pizzas for all the people outside on my dime?"

"No, that was Lupita's doing. I did eat some of it disguised as a 'Keep on Enslaving Tibet' protestor. She left right after that to catch a doctor's appointment."

"Doctor's appointment, what's wrong with my secretary?"

"She was waiting on some important test results."

"Ain't she a little old to be taking the SATs?"

"I don't know. I didn't think it was my business to nose around in other people's business and ask her about her private affairs. I'm not a snoop, you know. By the way, according to your bank accounts, I see you're living a very impecunious lifestyle at the moment. You might consider cashing in a few of my Vitcoins."

"Mr. Smith, or whichever one of your twenty-five identities you are today, please go back to tilting at the windmills of Internet conspiracy gossip and leave me alone. I sense there's no one actually trying to kill you anymore, and you know it. You're just here to bother me. Don't you see there is a real pile of shit outside there trying to make my life harder than it already was? I don't need you and your fake drama, as I got a dozen people telling me what I'm doing wrong just outside the front door."

Josh shook his head. "Those people out there are all tools to the masters. It is simply easier to make a man look down at his feet than up at the sky. The sky is huge and vast, and everyone has glorious dreams of flying. But the man already up in the air desires no friends. There are only so many wings that can be handed out. So the man in the sky tells the man on the ground that it is not those in the sky holding him back, but the very ground at his feet that is holding him back. Alas, the man on the ground gets angry at the ground, because he wants to fly. In his anger, he bitterly stamps at the ground below his feet. The more he stamps, the lower he sinks into the ground, and the farther from the sky he is. A man can sink himself deeper and deeper until he can't get any lower. When there is no more ground below him, he will still blame the foul ground and those others that live sunken inside the hole with him for all his problems. Those in the sky don't need conspiracies to remain where they are, because the man on the ground can't look past his own pair of feet to see that the person keeping him in his hole isn't anyone sunk in the hole with him. It is the man in the sky that feeds him the lies that made him angry that is the source of all his problems. The masses will trample themselves to death just to please the man in sky, but they'll never be joining him."

"I liked your porpoise story better. Now get back to your cell! I'll be down there in the cell block before you know it to come and fetch the doomed one. You wouldn't want to miss the show."

Josh for once took the hint and quickly vacated the desk. No doubt he was hacking into something from Lupita's computer. What could Gus do to stop him from doing it? Nothing, as he certainly didn't have the budget to hire a good computer expert to keep Josh Hansen out. It would be nice to see that man get what he deserved, but exactly what he deserved was very much in the air. With Hansen going, Gus turned his attention to his office door. He reached for the handle, and Hansen shouted out, "There's a lawyer in there."

"I figured Wilton McDermott would be down here to earn his paycheck."

Hansen smiled, "Not him, but another man. The top third in a law class become trial lawyers, the middle third become judges, and the bottom third become politicians. This one's a trial lawyer, but judging by his comb-over, not a very good one."

Curiosity overcame Gus, and he went into his office. There was a plump, balding man in a decent-enough suit waiting for him inside. The man had a briefcase full of papers that were no doubt all very important. The man stood up to shake Gus's hand, but Gus simply ignored the gesture. He circled around to his desk and sat down. The man hovered between joining Gus in taking a seat and saying something to Gus.

Some people needed the extra encouragement of grumpiness to get them over the edge, so Gus grumbled to the man, "Who are you?"

"I am Nigel Westinghouse. I represent the Topanga Pharmacy."

"Do you represent them often?" asked Gus.

"What do you mean by that?"

"I just wanted to know how many of their representatives are criminals and how many are the lawyers keeping the criminals out of jail, is all."

The lawyer wasn't up to the game. "All you need to know is that I'm Mr. Tang's lawyer." He circled around the desk to once again try and shake Gus's hand. Gus pointed to a seat on the opposite side of the desk. The man was an obedient sort and did what he was told. He talked the whole time he was sitting down. "You are, I assume, the person put in charge of this place. I have gotten a county judge to set a bail hearing for my client for tomorrow afternoon. My client is innocent of the charges before him, and I want him released as soon as possible, if not sooner. The people I represent on the West Coast would like it if my client didn't have to go through all the stress of a bail hearing and a trial. I've heard the DA isn't eager to pursue charges. It is perhaps possible an understanding could be reached before that happened. It might save the local DA's office from a few headaches and you from a possible lawsuit."

"I wouldn't like wearing a suit, particularly a law suit. The off-the-rack kind don't have much talent, and the quality stuff is so expensive you have to compromise your lifestyle to afford them," replied Gus.

"I am not kidding," said Nigel sternly as he clicked the latches on his briefcase. No doubt those very important papers were going to soon be making an appearance.

"Don't get all acerbic already. What I mean to say is that there is no reason for a hearing." Having calmed the lawyer's nerves, Gus pulled out a manila folder from the in-box on his desk. He opened it to pull out a piece of paper. He had been waiting to hand it over to whatever scum represented Terry Tang. When there's enough money involved, someone will defend anyone from anything. Gus smiled pleasantly to the man and handed him the note.

"What the hell is this?" yelled the lawyer, standing once again and shaking a fist in the air to express what might be misunderstood as an emotion.

Terry Tang would have been better off with a public defender, thought Gus. This lawyer had gone from all hello and smiles to white-hot anger with no sense of proportion. A court-appointed attorney would be smart enough to not care at all about Terry Tang. No one should care about Terry Tang. The Terry Tangs of the world don't drive people to fiery defense. He was just a paycheck for this guy, and Gus knew it. Gus laughed, "Calm down, man, it is a release form; your client is free to go. The other day he claimed to have a prescription for the drugs we found on his premises. My crack staff has tracked down and verified that he did indeed have legal prescriptions. Thus, we have no further need to hold your client. We, of course, apologize to the fullest extent of that word for the inconvenience of Terry Tang being arrested unnecessarily."

"There is the matter of the money…"

"I don't know anything about any money. We arrested Mr. Tang and took the drugs we thought were illegal. We left his money in his house, of course."

"But the money is gone!"

"Stolen?"

"Well, are you sure you don't have it?"

"I got a manila envelope right here with all the paperwork of what we took from that house. We didn't touch any money. I'm sure you know, as a suspected drug house, we could have used legal asset forfeiture to take your client's money, but we didn't. We're a fair bunch of even-minded people here in this county. I wanted to make sure Mr. Tang got a fair shake of the law before I'd do something so heavy-handed as asset forfeiture. Still, it's awful strange, this money disappearing. Do you know who might want to steal it from your client?"

"It could have been…"

"Yes?"

"It…it doesn't matter. All that really matters are the drugs…ah…I mean, is my client."

"Well, then your client is free to go."

"My client and, of course, the drugs you seized from him! You have no legal right to hold them, and they…I mean, my client would like them back."

Gus pulled open a desk drawer and pulled out two prescription bottles of OxyContin. He placed them neatly on top of his desk. He then pulled two prescription forms from the manila folder. They were signed on the dotted line from the company's quack medical practitioner, Dr. Smith. Gus placed one prescription on top of each bottle. He then said, "Here you go. I got two prescriptions written out for a Terry Tang, and you get his two bottles of pills back. Everything is legal and aboveboard. It all works out just fine for your client. We can go retrieve your client from my jail cell any time you want."

"But…I mean, yes, I would naturally like my client back on the streets a free man. It is just that…I know for a fact that there were more than two bottles in his place."

"Really?" replied Gus as he snatched the release form back from the lawyer. He pretended to read the form. He then dropped it back onto his desk. "That just can't be right, because I only got these two bottles to match these two legally written prescriptions. I mean, it wouldn't be legal for him to have more than these two bottles that we have these legal prescriptions for, now would it? Are you trying to tell me that your client did indeed break the law after all and did have more drugs on his person that weren't legally prescribed to him?"

"Ah…no, I mean…no. I'm just saying these bottles feel a bit light. I would say his friends on the West Coast won't be happy to hear his bottles were returned a little light. Some people might think this sheriff's office skimmed a few pills off the top."

"Not true, I can assure you. That bottle says fifty pills inside each container, and I counted out exactly fifty inside each container. I even got a deputy to double-check the total, and you'll see on this release form the verified total. I assure you these bottles aren't light," replied Gus.

"Still, it feels to me like there should be more stuff."

"I understand your problem, Nigel." Gus got up from his desk and quickly circled it. He patted the lawyer on the shoulder and dropped the release form into the lawyer's briefcase. Gus snapped it shut for him. "You got far too much feeling for your job. I suggest you try taking a few Oxy-Contin pills, and I assure you they'll help dull that feeling. Follow me, and we'll go fetch your client."

Gus walked back out his office door. The lawyer followed him carrying the two bottles and his briefcase. They wandered to the cell block. Deputy Costner was at the monitoring desk. The deputy sprang to his feet when Gus showed up. Gus looked over his chalkboard. He barked an order to the deputy. "Terry Tang in cell number one is free to go. Make sure you tell him a fond farewell from me." Gus turned and pointed to the roll-up metallic door that led to the back parking lot. He continued, "You better take him and his lawyer out the service entrance here, as there are far too many fools out front."

Nigel said, "Thank you."

"You're very welcome."

The deputy put the key into the lock and typed the security code on the door. In went the deputy and the lawyer. Gus picked up the eraser and erased Kyle Minnelli's name from the chalkboard. One prescription-drug dealer was very much like another, so what did it really matter which one was still in his jail and which one was freely released due to lack of evidence? It was just a little white lie written on the chalkboard in white chalk. Gus unlocked the service door and rolled it up. The deputy walked past Gus and left through the door. The deputy smiled to Gus as he passed.

Nigel and his briefcase filled with very important papers walked by with a blank expression on his face. His fake passion was sedated now by his partial victory. Terry Tang followed them with a scowl. He gave Gus a single-digit salute and shouted, "I'm getting my drugs back. This shit ain't over! It ain't over by a long run. I'll kick your ass to get them back." When he was done verbally threatening an officer of the law with violence, he was smart enough to walk out the door to his freedom while he still had a chance.

Gus typed into the keypad and walked into the cell block. He strolled down the block. It felt cold inside. There was no one between him and his destination. Jennifer Louis Bachman was standing in a corner of her cell. She wasn't crying, nor did she appear scared. Time had already worn her down. She only appeared very bored. She was just standing there helpless, dressed in an orange jumpsuit. Her high-priced lawyer sat on her bunk. Wilton McDermott was dressed to the nines. Even in jail the man looked like a million bucks, which was probably just a drop in the well of what he made from all the coverage of the Sheldon Nickelback trial. He was rolling in it, and yet there wasn't anything a lawyer wouldn't take from you to pay his fees, and that included your cell's only seat. Gus put his key in the lock and unlocked the door. He slid the door open.

Wilton McDermott stood up and straightened his suit. He pulled his cuffs taut and flashed Gus a little sight of his gold cuff links. He was a very Dapper D type of man. He casually asked, "Is it time?"

"Yup, it's getting to be about that time," replied Gus. Gus went over and snapped one handcuff around Jennifer's wrist. He clicked the other to his own. There was still no expression on her face.

"There is no need for that," protested the lawyer.

"I don't think she'll run, but I don't know what those people out there might do. If she's strapped to me, they will hopefully be less likely to do anything."

"Those people out there spooked the governor. She wouldn't listen to reason no matter how much I tried. They threw every lie in the book at her: abortion causes cancer, abortion causes infertility, most women regret having an abortion, once women see an ultrasound they won't want an abortion, abortion is psychologically damaging to a woman, abortion endangers a woman's life, most women lie about medical needs for an abortion, and of course that they sell the baby parts for profit. I don't think in the end the substance of what they said won the governor's heart, though. She was just spooked by the huge crowds filled with lie-induced anger."

"I know; she just wanted all you assholes to leave her alone," said Gus.

"We'll do better in Kansas," assured the lawyer.

"Yup," replied Gus.

"It doesn't seem real," said Jennifer to the air.

Gus replied to her, "Yup, it is time to go."

Gus led her out of the cell with him and back down the cell block. None of the other inmates made a sound. The lawyer trailed her, rattling on and on about his strategy for winning in Kansas. Wilton McDermott only had his word salad to offer her when all she likely needed was a touch of sympathy. That was more than Gus could offer. He was only doing his job. Deputy Costner had returned to the guard desk. "You taking her away?" asked Costner.

"Yup," replied Gus.

The deputy unlocked the door and let Gus return to the land of the free. Gus paused at the chalkboard and erased Jennifer's name from it. Gus glanced at the chalkboard. The names were still arranged made to order. He then marched her through the station without saying a word.

Outside the front door, the press had set up a podium as if they were expecting Edward Everett to show up to make a brief oration. Major Scott Dundee loomed on the edge of podium. The crowd erupted with an unholy howl of condemnation at the appearance of Jennifer. She had just spent the better part of a week in a cold, dark place already, so you'd have thought she'd be used to it. To her credit, she didn't shrink back from the jeers. She placed her free hand over her eyes to shield them from the sun. Perhaps the light of the postmidday sun was more intense than the darkness of the crowd. Someone from the press gaggle shouted for a statement. Then another screamed over the crowd for Jennifer to give a statement. Gus held her firmly away from the podium and ignored them.

Jennifer couldn't have reached their microphones had she wanted to, since she was tied to Gus by the cuffs.

Wilton McDermott was free to make an ass of himself and gladly stepped up to the microphones. The crowd rained a chorus of boos toward him before he spoke. The seasoned lawyer acted like a villain at a wrestling match. The more the crowd booed him, the more McDermott liked it. He was used to defending unpopular clients. The crowd didn't understand that in some situations it is best to do nothing. Every boo they uttered would be on television and would help jack up the trial's ratings. The higher the ratings' the more money Wilton McDermott would make in the end.

Wilton gave a discourse on civil liberties to the uncivil crowd. Occasionally Major Scott Dundee interrupted him with vile hate speech that no doubt made Wilton more sympathetic to the people at home. They were the unseen jury that was far removed. A person was innocent until proven guilty in a court of law. The court of public opinion was what Major Dundee and Wilton McDermott were both currently appealing to. In that court your guilt or innocence was often decided by the flimsiest of evidence, and there was never a need to wait for the trial. Gus just stood there waiting for the damn trooper car to arrive with the papers so this farce could end.

It could have been fifteen minutes, or it could have been forever, but finally over the din of the crowd a horn bleated. Major Dundee left the podium to stand next to Gus. Gus pulled the keys to his handcuffs out of his pocket. The Kansas patrol car plodded through the throngs of people toward the parking lot. The protesters gladly parted the sea to let the patrol car through. Members of the national press reluctantly gave up their prime spot they had staked out for just the best angle to allow the patrol car by. Trailing the patrol car were three separate news helicopters overhead that apparently had filmed the car's progress all the way from the capital to here. People gawking at it probably explained the traffic delay. The papers had finally arrived, and they were now the star of the show. The patrol car pulled right into Gus's assigned parking spot. It ran right over the plastic swimming pool with its few floating plastic babies. A tire crushed a doll beneath it as the patrol car halted. The patrol-car door opened, and out stepped a blond man from Kansas with a packet of legal papers in his hands.

Pastor Voce broke into a recitation of a psalm. "For you created my inmost being; you knit me together in my mother's womb. I praise you because I am fearfully and wonderfully made; your works are wonderful; I know that full well." Gus was impressed to learn that the man knew any part of the Bible.

Had only the God almighty not knitted the fetus with trisomy 13, none of them would have had to be here today. The Lord worked in mysterious ways that often seemed pretty pointless and stupid to Gus. The stupidity of God's creation was only mysterious if you believed that the Lord wasn't as susceptible to doing stupid things as anyone else. Gus ran his eyes over the chanting crowd, the camera-hawking orating lawyer, the judgmental Kansas lawman, and the ratings-oriented third estate. It was hard to think that this country with sixteen million children struggling to find a daily meal could find the time for all this nonsense if the Lord didn't have his share of the stupid. Well, it was all going to be over soon now. The crowd seemed more than pleased with that knowledge.

Gus held out his free hand to receive the legal papers. He was left hanging, because Major Scott Dundee hadn't cooled his heels waiting for nothing. He ignored Gus's hand as he took the papers on over to the podium and proceeded to give his own speech to the microphones. While Major Dundee lectured the crowd about his ideas on traditional values, three rather slim dark-haired gentlemen in three-piece suits stepped out from the crowd. They moved swiftly to intercept Sheriff Gus. While Major Dundee postured for the cameras, they slipped their own legal papers into Gus's waiting hand. When they were done, they walked over to the podium. Two men shoved the rather cross Major Dundee out of the way. The tallest of the three men manned the podium and spoke to the crowd.

"The United Mexico States has just placed extradition charges in the hands of the county sheriff. The United Mexico States will be taking the accused Jennifer Louis Bachman back to Mexico to face charges on account of her having an illegal abortion past the twelfth week of pregnancy. This is an affront to all the people of Mexico. Mexican justice will be observed in this case!"

The crowd erupted in boos. Major Dundee wrestled the microphone back from the man. He shouted at him, "Your country's request is impossible to fulfill, because the great State of Kansas has first claim to this prisoner. I will not stand here and allow this gross miscarriage of justice to happen!"

The crowd cheered him on, but the representative from Mexico was quick to reply, "But surely the crimes in this case happened in Mexico and not this Kansas place." The crowd hostilely replied to that fact with jeers.

Major Dundee insisted, "The alleged fetus was American, and more than that, she was a Kansan, and we refuse to have the murder of our Kansan be tried in Mexico instead of America! We need to keep murder in America where it belongs."

"Keep murder in America!" cheered the crowd.

Major Dundee angrily turned from the podium and placed his own signed extradition papers into Gus's hand right next to the papers from Mexico. The major insisted to Gus, "Now I'm taking that murderer!"

Gus looked at the two sets of papers. He shrugged at the uselessness of all this. Gus jiggled the handcuff that linked him to Jennifer. He held the papers out for Major Dundee to see. He replied, "I can't let you do that. I don't know who has the legal right to claim her. What I got here is two separate requests for her corporeal body, and as far as I know, she can't bilocate. I see no alternative to this situation than to keep her here until the courts figure this shit out for me." Dundee angrily grabbed Gus by his lapels, and then, remembering the cameras were still rolling, he backed off. He turned and faked a smile to the cameras. Wilton McDermott was off and running quick as a jackrabbit. No doubt he suddenly had legal briefs to file and was not about to stand around this hot mess when there was a chance to practice his rhetorical skills in front of another judge. Gus tugged at Jennifer's handcuffed hand. He said to her, "Come on, we're heading back to your little cell in my office where you'll be safe from all this."

The crowd screamed for bloody murder. Major Dundee was back at the podium stirring them on to call the governor, call the Supreme Court, call the president of Mexico, and most important of all, call for justice. The cameras were rolling the whole time. What the people thought at home was anyone's guess. It probably beat watching reruns of *Gilligan's Island*. They never got off the island, and Jennifer Louis Bachman was never leaving Gus's jail at this rate, so it seemed an appropriate remark.

"This is complete madness," was all Jennifer could say as he led her back through the front door.

"Nah, all this ain't crazy; it's just plain, basic stupidity," Gus replied.

CHAPTER 6

Couldn't help but make me feel ashamed to live in a land where justice is a game.
—Bob Dylan

The Moirai had woven their thread of fate, and tonight it would be time to see if they had allotted enough rope to get out of this sticky situation or if it was only enough to hang Gus with. He didn't know if he could avoid the inevitable freckled hand of justice or not. Neither the powers of Dike's randomness nor Themis's absolute certitude had been granted to Gus in his many attempts to deal out a modicum of justice lately. He had played his hand as best he could so far, and he felt he had chosen to follow the most logical course open to him. Indeed, things had worked out so humorously well this afternoon that even he couldn't believe it. The stage was now nearly set. The absolute destination of his intended course was known, but the success or failure was yet to be determined. If Gus had been granted the gift of clairvoyance, then he'd be in Las Vegas forecasting his way to a richer tomorrow; instead, he'd let things play out tonight and know if it all worked out tomorrow morning when the future had become the past.

Gus sat on his couch eating a frozen dinner. It was a healthy dose of microwaved fried chicken with peas. You could barely taste the freezer burn through the salt. Gus drank the last of the expensive microbrew. The bottle was one last generous gift from Sedric Hedgecock. Gus had promised the judge he'd look into the theft, and he looked into it as hard as humanly possible. Unfortunately, the beer evidence was going away far faster than he could keep up with it. In a few more minutes, the evidence would be totally consumed. It was one case Gus had quickly gotten to the bottom of, and yet it was destined to remain another unsolved mystery in the county's history books. It was just a fact of life that unsolved cases happened to even to the best of detectives. Time was standing still, or so it felt as Gus waited for the witching hour to begin. It was then that the Mexican mob would be out to howl at the moon. Gus reached over to grab his home phone. He had one more important task to complete. He dialed up State Police Commissioner Brian Hartline to update him on the state of the state's ongoing natural disaster. He dialed up the secret law-enforcement emergency natural-disaster number that he knew went straight to Brian. If this state was ever in a natural-disaster type of an emergency, then the time was now. The phone rang and rang, but Gus was determined to talk to him. He wasn't going to hang up.

Finally on the twentieth ring the line answered. "Who the fuck is this on the emergency line? You idiots can't fucking use this line except during a goddamn emergency. I know it's supposed to rain tonight, but you better be calling this fucking number from an ark, or I'm going to throw charges your way! Has the predicted monsoon started? Are the floodwaters rising? Come on out with it; what is the fucking emergency, asshole?"

"This is your old friend, Sheriff Gus. Remember me? I'm the man you left holding the front line of the national circus," replied Gus.

There was a pause on the other end of the phone. "Oh, so it is a disaster after all. How is it my fault you went on parade with a fuck idiot like Sheldon Nickelback? If you lie down with a dog, then you expect to get up with fleas. You're a big boy, so I know you know that. Anyways, what the fuck is wrong with you? I saw that other shit on my TV this afternoon. Hell, idiot, do your job; just give that girl back to Kansas and then let the Mexicans try to take her from them. You blew it. I knew I should never have tried to do something nice for you. When our esteemed governor called me up for advice on the legal ramifications of this abortion crap-trap, I told her to give the burden away and don't listen to the fuck-stick lawyers and their San Francisco bleeding hearts. I do you that big favor, and what do you do with it? You got your ass wrapped up in international bullshit intrigue instead, and that girl's still in your fucking jail. Fuck, don't call me. These are all your problems now through and through."

"Don't hang up just yet. I have another nice thing to ask from you."

"I don't do nice things for a living; that's why I became a police officer. If you want nice things, go shop at Tiffany. I'm hanging up now, because this number is only supposed to be used for real emergencies and not stupidities."

"The thing is that I reckon I'm going to be driving down the interstate tonight heading south sometime way past midnight. I believe I've got the situation figured out right, and thus I know there will be another vehicle following me on my way south. I don't want that particular vehicle from the great state of Kansas following me. You might do me a favor and make sure that little scenario ends someplace close to where the heights begin on the interstate. Do this little thing for me."

"Gus, I honestly don't give a fuck about you and what you want. Why do you want to head south of the border anyways?"

"There are certain interests on the other side of that highway. I have a package to deliver to them that they have a real hankering for. They wouldn't be happy if my cargo arrived having been molested by the hands of the lawmen of Kansas. I won't have that worry if there's a state-patrol boy waiting on that highway ready to pull that out-of-state vehicle over that is going to be following me. I'd appreciate it. I got far too many problems to have these unfriendly elements from the north bothering me tonight. I need to pacify the drug gangs tonight. The last thing we both want is the kind of violence a Mexican drug gang can start up to occur in the middle of all this national press."

The line was silent again for a good minute. Brian Hartline finally answered, "Fuck it, you can't count on me to do something like that. I repeat, you can't count on me."

"Thanks, I appreciate it," replied Gus as the line went dead.

Well, that was that. Gus hung up the phone. He already had Deputy Drew clearing the law-enforcement-complex back parking lot of people.

He needed that back service entrance to the cell-block area cleared out tonight if he was going to remove Kyle from his prison unseen. He had taught Antonio enough of a lesson, and now he was going to return his stolen goods for a small share of Antonio's stolen goods. It did only seem fair. He was sick of Antonio and Big Gustavo thinking they could hurt him any time they wanted. Gus had hurt them a little where it counted—with the family. Now that the lesson was taught, it was time to end it before things got messy in front of the national media's cameras. Antonio would also be paying him a little money to end it, and that was just icing on the cake. Hell, it was enough money to be a whole cake. Antonio would have the bribe money together by now, so tonight was the right time to return his son. Gus was sick of playing the game, and the money would be his reward for playing it all these years. If it came to him criminally, then so be it. It was, after all, just a small injustice among so many wrongs.

Gus returned to his sofa. He pulled the wooden television tray near him. Somehow the reheated previously frozen peas just lacked flavor tonight. Gus shook a bottle of Tabasco sauce over them. It was a cheap way to cover the flavor of an inferior product. Speaking of inferior products, on the television two flavors of pundit were on the twenty-four-hour news arguing over the ramifications of the scene at the law-enforcement complex this afternoon. Gus had the sound off. There was no point in listening to them, as he figured they didn't know anything worth hearing. It was just fun to watch them think they did. One pundit had a degree in history, and the other was an Ivy League graduate with a medical degree. Neither man knew a damn thing about the law or the feelings and lives of real people forced into the news without being asked to be there, but it didn't stop them from pretending they did for the television audience at home. They were likely horrendously wrong, as they had been countless times before. They were just two men playing the role of an expert with no real expertise, and it never apparently mattered to the network. When actual expertise was needed, they so often turned to the same recycled highly educated idiots over and over again. The men believed their education insulated them from the foolishness of the uneducated lesser people.

They were sadly wrong. There is often no better audience for a con man than the intelligent and educated.

A magician and avid three-card monte huckster named Ernie Ball had taught Gus that in grade school. The best person to get into a con game wasn't the uneducated but instead the intelligent, well-educated man. Old Ernie always set up shop near places he could find them in droves. The educated man thought his inflated opinion of his own intelligence protected him from being fooled, but on average he was just as likely to be fooled as the next man. No one was immune from stupidity, in Gus's experience. Educated men's egos made them ideal targets, and better still, their education trained them to be highly skilled at defending their beliefs even when they had arrived at these beliefs due to very stupid reasons. Ernie would take those types of men to the cleaners over and over. The best part was that they'd come back for more, because they just knew they were right. They'd have been a whole lot smarter to remember Socrates, who knew he knew nothing absolutely but nothing itself.

The network only displayed the pundits because they already knew these men's egotistic pompous asses were entertaining to the audience at home. Half the audience was nodding their heads in silent obedience of what they believed were founts of wisdom flowing from their mouths, and the half like Gus watched to convulse on the floor in giggles knowing that it wasn't likely to be wise what these men said. In either case the audience was entertained, and that was the role that the educated expert was really playing. Meanwhile, people like Jennifer were only fodder to feed the fake reality-entertainment industry disguised as news. That their lives were often destroyed in the process neither pundit seemed empathetic enough to notice. Perhaps Sheldon Nickelback, while a rotten bastard, wasn't so wrong to try and cash in off these fools. No, Sheldon Nickelback wasn't much different from that old magician Ernie Ball. Gus sat back with a spoon of hot peas, wondering what had become of that old magician. No doubt that old man would be proud if he knew about the magic trick Gus was trying to play tonight.

The doorbell rang. Gus wasn't actually expecting a guest, but after what had happened that afternoon, just about anyone could be at his door searching for him. There were likely a lot of locals with opinions to express about rapid rebranding of Main Street into sit-in-protest central. Gus didn't want to hear them. Gus slid his television tray back and eased off the sofa. The knees were sore but functional, and the horse sitting hadn't done them or his rear end any permanent harm. He walked over to his front door and pulled back the curtains on the vertical framing windows that surrounded it. Those windows were designed to accent the doorframe, but they were functional as well as decorative. Standing on Gus's stoop was the prodigal son. Lupita was back from testing and standing there waiting to come in. She hadn't been to his house in fifteen years. He wondered why she was here now. Gus snapped back the curtain and opened the door.

Gus put a wide campaign smile on his face, not because it would work on her, but because he knew it wouldn't. He greeted his secretary, "Lupita, it is so wonderful to see you here. The office just hasn't been the same since you went in for testing. I hope your battery isn't running low."

"The office is an absolute madhouse of sin and depravity. I've always done my best to place you on the righteous path, but you won't have me around there anymore to help steer it properly. I would have come to the office to tell you, only there are so many locos down there at the moment. Now may the Lord of peace himself give them all peace, at all times, and in every way, but not when I'm trying to get things accomplished; then, Lord, get these idiots to their own home. You understand that being around so many sick people isn't good for a person in my condition."

"Why'd you buy them all pizza?"

"Naturally I sympathize with their cause, but I also thought they were leaving today. Now things are different in more than one way."

"I take it you weren't taking the SATs."

"I came to tell you the doctors say that I have cancer. Your protestors aren't leaving you, but I have to. Lord knows what will happen to your fat ass without me to guide you from doing such stupid things."

Gus didn't know what to reply. She looked healthy enough standing there by porch light. He rubbed his temple. His mind was blank. He hadn't expected that response from her. He was old enough to have known many people who had died from cancer. You get used to people coming to work day after day. You don't think they're ever going to leave, but they do leave. Everyone has a last day at the office one way or another. She was the last one left who was working in the office from before he arrived. He quietly muttered at long last, "I'm sorry."

"I didn't come here for your sympathy."

"Well, then I'm not sorry."

"A thing like this shouldn't have happened to a person like me. I have done nothing but good in this life. I've prayed the right way, voted the right way, donated my time for the right causes, and raised my children to abide by the laws I've always worked hard to enforce. A thing like this should happen to someone that deserves God's formal justice, a person who doesn't know godly right from wrong. You know, a person like you."

Her words failed to strike home. Gus figured if God had all eternity to judge you for your action here on Earth, then you'd think he'd give you longer than a blink in the eye's worth of data points to know when a man was worth the ultimate prize of sharing eternity. This God hadn't even given Robin a blink, and yet he was supposed to sit in judgment of her just the same. All he could say in return to Lupita was, "I think it happens to all of us. My time is coming eventually. I know it as well as you."

She bit her lip. There appeared to be nothing more to say. She replied with a matter-of-fact voice, "I just came to tell you personally that I have to take time off until the cancer is gone. I want to assure you that I will be back at the office. I am not going to lose to this cancer."

"Yup," replied Gus. Lupita left his porch and headed down the walkway toward her car. Gus stood in his gaping door, wondering if a life was a thing that could be won or lost like a game. It was all fun and games when you watched media shows on television, but he wasn't much different from the pundits on television. He didn't really know anything about anything important. He felt bad for Lupita, but honestly he couldn't feel her pain. There was no comprehending a thing like finding out you had cancer when it was someone else facing the sentence.

The news about Lupita soured him on his dinner. He hadn't figured the tests were so serious. Then again, her having a serious illness kind of fit in with the general state of things as of late. Had she been healthy, no doubt, she'd have been out there protesting with all the other good Christians she said she had grown sick of. Lupita had always been a strong woman who thought justice was not served until those who were unaffected by the alleged crime were as outraged as those who actually were. He had just used the past tense in thinking about her, and yet she was on the edge of his lawn getting in her car as he thought that thought. She had cancer, yes, but she wasn't dead yet. There was always hope, wasn't there? No sentence was a death sentence until the final bell tolled. After all, that was the theme of the night. Right now wasn't the time for pessimism, as there was a drug dealer's son to break out of prison and illegally transport across the border for the sake of a few dollars. Suddenly the money didn't feel so exciting.

It was still a little early to get the plan running, but dinner was now off, so he headed for the sheriff's truck. Gus started up his truck just as another vehicle roared up the driveway and parked dead behind him. The vehicle blocked Gus's pathway away from his house. Gus checked his side mirror, but Lupita's car was long gone by now. A man from the vehicle behind Gus got out. The man wore a long trench coat with a silly brimmed hat. The hat was pulled down low, so Gus couldn't make out his face. The man was walking up to Gus's truck's driver's-side door briskly. Gus watched him in the side mirror. The guy was acting nervous. He'd stick his right hand into his trench coat's pocket, and then he'd pull it out. He repeated the action over and over again as he slowly walked up the driveway. Gus slid his own hand down to where he kept his gun. Gus held on fast to the handle of the gun. It could be one of Antonio's thugs. That didn't make sense to Gus. Antonio wouldn't kill him, not now. He'd wait until his son was released from prison before he'd try that. It was possible the thug only had a message to call tonight's game off. Perhaps it was one of Terry Tang's West Coast friends. There were many other potential innocent reasons as to why this man was here, but then again there was that hand that kept dipping in and out of the trench coat's deep pocket. You couldn't take any chances on what exactly this message was going to be.

The man arrived at Gus's driver's-side window. He paused by the window and dug once more into his pocket. His head was down, looking straight into that pocket. It was a mistake on his part. Gus popped the door hard and leaned all his weight into it. The force of the door's striking the man flung him several feet off the driveway and onto the front lawn. He landed hard, making an expensive divot in the turf. His hat had been knocked off his head. The man's hands were free of his pockets, as he had desperately used them in vain to try and break his unexpected fall. Gus came out of the truck, held out his gun, and pointed it at the fallen man. Gus ordered him, "Get your hands up where I can see them. I want no fancy stuff. I'm not in a fancy-stuff kind of mood this evening."

"What the hell was that for?" complained a familiar voice from the ground.

Gus put the gun away and put hand out to help the man up. "Sorry about that, Frank. I didn't know it was you. You have to have more common sense than to dress like that and walk up on a sheriff unexpected-like."

Frank didn't put his hand in Gus's hand. Instead, he reached his hand back into his pocket and pulled out a stack of papers. He placed those in Gus's hand. Frank yelled from the ground, "I didn't come here to start something. I came here to stop things before they get too far."

Frank Patterson climbed to his feet. Gus went into his truck and pulled out his reading glasses. He put those broken reading glasses on and pretended to read over the slips of paper Frank had handed him by flashlight. Deputy Lopez was a fury when it came to vengeance. He had sent her out to write tickets, and she had gotten a lot more than tickets. She had delivered the news to Frank about the forfeiture. Gus whistled and then said Frank, "There's a lot of trouble here for your bank. Don't worry, though; I haven't filled out all those papers about the forfeiture just yet. There might be a valid reason for all that money I found in your car when I broke into it."

Frank dusted the lawn off his clothing. "My bank employees got a thousand dollars' worth of tickets today. A thousand dollars! You stole five thousand dollars from my BMW as well. It is my client's money. This stuff has got to stop. Most important of all, you can't tell people who lie about laundering drug dealer's money."

Gus turned to face his neighbor's house. "Frank, do you know whose house that is right next door?"

"In a few days it will be the bank's house," replied Frank.

"How much is my neighbor's house worth to the bank at auction?"

"I'm not at liberty to say," replied Frank.

"Why not? It's a free country."

"Fine, the bank will probably get one hundred thousand give or take twenty-five thousand at auction for that house. I mean, look at it. It's not worth that much, but one hundred thousand is one hundred thousand."

Gus fanned himself with the stack of tickets and whistled. He replied, "That's a lot of money to be made off of just the lack of a two-dollar payment. I'd say your parking problems will easily be ended by me. Don't you worry about them ending; I'll personally take care of it. I'm sorry for the inconvenience."

"I should say so."

"Let me finish. I'm sorry for the inconvenience of the next hundred days or so. I figure at the going rate of a thousand dollars a day, it will take about that long to repay the bank in sum for the lack of taking my two dollars when I tried to give it to you for the sake of my neighbor. I did it as honestly as I could, but you just wouldn't take it. Of course, there is also that news about the laundering of money…that might cost the poor bank even more than that if I did file my report about laundering money for drug dealers."

"You can't do this; it's against the law."

"I am the law in these parts. I think you'll find everything I'm doing to you is perfectly within the letter of the law in this state. I'm only following the letter of the law, which you hold dear, Frank. The letter of the law will be following you very carefully for another ninety-four thousand dollars' worth of fines and forfeitures."

Gus reached his hand out to give Frank back his tickets. Frank's hands didn't reach out to take them. Gus put the tickets into his own pocket. He pulled out his wallet. He took two one-dollar bills out. He reached them out to Frank. Frank frowned at the sight of the money. Then Frank took them with an angry jerk. He shoved them into one of his trench-coat pockets.

"This isn't right," complained Frank.

"Nope, it don't seem right," agreed Gus in sympathy.

Frank didn't say another word. Gus reached down and popped the back latch of his truck open. He said to Frank, "You'll find seven bags in the back partially filled with money. Take it; it's your clients'. I think I'm convinced that they're not proceeds from a drug deal all of a sudden."

Frank took the bags out. He stormed back down the driveway to his own vehicle carrying the money. Gus walked over to the edge of the grass. The sun was totally gone now. He turned his flashlight on the lawn. The place where Frank had landed hard was now another hole that would need to be filled. Gus held the light on the hole as he tried to kick the large divot back into place. Frank's vehicle started up with a roar of the engine, and then Frank tore away down the road as fast as he had come. Gus frowned at the thought of another expensive lawn repair. It didn't seem right. In disgust he headed back inside his truck. He dumped the tickets into the glove compartment. He'd void them all in the morning. Finally his path was clear, and he started his truck up on his mission to return to the law-enforcement complex to pick up his cargo.

He calmly drove down the street. It was a nice, quiet night besides the few gathering clouds in the sky. He could make them out by the lightning strikes far off in the distance. Good, a little rain would mean fewer fools on the road. The oncoming rainstorm meant that not a soul was on the sidewalks of the local neighborhood as he drove back to work except two little girls. They were about three blocks from his neighbor's house. One girl was chasing after the other in a fury. It didn't seem right for two young kids to be running around after dark creating mischief. As Gus paused for a stop sign, he saw the girl of unknown origin jump and tackle the neighbor's daughter. They both toppled onto someone's lawn. They were illuminated in full view by a streetlamp. They appeared to be physically roughhousing with each other as only young children can. It could have been just playing, but it sure looked like a good solid fight. Had it been day-light, Gus would probably have just kept driving. He would have chalked it up to kids just being kids. But it was past dinnertime, and kids shouldn't be out fighting each other in the neighborhood after dark. Who knew what could happen to them under that streetlamp. As the two girls swung fists at each other, Gus thought about Sheldon Nickelback and his incident. No, Gus would break this up, because only trouble happened to children who were outside after dark.

He accelerated from the stop sign and pulled the truck over to the curb next to the two combatants. Gus sprang out of the truck and grabbed the two girls by their arms. He had the neighbor's girl in his right hand and the girl of unknown origin in his left. He forced the two girls apart. The girl of unknown origin managed a few leg kicks as Gus separated them. The two girls squirreled around beneath his iron grip, but they couldn't break free. They both cast an angry gaze up at Gus. Gus calmly lectured the two miniature combatants. "Now what in the name of Sam Hill are you two doing? You are supposed to be the best of friends, and yet here it is I see you two fighting tooth and nail on the city sidewalks after sundown! That just won't do, little ladies; do you hear me?"

"But we were just playing like the Minimite and the Darvelak in the new sequel to *Death to Hungry Kids: Uprising of Driedel*. You see, Mister Sheriff, the super fighter Danica finally figures out in the third movie that the Darvelak are just using the Minimites when they were getting them to fight among each other. Driedel knew the Minimites would never team up to overthrow the unjust Darvelaks without a leader. Driedel is the bestest and wisest, as he's the one that convinces Danica to bravely lead all the Minimites into mass rebellion!" explained the girl of unknown origin as she tried another kick in the neighbor's girl's direction.

"Isn't it just horrible? The Darvelak at the end of the movie are being forced to actually pay the Minimites, and even worse, let them play with their own dolls. It just isn't fair! After all, the Darvelaks didn't do nothing and would like to keep it that way. Who would ever think this bestest movie series was going to end like that? They took a perfectly good movie series and ruined it!" complained the neighbor's girl, who added a kick of her own to the end of it.

Gus reasoned, "Well, perhaps you two girls should consider that it is only a movie. Don't you think it would be wiser for you two to both pretend to be Minimites and team up and defeat the Darvelaks like in the movie?"

"That's stupid; I have always played a Darvelak, and a Darvelak I want to stay. I'm pretty sure no noble, rich Darvelak would want to be a dumb old poor Minimite! The first two movies were so bestest, why did they have to go and ruin it? I want to be a Darvelak now and forever, not a stupid Minimite!" shouted the neighbor's girl.

"That's stupid; I'm a Minimite, and I ain't letting nobody force me to watch them play with my dolls again! It is time for a rebellion. Death to the Darvelaks!" screeched the girl of unknown origin as she finally broke free of Gus's grip. The neighbor's girl wiggled out as well, and down the street they chased each other, shouting rebellion at the top of their lungs.

Gus shook his head. Kids, they just never learn, do they? He did the best he could to bring a little control to the neighborhood, but he didn't have the time to go chasing after two little girls who just didn't understand how the real world worked. They'd figure it out eventually. The rainstorm would chase them indoors soon enough. Gus climbed back in the sheriff's truck and headed back on course to his rendezvous with destiny as the first few drops of rain fell from the sky.

Sophie's Ice Cream Parlor had been in business since 1957 when Sophie Jordan's husband, Pete, had opened up the shop. Neither of the original owners of the parlor was around anymore. The ice cream hadn't lasted either. The parlor hadn't served an ice-cream cone in nearly ten years now. Ice cream had gone out with the Pilates fitness craze. Then again, it might have been the Thai boxing fitness craze that did it in, or perhaps it just might have been the latest fad exercise of yoga that ended ice-cream cones in Sophie's Ice Cream Parlor for good. Modern hipsters don't sully their lips with such mundane things as ice cream. These days Sophie's Ice Cream Parlor only served up gelato or frozen yogurt sprinkled with all-natural-grown fresh fruit, smashed-up wheat-free whole-food cookie dough, or organically farm-raised vanilla extract. Luckily for Gus, whatever it was they served, it still packed in the same amount of sugar, cream, and vanilla flavor as the passé ice cream had. Sophie's was located back-to-back with the law-enforcement complex. No doubt they were doing a pretty good business at the moment with so many people in downtown. Nothing works up a good gelato hunger like a little firebrand protesting of a seventeen-year-old woman's imagined sins. Gus would have snuck in for a gelato himself right now, only it was well past closing time for the parlor. Gus had made sure there would be no backdoor foot traffic behind the ice-cream parlor tonight by placing a barricade to bar the protesting people from the back parking lot of the law-enforcement complex.

Gus was driving by Sophie's for a non-gelato-related emergency. Sophie's conveniently had a narrow alley that ran between it and the back lot of the law-enforcement complex. Normally it was only used to roll the big green garbage Dumpsters to the curb and to deliver things to the roll-up back service door of the law-enforcement complex. Tonight Gus was going to be using it to sneak Kyle Minnelli out the back way, unseen by the eyes of those who claimed to see God. It was a mission of garbage in, garbage out, so it wasn't much different from normal back-parking-lot operations. Then again, no one had proved in a court of law that Kyle was exactly garbage. Gus slowed the truck to a crawl as he navigated the tight space between buildings. Sophie's shop was on left side of the alley, and a place named the Yoga Gym was on the right. A few sparks were coming off the truck's side mirrors as Gus navigated the tight fit. There were advantages to driving a twenty-year-old rusting truck. You could spark up a side mirror on the cement side of a yoga gym and not get all bent out of shape over the fact that it was getting all bent out of shape.

Finally, the truck was free of the tight alley walls and arrived in the small back parking lot of the law-enforcement complex. Deputy Drew had done his job very well. He was holding the barricade line, and the back parking lot was completely free of gawkers and protesters. The din of them singing hymns loomed just beyond the far corner of the parking lot. They were out of sight, but not out of mind. Deputy Drew had set up a fair number of orange cones and yellow caution tape to basically surround the whole back area. He had also set up the little white tent like the one they had used during the drunk-driving trap so many nights before. It seemed like ages ago. The tent was set up right in the middle of the small back lot. In a folding chair under the tent sat Deputy Drew guarding the area from any possible onlookers. Gus pulled the sheriff's truck right up next to the tent and waved hello to the deputy through the truck's window.

Gus exited the truck and walked under the tent. "Deputy, I don't believe I've ever said this before to you, but good job in keeping those damn protesters away from here. The only thing I don't get is the need for this tent."

"Don't you ever read the Internet weather report?" asked Deputy Drew.

"It's just a little rain. You're not made of sugar, so it can't hurt you," replied Gus.

"Tonight the surf is going to be up. The monsoons are coming in full force for sure, according to the weatherman. All the weather sites agree on the possibility of extreme heavy showers."

The old man at the ranch this morning had been right about the weather. Gus looked up into the sky and affirmed that there wasn't a star to be seen. The blackening clouds were dead overhead, but it wasn't much more than a sprinkle coming down. It was just nuisance weather, but nothing to get worried about. It didn't seem so severe at the moment. While the clouds were packed in tight, the thunder and lightning was still pretty far off. It was raining hard somewhere in the county, but possibly it would not rain very heavy here. Gus said to Drew, "It doesn't seem to be too bad. I got a feeling the weatherman is wrong and the worst of it will miss us like it typically does."

"You don't mind if I take your word for it but stay under my tent just the same?"

Gus watched small drops fall onto his truck's windshield. Gus instructed Drew, "Nah, I don't mind. Just keep the fort safe. I'm going inside to pick up the cargo. Oh, and one last thing, there's no need to ask what's going on and no need to wonder why I'm doing it."

"If my dad has taught me one thing in life from all the years he's been our mayor, he's taught me that when you don't know what is going on, you never have to pretend to care about what is going on. I've never seen him know or care once in all these years."

"That sound reasoning is why I voted for him twice last election," replied Gus.

Gus placed his key into the service door of the law-enforcement complex and opened the lock. He slid up the rolling door to the cell block and stepped right in. The guard desk was vacant, because the man who was supposed to be at it was sitting under a tent in the drizzle not caring. Gus examined his chalkboard. Cell one allegedly had Terry Tang. No one had noticed the slight clerical error that Terry Tang was currently a free man, and Kyle Minnelli wasn't. That was the burden of poor office work that a place gets when your secretary is stricken with cancer. That was the current excuse for tomorrow's discovery that there had been a mix-up, in the paperwork, and it was actually a good one. Far better than anything Gus could have made up on his own. Gus smiled at the chalkboard momentarily, but the moment ended as he inspected the other two names on the board; cell three had Jennifer Louis Bachman, and cell five now had Mr. Smith. The three people in stir were locked up safe for the night. That meant his jail had two innocent people and one criminal. Who was who was a matter of opinion; Gus had his opinion on the matter, and he was acting on it. None of them had actually been convicted of anything as of yet; still, only a fool thought a man like Josh Hansen wasn't guilty of many things. Granted, no matter how guilty he was, this hacker wasn't supposed to be in his jail at all. The only criminal in it was technically the only free man. Gus was here to free the poor innocent inmate so he could get money from his father.

It didn't sound very noble an act when it was put that way, but the nobility had money, so they could afford to put things any way they wanted. A poor working man like Gus had needs, and thoughts of being part of the lofty nobility got in the way of fulfilling those needs. Gus always found that mercy bore richer fruits than strict justice. It helped when the fruits it produced were papery and green. Gus placed the key into the lock, punched in the code, and opened the cell-block door. He left the door hanging open by propping it with a chair. He didn't plan to be in here long. He walked down the cell block to cell number one. He had moved Kyle into it before leaving work earlier that night. He placed the key into the lock and unlocked it. It was time to free Kyle from his false burden of having to be Terry Tang for the day. Only as he slid the cell door wide open did he realize that Kyle wasn't actually inside his cell.

A blond man's head was resting on the cells bunk's pillow. Gus was angry and yelled, "Hansen, what the hell are you doing in this cell!"

Wiping the sleep from his eyes, Hansen lifted his head from his pillow. He squinted at Gus. He then replied, "I was sleeping. The pillows in here are much softer than my cell, so I traded bunks with Kyle for the night. By the way, your chalkboard is wrong, but I figured you know that already. You're not up to no good, are you, big boss man?"

Gus laughed. "I'm up to my neck in no good, but you all won't leave me alone. That suck lawyer of Terry Tang had a briefcase full of papers but never read the most important one. Thanks to that mistake, tonight I'm just ridding my jail of the good that only are falsely labeled no good. It is all I can get rid of unless you leave voluntarily."

"If you don't mind my asking, why'd you arrest him in the first place if you were just going to let him go?"

"The reasoning is between my aching knees and his father. Don't you hackers ever learn to stick to your own business?"

"Of course not, it's my business to nose around into everyone's business. Once I know your secrets, I tell everyone about them. How else am I going to topple the oligarchy? I've worked from the outside hacking in and from the inside leaking out, so I know the game very well. I'd say I'm watching a little inside job right now. So it was a business arrangement, was it? I'm sure I offered you much more in the form of shit coins than his father did in real currency, and yet you still want me to leave! I have to say my heart will go on, even though you've broken it some. Do you want to hear a story?"

"No."

"Did you ever sit at the kids' table at family functions while growing up?"

"I said no stories," warned Gus.

"When I was young, I always sat at the kids' table and dreamed about having a seat at the grown-ups' table. They were older, bigger, and wiser than me, and so who didn't want to sit with them? I thought the grown-ups' table would be a place where intelligence and science got a seat. I'm not saying they have the whole table to themselves, but I assumed being grown-ups at the table, they'd reserve such things as wisdom a seat at their table. The laws of the table would be just and fair laws, because the policies of the table would be those that had been proved to work over the years, and those that proved to be failures would be quickly removed forever and abandoned. I grew up eventually—some people do, but most people don't, judging by who is really at the grown-ups' table. At the real grown-ups' table, you'll find that intelligence and science rarely get a seat at all. The spaces are all reserved for dogma, jealousy, greed, superstition, and hate. The law is filled with bad ideas that are sometimes overturned but rarely abandoned. Like a bad penny, they turn up over and over again, and each time they churn to the top, the grown-ups at the table pretend this is the time the failed idea will work. Now that I'm grown-up, I wish to go back to sit at the kids' table. I'd rather dream that this world of ours is a just place than to know our petty self-induced ignorance will make sure it will never be."

"I still like the porpoise story the best." Gus pulled his gun out and pointed it at Josh Hansen. "You know what, Hansen, you're leaving tonight as well. It's a small change in my plans, but I think I can swing it."

"But I don't want to go. I like it here, and besides, if you remember my lie I told you, then the climate scientists are still trying to kill me. Did you forget that part, or do you just not care about me? Do you want them to kill me?"

"I was fixing to rid myself of the inmate in cell one, and you're now the man in cell number one, so you're leaving tonight. You can choose to leave in a knotty pine box or out my back service door, but you're leaving nonetheless."

"You won't shoot me."

"Why not? You're a thief, a spy, a philanderer, a megalomaniac, and likely a murderer. If you've forgotten about the dead girl you left behind

226

on your last visit to my county, then I'd like you to know I didn't. I would be doing the world a favor if I killed you here and now."

"I was under the impression you weren't the type of man to do this world any favors."

Gus frowned at that remark and put the gun down. He tucked it safely back into its holster. He hung the cell door open. He grumbled to Hansen, "This door is all the way open, and you're an optimist, so I know you see it that way. Pack your bags, because you're leaving tonight."

Hansen hopped off the bunk and pulled out his trunk that was stored under it. He explained, "They're already packed. I figured I've cooled my heels here long enough. There are people trying to kill me. Not those climate people, obviously, but real people who are good at killing other people. They'll find me here eventually if I don't keep on moving. I figure that I've stayed here just about as long as I could."

"All right, smartass, which cell is my boy in?"

"Cell number five."

Gus pulled his keys out of the lock and made his way toward cell number five. He walked by Jennifer sleeping uncomfortably in her bunk. There was no telling how long she'd be stuck in jail now. The whole Mexican thing had come as a shock to everyone, or almost everyone. Someone had set that stage up this afternoon. It was probably her slick defense lawyer. Josh whispered into Gus's ear as they walked by, "You know, Sheriff, why don't you take her with us? They say it is better to risk saving a guilty person than to condemn an innocent one."

Gus replied, "Need I remind you that I am risking saving a guilty person already? Plus, don't forget that I'm risking myself in all this mess as well. I'm the most innocent person I know. I could lose the next election if people found out what's been going on here, or worse, I could go to prison. Prison is no place for a man like me, because it should be filled with people like you."

"Yeah, but I bet you anything Kyle's dad is paying you awfully well for the privilege of risking your guilty neck. You wouldn't stick your neck out without getting something good in return."

"Who told you that?"

"Kyle did. He told me you planted some drugs in his apartment. The Kyle kid isn't that bad a fellow. Kyle figures you did this because you don't like successful Mexicans. I think you did it to get a bribe out of his father. I heard he's the biggest avocado dealer that this neck of the woods has ever seen. I imagine you need to replace avocado with cocaine in that story to get nearer to the truth, but it rings true to me in dollars and cents all the same. Kyle's a nice lad, but a bit too trusting of his parents. I do like him all the same. That other drug dealer, Terry Tang, was the pits. All of us on the prison block hated him. I'm glad he's gone. This drug dealer's son, though, seems like a decent fellow. Using Terry's drugs to do this to him just for some money when you could have put Terry away in prison is wrong. You disappoint me, Gus. I had a very high opinion of you when I broke in here. I don't hide among every sheriff's jail cells, you know."

"I was worried you wouldn't approve. No need to stand around here; let's reunite the father with the son and get rid of you at the same time."

Hansen lectured him further, "Right is right, even if everyone is against it; a wrong is still a wrong, even if everyone is for it. Everyone wants money, but there are right ways and wrong ways to go about getting it. I'd say planting evidence against a drug dealer's son just to bribe him of money is rather wrong. It seems to me a lot worse than anything that Jennifer is ever going to do to offend this world. Come on, what do you say? Let's fuck them all and let her go."

Gus jammed the key into lock number three and unlocked the door. He slid the cell door wide open. He instructed Hansen, "I want you to know I'm doing this under protest. Wake her up and tell her she's being moved to a more secure location. She is your responsibility now. Take her out of here and put her in the sheriff's truck outside. Now, if there are no further delays, I'm going to get the only person I came in here for tonight."

Gus left Hansen and finished the journey to cell number five. Kyle Minnelli was asleep on his bunk. Gus opened up his third cell of the night. He cleared his throat, but Kyle remained asleep. Annoyed, he put his hand on the boy's shoulder and gave him a little shake. Nothing stirred. Gus started kicking the bottom bunk with his foot. On the third kick, Kyle reached out his hand and caught Gus's foot. Kyle easily turned Gus's foot and put Gus off balance. Gus spilled onto the cell floor.

Kyle clung to the bunk with his hands, daring Gus to drag him out of the cell, "Mr. Smith told me what you were up to tonight. I will not leave with you; not tonight, not tomorrow morning, not ever. I will not let you blackmail my father just to let you have some blood money. You can go to hell, you corrupt, fat bastard!"

Gus sprawled on the floor and reconsidered shooting Hansen. Unfortunately, Hansen was taking Jennifer to the truck at the moment, so he was safely out of range. Instead Gus slowly sat up on his butt. He turned around to face Kyle. He could see the defiance of youth in his eyes. A lot of wasted energy the defiance of youth had cost the world, but Gus didn't hold it against the kid. It was the logical conclusion Hansen had drawn. It wasn't exactly accurate, but then Hansen was too criminally oriented to understand the truth. The truth was far stupider than he could imagine. Gus rolled up his pant legs until he exposed his bare knees. The black-and-blue marks were still very visible.

"See those marks on my knees?" asked Gus.

"I do not care!" yelled back Kyle.

"Denial doesn't become you. Your father had two goons beat me pretty good the other night. He did it because he was worried about you. He knew there was a killer about to be set loose on the community. A killer he thought killed young men like you. I think he was wrong on that part, but he couldn't have known it at the time. I took you, just for a little while, as revenge, but also for something more. It was a stupid thing to do, I admit that, but your father deserved it. You didn't deserve it, so I'm releasing you tonight. There are no charges against you, so there is nothing to get money out of your father for. You could just walk out of here a free man at any time you had wanted today had you known. I'm sorry to have kept it a secret up to now, but I had to."

"I don't understand…why all of this then?"

"The sneaking around late at night? Well, let's just say you're not the only one I wanted to get rid of. Your father isn't the only man with money.

I do have my reasons. They might be stupid reasons. I won't argue over that now, as we have to be going."

"How do I know you're telling me the truth?" asked Kyle.

"Come see for yourself. I checked you out of here this afternoon when Terry Tang was discharged with papers with your name on it. As far as the official paperwork knows, you're a free man, and Terry Tang is still in my jail. Tomorrow morning I will say Terry Tang escaped this prison cell tonight, and no one will ever know you were suspected of any crime. Terry Tang and his lawyer will protest, but by the time the confusion is sorted out, you will be long gone. There are no charges pressed against you."

Gus took the great effort to stand up. He waved his finger to Kyle to follow him. Then he left cell number five. The cell door was wide open. Gus never turned back; he just walked down the empty cell block, leaving behind the allure of freedom. He reached the open cell-block door and went through. He paused at the vacant guard desk. Kyle was about fifteen seconds behind him. Curiosity simply had gotten the better of him. Kyle examined the three names on the chalkboard. He interjected, "Anyone can write anything on a chalkboard."

Gus opened the guard desk's drawers. He pulled out a copy of the discharge papers. He handed them over to Kyle. "Here's the official paper-work. Terry had a real fine and dandy lawyer. He was so angry about me letting your father's boys steal his client's money and not even getting the drugs back in return that he never bothered to look at the name written on those forms. If you ever get in real trouble with the law, go get yourself a real good lawyer, kid. A bad lawyer that cares more about illegal drugs than your safety will do you an injustice every time. So you ready to go?"

Kyle was ready. The two of them went out the back door. Gus saw that Josh was ever the gentleman. He had loaded himself into the passenger seat of the truck and left it up to Jennifer to load Josh's traveling trunk into the back of the truck with Deputy Drew's help. Poor Deputy Drew was aiding and abetting a crime, but luckily he'd never figure that fact out. Gus motioned Kyle into the back of the truck. There were no seats back there in the truck's bed under the covered canopy. Technically it was illegal for riders to sit back there. It was a small crime, all things considered.

The final passenger was loaded up, and Drew closed the back hatch. Gus checked his watch. He was right on time. The plan was unfolding beautifully. In another half hour, he'd have dumped all his burdens over the border. They'd be Mexico's headache to deal with. He was honestly giddy at the prospect, but he kept a stern face.

Gus asked Deputy Drew, "Everything all set to go?"

"I figure they are, but I don't understand why you're letting the whole jail out tonight."

Before Gus could answer, a new voice broke in the night air. It was a female's voice. The sound of the voice was something like, "*Zdra-stvooy-tye.*" Gus spun around. In the open service door was standing one Deputy Chiquita Lopez. She was holding her gun outstretched in her left hand. Its barrel was pointed at Gus. Deputy Lopez spoke again, "I can't let you simply drive away from here. I have come too far and searched too hard to find Josh Hansen. When word got around that Josh had arrived in these parts, they called me up immediately. His path wasn't hard to follow here to this county. I was very fortunate to find this lovely position from which to search the county far and wide for Josh without drawing any suspicion. How silly of me not to start my search here at the law-enforcement complex. I've been every other place in this county but this cell block. Until now, that is. I've found him. I guarantee I will end him here tonight."

Josh Hansen rolled down the driver's-side window and poked his head out. He shouted, "Why, if it isn't Chiquita Lopez, my friendly daughter of an old Russian agent. Gus, she's good, real good. She's the daughter of the best Russian-trained agent inside of Mexico. Her family's been down there since the start of the Cold War. I'd hire her if I were you. You couldn't find a better worker. It's been a long time, no see, Chiquita baby."

Gus rubbed his temple. "Hansen, if you actually tell me she is a paid assassin of the climate scientists, then I'll shoot you myself."

Chiquita replied, "What is this climate-science thing? I have stalked Josh all this way for revenge. I was placed in charge of keeping Josh safe while he conducted some hacking business for Russia. He told me he loved me. He told me he'd never leave me. He made love to me, and then he had the nerve to leave me. He stole the information he was gathering, stole the money Russia was paying him, and he stole my heart. No words of even good-bye."

Hansen explained, "Chiquita, baby, trust me; I loved every minute of it, but you've got to understand I was just lying to you when I said I loved you so I could sleep with you. You are fairly hot, as Russian-trained Mexican assassins go. You got to understand that to me, it was just a little hacking assignment with the added benefit of sex. I don't give a crap about your shit-ass government or your people who help protect it. I fucked you, and then I made up all the data I leaked to your government and stole the real data, so in a way I fucked them too. I fuck people over for money; that's what I do. I'm a hacker, baby. It is no big deal, right."

"You wronged me, and I never forgive a wrong. A person should pay for their mistakes. I would never let a man violate me and not pay the ultimate penalty for it. You said you loved me, and you didn't. I have been wronged, and I shall right that wrong tonight. There will be no negotiations on this point, no trial, no courtroom, and no judge. There will only be justice on this matter."

Gus interjected, "Well, okay then, out of the truck, Hansen, and let this pretty lady shoot you. I've got a schedule to keep, and I can't waste time yakking about your sordid sex life all night."

Chiquita replied, "I am sorry, but there can be no witnesses. You will all have to die."

Gus reasoned with Chiquita. "Look, you said you wanted justice. Justice is about making the criminal pay for creating suffering, but revenge would be making all of us pay out of your anger. Hansen's right; you're the best deputy I've ever had. Don't throw away a promising deputy career away over this…man. He's not worth it. He is just another Vitcoin. He looks all nice on the computer screen, but he's shit and not worth the investment."

Chiquita didn't answer. Instead, a new voice shouted out from the small alley that lay between the yoga gym and the ice-cream parlor. The back parking lot was getting to be a rather busy little place to have a very discrete late-night rendezvous. At this point Gus might as well have let all the protestors just stay here so they could enjoy the show. Gus slowly circled in the direction of the alley. Terry Tang, carrying a gun in his outstretched hand, arrived from the alley. Terry Tang instructed the mixed crowd, "No one is doing anything to anyone until I get my drugs back. I saw you load them inside a trunk onto that truck. I see that trunk right there. You were going to take them over the border and into the care of Antonio's bastard son. Big Gustavo already has my gang's money; he will not have my gang's drugs too. I'm afraid that isn't going to happen, because I'm smart. You thought you were smart, Sheriff, but I'm way smarter."

Gus replied, "You're pointing a gun in the direction of a Russian-trained Mexican assassin, and you want me to be impressed by your intelligence?"

Chiquita now shouted, "I remember you, Terry Tang. You are the criminal drug dealer from the other day. I do not care if you want to die with them. You are all filthy criminals, and none of you deserve to live."

Hansen now interjected, "Even me, baby? I'm the one that stole the passcode to the Pentagon's squash court for you. I'm the one that told you he loved you. I do love you, baby, only not that much. Is that really a crime?"

"You're not really helping things, Hansen," interjected Gus.

Terry was walking closer and shouted, "Shut up, all of you! No one is shooting anyone until I get my fucking drugs. You, the fat-ass sheriff, retrieve my drugs for me."

Chiquita replied, "Men, they are so confident of themselves. They always think they have fooled you with words of love or authority. They are always so in the wrong on these things."

Terry pointed his gun directly at her. He said, "Listen, bitch, shut the fuck up. You're just a stupid-ass deputy of this stupid fat-ass sheriff. Both of you stupid fat asses pull that trunk full of my drugs from the back of that truck now, or I shoot you both!"

"I have a gun. I will use my gun," she replied.

"What? Do you think I'm afraid of a woman? You should be home baking brownies, bitch," replied Terry.

Chiquita answered that statement with her gun. She shot. Terry Tang pulled his trigger a split second later. The moment happened so fast that

Gus didn't have time to do anything. He just stood there perplexed between the two gunmen as the comedy of the situation unfolded. It was over in less than a second. Chiquita crumpled to the ground as her gun skittered across the parking lot. Terry wasn't any better a shot than he was a drug dealer and had hit her in the shoulder. At least it was the shoulder to the arm that held the gun. Terry Tang was shot through the heart. He dropped to his knees. He raised his gun to fire a second time. He pointed his gun straight at Gus. There was hate in the man's eyes, but nothing but a hole in his heart. By the time his arm reached the vertical position, his heart had stopped pumping. He crumpled into a pile. He was dead. The pain in Gus's left earlobe followed a split second later. One of them had nicked it in the fray. The earlobe bled freely down the side of Gus's head. Gus examined his load tucked away in the sheriff's truck. They were all safely out of sight, ducking their heads below the truck's windows.

A maddening crowd of pro-life protestors, media reporters, and just hangers-on had heard the shots. They started to pour past the corner of the parking lot and enter the back parking lot. Pastor Voce was in the lead. He stopped dead at the edge of the yellow caution tape. He gasped at the sight of the blood gushing out of what used to be Terry Tang. Gus looked at Terry, he looked Chiquita, and then he looked at the truck with everyone ducking out of sight. He glanced at Deputy Drew, who just stood there doing nothing. You could always count on Drew to do what he did best during a pressure packed situation. Gus had to think fast. Gus turned to face Pastor Voce and yelled out, "I want your people to watch out, as there are dangerous gang members on the loose. It appears that a pro-abortion terrorist group has just burst into my jail and unfortunately busted Jennifer Louis Bachman out. Deputy Lopez here was able to take one of the scumbags out, but the rest got away with our criminal from Kansas. Don't just stand there; some of you call an ambulance for my deputy, some of you go through the front door of my law-enforcement complex and get some more of my deputies, and lastly some of you call nine one one and tell them to be on the lookout for a yellow Porsche with Canadian plates. They'll be driving north to what they think will be their Canuck-flavored socialist freedom."

234

There was dead silence in the crowd for a few brief seconds. No one seemed to believe the news, Gus most of all. Then in unison some of them pulled out their cell phones to call 911. The media members in the crowd started yelling to studios on the East Coast to go live. Others in the media started shooting pictures of anything that was in front of them, even the heads of other people standing in front of them in the crowd. People were taking selfies. It was decaying fast into pandemonium. One media member was so enraptured by the thought of what was sure to be the biggest total dump of news bullshit to hit the airways in years that he simply peed in his pants and then fainted from the sheer excitement of the event.

Deputy Drew came up and offered Gus a rag to place over his bloody ear. Gus barked to him, "Drew, go keep those people out of here. Use force if you have to. We got a crime scene and an officer down. Chiquita is hurt, and I don't want her to bleed to death while these gawkers look on."

"I'm confused, boss," replied Drew.

"No need to be; just let it all happen and see to it about keeping those people out of here," replied Gus.

"You can count on me." Drew went over to try and quell the crowd. Pastor Voce was doing his best to keep his people in line. Oddly enough, the crowd didn't crush in on Gus. The yellow tape of authority held them back as if it had magical powers. They stood on the other side of it gawking, filming, and praying for the violent death of the rest of the corrupt Canadian terrorist pro-abortionist group.

Gus walked over to Deputy Lopez. She had managed to sit up. Her face had the look of being in a lot of pain. He handed her his rag. "Here, you need this more than I do. Congratulations, Deputy Lopez, you're about to become a national hero for killing that pro-abortion terrorist. How does it all feel to be a hero?"

"My shoulder hurts."

Gus bent down on his knee and looked at her wound. "Clean, through the muscle. You should live."

"I…"

"Don't need to say any more; there are cameras rolling. I'm leaving now, because I really need to be in hot pursuit of those terrorists at this moment, but you take care now. I owe you my life, as I think that Terry Tang guy would really have killed me."

"What about me?" she asked.

"You almost died just to get the opportunity to kill the worthless Josh Hansen. Do you think it was worth it?"

The lights flashed from the reporters' cameras. The crowd was singing a lovely hymn of retribution against those darn Canadians. Chiquita looked into Gus's eyes and said, "No, it wasn't worth it. Had I done what I threatened to do, it wouldn't have been justice. It would have been murder. I'm sorry I tried to kill you."

"I'm sorry you got shot."

"What stupid things I've wasted my life doing."

"I got a feeling there will be more interesting opportunities coming your way from now on," replied Gus. Deputy Wilson and Deputy Costner arrived out of the back entrance of the jail, which distracted her from saying more. Gus yelled over to them to help Deputy Lopez. The crowd began to reluctantly part as Gus heard the sound of an ambulance arriving. The hospital was only a stone's throw away from his station, so he wasn't surprised they had gotten there so fast.

He tried to go over to his truck, but Chiquita held on to his arm with her good hand. She whispered to him, "Don't worry; I'll stick to your story."

"Why?"

"Justice should be done. I owe you something for my mistake made in anger tonight. You better leave in hot pursuit of those suspects now."

She let go of Gus's arm. Deputy Wilson knelt beside her and said, "She'll be all right."

Costner asked, "Should I head out in pursuit of them suspects too?"

"Nah, I'll go it alone, I think. You boys make sure to take care of her and keep this crowd pacified. I don't need any vigilantes. Have no worries; every state boy on Brian Hartline's force will be on the lookout for that yellow Porsche. We'll catch them."

Gus left it up to his deputies to do their job and walked over to his truck. He opened the door. The three passengers were all hiding out of

236

sight. Gus sat down in the driver's seat. He hit his sirens and the emergency lights on. It all looked like one crazy mess outside his truck's windows, and yet somehow the plan was still together. He had his load packed up and ready to go, and with word out there were terrorists moving north toward Canada, not a single honest lawman, but hopefully one, would be south of his station. Gus turned over the truck's engine, and he departed the scene of the crime.

Fully loaded with its illicit cargo, the sheriff's truck emerged from the alley. Gus took an immediate left and drove parallel to Main Street. The goal had been to escape the law-enforcement complex unseen by the masses of protestors, and it had been a rather unsuccessful execution of that plan so far. A drug dealer had been shot, and Gus's deputy was wounded in the affair, but you had to take the good with the bad. The good being Deputy Lopez, even if she was a fake, and the bad being Terry Tang, who had been genuinely an ass. Gus felt bad about Chiquita being injured, as she likely had saved lives tonight even if she had also threatened to take those same lives away. None of that stuff mattered now. What mattered to Gus was that no one at this late date appeared to suspect Gus's greater plan.

The sheriff's truck arrived at the end of the street. Gus checked his rearview mirror. There was no one behind him. The rain increased in volume, and Gus turned his windshield wipers to full. He was growing a little concerned. A little rain was okay, but a monsoon was not. Too much rain would flood the arroyos, and the dry washes would not be passable until late tomorrow or the next day. His cargo needed to leave both the county and the country in a hurry, and tomorrow night wouldn't do. The passengers all sat listening to the rain beat down on the roof of the truck in a sort of odd, quiet calmness. They were heading to a destination unknown to any of them, and none of them seemed to be objecting to the fact that they were clueless as to where Gus was taking them at this late date. They all just seemed happy to be going anywhere that was out of his jail. Gus turned to the right, heading on a path toward the interstate. They were only five miles from the junction between the two main interstate roads. That was five miles between Gus and the road that lead south. Down south was the promised land of freedom.

There was chatter on the radio. It told Gus that the authorities were setting up the state police to block the major routes north out of the county and also that Deputy Lopez had gotten to the hospital okay. The truck reached the start of the interstate, and Gus pressed down on the accelerator. The road south was as clear as it could be hoped for. He accelerated up to the speed limit. The old "fifty-five saves lives" speed-limit signs were now all tucked safely away in a storage closest in the basement of the law-enforcement complex. They were keeping company with all the metric signs that the rest of the world could read, but American drivers could not. The effort to save lives and fuel consumption had lost the battle to people's desire to get where they were going slightly faster. If slightly faster increased traffic deaths by a few percent, then no one still alive in America appeared to care. Gus accelerated the truck up to the speed limit as it increased past 70 mph or 112.6 kmph. He pushed the old truck as hard as its tired twenty-year-old frame could handle with this full load in it.

Jennifer broke the long silence. "Is this illegal?"

Josh Hansen replied to her, "Only if we get caught."

"I don't want to do anything illegal," Jennifer said.

"Then I'll make sure to not get caught," added Gus.

"You might have a hard time delivering on that promise," said Josh Hansen. He didn't deliver good news. "I believe there is someone behind us, friends of yours?"

Gus glanced up to gaze at his rearview mirror. Sure enough, a vehicle had made an appearance in his rearview mirror. The headlights shone bright. They were easily keeping pace. They must have had their headlights off the whole time until the increased speed forced them to turn them on. They had been stalking them for a long time, and they weren't about to lose them now.

"Who's behind us?" asked Kyle, sounding worried.

"Not another killer, I hope. I'm starting to feel I would have been safer had I remained in the jail cell," whispered Jennifer.

"Don't worry, because we're with Sheriff Gus, the man that has shot dead more people than anyone else in the state! How much safer could we be than with him?" offered Josh Hansen.

"Somehow that additional information didn't reassure me," replied Jennifer.

She was right; that fact offered by Hansen, while true, wasn't a helpful one, as Gus was trying hard to avoid another killing tonight. Gus hoped that the people behind him were the people he expected to be behind him. *Just don't let them be media.* The swarm of people on Main Street and the ambulance moving about on it would prevent any media members from keeping pace with him. They had a wounded deputy to film and a dead body on the ground, so he should be safe from them. Plus, their helicopters wouldn't be flying in this rainstorm. Anyway, any media van that did manage to shake free would logically be moving north to film the roadblock. All that information meant the vehicle behind him just had to be who he was expecting. He didn't need more surprises on a night full of them.

The lights on the top of the trailing vehicle went off. Their sirens pierced the night air. No, it wasn't the climate scientists coming to murder Josh Hansen. It was the Kansas state troopers come to acquire Gus's load before Gus gave them away to Mexico. They wanted justice, and they were willing to arrest good ole Sheriff Gus to get it. Their car was newer, faster, and carrying less weight. The only advantage Gus had was that he knew the road and had driven it in the wet weather many times before. The patrol car pulled alongside the driver's side of the truck. It nudged Gus's truck with a slight broadside kiss of the two vehicles. The patrol car pulled away, readying itself for an even greater side-to-side impact with the next attempt. Gus didn't give them a second chance. At the last moment, he swerved the sheriff's truck onto the on-ramp of the southbound interstate road. The Kansas troopers, not knowing the roads, did not expect the maneuver and overshot the exit. It bought Gus and his occupants only a few minutes. Soon the patrol car would roar back into the view in his rearview mirror.

Josh Hansen asked, "Do you mind if I ask you what your plan is to get out of this? You're going to look pretty bad getting pulled over with this particular payload in your truck."

"What makes you think I have a plan?" asked Gus.

"Everything's been so well arranged so far tonight that I naturally assumed there was a grand plan to it all."

"You mean the dead body we left back at the station…" grumbled Gus.

"No plan is perfect," pointed out Josh.

The patrol car roared back into view of the rearview mirror. Gus replied, "Well, if you must know, I was figuring on pulling our pursuers over for speeding and reckless driving." The troopers rammed into the back of the sheriff's truck. The truck jerked forward; then the truck went into a sideways skid. The tires smoked hot, black smoke, and the young people in the back of the truck bed screamed. Gus stayed calm. He wasn't much for horse riding, but he'd been speeding down these interstates rain or shine since he was fourteen. He pulled the truck out of the skid as the trooper's vehicle pulled alongside the passenger side of the truck. It hammered broadside into the sheriff's truck. You had to admit they were persistent people who lived in Kansas. They really wanted his passengers to answer to their state's laws.

Hansen spoke again, "I believe your plan has one minor defect. It certainly appears that they're planning to pull us over and don't seem that worried if you pull them over first. Indeed, pulling them over might suit their plans just fine."

"Things don't always go as planned," grumbled Gus as he kept his eyes on the rain-soaked road. It wouldn't be much longer now. They were driving through the pass that was cut through the heights. The heights were a huge limestone monolith that ran through the southern part of the county. The people from the great state of Kansas rolled down the driver's-side window on the patrol car. A hand with a gun extended out of it. Major Scott Dundee was a determined man. The hand momentarily waved at Josh Hansen, who was taking ample notice of the display of weaponry. Jennifer's voice screamed from the back of the truck. The gun fired and missed the truck's tire. Instead it blew out the right front headlight.

"Why did they have to do that? Do you know how much a new headlight costs?" grumbled Gus.

Josh Hansen screamed, "I think those bastards aim to shoot us next!"

Jennifer pleaded from the back seat, "Just pull over. I don't want anyone getting hurt over this nonsense. I can't be worth all this to you all."

Gus replied while watching the road, "No one else is getting hurt tonight…well, more hurt. We're almost there. He's not gonna shoot anyone. The brave man is only going to try and shoot out our tires. He's apparently a rather lousy shot."

The road turned again, and now it ran adjacent to the heights. The large monolith of mountains that ran east to west loomed just outside the passenger-side window. In the dark you couldn't see it. Gus knew that on the other side of the road opposite those heights was a long, flat plain that extended about six hundred feet until it hit the border fence. Gus braked hard on the road. The patrol car sprang ahead. The arm with the gun went back into the patrol car. The driver needed both hands on the wheel to maneuver back to get to the sheriff's truck. Gus swerved as the patrol car tried to slow back down and get alongside again. Gus wasn't going to let it do that. Instead, he rammed the patrol car in the back bumper. It was just a little tit for tat. As the patrol car swerved, trying to regain control, Gus roared back ahead of it.

Just at that moment, a new pair of lights on the side of the road came to life. This new car pulled onto the interstate and joined the chase.

"Who's that?" asked Josh Hansen.

"State police," replied Gus.

Hansen replied, "I thought those other guys were the state police."

"They are, but they're from the wrong state. The Kansas troopers weren't about to let Jennifer Louis Bachman go without a fight. An officer out of his state is like a fish out of water. You can flop around some, but in the end all you make is a hell of a mess for yourself."

The new patrol car maneuvered between the two embattled vehicles. It was only a matter of time before the Kansas patrol car would give up the pursuit. They might not know it yet, but they were beaten. The state police were forcing the car from Kansas to the side of the road. The Kansas patrol car gave as good as it got for a few moments; then reality sank in. They had no leg to stand on against that state police car. The sheriff's truck was hauling away precious cargo, and maybe they could make their actions appear right in a court of law, particularly a court of law in Kansas, where they would have ended up if they had gotten Gus's truck over to the side of the road. These state police were different. It was going to be hard to explain why they had resisted being pulled over by a state trooper from a different state that was only doing their job. The patrol car from Kansas gave in to that reality at last. Without Gus and his truckload of evidence, they had nothing to stand on to defend their actions. They didn't likely go over willingly, but Major Scott Dundee accepted reality and finally pulled over. He couldn't risk it. Brian Hartline had repaid Gus for sticking him with this mess. He had lied on the phone, but you don't become commissioner of the state police by telling too much truth over a phone line. After all, these days a person like Josh Hansen might be listening in on you. He had placed the patrol car right where Gus had wanted it. Gus drove on finally alone on the interstate at night in the torrential rain.

Gus only drove another five minutes before he pulled the truck to the left side of the road. Gus turned the engine off and opened his door. "All right now, we're here, so everyone get out and enjoy the view." He then stepped out into the rain. He went around back to open the hatch to let the passengers out. He dug around in his black bag that he stored in the back of his truck. He wanted his flashlight. It was a big industrial-size flashlight, but it wouldn't make much of a dent in the barren black desert, particularly with this heavy rainstorm. He clicked it on and took a few steps into the water-filled high plain. The dried, parched earth didn't absorb the falling rain. The ground had dried too hard to allow rapid permeation of the precipitation, so the water was sitting on top of the dirt, making for a sloppy little hike. Gus turned around to examine his cargo.

Josh Hansen made his way into the downpour. He complained to Gus, "We're where exactly? This is the middle of nowhere."

"Everywhere is nowhere to somebody. Time to go," replied Gus.

Josh looked over to the two kids hanging near the truck. He instructed them, "Get my trunk, guys; we are going off for a little rainy night hike in the slowly flooding plain."

Gus barked to Josh, "Aren't you the man always preaching about freedom and liberty like you own the concepts?"

"You know I am," replied Josh Hansen.

"So you're free to carry your own trunk from now on. You brought it here, and you can take it out," ordered Gus.

Jennifer asked, "What is out there for us?"

Kyle responded, "Home."

"Well, no point delaying a happy homecoming any further. Everyone, follow me," ordered Gus.

They stepped out of the area near the truck into the pitch-black high plains. The puddles splashed at their feet as the rain drizzled down from above. Gus stood out front making pace for the group. It was a short and very lonely distance in the dead of night until they reached the fence. His flashlight illuminated a small swath of ground in front of them. Gus scanned it side to side. He was on the lookout for trouble. Only there wouldn't be too much trouble tonight. Not with the rainstorm and the potential for flash flooding. The coyotes of all varieties, human and animal, would be smart enough to stay at home on a night like tonight. A quick flash flood would wash fools away if they took a wrong step. Only someone following a very stupid plan would even dare to be here.

They hit the chain-link fence before they knew it was there. Gus walked right into the damn thing. The fence was twelve feet high in these parts and covered in razor wire on the top.

Josh Hansen dropped his trunk into the mud and complained, "Great, how do we get over that thing without being ripped to shreds?"

"You invited yourself on this trip, remember," grumbled Gus back. Gus grabbed a handful of the chain links and rattled the fence. The area immediately illuminated as if it were daylight in a twenty-five-foot radius around him. From out of the black came men carrying assault rifles and huge high-powered lamps. They closed in, forming a tight circle around the group. There were twelve of them in all. They were big Mexican men wearing desert camouflage. It wasn't clear yet if they were the jury, the judge, the executioner, or just the gallery. The indecision didn't last long, because the roar of a powerful truck engine came from the other side of the chain-link fence. Two headlights illuminated in the distance. Gus knew the sound of that engine. It was an engine that belonged to a black SUV owned by one Antonio Victor Minnelli. The men wouldn't do anything until Antonio told them to.

A snip could be heard, and Gus focused on the fence. Two men were hastily cutting a larger-than-man-sized hole in it with wire cutters. Through the hole came three men—two thugs carrying umbrellas and one large man standing under those umbrellas. He was dressed in a white Italian suit even in the night's rainstorm. As soon as he came through the fence, Kyle shouted," Papa!" and ran to his father. He gave his dad a huge bear hug. They were a comical sight to see. The huge, obese middle-aged Antonio and the fit, sleek, handsome Kyle standing there celebrating Kyle's liberation.

After the moment had passed, Antonio pulled his son to the side and pointed to Gus. "Tell me, my friend, why I should not kill you right here and now."

"No man is justified in doing evil on the grounds of expediency. Anyways, there are also too many witnesses."

"I don't see why that should worry me," replied Antonio.

Gus quickly added, "Remember, avocado dealers don't kill people in front of certain witnesses—good witnesses. It's late, it's raining, and I'm a little tired of all this, so let's cut to the chase; did you bring me what I wanted?"

Antonio looked at his son standing beside him and laughed, "Some witnesses you have there. To use a good son against a bad father is not a very fair thing to do. You and I, we are just a couple of old criminals, so it is smart to bring an honest man to the meeting, Sheriff. Bravo, I salute you for you cleverness. What about the others? Does it really matter if they go to jail in your country or mine?"

Jennifer ran up to Gus in tears and tugged on his sleeve. "I would rather go to jail in America, if it is all the same to you. I'm not sure why you brought me here. I don't want to go with these men."

Gus grumbled, "Quit your worrying; you didn't kill anyone. You're not going to jail anywhere, and that includes particularly going to jail in Mexico. I wouldn't have brought you here otherwise."

Antonio laughed. "My men were *muy* good actors, were they not? I found them in a Spanish production of Hamlet. You haven't seen Shakespeare until you've heard it in its original Spanish. It made me feel like I was in Denmark itself. I figure tomorrow morning the lawyers and the judges will sort out the confusion with the Mexican embassy, who at this very moment is too confused to deny ever wanting to extradite her to my country. There was enough money to insure that their confusion won't clear up until morning, and then they will say that they never heard of those three men, and they have never have seen those papers before either. It will be chalked up to a cruel American hoax against my country. It costs a lot of money, my friend, to bribe embassy workers to delay an international story like that until tomorrow morning."

"Yeah, but the fact is Terry Tang's gang will take the rap for the fakery. You see, as an unplanned bonus to the grand plan, he got himself killed tonight in an inconvenient way for him, but a rather convenient way for you. They're going to trace all this muckraking to the wrong muck. They're going to trace the mess tonight back to those gangs on the West Coast when it's all said and done. That will be a harsh enough lesson to keep them out of here."

"I guess I should thank you eventually for all this then," replied Antonio.

"You can thank me now, do you have my money?" replied Gus.

"You kept your side of the deal, so I will keep mine in full." Antonio lit up an electronic cigarette. He laughed and clapped his hands. Two thugs came through the hole in the fence carrying two large brown briefcases. They dropped them at Gus's feet.

Gus carried one over to Antonio and dropped it at his feet. He explained, "That one is for your troubles and expenses."

"And the other one, my friend, is it for yours?" asked Antonio.

"No, that one is for Jennifer's trouble and inconvenience. I want you to help her start all over again somewhere else. You'll arrange that and make sure her money is safely stored in a Swiss bank account."

"Sure, my friend, sure. We avocado dealers are such an honest bunch. Almost as honest as you sheriffs," laughed Antonio.

Gus took the other briefcase and handed it over to Jennifer. Jennifer replied, "I don't deserve this. I don't understand. I'm nobody. It was a tragedy what happened to my child's father. It was just chance my child came down with a rare fatal disease. Why would the law care so much about judging me for choosing a rare medical decision? Why did all those people care about what happened to me for choosing it? What business was it of theirs? Why would you break me out of jail and give me all this money for nothing? I'm nobody special, and yet everyone has professed so much about caring about what happens to me. Where were they all when I really needed them? When I was a seventeen-year-old pregnant girl fearing how I'd raise a child with no father?"

Gus replied, "I can't answer your questions, because I don't know the answers. I don't think those people can either. They never could. Bad things happen to people who are nobody for no particularly good reason. It had to happen to someone. This week that someone just happened to be you. There are a lot of people with several million dollars that are nobody special, even if they don't appreciate that fact. Being no one special doesn't make you any less worthy of help. I find it is often the case that the no-one-specials of the world tend to need the most help. You have two options at this moment and I won't force you to do anything you don't want to do from this point forward. You can continue to be no one special and take that money and leave or you can do the law abiding thing and go back to jail with the near certitude you'll be a very poor, but very special prisoner in Kansas."

Kyle walked away from his father. He took Jennifer by the hand. He said to her, "Do not worry; we will take care of you. My father is a very important man in the avocado business in our country. He will see that you are safe. We will both see that you are safe. Go with me and my father, and

we will take you away from this diseased country and its foul criminals."
Jennifer picked up the money and they both walked together through the
fence headed for the black SUV.

Josh Hansen coughed. All remaining eyes circled over to him. Gus
yelled to him, "Hansen, you're like a birthday card. The people who send
them imagine the people who receive them are happy to see it when it
arrives, but they aren't. The truth is all anyone really cares about is if there's
any money inside it for them. If there isn't, then they discard the birthday
card in the trash. Your enemies keep trying to discard you, but you're a
pretty lucky guy. I wish your luck would run out, or at least out of my
county. I'm tired of keeping you alive."

Josh Hansen replied, "I think if you remember correctly, I did offer
you money to do your task of keeping me alive."

"That's my point, I opened your card and I took it. I don't understand
computers one bit, but I remembered everything you told me the other
night. I wrote it down and gave it to Antonio. I figured he had boys who
know how to take your shit coins and turn them into cash. Sure enough,
Antonio cashed in all your shit coins to pay for those two briefcases filled
with cash. I don't take bribes from criminals, but you're a pain in the ass,
so I took your money and did what I wanted with it. It's not like not taking
it would have made you go away any faster. Take your trunk and follow the
rest of the jailbreak to Mexico."

Josh said, "I've done a lot of risky things in this world, but I don't
know how I like the sound of traipsing off into the rainy desert at night
with a bunch of assault-weapon-wielding banditos."

Gus replied to Hansen, "In a perfect world, there would be justice. In
this world, there's only this. Take it or leave it."

Josh Hansen laughed. "Ah, I see now; you claim that I face Plato's
conundrum that true justice can only be found in the land that is reduced
to not needing it at all. Given the world as it stands, I think I shall take
your kind offer and leave. I know you'll miss me, but I choose to live where
assassins are not on the deputy force."

Gus stood in the high desert next to the border fence. Hansen was
escorted by Antonio and his heavily armed thugs to his awaiting SUVs.

The rain fell hard now around Gus, but he stood there in the dark watching and waiting until the vehicles drove off into the Mexican night. He hoped that was the last he would see of any of them. Once they left his sight, he used the flashlight to make his way back to his truck. It was a short walk through the mud and puddles. He reached his truck and didn't jump right in. He walked around the truck in the rain, surveying it. The Kansas lawman had put a beating on the old thing. The right and left sides were heavily dented. The rear bumper was hanging by a thread. The right headlight was out. Gus walked up to his truck and gently patted it on the roof. Everything had worked out for the best tonight, but his poor truck didn't deserve the fate it had received.

CHAPTER 7

I'm really very sorry for you all, but it's an unjust world, and virtue is triumphant only in theatrical performances.
—W. S. Gilbert, *The Mikado*

he monsoon rains were rare, but when they hit, these winter rainstorms brought their rain in waves. Naturally the last heavy wave had circulated through the county just when Gus was standing out in the mud by the border fence. Now that he was back safely in his truck, the rain was falling lightly again. Gus had his windshield wipers set to low. He was in a somber mood despite everything more or less working out. It may not have gone strictly according to his grand plan, but a plan was only set in place to lay the seeds of ideas that you hoped came to fruition. Rarely did all the seeds planted grow to fruition, and yet just as rarely did a field once sowed completely yield no crops at all. The activities of the night were over, and the headaches that had plagued Gus were all long gone to parts unknown in Mexico. The bad guys in charge were the type that could easily make Jennifer disappear for good with another name, passport, and life. It would only cost money, and she had a lot of that stuff now. If that was the way it ended for her, then one should count her blessings.

That all sounded good in the back of Gus's mind, but it did nothing to ease the remaining problem. The problem was that with all his problems in his rearview mirror now, his job remained. He had let his problems walk away along with all the cash. It was ill-gotten goods, so did he really want them? Well, yes, he had wanted them. Only a fool doesn't want wealth in a world where wealth is there to be obtained. Wealth and honor in an unjust society is a form of disgrace, but the wealth sure made the disgrace easier to bear. He imagined Jennifer would find more happiness being disgraced, rich, unknown, and free than she would have been being famous as a poor man's martyr for multiple causes while enduring life locked up inside a jail cell.

Gus turned the corner and was now driving in his own neighborhood. A few more blocks and he'd return home. Tomorrow would bring the paperwork over the shooting down at the law-enforcement complex, paperwork over the jailbreak, and perhaps the search for a new deputy to fulfill Terrance's rebranding effort. He might want to keep Chiquita, but she'd be a hot commodity once the media got done with her—a real hero, of a sort, she was now. The talk radio went on and on about her the whole drive home. Gus pulled into his driveway. He was exhausted, drenched, and still partially covered in dried blood from the ear wound. He contemplated just reclining the truck's chair and sleeping in the cab. His back wouldn't appreciate it, but the rest of his drained body would. The radio gave a crackle. His radio announced that a dispatcher was searching for the sheriff. Gus's hand was on autopilot and reached over to the receiver before Gus's mind could stop it. Gus answered the call. He assumed it was just a call to inform him there was more news on the fatal shooting at the office. He already knew the truth, so no big deal in replying. "This is Sheriff Gus; what do you got for me?"

"Sheriff, Deputy Costner called in to report a fatal accident out by Wheatstone bridge. He wants to know if you could come down and assist."

"Do you know what time it is?"

"He only asked me to call you to see if you'd come down. He suggested it might be important if you came. There's been a two-vehicle accident there with fatalities involved. I know it isn't as serious as the gun fight at the law-enforcement complex. I can inform him that you are preoccupied on weightier matters and won't be able to assist."

"Nah, don't do that. Tell him I'm coming."

"Will do," replied the dispatcher.

The job, he could never escape the job. Gus pulled back out of the driveway. There was never any rest for the weary. The rain from the storm was waning, but the aftereffects were still to be dealt with. One storm wave had swept in, but another could just as easily follow it in a few hours. The northern parts of the country survived sleet, ice, and snow, and those who lived there laughed at the fear of those in Gus's small world who feared the occasional rain. They didn't understand the hazards a flash rainstorm brought with it. Sure, the dry roads often became slick with oil from months of accumulation without any rainfall, but far worse than the slick roads was the fact that the dry arroyos would fill up quickly, and many of them had no bridge to protect the roads from flash flooding. Even that wasn't the worst part of these storms. The worst part was no doubt the sheer lack of experience in driving in weather conditions. A brave person in the north learned quickly to deal with snow and ice, because it lasted months every year. That was a lot of unappreciated practice those people up north got, and practice makes perfect. The poor person down in Gus's county saw heavy rain rarely and sometimes not at all in a given calendar year. It all lead to the unfortunate truth that good people died from weather conditions down here that rarely caused troubles elsewhere. One of those tragic rare occurrences had just happened to pick tonight of all nights to materialize.

The rains remained light as Gus drove to the scene of the fatal accident. A half hour later, Gus pulled the truck to a halt next to the Wheatstone bridge that just happened to run over an arroyo. It wasn't the place you normally associated with a flash-flood death. It was all the roads without bridges that were trouble. Still, it had happened here; you couldn't doubt that fact. Gus got out of his truck and peered over the guardrail down into the embankment. He could see the water flowing in a trickle underneath the bridge. Most of the year this riverbed would be dry as a bone; still, there wasn't much water down there yet. It must be that the rainstorm hadn't been too bad up to now in these parts, or the arroyo would be fuller.

On the opposite side of the bridge, there was a small dive bar called the Water's Edge. It was not known as a very classy joint, but it was known to be one willing to serve alcohol even on a stormy night to just about any fool who happened to wander out to drink a lot of it. In the bar's parking lot sat a deputy car, an ambulance, and two emergency vehicles from the fire department. The tow-truck drivers would hopefully be there soon. The embankment was likely too slick with rain to try and pull the vehicles back up tonight, but they'd try all the same. From this side of the bridge, it seemed obvious as to what had happened. A driver had sped out of that parking lot of that bar onto the interstate. Either the rain was too heavy to see properly, or the driver's eyes were impaired by other means. Either way, the driver had failed to see the vehicle already heading down the road. The impact from the collision appeared to have sent both vehicles over the embankment and down into the arroyo below, where no doubt Deputy Costner was now. Gus could see the lights of men below the bridge working among the wreckage.

Gus strolled in the light rain over the bridge toward the flashing lights that belonged to the ambulance. He casually waved his flashlight in his hand as he walked. A lot of out-of-towners took this interstate route, so with a good bit of luck, Gus was hoping not to know the identity of the people in the ambulance. You only got so much luck on any one night, though. Gus knew the man sitting up on a gurney in the ambulance all too well. He rounded the back of the ambulance to come face-to-face with Skip Lipschitz. He wasn't exactly in great condition, but you could count him as lucky to be alive. Two paramedics were busy working on him. Gus casually watched the men work on Skip as he inched nearer and nearer the ambulance. Before long, he was right in there among the fray. No one seemed to object to his presence, so he took it as a signal it was all right to talk to his eyewitness.

Gus greeted Skip. "You look like hell tonight, Skip; what happen to you?"

Skip grimaced in pain as a paramedic played with his shoulder. Skip turned to Gus. "It is such a mess. We were out celebrating our good fortune."

"You said we; who else was in the car?" interrupted Gus.

"Sorry, I should begin at the beginning. I called up Sheldon tonight and told him the good news. The response to the cross-burning incident has been overwhelming. That horse-riding bit the two of you did this morning for the network TVs put it over the top. We've raised over a million dollars from hardworking Americans all over this generous country. Not only could Sheldon finally pay off his trial debts, but he could truly find the peace of mind the trial robbed him of. It just goes to show that Americans are decent people who respect the justice dealt out by a fair jury. Sheldon picked me up in the Corvette and said we ought to celebrate. I warned him about the slick roads, but he's not from around here. A little water falling from the sky didn't frighten a man like him. He was truly one of the bravest Americans I've ever met. He stood in front of twelve angry men passing judgment, and like Daniel in the lion's den, Sheldon walked out a better man for it. He wasn't afraid to go anywhere so long as he had his sidearm with him." Skip patted his own gun strapped to his leg when he said that.

"Where's Sheldon Nickelback right now?" asked Gus.

"I think he's dead, Sheriff. He was driving happy as can be. We were heading for the lovely convention-center restaurant for a late-night snack when blame out of nowhere a car just T-bones us from off the side of the road. I guess the other driver never saw us coming. It all happened so fast that I didn't see it hit us. Their lights might have been off. I had my seat belt on. You know me; safety first is my motto. I don't know if Sheldon did. I don't think it would have mattered. Just when everything is finally going his way and he'd shaken off something so awful as a wrongful arrest and trial. Blam! This terrible thing happened to that wonderful Christian man."

Gus nodded. One of the paramedics tugged at Gus's sleeve. He gave the go motion to Gus and explained, "This man has a few broken bones. We won't know the full extent of his injuries until we get him down to the hospital. Given the crash, it could have been a lot worse. We need to move while the rain is light."

"All right, all right; Skip, these guys are going to take good care of you, and if they don't, I'll come looking for them, so don't you worry."

Skip didn't really acknowledge Gus's attempt to cheer him up. He just sat on the gurney muttering to the air as the paramedics loaded him into the ambulance. The words were, "Just when everything is going good, this happens. I truly believe that there is no justice in this world." The ambulance back door shut, and they began to prepare to drive the survivor off into the light rain of the night.

Gus snapped his flashlight back on and walked into the roadway. There were thick layers of eight sets of skid marks, one for each tire involved in the collision. Plastic parts were thrown about the road. A small amount of glass was thrown on the road as debris as well. Gus followed the tire marks to the roadside. One set went right into the bar's parking lot. Indeed, someone had pulled out of there in an awful hurry. The person must have been driving a car with one hell of an acceleration capability. They left heavy skid marks in the road all the way through the impact zone. The second set of marks ran perpendicular to the path of the roadway. They started right there in the impact zone. The car with Skip and Sheldon in it clearly had been hit by a lot of sheer force and traveled against its will sideways off the road. The guardrail at the entrance to the bridge was gone. Gus followed the second set of skid marks to the opposite edge of the roadway. The ambulance turned on its sirens to a high-pitched wail and flew at high speed from the bar's parking lot. Gus watched the ambulances lights fade into the distance. Skip would be okay, thought Gus.

Down the slippery slope that started at the edge of the road was the dry wash of the arroyo. *Stay relatively dry a little longer*, thought Gus, but the night sky was betraying him. The next wave of the storm could be seen flashing in the dark clouds at a distance. The arroyo would soon be flowing profusely due to the sudden influx of rain. He directed his flashlight at the long slope down. The slope was mostly covered with dry grass and shrubs. Gus could see a large, muddy path had been cleared through the shrubs by something extremely heavy. He trained his flashlight down the gouged path the two vehicles had made in the muddy slope all the way to the bottom of the wash. There at the bottom, his flashlight illuminated the two vehicles. They were in a tangled mass stuck sinking into the mud of the lightly flowing arroyo. One vehicle was the remains of the generous gift of the city—a white Corvette. It was pinned under a red car that had T-boned it right at the driver's-side door. Gus couldn't tell much about the identity of the red car, since it was nearly obliterated by the impact. What it had been before that crash was a mystery at this distance. It must have been something fast, however.

Gus took his flashlight off the vehicles and fixed it on Deputy Costner, who was making his way up the muddy slope toward Gus. Gus decided to save him the trouble and began to make his way down to the deputy. He only took three steps before he noticed the red tarp on the ground. It was located just off the main path cleared by the tumbling vehicles and partially obscured by a barren bush. The tarp was weighed down by rocks, but it rustled in the wind. The rains meant the bush would spring to life once more in a few hours. That was more than you could say for what was under that red tarp. A pair of paramedics chatted away in the light drizzle near that tarp.

Deputy Costner caught up to Gus. The deputy was all smiles, oddly enough. "Sheriff, I heard from Deputy Wilson that the doctors say Deputy Lopez will be all right."

"That's good news. What about all this then?"

Deputy Costner's expression turned grim; he explained, "After the vehicles impacted, the driver of the red sports car must have been ejected through his front windshield. He was lucky that the mass of the two cars didn't go right over him. Still, he must have bled to death before anyone could arrive. He was not a pretty sight."

"Who called it in?"

"Some people at the bar; they heard the crash but didn't see it happen."

"Do you know who it was under that tarp?" asked Gus.

"People at the bar didn't know him by sight, and he paid in cash, so no credit-card records to use. There's not much left of him under that tarp to identify. I figure it could be just about anyone under there. You are free to take a look if you want."

"Nah, I trust you. Did you run the plates on the car?"

"I was just walking up the hill to do that. I got the plate right here in my hands. Found it buried in the mud of the river. It took me fifteen minutes to find the sucker. A few more minutes and likely we'd never have found it." Deputy Costner held up the plate to give Gus a good look at it. It was covered in mud from the river bottom. Gus scraped it off with his hands. He held his flashlight on it. The letters read "TWRKING."

"Given it was a personalized plate, we should narrow the identity down pretty easily," explained Costner.

"Too easy, I'm afraid. The vehicle belongs to Sedric Hedgecock. I figure that's the identity of the body under that tarp. No doubt the coroner will find he was full of alcohol; that is, if there's any blood left in him at all. The man had a way of getting out of a seemingly bad situation. Somehow, though, I don't think his lawyer will be able to fix this one." Gus took the flashlight and illuminated the white Corvette at the bottom of the ravine again. He asked Deputy Costner, "The other body still in the Corvette?"

"There's only the one body, Sheriff. The two people in the white Corvette survived the impact. The passenger is pretty shaken up. We have him up top being looked over by the paramedics. The driver is down there with another paramedic. He's still alive. I'm not sure for how long, though. There's a motor vehicle nearly sitting on top of him. The damn car went through the driver's-side door and nearly halfway through the whole car. It's a miracle he survived the impact, but he's alive down there. The tow trucks are coming to pull that wreck off him. If he's lucky, then he'll live to see it arrive."

"Well, get on the horn and hurry them along before the rain starts up again," ordered Gus.

Costner scrambled up the slope to do just that. Gus trained the flashlight back down at the two vehicles. He took a step downward on the slippery slope. He wasn't longing to see another accident victim. He was compelled to go all the same. The arroyo wasn't so much flowing as it had a trickle of water resting on top of a thick layer of slippery mud. The mud pack flowed in the arroyo bottom at a meandering pace. The two vehicles were sinking down into it. Gus reached the edge of the arroyo. He took his first step in and sunk down until the wet, sticky mess reached up to his midshin. The mud was almost up to the top of the vehicles' tire wells. In the monsoon season, the arroyo could rise nearly eighteen feet in a few hours of really hard rain. The thunderclaps were coming closer. He could feel the drops quickening their pace. Walking out into the arroyo was a bit risky, but Gus was paid poorly to take those kind of risks. Gus circled through the mud to the passenger-side door of the vehicle. He was now standing in the middle of the arroyo. The passenger-side door was wide open, and a paramedic was sitting on the passenger seat.

Gus instinctively asked him, "How's he doing?"

"There's about a ton of vehicle sitting on top of him. We have to get it off soon to work on him, or…" The man looked back inside the car and bit his lip.

No use telling the obvious to the victim, agreed Gus. Gus flashed his light past the paramedic into the vehicle. Sheldon Nickelback's battered face hung in the light. Sheldon's eyes turned toward the light. Gus gave a thumbs-up with his free hand and shouted into the vehicle, "Don't worry, Sheldon; we'll get you out of this." Gus stared into the paramedic's eyes after finishing his words of encouragement. Those eyes were poker eyes and gave nothing away. Gus rubbed the paramedic's shoulder and whispered to him, "Well, just do the best you can for him."

Sheldon groaned. The paramedic replied, "I'm going up top to get more morphine. Can you keep an eye on him, Sheriff?"

Gus just nodded. "While you're up there, hurry the tow truck along." The paramedic started to trot out of the mud and up the ravine, leaving Gus alone with the sinking vehicle. Gus wiggled into the passenger seat. It was a tight fit for a man his size even before the accident. You had to admire the custom Corvette's leather seats. The interior had real wood paneling. It sure was one beauty of a car, or it sure had been. He rubbed his hands on the custom dashboard and made a loud whistle. He turned to Sheldon. "Nice car. You'll be out driving it again before you know it."

Sheldon whispered into the air, "I got to make a confession."

"Now, Sheldon, you understand that I ain't no priest. You don't have to confess anything you don't want to. I can't give you absolution."

"Sheriff, is that you?"

Gus waved his hands in front of Sheldon's face, but he made no response. His eyes were dilating. He must have been losing a lot of blood internally. He reached out and grabbed Sheldon's hand. He moved in close and shouted into the man's ear. "It's me, Sheldon! Can you feel me squeezing your hand?" Sheldon nodded yes. Gus continued, "When this is all over, we'll go for another horse ride. You'd like that, wouldn't you?"

Sheldon blurted out, "I burned the cross in my lawn the other night. I wanted the money. I couldn't let that teenager with her goddamn abortion steal all my press. I spent eighteen months in the news, and I never got a damn thing out of it. Just when the money was gonna come to me, she has to fucking show up and threatens to take all the good press from me. I couldn't let her do that. I needed the interest of the press back, you understand; I didn't mean no harm to the people I falsely accused. I deserved the fame, money, and press, so I burned that cross."

"I know you did, Sheldon. I kinda knew it that night and confirmed it by the next day. I'm not stupid, even if I do occasionally do stupid things."

Sheldon squeezed Gus's hand. "You knew..." He coughed and then continued, "Why didn't you say something?"

"My job isn't to help people raise funds. I'm just supposed to enforce the law as best I can. It's not always easy in every case, but I try to, you know, allow justice and such-and-such to happen."

"Helping me raise funds was justice. I deserved that money. The biggest celebrity in America, and I didn't get nothing for it. It was my turn. I am a star, and a star deserves to be paid."

"Nothing? Do you think a man like Wilton McDermott would have been your lawyer if the media didn't turn you into a celebrity? Without the television and the cameras, you'd have gone to jail for murder. If you are confessing things, then maybe you should confess the big one and not all the little shit that doesn't matter."

"Sheriff, you still there? I hear you, but I can't feel you no more." Gus squeezed Sheldon's hand tighter. Sheldon continued, "It...it was self-defense."

"Aw shit, Sheldon, don't lie to me now. You were nobody, and you always wanted to be somebody. Becoming somebody requires luck. I think you tried your chance at luck the only way you figured you could. You can't act, sing, or dance, but you did own a gun. Sheldon, you left that house with a loaded weapon to confront a boy who was doing nothing illegal. You two got into a tussle on a public walkway. It might be that you planned on having that tussle all along. You're not a racist, so why do all that other than the fact that you wanted to be a star? You knew the media potentially could make you a star if you said the right things to the right people. It has happened for other criminals, so why shouldn't it happen to you? Many of them got off, and to become a star requires you take risks. I think you were willing to take the risk. It was a risk, but as you told me, you were nobody before this, so you had nothing to lose. I think you planned to kill someone all along, anyone that fit your model of a good victim. The right-sized victim just happened by one night, and you jumped at it. You left your house to start that tussle hoping the boy would fight back. The boy was very obliging and fought back a little, so then you shot him as planned. You don't think that's murder? You planned on having that altercation just like you planned on burning that cross. You carried that gun out there that night for a simple reason; you had the intent to murder someone and try to become a star because of it. Everything else was just part of a game: the racism, the alleged gang violence that plagued your street, the streetlamp story, and standing your ground in self-defense. They were words to seed the story to help make you famous. Wilton McDermott helped you craft them into a beautiful mosaic for the jury to hear, but the idea was always yours right from the start. You burned that cross for the same reason you killed that kid. You wanted to make a shitload of money. You wanted that right from the start. I'm right, ain't I?"

Sheldon shook his head from side to side in disagreement. The shaking was very weak. His grip on Gus's hand was failing. He whispered, "Self-defense. I have the right to self-defense."

"What about the boy? Didn't he have a right to defend himself from you? You became a star, and he became an afterthought. Now, Sheldon, you're a star. How does it feel?"

"You want me to confess?" whispered Sheldon.

"No, you told me you wanted to confess. I already told you I'm not a priest. Don't leave here tonight without being honest with yourself. I always figured justice was a matter of honor that people owed it to themselves as a form of the truth. If you can't be honest with yourself, then you'll never have justice. The jury might have found you not guilty, but only you know if justice was served. Well, do you feel justified, or do you feel guilty?"

The rainstorm opened up with full fury. The next wave of the storm had arrived with its vengeance. Gus could hear the drops beating on the hood of the beaten-up vehicle. The vehicle lurched a little as the floodwaters started roaring back to life in the arroyo. The whole surrounding area would channel its rain through this spot. There was no telling how much time they had. The paramedic was taking his sweet time getting back here with medical attention. Sheldon's hand was growing cold to the touch. He wasn't squeezing anymore. He was beyond pain. He was probably already in a euphoric state. They sat in silence for a few minutes, listening as the rainwater fell in the dark night. It was a trial by water. In the old days, they'd drown witches to determine their honesty. The trial was a simple one. They would dunk a lady in the water. If she sank and drowned, then she wasn't a witch. If she floated or swam, then she was a witch, and the mob would burn her alive at the stake. There was no escaping from the trial with your life. There is a point when justice only does injury. Sheldon would not escape the floodwaters alive. They'd never get him out of this mess in time. The tow trucks were no doubt delayed arriving because they were busy tonight towing all the stalled cars due to the floodwaters. With all the arroyos between here and town soon to be flooded by this new heavy wave of rain, those tow trucks would not be here anytime soon.

Sheldon squeezed hard on Gus's hand. He spoke in a soft whisper to break the silence. "Sheriff, I do have something more to confess."

"Well, go ahead. This rain falling the way it is means we ain't going nowhere soon." Gus perked up his ears and moved closer to the man to hear him over the falling rain. Sheldon Nickelback never spoke another word, though. His hand went limp. Gus let it go. He sat in the passenger seat waiting out the wave of heavy rain. In another fifteen minutes, the worst of the current storm cell had passed. It was still raining hard, but not hard enough to prevent Gus from escaping the sinking wreck. The floodwaters were up to the doorframe and leaking into the passenger seat. Gus waded out into the river. He held on to the car and used it to steady himself as he made for the shoreline. It was tough going, and he was soaked through and through. The paramedic, wearing a plastic parka, wandered down the muddy ravine to him with his hands full of medical devices.

The paramedic said, "The deputy says that there is no way to get the tow truck here until morning. This storm cell passed through downtown already. Everything between here and there is flooded. Even worse, there are two more cells behind this one. The deputy begged the tow trucks to come for God's sake, but they say it is impossible to pass the arroyos right now. They're not going to risk their trucks. We're all stuck out here for the night."

"He's dead," replied Gus.

"Can't leave him down there," replied the paramedic.

Gus shrugged. "No sense all of us dying in a flood to get a dead man out of a car. You guys can take care of it whenever the tow truck manages to arrive tomorrow. There's no crime here to investigate. It was just an accident."

"They do happen."

Gus nodded and started back up the slick, muddy slope of the ravine. A strong gust of wind blew through the arroyo valley and nearly knocked Gus off his feet. The paramedic did fall down and sunk partially into the muddy slope. Some of the medicine he was carrying blew out of his hands. The wind lasted only a few seconds but long enough for the fancy red sports car's trunk to open up. A lightning flash filled the sky, and Gus saw it in there. Gus sludged through the mud back down to the ravine bottom to retrieve it. It was a pristine case of Little Red's Mexican Ale sitting there inside the trunk. It had managed to survive the collision and the fall into the ravine. That beer was made of stronger stuff than men. Gus reached in and tugged it out. He continued up the muddy slope carrying his prize.

Gus stopped and stared at the body under the red tarp—a senseless death. He thought about Skip's sense of frustration on the accident. It did appear things had been going well for both Sedric and Sheldon up until tonight. Gus tried to feel some empathy for them, but there was none inside him to be found. It should have been inside him somewhere to feel.

He had felt it so strongly for the guilty young woman from Kansas who the law had said had done wrong. Yet he felt nothing for the fate of these two men lying in the muddy ravine who the law said had been justified in their actions. He certainly didn't have an ounce of guilt in his conscience for the lack of empathy. After all, they had gotten what they wanted out of this world, and that was more than most got in this life. He opened the case of beer and tossed a bottle on top of the red tarp—one more for the last trip on the road.

He finished the climb up the slick hill toward his waiting truck to get out of the rain. There would be a whole lot of paperwork to be filled out in the morning. There were a lot of accidents to be cleaned up by that paperwork. He thought about the ease of that task. He'd do this new paperwork with a clear conscience, and a clear conscience was where justice truly dwelt.

A pair of headlights shone in the darkness. Gus stood in the rain watching them approach. If the tow truck had made it all the way here, then the path home was likely clear. Gus wished for nothing else but to go home. The vehicle drove past Gus and parked on the edge of the road. It wasn't a truck at all. It was the energy-efficient vehicle that belonged to Dr. Chloe Armstrong. Her car door opened. An umbrella stuck out of it and opened fully. She then stepped out of the car. She immediately saw Gus on the side of the road standing in the pouring rain. She ran up to him.

Gus yelled at her, "What are you doing here? The roads are too dangerous to be driving around tonight. A fatal car accident is no reason to do something stupid like rush out here. The drivers will still be just as dead tomorrow morning."

"Gus, there's been a shooting at the law-enforcement complex. A drug dealer was killed, and apparently his gang kidnapped that poor prisoner from Kansas for God knows what reason. The first report on the television said it was pro-choice people from Canada, but now they know it was a West Coast drug gang. I just came from talking to Deputy Lopez at the hospital. She confirmed it was Terry Tang who was shot dead by her. It all sounds like madness."

"Aw, that. I know all that already. There's not much I can do about it tonight or most likely ever."

"You have to do something! Wilton McDermott is threating to sue the city for gross negligence on account of our losing his client. More than that, you have to find that poor girl from Kansas because you can't let those drug dealers take her. Going back to Kansas is better than being left to that fate. Those gang people, they must be crazy, Gus." Gus looked away from her. He stared down the slope into the rising, darkening waters of the arroyo. She continued, "You don't care, do you?"

"Don't worry so much about Jennifer from Kansas. I got a feeling she'll be just fine from now on. She won't be so famous no more, and that fact might hurt Wilton in his heart-shaped wallet, but she'll be better off for not being so famous. You got Sheriff Gus's personal guarantee on that."

Dr. Armstrong replied, "Gus, you didn't go and do something stupid tonight, did you?"

Gus turned to her and smiled. "Why would you ask a thing like that?"

"There's something wrong going on here, because I can't figure out why in God's name drug dealers would want her otherwise, unless someone put them up to this."

"Who cares what drug dealers want? That's not the important question. This damn week I've heard a lot from people telling me about what God wanted for my prisoner Jennifer, and I've wondered if all that stuff they said to me was true. If it was true what these people all said to me in God's good name, then I wonder, why does this God want any of us living in this just world of his?"

Dr. Armstrong didn't answer immediately. Finally she spoke as the rain fell down around them both, "Is that beer any good?"

"It's the bestest," replied Gus.

"Then let's get out of the rain and drink a few down while we wait for the roads to clear."

"That's the best stupid idea anyone has had this week."

She walked the umbrella over to Gus and covered his head. Together they headed over to the sheriff's truck to get out of the rain.

ABOUT THE AUTHOR

Raised in Saratoga Springs, New York, John D. DeSain received his bachelor of science in chemistry from Siena College before earning a doctor of philosophy in physical chemistry from Rice University in Houston, Texas.

DeSain worked in the combustion chemistry field before moving into the Californian aerospace industry. His current research revolves around existing and novel space propulsion systems and such environmental issues as green propulsion, space debris, ozone destruction, and climate change—issues that regularly creep into his writing.

As a reader, DeSain loves the work of Dashiell Hammett, Raymond Chandler, Agatha Christie, and Stephan Jay Gould—all of whom influence his writing, which somehow resembles none of theirs. His favorite comedian is George Carlin, which may explain his need to poke fun at the bizarre nature of politics and society.

Manufactured by Amazon.ca
Acheson, AB